Howls from the Dark Ages

Editing by P.L. McMillan and Solomon Forse
Formatting by Molly Halstead
Cover art by Joe Radkins
Cover design by Molly Halstead

Howls From the Dark Ages published by HOWL Society Press
ISBN: 978-1-7367800-4-6

Visit our website at howlsociety.com

HOWLS
FROM THE
DARK AGES

Edited by P.L. McMillan and Solomon Forse

PRAISE FOR
HOWLS FROM THE DARK AGES

"Chilling and horrifying, Howls from the Dark Ages collects multiple stories from a wide range of authors to bring the reader terror that transcends centuries. I greatly enjoyed this collection."

—Sonora Taylor, award-winning author of
Little Paranoias: Stories and Seeing Things

"A thrilling collection that pulls no punches, Howls From the Dark Ages returns the reader to the point in history when the human misery index was at an all-time high."

—Donnie Goodman, author of *The Razorblades in My Head*

"These stories offer a rhythmic pull, dragging its readers into the past through the lulling lyricism of woven words…you won't be able to tear your eyes, heart, mind, or soul away from its mesmerizing chaos—nor will you want to."

—Ai Jiang, author featured in *F&SF*, *The Dark*, and *The Deadlands*

"Howls from the Dark Ages offers a visceral assortment of medieval horror and dark fantasy stories from eighteen passionate new and established authors. I thoroughly enjoyed this anthology, which read like a gruesome sequel to The Canterbury Tales!"

—Christi Nogle, author of *Beulah*

PRAISE FOR
HOWLS FROM THE DARK AGES

"Amid crumbling castles and decaying flesh, come walk the wild woods, drag your feet through the black mud of perdition, face beasts from the aether, and fight for life and sanity against dark and terrible powers whose very existence deny both."
— Mike Adamson, author featured in *Weird Tales*, *Abyss and Apex*, and *Lovecraftiana*

"These stories brilliantly capture the magic, grime, and fever-dream faith of the medieval world. In the hands of these macabre wordsmiths, the Dark Ages truly live up to their name."
— Eric Raglin, author of *Nightmare Yearnings*

"Howls From the Dark Ages is a brutal, sometimes heart-wrenching exploration of medieval horror...The stories are compelling and unique."
— LP Hernandez, author of *Stargazers*, Cemetery Gates Media

"Moonlit castles, foggy moors, ancient religions, blood smeared knights, corrupt kings, woodland witches, and something unfathomable howling just outside the ramparts. This anthology has everything a Dark Fantasy fan could ask for. Atmospheric and uncanny through and through."
— Corey Farrenkopf, writer/librarian

TABLE OF CONTENTS

For a complete list of content warnings, please
follow this QR Code or visit our website at
https://howlsociety.com/anthology/
content-warnings-hftda/

WRITING MEDIEVAL HORROR FICTION FOR FUN AND...WELL, MOSTLY FOR FUN.

Christopher Buehlman

In the summer of 2010, I realized a lifelong dream and sold my 1930s Southern Gothic werewolf novel, *Those Across the River,* to Penguin, one of the biggest and most reputable publishers in the English-speaking world. Confidence seemed high at Berkeley, my division, that *Those Across* would be the next big thing in horror.

I was elated.

The book would come out the following year, and Penguin was ready to contract me to write a follow-up. When my editor asked me what I'd like to write next, I said, "I want to write about plague."

I had been weaned on Stephen King's *The Stand,* and as a teenager I would read any book at all about pandemics, from cheeseball *Stand* knock-offs to Michael Crichton's brilliantly understated *The Andromeda Strain.* But I wasn't interested in writing about a plague happening today.

I wanted to write about The Plague happening when The Plague happened. *The* Plague.

Capitalized, please.

That event in the 1340s that killed as many as two out of three medieval Europeans and, as one would expect, changed *everything*. By 1350, the time called the High Middle Ages was over, and with it went bright paintings featuring Summer and Spring; the colors of the art produced by the collective psyche grew autumnal now. The Dance of Death came into vogue, reminding us that bishops, bakers, mothers, and queens must all depart when summoned by that grinning, ubiquitous skeleton that tugged, and pulled, and sometimes bit them off the page. Laborers, their numbers thinned, walked off the farms where they had been effectively enslaved, and now sold their labor dearly. I daresay they sold it for something like what it was actually worth. Sound familiar? *Plus ça change...*

But rendering the summer and fall of 1348, the timeline framed in my second novel, *Between Two Fires,* meant understanding more than just the mechanisms and effect of the Black Death. It meant trying to understand, as best as I could, the mindset of the late medieval man or woman. It meant learning about the architecture of the period generally, and the layout of certain towns and neighborhoods specifically. It meant learning how people made war; what they ate; with whom they hunted, traveled, or made love; how they might be named; how they might be dressed.

First-hand accounts or illustrations were of course invaluable, as were insightful texts written after the fact. But the knowledge I needed would lead me to new depths of research. For example, I could find no sources in English telling me where bridges crossed the Seine in 1348 Paris. I knew about the ironically named *Pont Neuf,* or New Bridge, now the oldest bridge spanning that river; but since it dated from the 1500s, the *Pont Neuf* was not even a sketch when the Black Death came knocking. I knew about a big stone bridge called *Le Grand Pont,* but that collapsed in the 1200s. How the *hell* did 14th century Parisians get from the Right Bank to *Île de la Cité* to The Latin Quarter? To find out, I tapped into my college major — French — to read a French-language Atlas of Medieval Paris, which turned out to be the second most valuable single book I made use of, right after Barbara Tuchman's masterpiece, *A Distant Mirror.* A lot of work for a sentence or two, I know.

I could have just said "they crossed the bridge," and a lot of authors, understandably, would have done so in that situation. But I'm the kind of writer who wants to know *what* bridge, and to name it; not to show off or be pedantic, but to establish with the reader the kind of casual authority that true stories ring with. You don't go from Sausalito to San Francisco across *a bridge;* you cross the Golden Gate Bridge, don't you? You don't walk up *a road* to Holyrood Castle in Edinburgh; you walk the Royal Mile. And when you approach *Île de la Cité* from the north in 1348, you damn well walk across the *Pont aux Meuniers* with its thirteen water mills at the bottom, because the *Pont aux Changeurs* is just for wheeled traffic, and you'll get run over by a shit wagon. And no, I didn't research whether or not there were shit wagons before I wrote that, but, if I had put one in the novel, you can bet I would have.

I also engaged knowledgeable beta readers to watch out for inconsistencies—one of them caught me on persimmons (which originated in East Asia and weren't cultivated in Europe until the 19th century) and another on sunflowers, which are New World flora, and wouldn't have shone in France until at least the sixteenth century.

Nitpicking?

Maybe.

But poor research is a form of author intrusion, and nothing is deadlier to the complex business of crafting illusions.

And what are fiction writers, particularly those in the more fantastical genres, but illusionists?

If I want you to engage the cinema of your mind to see an eely abomination in a river, or a bunch of dead people harvesting grapes, or an angel of God, I can't also ask you to believe a little French girl in 1348 had a mule named Persimmon when you know she wouldn't have known a persimmon from an Xbox. That's a good way to make you remember I'm full of shit about angels, too. And, by extension, devils.

And, as a horror writer, I *really* want you to believe in my devils. Which brings us to the topic of medieval horror, the purview of this collection.

The first thing I think of when I think of what scared medieval Europeans is Hell. Certainly, individuals were scared of dying, getting old, illness, heights, spiders, snakes, or old ladies with moles. But the argument is compelling that a great many of them were frightened of the eternal torture promised to them by the Church should they fail to obey (wait for it...) the Church.

There's something delicious about medieval images of Hell too, isn't there? None of this existential *Hell is other people* hooey. When you come to medieval Hell, you're in for torture, devils, fire, and seas of the damned that are nauseating in their scope. Medieval Catholicism didn't fuck around. It was in a fight to the death, not only with Islam, secularism, and much older indigenous religions; it was amputating and burning mutations in the DNA of its own teachings. You would not only go to Hell for murder; you'd go for heresy. You'd go for believing Christ was only spirit and never had a body. You'd go for not believing the bread you ate at Mass *was* Christ's body.

So Hell had to be *really* good at being *really* bad.

It had to be worse than the short, overworked, oppressed, shame-filled, opiate-free life of war, famine and plague its underfed population lived from day to day and season to season.

And you know what?

It almost was.

Come and see, come and see.

Welcome, Dear Visitor, to my humble little museum of medieval oddities. I am the Curator. Care to join me for a little spin through these echoing halls? I have such sights to show you, if only you think you're brave enough. Follow me—but be mindful not to leave the lighted path. I cannot guarantee your safety should you stray into the shadows.

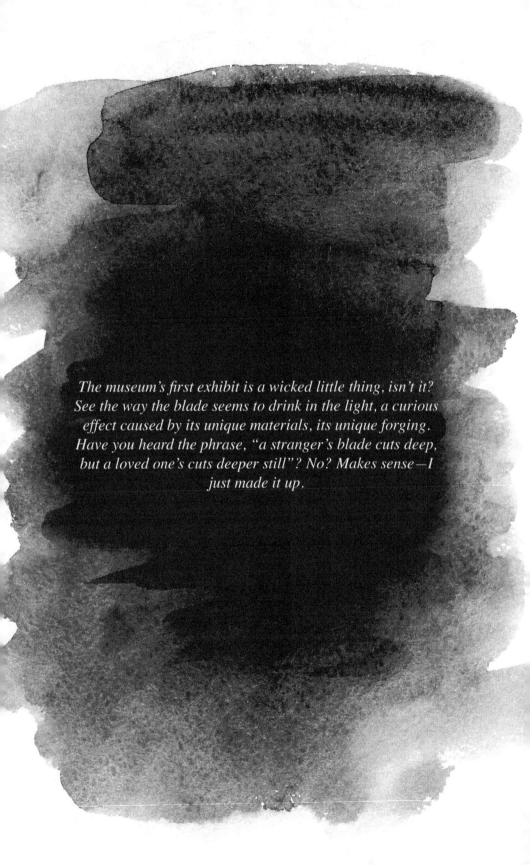

The museum's first exhibit is a wicked little thing, isn't it?
See the way the blade seems to drink in the light, a curious
effect caused by its unique materials, its unique forging.
Have you heard the phrase, "a stranger's blade cuts deep,
but a loved one's cuts deeper still"? No? Makes sense—I
just made it up.

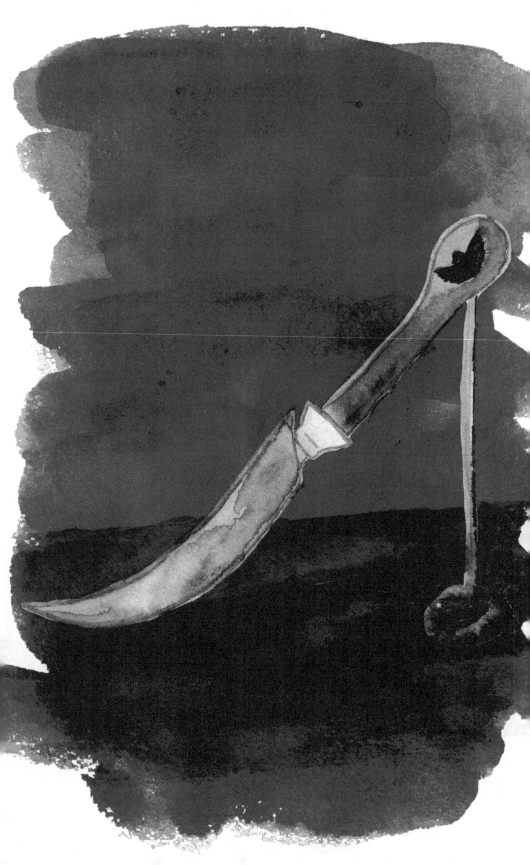

THE CROWING

Caleb Stephens

I mark my age in scars. A forest of white lines mar my forearm, and tomorrow, the day of the Crowing, the hags will cut the final one. Tomorrow, I am to die having never once glimpsed the color of the sky.

A foot in the ribs wakes me, followed by a harsh cackle. My eyes creak open to Mother Valérie gripping a torch, the light dripping across the floor of my cave-made-prison in dusty orange puddles. A cruel smile parts her beautiful lips.

"On your feet, Ronyan! The Black Well awaits."

Ronyan. The Old Crows' name for me, an insult given the scabs that fester my skin and pock my face. The welts and sores that ooze and blister no matter how I tend to them. Though I am only eighteen, I have a spine as crooked as a spinster's, with hair white as frost and skin wrinkled like a leather pouch. The Crowing requires the blood of a royal, and after thirteen years held captive, mine is nearly spent.

I grunt and look away.

"Ahh, feeling feisty, are we, girl? I've no time for your obstinance this morn."

I steel myself for another kick, but instead, she jams the torch into the flank of the goat lying next to me. Hob's screams mix with mine as I push to my knees and grasp her robes. "Please, Mother Valérie, do not harm him. I will do as you say."

Her eyes narrow, and she clucks her tongue. She is centuries old and beautiful beyond measure, her youth stolen bit by bit from mine and the royals the Crows bled before me. "That you will, Ronyan. That you will." She pulls a length of rope from her pocket and flings it at me. "Bind this filthy creature and come. It is time." With a flourish, she turns and stomps outside, a purple cloak trimmed in silver trailing behind her.

I crouch next to Hob and examine the wound. It has already blistered, the hair charred into a pocked ring. I stroke his coat, and he stops licking the burn long enough to give me a soft bleat. I trace my fingers the length of his jaw and then cup his face. His rectangular pupils quiver in place.

"I'm sorry, Hob. Their hate should not fall upon you."

But it will. They will bleed him first.

With a heavy heart, I loop the rope around his neck and give it a tug. He follows without hesitation, even now, marching to his death.

I have never had a finer friend.

I step from the cave and into the swirling fog that has swallowed Francia's sky for a millennium. It is the curse of the Old Crows, a veil so they may hunt unseen, frail shadows painted on the bedchamber walls of Carcassonne's children—there one moment and gone with the child the next.

They took me from the palace when I was five. Thirteen years later, the memory is like a fever dream: Father in our chamber, facing Mother Madeleine with his broadsword drawn, the emerald hilt flashing in the moonlight, Mother Madeleine staring back with her flawless hands wrapped tight around my neck and that of my brother Thomason's, neither of us able to move...to breathe. I can still hear her voice drifting like ice down my spine.

The sky is dark, and the hills are white, both in death as in life. Bring to me a royal's line, for in it, I shall make your kingdom mine. Where there are two, there must be one. Give us thy daughter or give us thy son.

And Father cast his cold, pale eyes on me.

Take the girl if you must.

I bury his hateful voice and hobble after Mother Valérie, every step sending bolts of pain through my ruined feet. The fog lessens as we near the witches' camp: a sea of shining tents and the apothecary full of glass jars packed with various herbs and roots. I know some of their names and uses. Acacia to steal a baby from its mother's womb. Hellebore or maleficium to fly. Nightshade to poison.

Beyond the apothecary, at the edge of the encampment, lie the dead woods—a dense maze of fog-scrubbed bark and desiccated branches. When the Old Crows first brought me here to Salt Rock, Mother Grimilda spoke of the Otherlings, the ageless creatures the Crows seduced and banished within. It was Otherling blood that forged the Black Well, she said, and it is only Otherling blood that can reclaim it.

Sometimes, in the early morning hours, I can hear them shriek. Distant, haunting cries muffled by the fog that crawl across my skin like a nest of spiders. There's a hunger to them, a seething, bubbling rage that bathes the witches in fear. They tell me I am never to speak of the Otherlings, never to mention their name or it will cost me my tongue.

It is said only a Crow may enter the dead woods and survive, and that anyone daft enough to do so will be devoured alive. But I know something different, because I've been in the forest, and I've seen an Otherling with my own eyes. A creature with skin black as the night sky and teeth like metal who spared my life in exchange for a promise—one I intend to fulfill today.

We break from the tents, and I hear the grating whispers of the Old Crows dripping through the air. They gather on either side of the first bone arch, the witches lining the cobblestone path in their ritual garb. Black cloaks clasped at the neck with silver brooches, banks of raven hair pinned in place with bone taken from sparrows. I am ugly in comparison, the old crone from a child's storybook, and if one were to see me now, they would think me the witch.

The Crows fall silent as I hobble forward and brace myself for what comes next. A hot glob of spit smacks my cheek. A warm cup of urine soaks my tunic. My eyes water against the bitter ammonia stench. A handful of rocks flung with force bite into my neck and shoulders. A stone cracks off my shin and sends a sheet of blood running down my calf.

They hurl insults with perfectly shaped lips.

"Bent-nose swine!"

"Wanton whore!"

"Vile filth!"

Fingers tear at my hair as more spit spatters my face. Hob bleats in terror behind me, yanking against the rope with flared nostrils. I go numb inside and force myself to continue. My joints ache as if they are stuffed with glass. At last, I reach the final bone arch with its forest of cracked antlers and press beneath it into the great amphitheater. At its center, bound to the iron latticework encircling Salt Rock, are the children.

There are always four—one for each of the seasons. This year there are three girls and a boy, all of them younger than ten, some closer to five. They stand gagged, their bodies cloaked in simple linen gowns. I do not know the girls, peasants by the looks of them, with ash-smudged cheeks and hair caked in dirt, but the boy's face is unblemished, something familiar about his square jaw and high cheekbones, his tuft of auburn hair. Before I can place it, Mother Valérie jams her gnarled cane into my back.

"Onward, Ronyan. No time to dally."

With quaking legs, I limp over the elaborate wings scorched into the amphitheater floor, the fan-shaped tail and curved beak, and ascend the white stone steps to Salt Rock. The Black Well rises from the stone's center. I can smell it, a stale copper scent that churns in my stomach. Hob smells it, too, bleating and jerking against the rope. I kneel and coax him next to me as the Crows filter in one by one. Their voices crackle with excitement as they take their places, their strength withered after a year without innocent blood.

Mother Madeleine steps forward wearing her feathered headdress and raises her hands.

"Be still, my sisters, be still!"

The buzzing stops.

"Today, on this most sacred of all days, we remember the torment and suffering of those who came before us; the brave sisters who were hanged or burned or torn asunder by the evil men of the south for nothing more than practicing their beliefs. *Our* beliefs."

Murmurs ripple through the coven. Heads nod.

"Today, as we have for a thousand years, we offer the children of Carcassonne to the Black Well as vengeance. With its power, we will renew the fog that chokes their kingdom and holds our enemies at bay. We will drape them in everlasting darkness and"—she levels a long finger at me, then draws it toward the boy—"drink the last drops of youth from their royal daughter and start anew with their princeling son."

A hundred lungs expel as one, the sound like an ocean tide scrubbing sand.

"My Black Sisters, remove thy cloaks!"

Shrouds fall to reveal a sea of milk-white skin. Legs and waists and breasts coated in gooseflesh.

Mother Madeleine slips a sickle from her sleeve and disrobes, the blade shining as she raises her arms overhead once more. "Let the Crowing begin!"

A low reverberating *bom...bom...bom* fills the amphitheater, the Crows at the base of each of the five marble pillars swinging thick elk-bone drumsticks. The sound vibrates my teeth as Mother Madeleine drags one of the girls forward by the hair. She squeals and Mother Madeleine snaps her head back to reveal a soft patch of throat.

"Shh, you stupid thing. Calm now, and I may yet spare thee."

It is a lie, but the girl goes still all the same, urine soaking her gown, fear clouding her gaze. Mother Madeleine nods toward the Crows standing naked before her and begins the chant.

"So what is above, we send below, for the life that is hers, we shall reap with a crow."

The coven echoes the verse, their voices shrill and ragged.

"So what is above, we send below, for the life that is hers, we shall reap with a crow."

And they crow.

"Ah...Ah...Ahhh."

It is the sound that has infested my nightmares for more than a decade. It starts slow, and then builds to a biting, inhuman cadence; a wall of shrieking noise that spills through my veins. The girl's eyes flash to mine a moment before Mother Madeleine carves a red grin into her neck and thrusts her into the well.

She repeats the ritual, wrestling the second girl forward. This one thrashes and screams, stopping only when the sickle parts her esophagus. The last girl flaps her hands and faints a second before Mother Madeleine slits her throat. My eyes burn as she topples into the well. Mother Madeleine smears the girl's blood across her breasts and flashes me a gleaming smile.

"Bring me the beast."

My stomach tears. I do not want Hob to die. He is my family and my only friend. But I have no choice, for it is with his death I hope to win my freedom. With a sinking dread, I limp forward and offer her the rope.

"Ahh, Ronyan, you sod. Today we begin with you."

She snatches my wrist and jerks me to her chest, the sickle coming to rest against my neck. My heart explodes. This is not the way, *cannot* be the way. Hob must die first. In all my years, I have never bled before the animal. My gaze falls upon the Black Well. A billow of acrid heat drifts upward, wet with rot, and my legs go weak. A memory flashes. The Otherling I met in the dead forest. The thing that found me at the base of a withered cypress when I escaped Salt Rock a year ago, its finger tracing across my cheek as it spoke.

Allow me to bind my blood with that of the beast's, then return to the Crows for their feast. Pour my blood into the well and light the fire that will summon hell. Until that time remain unseen, and when you call, we shall make you our queen.

It felt like a dream, the thing slowly drawing a talon across its wrist before setting it to Hob's mouth, Hob lapping at the Otherling's blood until his tongue blackened. I fainted then and woke to Mother Grimilda staring down with her spiteful gaze. She dragged me back by my hair and threatened to carve out my eyes. I begged her not to, swore an oath to never again flee. She smiled and said she wouldn't. She cut off my toes instead.

"Sisters," Mother Madeleine cries, her breath hot in my ear, "let us drink what youth yet remains in this pitiful creature."

I go rigid as the knife digs into my throat.

It cannot happen. It must not.

She begins the chant. "So what is above, we send below, for the life that is hers, we shall reap with a—"

A sudden rush of air skims my cheek, and the sickle falls from my neck. I whirl around to see Mother Madeleine crumple with an arrow protruding from her eye, the shaft fletched with green and gold.

The colors of the king…

A horn blows a haunting, solitary tone. More join it, followed by a great roar and the thunder of hooves. Rows of armor flash dull at the edges of the amphitheater.

"Ready," a voice cries. "Release!"

A storm of arrows rain from the sky and plunge into naked flesh. An Old Crow, one I recognize as Mother Renée, is hacked down near the sacrificial stone, blood streaming over her forehead and into her hateful eyes. Another Crow, one with raven feathers wound through her flaxen hair, bares her teeth and charges a soldier wielding a broadsword, only to be cleaved from behind by a battle-axe. A sea of blades spills through the Crows, men hacking and slashing, killing those who fight back and binding those who don't.

A man in a silver crown ascends the steps of Salt Rock. He is broad-shouldered, with piercing blue eyes, and dressed in a cloak bearing the royal crest of my family—a golden lion spitting a tongue of fire upon a grass-green field. My pulse races. I cannot believe what I am seeing, *who* I am seeing, for before me stands my brother, Thomason.

He strides for the boy and cuts him loose. The child wobbles into his arms with a cry, wrapping his still pudgy arms around Thomason's neck.

"Ah, Faustin, my boy," Thomason says. "Fret not, for we were never far. Sir Jean lay in wait for a fortnight to track the vile Crow who stole you. And here you are found and returned to me safe."

With a gasp, I rush forward and grasp my brother's cloak.

"Thomason, is it truly thee?"

My answer comes as a gauntlet to the temple.

"Do not presume to touch me, crone."

I scatter back, and his eyes scan the deep lines etched into my face and the pockets of sagging flesh planted beneath my eyes.

"What evil is this?" he says. "How is it you know me?"

"Thomason, it is I, your sister Cateline."

He strikes me again, harder, and I taste blood. "Do *not* let that name pass your lips again, witch, or I will carve out your tongue." He crouches in front of me, his eyes simmering with contempt. "Now, I will ask you again. How is it you know me?"

"Because Father had hair as red as yours and Mother colored your eyes."

"Lies." His beard twitches and he glances toward a nearby spearman. "Bind her. We will burn her in Carcassonne with the rest."

"Yes, milord."

The man jerks me to my feet.

"Wait, sire," I cry. "I can end it. I can end the curse. I can bring back the sun."

Thomason pauses, and I expect him to continue down the steps, but he returns and places a steel-tipped finger beneath my chin and tilts my gaze to his. "And why pray tell, should I believe the lies of a Crow?"

"Because I am no Crow, my lord. I too was once like your boy, a child with dreams of seeing the sky before the hags stole me away. I wish nothing more than to see their curse burn."

His eyes turn to slits, and he cocks his head. "I will grant you your wish, but whatever you are, creature, know this. I will not be mocked. If you indeed lie, I shall see to it you are flayed and strung upon the racks." He nods at the spearman with a smirk. "Release her. We shall have our amusement."

The man loosens his grip, and I scurry toward the corpse of Mother Madeleine. I pry the blood-stained sickle from her rigid fingers and then approach Hob and ease my arms beneath his soft belly. It takes all of my remaining strength to lift and set him upon the well's rim. He gives me a sorrowful look, his legs trembling, and my vision blurs. I do not want to do what comes next.

I press my forehead to his and take in a slow, jagged breath.

"Be brave, my dear friend," I whisper. "Be brave."

And I cut his throat.

He squeals. Blood spurts from his neck in a fine red mist that quickly darkens to something like tar, a black, viscous substance that stains my shift and drenches the stone. With a sob, I gently roll him into the well.

"What farce is this?" Thomason says, spreading his arms. "Do you take me for a fool, wench? The mere blood of a goat to appease a thousand-year curse?"

I stand to face him and think once more of the Otherling's whispered words, of its finger drifting across my cheek, cold as a winter spring.

"No, sire. I do not."

He waves to the spearman. "Seize the cursed bitch."

The man takes no more than a step before the first rumble hits. A sudden shearing rises beneath my feet. Cracks splinter outward from the well and race across the amphitheater. Soldiers and Crows slam to the ground. Great slivers of rock break from the stone spires and crush those unlucky enough to be caught beneath. Shrieks of pain split the air. Cries rise all around me. The cracks widen and spear outward through the amphitheater walls, carving jagged black gorges in their wake. It continues for what feels like an eternity, the earth grinding in place, the amphitheater walls crumbling into great plumes of dust and rock.

And then silence.

A blanket of pulverized limestone scorches my nostrils and coats my tongue.

The earth creaks and groans.

Without warning, a tremor greater than the rest shears through Salt Rock. A column of brilliant green light explodes from the Black Well and blooms outward across the sky in a radiant halo.

I have no time to marvel. A crackling bolt of green fire peels from the pillar and strikes my chest. Agony rips through my body. More bolts of green flame branch across the amphitheater to impale the Crows, both living and dead alike. I lock eyes with Mother Valérie, who watches me in horror as her face smokes and peels. Mother Grimilda's mouth unbuckles in a silent scream, her tongue rippling with green veins of light before dissolving entirely. And not just her. *All* of them—every Crow paralyzed and crumbling into ash.

The pain in my chest transforms to a sudden warmth. I watch in wonder as the boils peppering my arms firm to smooth flesh. A prickling sensation spreads across my feet, toes sprouting from the nubs Mother Grimilda's paring knife left behind. My spine pops and straightens until I can once again stand tall. My vision sharpens. The scent of smoke, sulfur, and ash invades my nostrils. My fingertips prod cheeks that have grown soft and full. I pull a length of hair from my shoulders and gasp at the color, the delicate red of my youth.

I cannot move, cannot speak, for I have been remade.

With a sudden *whoosh*, the column of flame flickers and snaps out.

Weapons clatter to the stone all around me. Shields and bows. I look for Thomason in a daze and find him on his knees next to his son, tears streaming into his beard as he gazes skyward in awe. They are all like that, every soldier staring up at a sight not seen for centuries: a lemon-yellow sun piercing a crisp blue sky. It is why they do not spot the black things creeping from the dead forest.

They are creatures twice as tall as any man with hands splintered into eight talon-tipped fingers. They move in crouched silence, tendons leaping across rivers of muscle, their teeth bared in jagged lines.

A soldier shouts and takes his feet with a call to arms. Horns blare. Sharp metal is drawn. It is too late. The Otherlings sweep through the soldiers with frightening speed, disemboweling the men, severing limbs and heads in between shrieks of terror and cries of pain. Thomason's men flee and scatter, and he watches in a daze as they are slaughtered one by one. Soon, he and his son are all that remain.

"Thomason," I say, approaching him.

He looks at me, blinking hard.

"C-Cateline?"

"Yes, Thomason, it is I." My voice is light and without strain. I barely recognize it as my own.

He attempts to stand but is forced back down by the Otherling who found me in the dead forest. His talons click off Thomason's chain mail, his voice leaking out like a wisp of smoke.

"What is to become of this thing, my Queen?"

Thomason's eyes flash, and I see in them Father's hatred: Father as he beat me in my bedchamber while Thomason watched…and laughed. Father who looked upon me with derision and scorn, a girl instead of an heir. Father who all too gladly fed me to the Crows in Thomason's place and whose cruelty drove Mother to take her own life.

With a steady hand, I set a finger beneath his chin as he did mine, mockingly, and tilt it higher. "You have grown cruel as Father, Thomason. You would have had me burned."

His eyes widen. "No! I knew not it was you, dear sister. The knight's guard scoured the land for months in search of you. We all thought you dead."

His mouth twitches, and I know it is a lie.

"Please, I beg of thee, spare my life, and that of my son, your nephew. We shall leave at once."

The boy looks up at me through a sheen of tears, and I nearly break. He is innocent as I once was, but I know with time the boy prince would come to hate me as his father does, and his father before him. I kneel and pull him to me, then take the jeweled sword at Thomason's waist and slide it from the scabbard.

"I will grant you your request, brother. You and your son shall live, but you will wish you hadn't. You will not leave this place. You shall exist as I have, in the dark alone. And you shall watch your son learn to love me in your place."

I nod at the Otherlings restraining him. "Take him away."

Thomason's face lines with rage, and he roars as they drag him from the amphitheater. His son cries and squirms beneath my arm, but I hold him close until he calms.

The Otherling from the dead forest eases next to me, its voice sliding out in a hiss. "What next, my Queen?"

My gaze drops to Thomason's sword, the emerald hilt sparkling in my hand, and I think of the great walled city of my youth. *Carcassonne*. I stare back out over the now unblemished horizon, past the death and slaughter of the amphitheater, and I know my answer.

"We will take back what is mine."

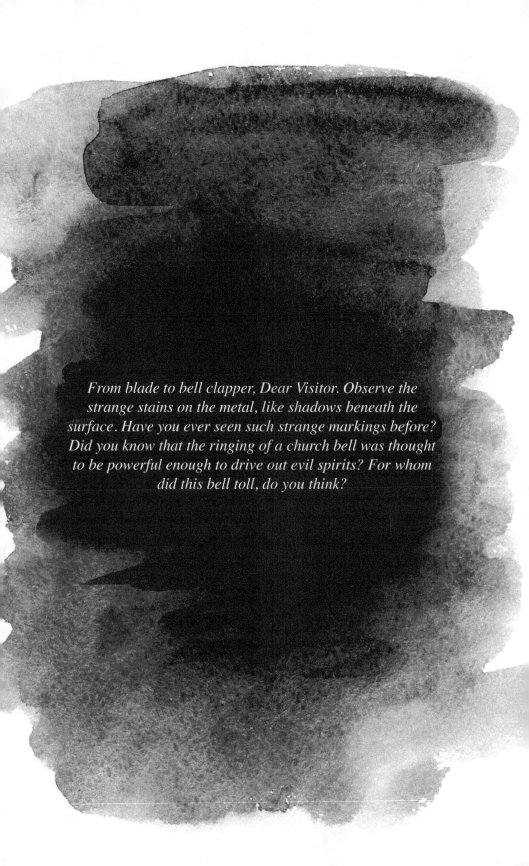

From blade to bell clapper, Dear Visitor. Observe the strange stains on the metal, like shadows beneath the surface. Have you ever seen such strange markings before? Did you know that the ringing of a church bell was thought to be powerful enough to drive out evil spirits? For whom did this bell toll, do you think?

ANGELUS

Philippa Evans

We did not arrive in time to save the child from the violence of the mob.

Indeed, by the time Father Adelard and I reached the field, most of the participants had returned home for dinner; the flames of the pyre were already settling down like the family dog to gnaw over the last of the small bones. Tomorrow, someone would come to rake through the greasy ashes, careful lest a single shard of the witch's body survive the fire.

My mouth filled with saliva, and I gagged as the stench of the morning's cruel activities cut through the sweet, golden fragrance of the nearby bales of hay. Father Adelard buried his face in his hands.

"Not even time for a trial, Elias. She was a mere child!"

"But a wicked one, Father," a sly voice croaked, an elderly woman approaching from the village. "Haste was required to save my son from the she-devil's curse."

As she spoke, I noticed how she turned over and over a curious object in her hands. Catching my gaze, she thrust it out towards me. A crude wax figure—no, two figures. A man and a woman, clumsily shaped, their backs melted together, Janus-like. I recoiled from the baleful thing, my hand instinctively darting to the cross around my neck. Laughing grimly, the old woman tossed the twisted poppet into what remained of the flames.

"The girl's death has freed my son of her charm's effects," she said, "but I don't want witchcraft under my roof."

Adelard looked away from the poppet as it warped and melted to nothingness. "You carry your curses with you, I fear. I will pray for your forgiveness. Come, Elias."

The woman's face curdled in distaste. "And who are you to talk of forgiveness, Adelard of St. Augustine? I've heard the stories: 'the scholar who communes with angels.'" She spat onto the black earth. "Dark magic! I know what a nest of sorcerers Canterbury nurses to her breast."

"I am no necromancer, only a man," the abbot replied, not turning back. "And if the angelic orders have ever considered me worthy of conversation, I have not been blessed with the hearing of it. Certainly not today."

We had been walking an hour before unhappy realization stopped me short, my hands flying up to pat clumsily about my neck and habit. In agitation, I cast my eyes to the path winding behind us, its twisted curves choked with betony and hyssop.

"Whatever is the matter, Elias?" asked Adelard as I rooted among the purple flowers.

"My cross, Father. The one given to me by my mother. I know it was about my neck when we were in the village but…"

Adelard knelt to help me look, his mild blue eyes still clear in spite of his advanced age. He had been our abbot some five years, journeying to our highland wilderness after spending most of his life within the exalted walls of St. Augustine's Abbey. Why anyone might leave such a sanctuary to end up puttering about the weeds with a novice monk, I couldn't guess at the time. I was barely into my twenty-first year, and if it was a sin to yearn for the stained-glass dreamscapes of St. Augustine's, I think most would pardon it.

"I suspect your cross lies some way behind us," the abbot said. "Would you like to go back the way we came?"

I shook my head, grieved at the loss of my mother's gift, but unwilling to return to the scene of the execution. "What was that doll, Father?" I asked. "Was it really—"

"—Black magic?" Adelard hesitated. "It was magic, Elias, but the intent behind it was not evil. Those two waxen figures, back to back, were a charm to cause distance between the people represented. The supposed victim was the girl's uncle, I understand."

"Why would a child wish to lose her uncle's favor?" I wondered aloud. Adelard did not reply, and we walked in silence for some way before his expression thawed.

"Pray for the soul of that poor child, Elias. Her actions were unwise: it is not for laymen to be invoking the Lord's power through means of magic. Only those with the protection given by study and lives lived in holiness can use such tools. Yet she was not evil, and deserves nothing but our pity."

We breached the walls of our abbey, and he turned to me, smiling at last. "Enough of this unhappy topic, my young friend. I find myself in need of an assistant for a new project."

I looked up at him, my cross and the whole sorry day temporarily forgotten. "Me, Father?"

"You indeed! Following the loss of our abbey's precious bell, it has been an inconvenience and a shame to make do with handbells, practical though they may be. After some thought, I have a mind to forge a new bell for the tower, so it might stand empty no longer."

"Are you commissioning it from one of the villages, then?" I asked. "Do you need me to carry a message?"

"Our abbey lacks the funds, and so my plan must be more ambitious. I intend to forge the bell myself. Indeed, I have already made a start."

"Yourself?"

"My father was a blacksmith. A renowned one, in fact, although part of my praise may be attributed to a son's pride. I used to assist him before I was chosen for a monastic life. However, I lack the strength I once had. The spirit is willing, but the flesh, alas—" he sighed. "Let me show you."

He led me to a small workshop which lay just inside our abbey walls. The work itself consisted of a simple oak spindle lying horizontally on a lathe supported by two wooden horses. Around this spindle Adelard had wrapped a sturdy rope in neat coils, and, to this, he had begun applying loam, layer by layer, to form a cylinder.

"What I'm making now," he said, his voice carrying the same reverence he might give to an explanation of the sacraments, "is actually the empty space of the bell. A wax mold will be shaped around this cylindrical core, and a loam shell will cover the wax. Molten metal will then replace the mold, forming our new bell."

As he spoke, he began to guide me, showing me how carefully he applied the layers of loam, allowing time for the wind blowing through the open door to dry his work. So we spent the remainder of our free hours, the abbot telling me tales of St. Augustine's myriad wonders to distract me from the grief and shock of the morning.

We finished the core just as the bells rang for Vespers, the setting sun casting a shroud of amber over the firmament. It was late spring, and the trees stood stark against a sky glowing like a stained glass window, the lights of heaven illuminating the stubbled fields lying fallow in the distance. The evening's embers brought back to me the failure of our morning journey.

"Is it true then, Father, what that woman said about you being a—a sorcerer?" I asked.

"St. Augustine's Abbey is the greatest library of magical texts in all of England, my dear Elias, and I had the good fortune to study and pray there for many years."

"Forgive my ignorance, but are there not injunctions against practicing magic?"

The abbot paused to consider, his expression gentle in the gloaming. "You are right to ask such questions," he said. "Magic is a subtle art. Only those who walk a straight path are able to perceive the line separating Christian magic from necromancy—or frivolity. In my time at St. Augustine's, I saw my fellow monks use their learning for empty tricks and worldly gain. I hope I might impress on you the lesson that one should only make use of such things in times of great need."

"But you maintain the girl they burned was innocent of evil."

"Was her suffering not great enough to warrant any assistance available? Even that of the magical arts?" Adelard frowned.

"Surely it was frivolous when…when compared to magic used to aid kings, or achieve great works? What is one girl's needs in the face of—"

"The suffering of one poor girl, Elias, is worth more to me than the petty concerns of all our worldly rulers. We are told our Lord cares for every fallen sparrow; it saddens me to see this is not the way of men."

"But there's an order to things," I argued. "Divinely ordained by

God, everything in the cosmos has its place, surely. Kings above the common man; men above women; human beings above the animals. God and His angels above all. Some cares must take precedence over others."

Adelard smiled at me, although it seemed a bitter one. "The Chain of Being. Where some see divine order, I fear I see cunning design. Why should a king live in luxury, or monks feast in palaces, when other people are consigned to lives of misery? If there *is* a Chain of Being, it is a chain that strangles some while sparing others. It is a chain that binds the many to the service of the few. Now a spell to shatter such a chain—"

It was only when Adelard broke off with a sigh that I recognized the tension in my own body. A voice howled within me. Some unnameable emotion held down my tongue although it could not still my shaking hand, which reached for the absent cross around my neck.

Adelard watched me intensely, his eyes bright.

"You are the most precocious monk in my care, but perhaps too young for me to have voiced such concerns. I would spare you this, but your time of struggle will come, when you will doubt the providence of a loving Father. But there lies another conversation which will come in its own time. Let us move on; it would be unseemly for either of us to be late to Vespers."

Sleeping in a dorter full of other monks is a labor in and of itself. Despite the anonymity granted by blind night, there can be little privacy, and a continuous wall of sound renders the infinite dark more constricting than one's bedclothes.

Still, the years had accustomed me to the whimpers of my brother monks, the mumbled visions of the dream-dazed, the flatulence, the snores, and the restless susurrations of the sleepless.

This night was different.

At first I thought someone was waking me for Matins. A white shape hovered above me in the gloom, its face indistinct despite my repeated attempts to fix my eyes upon its features. Although within arm's reach, it felt somehow far away, like a pale fish twisting in deep, dark waters—its normal size an illusion of distance.

More than anything, I prayed it would come no nearer.

A sound seemed to emanate from the figure and I realized I had not heard the familiar noises of my companions since awakening. Instead, there was the muffled hiss of snowfall and, beyond it, a high keening sound—neither voice nor music nor a ringing in my ears, and yet all of these.

The cresset lights that burned continually did little more than illuminate the shadows. But as I moved more completely into the waking world, my mysterious bedside companion grew more distinct.

The blood beating in my ears drowned out all else as I finally saw its expression, awe and terror washing over me. My eyes widened to match its stare, my mouth mirroring its own in its stretched, silent scream as tears of dirty wax burned its beautiful pale cheeks.

"And then what happened?" Adelard asked. As I related my nighttime adventure, he had kept his eyes on his work, molding strips of wax to the bell core with his weathered hands. Unable to go back to sleep, I had found him already hard at work on the bell. Now he turned his face to me, frowning when I found myself struggling to answer his question.

"My memory of what follows is confused, Father. We seemed frozen for a long time, the being and I. And yet Circator Thomas says he woke me when he first heard me scream."

"You did not relate this story as if it were a dream," the abbot prompted.

"I am certain the visitation of that strange figure led me from sleep to the waking world—not the other way around."

Adelard reached for another long piece of the supple wax. I noticed the underside, which he quickly placed against the bell core, had deep indentations scratched into it: a crawling script I did not recognize.

"Magic again, Father?" The words felt wrong in my mouth. A sense of struggle arose in me, as if I were resisting a wrenching wave of nausea. An overwhelming smell of aloeswood and ambergris brightened the warm air of the workroom with musky sweet notes. Seeing my distress, Adelard placed a hand on my shoulder, as if to anchor me.

"Do not let it concern you, my son. All bells harbor intrinsic power, you know. Church bells are commonly dedicated to a particular saint, or a specific purpose. The chimes of our old, cracked bell were known for casting out demons and perhaps, when this new bell is in place, you will find your nighttime visitor no longer troubles you."

"This being did not strike me as demonic," I murmured. "It felt...holy."

Adelard said nothing as he showed me how to perfect the wax mold, scraping off the unseemly bumps by pressing a sharp, flat piece of iron to the shape as he turned it on the spindle. To the casual observer, he wore a look of absorption on his face, but I who knew him better could see he was deeply troubled.

Later that night I came to my senses in the infirmary garden, three winged creatures at my side. I was on my hands and knees like a beast, my fingers tearing at soil and sage, releasing its cool scent into the night air.

The first figure—my visitor from the previous night—was frozen, its eyes white with blindness, one finger pointing down to the earth. Wax clogged its companions' mouths, but I could hear a trapped angelic music within them, begging me in escalating waves of harmony to dig deeper. What choice did I have?

Fetching a spade, I shifted more soil, rooting up sage, comfrey, and rue as my tool bit deeper and deeper into the ground. Before long, something pale emerged from the dark earth.

I thought it was a baby at first, small and white against the soil. Yet it was more unyielding than human flesh. I soon realized my mistake—and the extent of the abbot's evil. Two wax figures, facing one another, their fronts melded together in an eternal embrace. Looped around them was my silver cross. My love for the abbot seemed sick to me, then.

Repulsed, I made to drop the cursed thing, but my angel was at my side before it could fall once more to the ground. Taking it from me, it brought the doll up to its mouth and chewed through the wax, its screams of anger and pain transmitted directly into my mind as the wax liquified on its tongue and boiled inside its throat.

I screamed with it, tasting blood. When I was next able to open my eyes, I was alone in the garden with nothing but the silver cross in my dirt-smeared hand.

I ran through the cloister, my feet slapping against a stone floor dappled with dawn and shadow. I could hear the roar of blood in my ears as my heart pounded in time to the ringing bells. Bells. In spite of my discovery, my body thrilled with mortification: I was late for Lauds.

When our communal devotions were at an end, I wandered to the workshop, unsure of how best to confront the Father I had loved so dearly. Afraid of his power, it felt easier to feign ignorance in order to determine his design.

I worried Adelard might sense my unease, but the labor was a harsh distraction from my fear, and I finally understood the abbot's need of me. He had completed the waxen form of the bell, preparing the crown in my absence, but a strong pair of arms was necessary to help Adelard remove the spindle from the bell core. Once done, he applied himself to closing the bell at one end, adding the sound holes, and covering the wax bell model with the finest loam, sealing his work away.

Anticipation mounted throughout the abbey as the bell neared completion. Adelard continued to work on the finer details of the bell while I dug our furnace. I was no stranger to working the soil, but the waist-high pit cost me many hours of labor and I felt faint by the time I had finished.

The work was easier afterwards. Adelard and I built a fire in the pit, lowering the bell so the loam shell might be hardened in the flames—enough to withstand the molten metal we would pour into it. We then filled in the pit, leaving nothing visible but the aperture through which we might pour the bell metal.

"The metal alloy will melt away the wax," Adelard explained, "and fill the space between the bell core and the loam shell I have packed around the wax mold. It's a kind of magic, Elias, and I cannot wait for you to see what we two have made."

"A kind of magic," I echoed dully. I could dissemble no longer, and Adelard recognized at last the anguish in my eyes. I reached into my habit and pulled out the silver cross.

"So you know."

Recriminations and accusations choked me in my haste to voice them. In the end, strangled with an irrevocable sense of betrayal, I could only ask: "Why?"

"You have always been my favorite," Adelard said, simply.

"Your *favorite?*"

"I spoke true, on our walk back from the village. I am no longer young, and I need assistance. Now more than ever. My greatest work is yet to be completed."

"And so you compelled me? Conjured my loyalty?"

"I was only magnifying something already present, Elias," Adelard said, his voice gentle. "The image magic was nothing more than security. You were so interested in magic, so suspicious. My spell was only to ensure your acceptance. I had hoped, by the end, such magic would no longer be necessary, as you came to understand and agree with my design."

"But what are you doing?" I cried. "I don't understand what any of this is for!"

Adelard was amused. "What else but the bell, my son? One toll will shuffle the Divine order, shatter the links in the Chain of Being." He held out his hands, palms up in supplication. "I wish only to free mankind from a monstrous God."

"You'd sell your soul on account of one she-devil's death?" I cried. "You are not the first Accuser to revolt against his Master out of misguided feelings over what is right!"

"What God sets a ravening wolf upon a child who trusts her uncle, Elias? And then lets her burn for his guilt? Do you know they doused her in pitch before they set the flame to her skin? Can you imagine the ropes burning away as she exploded—a living hellfire?" Adelard unclenched his fists, his breath rasping against my silence. "You think we are beloved of God and His angels, my son, but we are nothing! Nothing but food, slaves, and sport. I know who exposed my spell to you, and I tell you your angels are monsters. They will devour you—in this world or the next."

43

I spat at his outstretched hands.

"As you wish," he sighed. "Do not think the destruction of the wax poppet has wholly freed you from its effects. You will love, hate, and obey me until my death."

I collapsed onto my bed, so tired and defeated I didn't feel myself crossing the border into dream.

I was in a world of fire and eyes and music. All around me seemed to fit into some holy machine of winged wheels that spun and turned, the rushing noise of their passing drowning out the hymns screamed by the Saints as they burned in eternal immolation. I no longer remember the words to the songs poured from those ashen throats like liquid gold, nor do I wish to. Stunned into horrified reverence, my eyes burned with this vision of Heaven.

When my angelic companions approached, I wept with remorse at my weakness, my botched confrontation with Adelard. I was little more than a pawn and a fool.

But God's grace extends even to fools. Resuming their familiar forms, the first angel took my cross from around my neck and consumed it. After speaking its own true name, it allowed its companion to tear into its torso to retrieve the cross and repeat the process.

They ignored me as I screamed, my ears bleeding with every syllable uttered until, at last, I found myself in bed once more, my spine arched backwards in an agonized wheel.

The day of the pouring arrived. If my mind was elsewhere during my prayers, I felt God would forgive my distraction.

My guardian angels had offered me the key to my prison cell, and I was careful to affect the same obedience I was accustomed to showing Adelard. Together, we fired up the little workshop furnace, mixing four parts copper to one part tin in the crucible.

It was sweaty work, and he failed to spy my hands as they slipped one last element into the alloy. I felt naked once more, without the protection of my silver cross, but I had faith it would serve its divine purpose. We navigated the tricky process of pouring molten metal into the small hole in the ground, battling the heat and fire as we tried to ensure none of the alloy was wasted.

This accomplished, we had barely enough time to rest, as the bell needed to be dug up immediately. Too long, and the cooling metal might crack against the shell, ruining our best efforts. Those few lay brothers our abbey possessed were tasked with exhuming the bell, its weathered shell looking for all the world like some relic long lost to time.

Adelard chipped away the dried shell with a hammer and chisel, working against time to free his unholy art from its loam coffin. Its form was true to his intention and he spent the following hours shaving away the rough edges of the bell and fitting the wrought iron clapper in its place.

I didn't dare to examine the bell's interior to see if the abbot's foul scratches had been transferred from wax to metal according to his design. But I knew by the way his shoulders sank in relief and he said, his voice tight, "It is done, dear Elias. It is done."

As curlews trilled their endless questions to the approaching evening, and pink clouds clotted the darkening sky, the bell was at last set in its place in the tower. We all gathered together before

Compline to honor the abbot's achievement and listen to his bell lend its lone voice to the evening song of the birds. Father Adelard stood to the front, his face raised up towards the tower, waiting for the first chimes that would bring about our liberty and ruin.

The hour came and the bell swung on its headstock. But there was no sound to chime out into the empty fields. Rooks rose in a crash of sound from a nearby copse of beech trees, startled by something that escaped our own confused senses. And then—nothing. We watched the bell swing back and forth, silence pealing into the looming dark.

Father Adelard turned around, his eyes meeting mine in accusation. He opened his mouth to speak—a question? A curse? I will never know. A bone-shattering gong shuddered forth from his open mouth, deep and resonant as the cry of some pain-wracked leviathan.

Waves of invisible force knocked us all to the earth, washing over us again and again until my brothers screamed against the relentless fury. Sprawled on my belly, I looked up towards our abbot. He stood alone as a tortured choir of bells resonated within his harrowed form, tumbling from his bleeding mouth.

The clear bronze tones of his own death knell beat again and again within Adelard's slowly unraveling flesh, tearing through his lips and forcing down his shattered jaw until it hung loose like a ragged stole. And yet, despite the dark gore spilling from his broken face and the excruciating crescendo of the bell, it was only when Adelard cast his eyes to the heavens that terror seemed to take him. I looked up.

It crawled down towards our ruined abbot—my angel, guardian of my soul—clawing through the fading clouds, dragging the gloaming in its wake. It met him as a lover, bending over Adelard to draw what remained of his face to its own. Blood and light flowed from their kiss, the angel's pale throat working as it feasted upon the abbot's dying harmonies.

At length, it was over. Adelard stood alone, swaying in the hushed half-light. As the new bell ceased its movement within the tower, one final *crack* echoed in the stillness. The bell, split down the middle, toppled from its perch. Father Adelard—one side of his body slipping from the other with the wet smoothness of a pared plum—collapsed, steaming, to the blood-dappled grass.

My fellow monks refused to touch our former abbot's corpse. I had to bury him alone, in unconsecrated earth. I didn't know what to do with the bell clapper I found within his entrails, transmuted from iron to purest gold, shining through the gore. I admit I kept it. Few men can claim to possess irrevocable proof of our true Father, and I hold onto mine with fear and trembling.

I have nothing further to confess. Indeed, I know not what sin I have committed, except perhaps some doubt of our Father's infinite mercy. I have spent the remainder of my life waiting to hear my Master's voice telling me: "Well done, good and faithful servant." If He has said it, I cannot hear it above the ceaseless ringing that has haunted me ever after.

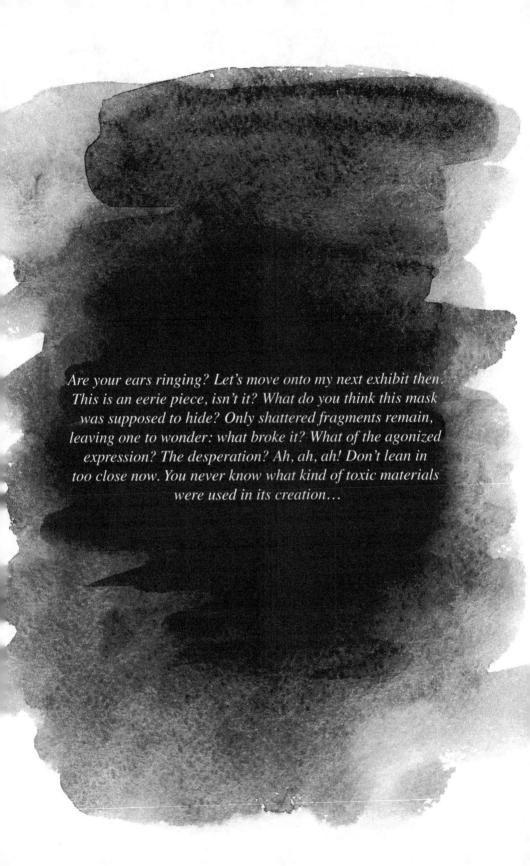

Are your ears ringing? Let's move onto my next exhibit then. This is an eerie piece, isn't it? What do you think this mask was supposed to hide? Only shattered fragments remain, leaving one to wonder: what broke it? What of the agonized expression? The desperation? Ah, ah, ah! Don't lean in too close now. You never know what kind of toxic materials were used in its creation…

PALETTE

J.L. Kiefer

he line etched across her forehead, deep as a vein, as if a string had been stretched against the skin. She rubbed it, but it would not erase; her young elastic skin would not uncrease.

It remained the next morning, deeper, darker. Fraying at the edges with little bird's claws. She examined it in her miniature hand mirror. It stretched the length of her index finger. She scratched her nail across it, in the groove, the only mar of her beauty. But she could fix it.

Every Saturday, she stirred the lead powder into rosewater. When it thickened into a dough, she would roll it into little pills and store them in a jar. She followed a recipe one of the nurses in the lady's estate had taught her when she had dropped off a swath of intricate fabric. Each morning she would dissolve one of these into more rosewater until it thinned back into a paste she could spread across her skin. This morning she poured less rosewater, the white paste thick enough to cake, to fill in the crack across her forehead like plaster, the bloodless ivory reaching up to her hairline. Onto her cheeks and lips, she rubbed bryony until they swelled, bright crimson. If she'd recently boiled Brazilwood and mixed in the alum to create a maroon dye for her yarn, she might dip her fingers into the cooling pot and swipe the color across her skin.

The girl had always been known for her beauty and for her madman concoctions, the lead paste long-lasting into the night, when she would remove it with yet more rosewater. Her beauty had been her obsession since she was a child, when her mother had taken her on a delivery to the manor, the large stone structure that loomed over the rest of the village like a giant boot about to stomp and trample. Her mother carted the fabric, one that had taken her months to complete. Washing the raw wool. Rubbing her finger-tips into angry welts spinning the yarn. Blooming blisters over the welts boiling the dye. Draining the boils while weaving the fabric, the needle growing slick and sticky. Along the edges were vined flowers which were mirrored in the opposing color on the back side of the bolt. A little dot of deep scarlet nestled against the wool. It had seeped into the only bit undyed, a dribble of her mother's own blood, diluted and mixed with the blister's serum when the needle had slipped and jabbed past the bag at the end of her fingers.

Her mother had taken her, then eight years old, to the manor to make the delivery and collect the money. It was some unusual arrangement with the lady, who wished to inspect the fabric before purchasing, but who could not be bothered to trek into the village herself. Just a child, the girl felt as though she were being swallowed as she followed her mother into the foyer, each little stone set into the wall like a chipped and rotten tooth. The expansive mouth of the manor house dissipated from her mind when the lady entered. The girl's breath caught in her throat. The lady's dress flowed along the floor as if she hovered inches above the stone. Her face was pure white. Paler than anything the young child had ever seen, the stark expanse led all the way up to the high hairline along the top of her skull. The effect was broken only by little spots of rouge on her cheekbones and lips.

The lady's uncalloused fingers petted the fabric. Her lips, dark as blood, twitched into a scowl when she lifted her head and caught a glimpse of the woman who wove the fabric, the woman with hair matted into nests, with fingers cobbled into thick knobs of skin and scabs. The lady's fingers jumped from the fabric and her nurse gathered it, scurrying away at her command to have it cleaned.

The girl vowed to never receive such a scowl. She would remain perfect and porcelain—and hide her own wrecked hands inside gloves.

Before she had been taught how to craft the makeup by one of the lady's nurses, before she could source all the little ingredients needed to paint her face, the lead, the orpiment, the quicklime and quicksilver, she would sneak into her mother's workshop. She searched for one of the long threading needles, and she would prick her fingers, a singular dot on the pads, letting out blood enough to leave her face ghostly.

Once her mother caught her, hands wet with her own blood, she pried the long needle out of her daughter's fingers. Then she locked the thin rods away in a wooden chest. Her mother would unlock it only during working hours, only when she needed to retrieve the needles to sew, the long, sharp things harvested and the box relocked. But the girl had discovered a stray needle on the floor. She poked it into the hem of her skirt. Each morning before dawn, she pushed it beneath her skin, its pointy fang ripping between the wrinkles on her palm or the ridges on her fingertips. It let out the blood like a fountain, the deep crimson bubbling to the surface. An old trick to leave her face as she desired—a colorless palette with ruddy cheeks. A poor comparison to the beauty of the lady, but it would suffice. Her fingertips had healed, now only letting out blood when the needle strayed, when it was a true accident.

Now, the crease on her face pulsed beneath her mask, and when she wiped away its cover, it had borne a twin. A second fat wrinkle stretched across the space above her eyes.

In the passing days, the marks multiplied as if her skin had been folded and a hot iron applied: tiny scars spanned from the edges of her eyes and at the corners of her lips; pockmarks lined her cheeks, like little craters scooped away. Soon, she applied her first layer of paste blind, not lifting the little round mirror until it could at least dampen the effect, could erase the years her face had inexplicably gained. Soon she dissolved three or more of the lead balls each morning. But her art was exquisite, as precise as her fabric. With a practiced hand, she filled in the cracks, the scars, the dimples, the ever-deepening craters.

Pain bloomed beneath her perfect mask. It became a throbbing metronome while she twisted raw wool into strands thin as web, to be dyed and then woven into an intricate fabric for the lady of the village. This commission would feed her for a full year, and, she hoped, would fashion a grand gown or cape that would inspire more from the upper echelons of the kingdom. With a screw of her neck, a wetness pooled against her skin. Beneath the lead shield, there was a sudden pop against the top of her cheekbone where she'd rubbed the bryony and honey to redden. A sharp agony invaded the spot, as if a rogue dog had clamped its wet teeth into her face. She slapped her hand over it, sure that the wet, the pus, was eating the lead, leaving a dark blemish. She abandoned her wool, her workshop. Her mask was eroding. She could feel it dissolving as she stomped up the stairs to her bedroom.

The spot seemed to vibrate, the angry rash tinged at the edges with green. When she wiped at her skin, thick swaths of the makeup fell away like an avalanche, caked by sweat. A pustule had broken. The thin membrane still cupped the yellow mucus in a sack, having ripped at the top, the little bag drooping against a wrinkle. Its exposed innards screamed with invisible daggers, and when she pushed her hand mirror up close, she could see the raw, rotten skin inside the boil writhe and squirm, pucker.

Soon a whole crop of these blisters freckled her face. A row dotted her forehead, swelling and expanding with sticky liquid overnight. In the morning, sunlight piercing through the window, she pricked each one with a sharp needle. Each expelled its glossy innards, deflating into concave redness that she could fill with lead, little wet mouths she could stuff with so much of it that they'd choke.

By the third day of pricking and emptying and refilling, she'd stopped removing the powder entirely. She'd stopped uncovering her ruined face. Instead, she caked on more of the lead. Her features blurred to the outside world while her skin writhed underneath, while it simmered and throbbed, her pores ballooning with milky pus until they flattened beneath the stiff mask, until they had no choice but to break and burn and further plaster the lead to themselves. While she wove on the loom, the thin threads transforming to delicate roses, her skin slithered. Raw boils emitted muffled screams. Tendons and stringy muscle twitched as if her skin had melted, as if it had dissolved entirely into the lead.

The thick paste surrounded her eyes, leaving a pinprick through which to see the tiny needle. She bobbed it through the long cords strung vertically. Then she pushed it straight into the middle finger of her opposing hand, the sharp tip sliding cleanly between her nail and flesh. The automatic jerk to her mouth splattered not only her crisp mask but the work in front of her, the blood worming its way deep into the thread, the pink rose now wilting.

The fourth day, she hovered over a hot pot of dye, agitating it with the long handle of a wooden spoon. She had to remake what she'd snipped away after bandaging her finger. The operation had become so practiced that she could dodge the steam and spittle of the pot with precise motions, knowing exactly the moment the turmoil of pink would overflow, would throw daggers up towards her pristine face.

A ruckus clattered at the edge of the street, the boisterous sound smashing into her shop, hovering above the sloshing of the dye. A street festival full of fools, each jester holding a paper mâché face over their own, blank slates with slits for eyes—the season's excess harvest an excuse to celebrate with copious ale and chaos. Before she could close up her shop to their anarchy, the drunk, faceless jesters poured into it, their grimy fingers plucking at the taut strings of her loom, snapping them and the roses in their crazed reverie, grinding clay into her skeins, clanging her tools to the ground.

In her sprint towards their commotion, a single drop of pink careened into her cheek, sizzling into the thick lead, a little eroding pond in the pale sand. But her own screams to stop were buried beneath their tumult and met with jest, with the masked figures pulling on her wrists, begging her out into the street as one of them.

As if a taut cord stretched from her fingers up her arm, around her elbow, through the stringy pieces of her neck, up to her chin, the fool's touch ricocheted up and vibrated through her perfect face, leaving a hairline crack. One more jolt and the crack fissured. A porcelain chunk shattered against the ground, sending up a cloud of chalk dust.

The exposed skin along her jaw wriggled as if on fire.

The hand pulling at her wrist became a limp hunk of meat. The eyes beneath the fool's mask widened before she slapped her hand over the spot. It tingled as though ticks crawled and wormed their way across the raw flesh.

She dashed inside, up the stairs, past more fools dirtying her wares, swaying and toppling the loom holding her magnum opus in their drunken reverie. The daggering pain of incoming air spread its tendrils across her face. The fissure sent out more cracks like a lightning bolt. A line of fire erupted across the bridge of her nose and over her other cheek, one million tiny screaming mouths across her forehead as more pieces tumbled away. An explosion of white sprang from the steps, each piece disintegrating upon impact. By the time she reached her bedroom, the entire thing had fallen away.

Now bare, her skin screeched with the sensation of pinpricks, as if all of the needles from her shop had flown up the stairs and straight through her cheeks, the tips digging between her teeth, poking at her gums. It felt like a pair of them, the curved ones, had slipped underneath her eyelids, the metal sliding up and over her eyeball, piercing behind them with such pain that her vision blurred. Feverishly, she mixed the lead with the rosewater. The jar of the little balls skittered, the glass smashing against the floor. She pressed the paste against her skin, rubbing it with her fingers, but something was wrong. As she dabbed the paste on, the skin stuck to her fingertips. The whole thing slid away in a rotten sheet, dotted with holes like moth-eaten fabric. It fell to the table in front of her, green and purple still milky from the lead.

A drip of blood splattered across what had been the skin of her forehead.

Another rained onto the former bridge of her nose.

Now, the stringy muscles and tendons exposed and throbbing, the pain howled and ricocheted through her entire body, a paralyzing zing, which she choked with lead, finding a stray ball of it on the corner of the table and pushing it into the pulp of her face until the sharp pitch inside her skull muffled, until she'd created a new skin, pink with blood. She covered it with more lead—she wouldn't let her face be ruined like her unfinished, ripped fabric.

She inhaled. Her beauty was restored. The pain dulled to a quiet throb. She lifted the little mirror to check—clean ivory with just a hint of burgundy at her cheeks and lips. Before she moved to return to her shop, to clean up the remnants of her former face and the fool's dirt from her yarn and loom, the tatters of her work, she spied it.

The welt on her wrist, the size of a pfennig.

It boiled beneath its thin lid, tumultuous as an ocean in a storm.

She reached for the small needle she kept upstairs and discovered another blemish on her thumb filled with green pus, full to bursting, the sheath stretched taut. And still, as she stabbed through the spots, vomiting their innards, thick like clotted cream, the raw skin screaming still beneath, yet another pustule appeared on her forearm. She found five more spots to hollow. She moved to cover them, to gag them too with the paste. Each moment exposed more of them, each one the same as the last, a whole crop of oversized pimples edged with green.

Beneath her, in the shop, the half-finished fabric—an elaborate commission for the lady of the village—bleached in the sunlight, the edges fraying for days before one of the fools snatched it from the loom. The skeins stacked along the wall disappeared into greedy hands. The pot of dye was upended, spilled a deep river between the cobblestones, the dregs breeding a foul odor, eating the thread she had shoved into it. Soon even the loom itself was dismantled.

Upstairs, as quickly as the blemishes emerged, she worked to cover them.

Prick. Drain. Choke.

Across her entire body, she plastered on the lead, until not an inch of skin was left exposed, until she entombed herself in it, unable to bend an elbow or knee or wrist to continue, lest she crack and her façade crumble. Underneath, her skin poached. The white nibbled at the raw skin with little invisible teeth until her epidermis melted, letting it soak into her muscles, then her bones, eating away until nothing was left but the shell of her own doing.

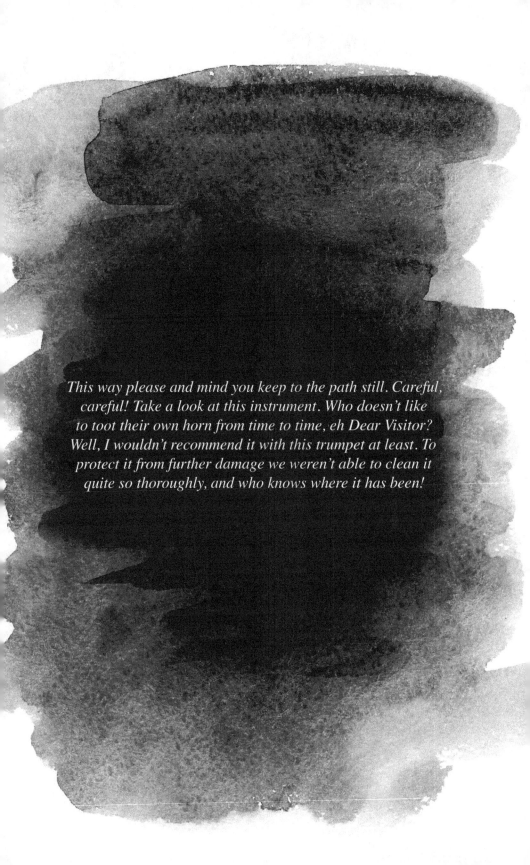

This way please and mind you keep to the path still. Careful,
careful! Take a look at this instrument. Who doesn't like
to toot their own horn from time to time, eh Dear Visitor?
Well, I wouldn't recommend it with this trumpet at least. To
protect it from further damage we weren't able to clean it
quite so thoroughly, and who knows where it has been!

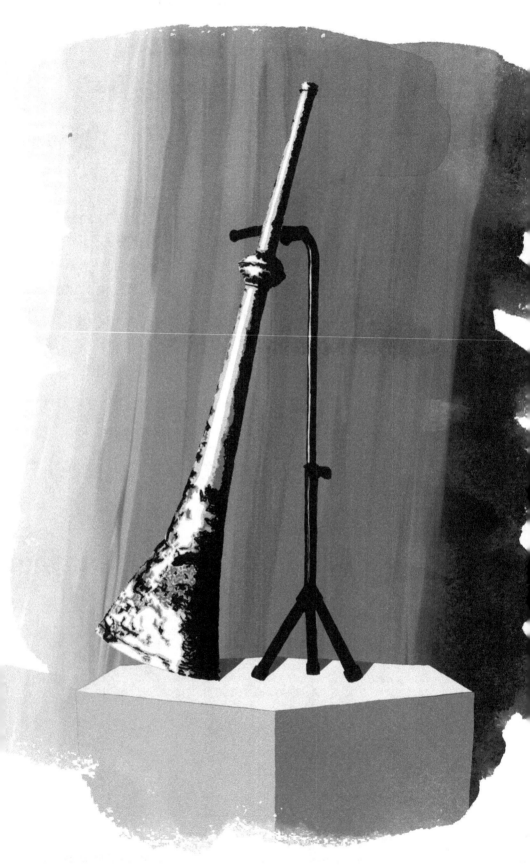

BROTHER CORNELIUS
Peter Ong Cook

onald and Kevin were expressly forbidden access to the room. It was hidden behind a bookshelf crowded with rusted musical instruments, which should have stopped them. But Kevin insisted.

"Prior Benedict did say we had to dust *every* corner," Kevin said. "Top and bottom."

Ronald rolled his eyes. They stood in the lowest basement level of the monastery, a dim stone-paved room, lit only with the lantern Ronald held. "You're still looking for that secret store of ale, aren't you?" asked Ronald.

"What of it?" Kevin polished a trumpet standing bell-down. "I wouldn't mind a secret store of wine, neither."

A ribbon of stale air seeped between the shelves, tickling the hair on Ronald's arms. He shivered. "Do you smell that strange air?"

"It wasn't me," Kevin said. "Not this time."

Ronald shook his head. On closer inspection, faint handprints in the layers of dust and the quarter-circle scraped into the floor indicated the bookshelves had been swung aside at some point in the past decade.

Ronald was bored. Monastic life should have been scholarly. Prior Benedict led him to believe his time would be spent illuminating calligraphic manuscripts. Instead, his hands were cramped from handling brooms with his obnoxious friend. "Indeed," he said. "Let us inspect the clearly clandestine chamber."

They pulled the edge of the bookcase. Brass trumpets clamored to the granite floor in a cloud of dust. They were so deep beneath the surface that nobody would hear the noise.

Ronald crept forward into the chamber lantern first, its stone corners hidden by shadow. The room was already dimly lit by an unusual red lantern. An angular silhouette sat at a desk before him.

Kevin began chanting his plainsong.

"Quiet," Ronald whispered.

"You know I sing when I'm nervous," Kevin replied.

"You sing when you're nervous, sing when you're relaxed, sing during quietude, sing during loudness. Prithee, silence." He wondered how a person performing Gregorian chants, which were practically hummed in monotonous flat tones, could sing off-key. The sound of flatulence was preferable.

Raising his lantern, Ronald shuddered. The light shone on a robed man who sat hunched so low he looked headless. "Pardon me for disturbing you, my brother," said Ronald. He held his breath, turning his head to see Kevin shrug and mouth the words "where is the wine?"

He tapped the man's shoulder, bones beneath threadbare robes. The tang of rot lingered, like a rat left in its trap so long it was no more than a matted husk. The hairs on Ronald's arms stood on end. He took a shallow breath. "Are you well?"

The body shifted forward like collapsing scaffolding, sending the stagnant air swirling in crimson-tinted particles. The body exhaled, "Oooaauuugh."

Ronald gasped, turned, yanking Kevin from the room by his gray hood and shoving the bookshelf door closed, more musical instruments clattering to the floor.

Kevin panted as they reached the ground level. "Gads," he said, tugging on Ronald's sleeve. "Ronald. We forgot to ask him if he knew where the wine was."

Ronald sought Prior Benedict in the rectory during dinner. The candlelit hall bustled with monks taking their bowls of potato stew and crusty bread to long rows of tables. He pushed aside monks to wedge himself onto the bench next to the pungent man. Benedict smelled like old spilled ale, old enough to stick to your sandal. Kevin forced himself in as well.

Ronald faced the prior. "Brother Benedict, I—"

"How was your day, Brother Kevin? Have you made much progress?" asked Benedict.

"*I'm* Ronald. *He's* Kevin." Ronald huffed, jabbing his thumb in Kevin's direction. They were often mistaken, even though Ronald was short with close-cropped raven hair, and Kevin was tall with a mop of red curls. "I wanted to ask about the bottom floor," said Ronald. "We happened upon a small chamber, in it a man—"

"I do not understand why postulates keep going into that room," Benedict sighed to himself. He had assigned them the task of dusting and sweeping the entire monastery, including all four basement levels. Benedict turned, pointing his half-eaten roll at Ronald. "That man would be Brother Cornelius. He is transcribing an important manuscript. That is the room the order forbade you from entering. It is intentionally obscured. Do you not listen?"

"But he wasn't moving," said Ronald. "He didn't respond when I talked to him—"

"That's because he's undertaken a vow," said Benedict.

Kevin tilted his head. "A what?"

"A vow of silence," Benedict said.

Kevin choked. "*Silence?*"

"But," Ronald insisted, "the man was gaunt, withered, practically lifeless."

"He's..." Benedict stuffed the remainder of the roll into his mouth, chewing slower. "Weak. From fasting."

"*Fasting?*" Kevin's ruddy cheeks blanched. "That poor man." He signed the cross. "Bless him."

"Anon, Brothers," Benedict said, the lump of bread slowly sliding down his gullet, "you are postulates, so I shall speak bluntly. Forget you ever saw that room. Forget you ever saw Brother Cornelius. Do your work. Be thankful for the clothes on your back, the food in your bowl, and the roof over your head. Be glad of God's grace." He signed the cross and turned back to his meal.

Ronald rose from the bench, his appetite gone. He pulled Kevin by his hood out of the rectory and into the empty cloister. "That must be what all of those rumors were about."

"Which rumors?" said Kevin.

"The rumors we heard—about dark magic, necromancy, all happening *here*, in the bowels of this monastery," said Ronald.

"I was hoping it was the rumors about the secret wine and ale," Kevin grumbled.

"We have to get to the bottom of this."

"*Bottom*," Kevin snickered.

Ronald scoffed. "Never mind. I'll see you at matins."

Ronald rapidly tapped his foot, waiting on the staircase to the chapterhouse where the order held nightly matins. This was Kevin's favorite time, for this was when everybody prayed in song. Monks made their way up the stairs.

Kevin approached. "Just in time, Brother Ronald," he said, slinging his arm over his shoulder.

"No, Kevin, I need to show you something about—" Ronald pulled Kevin's ear toward him and whispered, "Brother Cornelius."

"Brother Cornelius?!" Kevin shouted. A few heads turned toward them.

"Quiet, you," Ronald growled. "Come with me."

"Brother Benedict clearly told us not to mind him. You minded him, didn't you?"

"Hush, I have seen something," Ronald motioned Kevin to follow.

"Ale?" Kevin was ever-hopeful.

"Necromancy," Ronald whispered.

"Necromancy!" Kevin shouted. Heads turned again.

They descended to the fourth sub-level, fetid air escaping from the small room, Cornelius still hunched over his desk. Ronald crept around to face the man, Kevin intimately close behind. For once, Ronald was glad to have his friend so nearby.

"Hark," Ronald said, wincing. He covered his nose with one sleeve and gestured with the other.

Brother Cornelius stared down with dry pink irises, pinpoint pupils and hairline veins spread like wiry roots over the whites. He grimaced, yellowed lips flaking and taut to the gumline, exposing gray splintered teeth. Sparse hair floated around his wan dome, a halo of cobwebs.

The unblinking eyes focused on the pages of a thick bound book. Cornelius held a bone-white stylus, pointed and embellished with intricate geometric shapes. His hand was gnarled and lumpy with wormy blue veins. The stylus etched crimson lines that darkened to black.

There was no inkpot.

"Can you feel the evil?" whispered Ronald with shallow breath.

"And you want to do *this?*" replied Kevin. "Transcriptions?"

"Transcribing isn't supposed to be like this." Ronald's stomach churned, the combination of the stench, the ghoulish man, and an unsettling pressure in his ears that changed in tune with the flickering ruby flame. "Look." He pointed at the page.

Kevin's eyes widened, his mouth agape. "Blessed Mother. Is this what you brought me here to see?"

Ronald glanced down to the page. It was an illustration of a nude woman, reclined, her only garb a crown of black flowers.

"It's quite a fair drawing, Ronald. I like it." Kevin bent, his nose nearly touching the page. "Who do you suppose it's supposed to be? Mary?"

"Mary?"

"Saint Mary. Magdalena."

"By God's toes, not that!" Ronald pulled at his bangs. "This book, it's full of pagan symbols." He gingerly tugged at Cornelius' sleeve with two fingers, dragging the arthritic talon and stylus away from the page. Ronald flicked back pages, each filled with polygonal shapes and letterforms, vowels slashed and perforated, alien symbols. "The cover itself has the mark of the devil." He carefully closed the book to expose a cracked leather cover. A seven-sided box composed of serpents scorched the center, surrounded by dark, braided symbols. "He's practically mummified down here."

"Well, the man is fasting, what would you expect?" said Kevin.

"This could be us. Sacrificed for what? This is the occult magic the rumors warned us about."

Kevin squinted at Ronald. "Rumors…you mean…"

"Not the hidden ale. The necromancy. The brotherhood's search for unholy immortali—"

Cornelius, unanchored by his writing hand, teetered forward. Ronald reflexively caught the body and shuddered. It felt like a pile of bones wrapped in burlap. A lump formed in Ronald's throat, a mixture of fear and nausea.

"Oh, he does not look well at all," said Kevin, lifting the body up. "Light as a feather. We can't leave him here, poor soul. Say, do you think we can take that picture with us too?"

The monks slept in the dorter, a second-story hall divided into rooms of a dozen straw-bedded cots. Now it was empty, the others still participating in matins, the low hum of prayer and song carrying through the building.

Kevin lay Cornelius in his own cot. The body curled, shivering beneath a thin sheet, wrists spastically twisting deformed hands. "What do we do now?" Kevin asked.

Ronald paced the length of the bed. "If this was unholy magic, we must alert the Bishop."

"Surely the Bishop," said Kevin. "Why not the Archbishop? The Pope?"

Ronald could not tell if Kevin was mocking him or actually serious.

Soft leather sandals strode into the dorter. Ronald knew it was Benedict from the odor of acrid ale that preceded him. Ronald tensed, and his hands slicked with cold sweat.

"Brother Kevin," Benedict said, forcing eye contact with Ronald. Benedict was flanked by a tall monk with small eyes and blond tonsured hair. "Did you enter Brother Cornelius's chambers? Again?

Despite my express prohibition? Apparently, you left the chamber wide open."

"Me?" Ronald shook. "Do you mean *me? I'm* Ronald! *He's* Kevin! *I'm* the short, erudite one! *He's* the tall, stupid one!"

Benedict squinted between Ronald and Kevin, unconvinced.

"You've been practicing ungodly magic," Ronald sputtered. "You used poor Brother Cornelius to draft nitheful spells in that pagan tome. You've cursed him, mummifying his living body."

Benedict rubbed his face. "Ronald, or Kevin, whichever you are. Cornelius is there by choice. He was once a missionary to a leper colony in Andalusia, where he was afflicted. He's quite content isolated, meditating, voluntarily silent and fasting as he transcribes the Gospel into Nordic runes. What you think you saw—you are quite mistaken. His wish was to die in solitude. Do you understand?"

Kevin stepped forward, his face a mask of disgust. "Did you say *leprosy?*"

Ronald's hands pleaded, exhausted. "But—the eldritch inscriptions—"

"Norse runes," clipped Benedict.

"The magical stylus?" Ronald tried.

"A holy relic, of course."

"The demonic symbols—"

"Symbols are just that, they have meanings that I can assure you have naught to do with demons."

"But his teeth, his hair, his skin—"

"Leprosy." Benedict rubbed his forehead. "Do not blame yourself, young one. You're not the first postulate to question Brother Cornelius's station. While we encourage curiosity, this is one instance in which we seek your bliss."

Ronald's mind spun. He slumped down onto the foot of the cot, defeated.

Cornelius wheezed a hollow exhale ending with an abrupt squawk, causing Ronald to shoot back up again. He forgot the decrepit body was there.

Benedict's eyes bulged. "What was that sound?"

Ronald's eyes glared at Kevin before settling on his own feet. "That would be Brother Cornelius. We brought him here."

"You mean to say," Benedict ejaculated, "that he is not in the room right now writing into the Book of Craven Ruin with the holy relic as we speak?"

The blond monk, mouth agape, scampered to the bed.

"Book...of...Craven Ruin?" Ronald repeated. "Holy relic?"

Benedict looked past Ronald, short of breath. "Brother Tobias? Is it he? Cornelius?"

Tobias craned his head to meet Benedict's eyes, nodding. "He's dead."

"But we sent Brother Jacobus to investigate the tomb. He is alone." Benedict inhaled deeply. "Tobias, are you prepared?"

Tobias, his scalp dotted with sweat, nodded.

Benedict pointed at Ronald. "You, Brother Kevin, stay right where you are. We will take care of this. I will deal with you by the by." Benedict and Tobias hurried away.

"Well," said Ronald, "you heard the prior. Stay behind."

Kevin frowned. "But he meant you!"

Ronald shrugged, walking toward the stairs.

"Wait, I'm coming too." Kevin followed Ronald. "Incidentally, do you think they'll need this?"

He raised the bone stylus in his hand.

Ronald and Kevin scuttled down the stairs toward the fourth level, stopping when they heard voices. A song carried up the passageway. It was not Latin.

"*Segjöndum fló sagna, snótar ulfr at móti.*" Ronald recognized Benedict's voice singing in deep, harsh syllables.

Kevin hummed along, Ronald slapping his hand over his mouth. "They do not know our presence, prithee silence," Ronald pleaded.

Kevin tore his hand away, whispering, "Yet I know this song! Learned it as a lad."

Below them, the arched doorway to the storage room flickered with bright lantern light. They could hear muffled conversation, the hushed voices of Benedict and Tobias.

"Did Cornelius really have leprosy?" whispered Kevin.

Ronald shook his head. "I think the prior was lying."

Kevin's eyes widened, aghast. "No!"

A cacophony of brass instruments clangored to the stone floor, and a deep, throaty roar rose in pitch until it tapered off. Ronald flinched backward into Kevin, who wrapped his arms over Ronald's shoulders.

"*S-setisk ǫrn,*" the foreign chant continued, wavering.

"No!" A desperate echo from the doorway. The lantern's glow dimmed as it clacked to the floor. "Jacobus, please—" Tobias's sentiment ended with an abrupt gurgle. Then the sound of ripping wool was followed by the wet snap of bone.

"Christ beseech thee," cried Benedict's voice.

"Chrissst isss not here," a glottal voice hissed.

Benedict howled before falling into silence amidst the sound of clanking trumpets.

The commotion ended.

Ronald held his breath, stylus in hand, and peered into the room. Lantern light pushed shadows across the floor. A disembodied head lay sideways, its small eyes rolled upwards, tongue swollen between purple lips. Brother Tobias.

Benedict was still alive, crouched on shaking hands and knees against an empty bookshelf, surrounded by brass instruments. His habit draped above his waist exposing his lower half, and from his rectum protruded a trumpet. Benedict buried his striped beard into his chest as he muttered a prayer. There was no other being in the room, Jacobus or otherwise.

Ronald gaped, brain floating, thoughts distant, throat parched. A constant tap on his shoulder prodded him back to consciousness. Kevin, pale, shook his head, turned and fled up the stairs.

Ronald's lips quivered. "Coward!" Bracing himself, he crawled into the room. "Brother Benedict? What can I do?"

Benedict fell to his side, the trumpet bleating hollow wheezes. "My son," he rasped. His eyes focused on Ronald, and his face slackened. "Oh. Kevin." He coughed. "The relic—the bone stylus—you must find it, use it to write in the Book of Craven Ruin to contain that malevolent spirit." Benedict pointed a wobbling finger into the dark entrance of Cornelius's room. It gaped open, exhaling cold, pustulent breath.

"In-in there?" Ronald stammered.

"First, it took Jacobus. Tobias went in, but he could not find the stylus. And now—" he sobbed. "Forgive me, my brothers, for I failed." He collapsed to the frigid floor.

Ronald had gotten them into this situation. Cornelius and Tobias were dead, Benedict defiled by a musical instrument, and an evil ghost unleashed. He had no choice. As he crawled into Cornelius's alcove, he wondered if he should have carried a rosary or a bible with him.

Stopping just inside, his eyes adjusted to darkness. The red light was gone. Tobias's headless body slumped askew against the wall next to him, his blood smeared and spattered on walls and floor. Ronald crawled toward the desk, hoping the book was still there.

Suddenly, a hand shot out, pale fingers with purple nails. Ronald swatted the hand, scraping it with the stylus, and watched as black blood oozed from it like sap from a tree. A voice screeched, retracting the hand.

Ronald fell backwards into Tobias's decapitated body, frozen, fist tight on the stylus. Cold sweat dripped down the back of his neck.

"You possesssss it," hoarse syllables rising from the shadows.

Ronald craned his head to see Brother Jacobus, a stout, bald monk with no eyebrows. He stood, face pale, eyes sunken, pink and bulging. His shoulders were lopsided, the left sharply touching its ear, the other limp, hand dangling. Inky blood dripped like tar from his nose.

"B-Brother Jacobus?"

It tilted its head. "Ahhh. Your monk. Ja-co-bussssss." A black tongue slithered out, licking pointed teeth.

This was no longer Jacobus. As Benedict said, the demon had taken him.

"I'll make you a deallll," the Jacobus-demon gurgled. "Break that filllthy bone, and I willll not eat youuu."

"Bone? You mean the stylus? The holy relic?"

It hissed. "Yessss."

"And what then, you'll just leave the monastery? Leave us alone?"

It snorted. "Tellll me what you want, monk. Anything. Food. Women. Spiritssss."

Ronald chuckled humorlessly. This demon also seemed to have mistaken him for Kevin.

"Burrrn it. Defiiiiile it. Smashhh it. Lest you be doomed as Cor-neee-leee-uhssss."

Cornelius's visage popped into Ronald's mind, with its hollow pupils and papery skin, a sarcophagus of a human. Would that be his fate? "I've only ever wanted one thing, demon." Ronald stood. "To write. I joined this holy order so I could write."

The demon's face scrunched into a stray dog's snarl, then it opened its mouth wide enough to see deep down its pink gullet. It croaked in displeasure. "Then you diiiie."

Ronald darted to the table, to the book, open on blank pages. Jacobus's misshapen body lurched at him. As Ronald stretched his hands to the paper, the demon's hands circled his throat like cold iron chains, rooting him in place. Long, jagged fingernails dug into Ronald's neck. Ronald strained, almost touching pen to paper, but he could not reach. He could not breathe.

"The bone will drop from your dead hand before you spellll a singlllllle word." Its decayed breath swamped Ronald's face.

Ronald could barely keep his eyes open. Then, a loud, warbling sound came from the doorway, along with a golden light illuminating the opening.

"*Segjöndum fló*," a silhouette sang in strange Scandinavian speech. "*Snótar ulfr at móti*."

It was Kevin. He held a lantern high, brightening the caliginous corners of the room.

Ronald's lips parted into an affectionate grin.

The demon craned its flaring nostrils toward Kevin, whose voice trembled—Ronald had never heard it tremble. It screeched at Kevin, primeval hatred for the song, and Ronald almost commiserated. The demonic Jacobus let go of Ronald, leaving behind a cold sting, and sprang at Kevin. Ronald collapsed, his knees liquid.

Kevin swung the lantern at the Jacobus-beast's face, connecting with a satisfying thunk, but it was not enough to stop its attack. It heaved forward, getting one hand around Kevin's throat. Kevin grappled its other hand and kept singing. "*Settisk ǫrn, þars æsir*," Kevin quavered.

"I'll rrrrrip out your larynx," it shrieked.

Ronald pulled himself into the chair and stabbed the stylus onto the blank page. Crimson ink bled onto aged parchment, drying black. *Paternoster,* he wrote in careful lines.

The demon wailed in response. With each of Ronald's strokes, the pale face squawked, hacking, bleeding blood-red smoke from its mouth like a soupy mist. It staggered away from Kevin and his song.

"Sing," Ronald pleaded. "For once in your life, sing for me, you blessed, gallant man!"

"*Í gemlis ham gǫmlum,*" Kevin roared.

Qui est in, Ronald continued. *Sanctificetur nomen tuum.*

Between the chanting and the writing, the pallid Jacobus-beast backed against a wall, yelping, hissing, weeping carmine effluvium from its orifices. A brume of scarlet fog engulfed its body as it crumpled into itself, releasing bitter fumes, until nothing was left but a flickering ruby flame in the dissipating cloud.

Kevin, still singing, brought his lantern to the fire. He captured the flame, bathing the room with its familiar vermillion luminescence. Placing the lantern next to the Book of Craven Ruin, he finished his song as Ronald scribed the last words of his prayer.

"*Bleyði vændr — á seyði.*"

Sed libera nos a malo. Amen.

Kevin walked into the room, a plate of food in one hand and a trumpet in the other.

"I've decided to learn to play this," he announced, replacing Ronald's bowl of uneaten soup with a plate of bread and vegetables. "I figure I can practice down here, so as to not bother anyone upstairs." He brought a trumpet to his lips and blew out a discordant blurt, then removed it, licking his lips. "You don't suppose this is the one that was stuffed into the prior's rear?"

Ronald did not respond.

Kevin had been coming to the room for weeks. He visited when he could, watching Ronald write and draw illustrations in the book. Kevin particularly enjoyed his drawing of Benedict playing the trumpet from his buttocks, but did not like the images of devils and malignant spirits.

Ronald never touched his food as far as Kevin could tell. His skin was now sallow, veins dark and pronounced. His tidy dark hair now wisped, his eyes recessed in bruised sockets, dry and unblinking. His bloodless hand perpetually cramped onto the scribbling stylus.

"I've got something for you." Kevin looked over his shoulders before producing a jug of ale and two small bowls from beneath his robe. "From Benedict's secret store."

He filled each bowl with the brew, resting Ronald's in front of him. "Wassail!"

Kevin drank deeply and began to sing a low, solemn hymn.

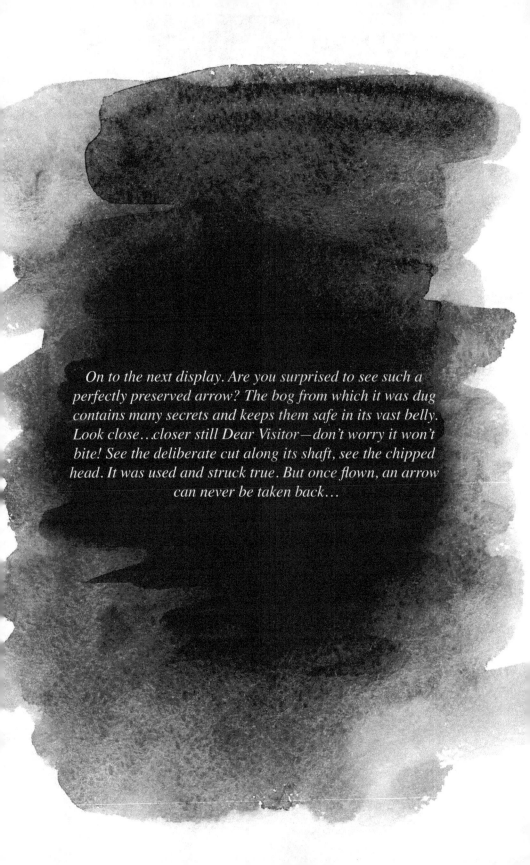

On to the next display. Are you surprised to see such a perfectly preserved arrow? The bog from which it was dug contains many secrets and keeps them safe in its vast belly. Look close…closer still Dear Visitor—don't worry it won't bite! See the deliberate cut along its shaft, see the chipped head. It was used and struck true. But once flown, an arrow can never be taken back…

IN THRALL TO THIS GOOD EARTH
Hailey Piper

utter hadn't meant to speak aloud, half lost in his head when "Points at the castle, doesn't it?" spilled from his lips as he passed the towering mound of rock. Now the other men turned back to stare at him.

"Meaning?" Jackson asked. Most days he seemed more hound than man, which gave Cutter the luxury of daydreaming on hunts, but now Jackson's pale eyes shined with curiosity as he awaited an explanation. His pointed face wedged out as if aiming one of his arrows.

The wanderer everyone called *the Fenner* slipped closer. "Thorn Rock?" Fenner asked. He had thick wild hair, a man aged little more than half either hunter's forty years.

The mound was far older, a moss-coated clump of smooth rock rising above the tangled field of high grass. A lengthy shaft of boulder jutted from the middle and formed the mound's namesake as it aimed north. To the south, the countryside descended into wetlands, but rising greenery covered the north, and beyond it, the village and castle from where the trio had headed out this morning.

Fenner mumbled to himself and then said, "I've passed by too many times to count, never noticed. Could point castle-ward, yes."

"And?" Jackson asked, shouldering his quiver. The arrows clacked together.

"A cry up top might sail clear over the trees," Cutter said, aiming a finger from the jutting boulder to the green-headed thicket. "Might even see the castle if we climbed it."

Jackson eyed Thorn Rock's foundation and then turned away. "No," he said.

Fenner followed. Disputes weren't his problem; he was only a hired guide.

Cutter gave Thorn Rock a hard stare, as if it might shout agreement with him, and then followed Jackson and Fenner out of the field and down a copse-riddled slope. Partnering with Jackson meant leaving Cutter to parse through conversations Jackson seemed to have with himself but rarely gave voice.

Couldn't blame him for a sour mood when this entire hunt was a pot of shit.

Baron Cogan's men had laid out the whole affair when Cutter and Jackson went asking around the village. Over the past month, the baron had woken in the night to some distant wretched wailing. Much as his pregnant wife and their advisors had assured he might be hearing wildcats in the thicket, Baron Cogan had already made up his mind—he was haunted.

Wailing ghost of the ban, courtiers had repeated. *Calling for the death of his unborn heir.* They didn't look to believe it, but they didn't look to disbelieve, either.

Smart men, considering the baron's reach and power. Cappamore was a rich barony, its people busy in their work and festive otherwise. Chatty local women said the baron's cows and ewes always bore healthy calves and lambs, the hens spat eggs faster than you could blink, the harvests were ripe and yielding, as were the women, Cutter found. The baron had wealth to place a tidy sum on the wailing demon's head.

Cutter and Jackson had only been passing through, off to regroup with a mercenary company from England, when they heard talk of riches. Lordly opportunity drove them to hire Fenner and set off into the barony's wilds, where this ghost would turn out to be a couple of wildcats after all, or some she-wolf in heat with no mate this side of Ireland.

But had she climbed Thorn Rock? Jackson must have eyed the smooth stone and decided not, but Cutter had seen village dogs scrabble up steeper stones in a quarry by the earldom where he was born. Wolves were stronger than feral mutts.

Glancing over his shoulder as trees shrouded Thorn Rock, he almost mistook the great leaning shaft for an enormous canine snout, aimed north.

At prey.

The sun had slid partway behind the western trees, lacing their green leaves with burnt umber, when Cutter noticed the rabbits.

He had followed Jackson and Fenner without question over slopes, around thick oaks and rowans, in and out of the thicket. No signs of wolves, or wild dogs, or any beast on four legs that might howl in the night. If there were cats, Cutter didn't see them.

"We should circle back and try south of the rock," he'd said.

Neither Jackson nor Fenner disagreed. They were exhausted, and the air weighed on their skin with unseasonable wetland heaviness.

Movement snagged the corner of Cutter's eye, where dewy grass shimmered with waning sunlight. The rabbits were little more than two small brown shapes tucked together in a tree-circled meadow. One beast nestled atop the other's rear half, their long ears slashing back from their sloping heads.

Nothing unusual to see animals rutting in spring, but a damp chill settled on Cutter's skin as if he'd emerged from a light rain. His heart thudded with rabbit-like quickness.

Why this strange feeling? He had seen dogs and rabbits and even cows in heat before. As a child, he had pretended to sleep while his father and mother moaned animal sounds. He had listened as frightened men and women found each other within stone walls during his last siege, hired among other mercenaries by one clean-handed English earl to break the king's peace against his neighbor. These were ordinary facts of life.

But here, his cooling blood told him he'd intruded as if breaking into the rabbits' home. No, worse—as if he had come upon them after someone else had found them first, someone still peering at the meadow. To watch the rabbits was one thing, but to interrupt a prior watcher was another.

Cutter scraped one boot across the soil, scattering pebbles through the grass. Had he and Jackson come hunting rabbits, they would have been silent, but Cutter wanted them gone.

They did not go. Their eyes and ears kept oblivious to predators.

This driven dedication felt too passionate, more like people than small game. Their inattention said there might be no predators here, which meant either Fenner had led the hunters to an impossible place in nature, or a worse creature than a wolf might howl in the Cappamore countryside, something that struck no fear in rabbits but plenty in men.

"Flee!" Cutter snapped, and he clapped his hands.

Nothing from the rabbits, not even an ear twitch. He didn't care to save them, but they needed to give a damn a man was here, like normal beasts.

Neither noticed; neither cared.

They only stopped when Jackson's arrow hissed through the air and pierced their necks. Both fell in a clump, and Jackson bounded toward them, laughter spewing from the black pit in his beard. He wrenched the two-in-one arrow free and waved it high overhead.

"Lucky!" he shouted. He drew his belt knife and scraped a line in the arrow's shaft to mark it as special.

Fenner waded into the grass. "Only needed the one," he said.

Jackson stashed his knife, bow, and lucky arrow, and then he lifted one rabbit by the hindlegs. "Supper," he said, and then he lifted the other. "Bait."

Fenner nodded, impressed.

Cutter forced a mimicking nod and tried to look unfazed. He would keep the rabbits' strangeness to himself and swallow any hint there might be no carnivore to enjoy Jackson's bait in these meadows and thickets. Quiet, in his head, no sense of another watcher in the woods.

But that damp chill across his skin lingered into the dusk.

A dancing campfire chewed the wet air, and Cutter sat close as he could to its burning tongues. He and the others had almost reached the copse near Thorn Rock when Fenner urged they make camp. He'd gathered stones while Cutter had gathered leaves, twigs, and branches, and Jackson had taken his knife to both rabbits.

Only meat, Cutter told himself as he bit down on fat and bone. Whatever atmosphere had spread from the live rabbits was dead like them. Food now, nothing more.

"Wolf will come for the other," Fenner said, eating his portion with a black slice of tough village bread. "Used to find more of their like when Thorn Rock was known as Carraig Bod, so they say, and she'll come prowling. Even if she's in heat, or wary of us, she won't shy from an easy meal."

A good plan, simpler than finding the wolf themselves when she left no trail. No one in the village beneath the castle's shadow, its nearby market, or the crisscrossing roads beyond had mentioned losing calves, lambs, or even chickens to wild animals despite the baron's vast wealth in livestock offering plenty of opportunity. Seemed as if every carnivore in Cappamore were either sated or dead. In the wolf's case, she might be starving.

If she existed at all. Cutter had seen no tracks, no wolfen fur. The nightly howling could be foxes or cats, but was it? That prickly sense of a watcher in the woods haunted him as he swallowed the last of his portion.

"Baron wants a ghost," Jackson said. Gristle haunted his teeth. "Bring him wolf's head, lowers the price? No."

He had a point, in his miserly way with words. Baron Cogan believed some otherworldly creature called for the death of his unborn child and had set a bounty to match. He might balk at learning he'd feared a mundane creature. The reward would shrink to the price of a wolf's pelt, nothing more.

"We'll sever and shave the head," Cutter said, clinging to the hope Cappamore indeed hid a she-wolf in heat and nothing worse. "Muss her teeth. Give the baron reason to wonder."

Jackson grunted agreement. Fenner didn't argue.

Cutter chucked a slender bone into the fire, where embers spat and swirled. He'd eaten gamey rabbits before, but these were plump animals, grown off good land. If the baron offered property in lieu of payment, Cutter might take it, settle down, at last find a woman to call his wife and take her home. Past time he had sons of his own—ones he knew of, at least.

After supper, Fenner held Jackson's quiver while he counted

arrowheads. The lucky arrow lay beside Jackson, awaiting opportunity. They sat thigh against thigh, as if neither could make out every arrow without both sets of eyes in the thickening darkness. To fire any of them seemed foolish, but the wailer came at night, and so would the hunt. Their quarry would either snag the dead rabbit or call out to them in the dark.

Come and get me, the howling would sing. *Come and kill me, if you can.*

A pounding rhythm thrust through the trees and stamped across Cutter's bones. Cappamore was wrong, he knew it now, less a land of fields, slopes, and thickets than a sickly heartbeat disguised as a barony. Unseen tides crashed across these woods as if plunging wet surf into writhing undergrowth.

Cutter sat straight up, his blood screaming a painful stiffness between his legs. He hadn't realized he'd fallen asleep, and now the campfire burned low beneath the black sky.

Jackson and Fenner were gone.

A trembling wail tore Cutter to his feet. His hands tensed in pins and needles. The wailer must have lured the others off, and they couldn't wake him fast enough. They meant to catch their wolf before the howling ended.

Cutter should be with them. One hand grabbed his hatchet, the other his sword, and he waited, his blood both chilly and throbbing at once.

There, another wail, and he dashed from the dying fire. Every step hammered another aching beat between his legs, but he let the pain drive him—charge, bleed, kill. Harsh wind whipped his face. Frail light dappled the moving night clouds as he slid past a familiar copse and realized he was headed west.

Toward Thorn Rock.

He'd been right to wonder about it. No need to wait for the guiding wail—he dashed west, fast as he could no matter the ache. Clouds abandoned the moon as he reached the shadow of Thorn Rock, where the writhing shapes between himself and the stones froze his legs in place.

Animals filled the tall grass. High-antlered bucks mounted rigid does. Rabbits jerked between blades of grass. There were hares, too, and foxes, cats, the skittering shadows of fieldmice, blankets of insects, entwined snakes, and a myriad of sparrows and owls hidden in the crooks of Thorn Rock.

All fucking the life from each other. A steady heartbeat thrummed in their grunting screeching chorus.

At Thorn Rock's foundation, Fenner curled against a mossy bed of stone, with Jackson hunkered atop him. They swayed to the barony's cacophonous rhythm, the same pounding need that carved through woods and blood and Cutter. He opened his mouth to shout at them.

Another voice drowned him out, its sunken howl jerking his hands. He dropped both sword and hatchet as the noise dragged his gaze skyward.

She thrashed in the wind like a tattered war banner, but no pole anchored her to the world. The wind tossed, and her earthen claws clung to its immaterial gusts. Cloaks of yellow and brown and shadow slashed from her shoulders, tangling and untangling around her legs. Moss-green hair jittered along her limbs, and some rich wet maw between them sent curling fingers of must through the air. Her toothy face thrust from the fabric storm and stretched wider than Cutter's skull as she let out another blood-chilling wail.

His knees wobbled, and his vision swam black. Better that way; he didn't want to see her float impossibly airborne, wild and defiant as a wasp. Her musty damp scent filled the atmosphere, and that sense of intrusion hung over him. He should either fall into the wailing witch's rhythm or avert his eyes. Join this land, or be noticed and be damned.

The she-wolf in heat—right idea, wrong breed. This creature's cry had drawn all virile creatures to her lair, yet what she needed hadn't joined them. Not yet.

Come and get me, the howling sang, but not the way Cutter had thought at the campfire.

He wouldn't stand here to see what kind of mate she lured. He didn't want to see her at all. His gaze slid toward the ground, and he charged past knotted serpents and screeching hares until he reached Jackson and Fenner, both moaning against Thorn Rock.

"Jackson," Cutter snapped. "Quit this. Help me."

Jackson grunted a non-answer. His eyes and muscles focused solely on Fenner, hellbent on making impossible children. Bow and quiver lay in the grass beside them.

Cutter slung the quiver over his shoulder, grabbed the bow, and retreated across the field. Every step pounded another ache through his core, his blood carrying the wailer's cry. He nearly rammed against one buck, the antlers grasping for the moon.

To linger or interrupt would draw the animals, and what would they do to him? Treat him as one of their own? A fresh chill filled his core, and he hurried on. Better not to find out.

At the field's edge, he swiveled in place and fell grasping at the soil. Another wail rocked across his body, and painful sores burst open at his elbows and knees. The beasts and other men had given in to the creature's cry, but Cutter—he looked to the field and then away.

Fresh sticky slits opened his knuckles. She wanted him to rut with something, anything, and to defy her strained at his flesh and bone. To prolong this night would tear him apart or send him into the field, to the beasts.

He knelt in the grass and notched an arrow against the bow's flax string. The arrow snapped loose early, cutting his finger as it sailed silently into the dirt. One more ragged wound to join his other drooly red mouths. He grabbed for another arrow, but darkness clotted his vision, and the drooping quiver spilled its arrows over the earth.

Moonlight glinted in one arrowhead, its shaft slit by knifepoint—Jackson's lucky arrow.

Skin burst open down Cutter's shoulder blades as he notched the special arrow and aimed across the stirring field. The moaning grunting cries grew deafening. Cutter screamed against them and then focused on the wailing witch with all the need these beasts and men drove into each other.

But Thorn Rock was no longer a handful of slippery boulders with a long shaft jutting from its castle-facing side. Its presence stretched across the air and around the thrashing witch, as if her wailing had called up the ghost of a grander façade. This field had once founded a castle in its own right, so immense it might swallow Baron Cogan's little stone hovel across the thicket. Cutter made out phantom parapets and towers that cradled the moon and stars.

And in the dead castle's grasp, this writhing wailing creature called all life beneath her, both what walked and rutted, and what would later spawn.

Cutter's head throbbed, sinking into his need. He could be her mate, lose himself in this wailing song. Never mind what horrors their children might be; the relief would overshadow them.

He shook his head at the musty scent, and the wind, and the wailing song. His ear busted against his shoulder until it screamed a shrill music. No, he was not in her thrall, and he wouldn't make strange children through her beasts or in her body. He did not belong here.

His fingers loosed the lucky arrow.

It whistled skyward, and its harsh note pierced both the wailer's rhythm and her thrashing body.

Her song cut off in a sharp shriek. Once-powerful wind melted beneath her, and she plummeted in a torrent of flagging cloaks. A soft crack echoed where she struck Thorn Rock's jutting stone, and Cutter guessed more than the lucky arrow's shaft had broken there.

The wailer's claws tore from her flaccid clothing and clutched at the boulder's smooth sides. No wolf could have climbed them, Jackson was right about that, but Cutter realized the rock's thorny namesake no longer mimicked a predatory canine snout. Its stiffness echoed the pain between his legs, and that ache waned as the stone crumbled down Thorn Rock's side, taking the creature with it.

Musty scent and invasive rhythm faded to grass smells and a quiet night. Snakes disentangled, rabbits tore from each other, deer bounded in separate directions, and the insects spread wherever they might touch. They had forgotten why they had come, thirsty creatures having drank a pond dry.

Jackson and Fenner did not break like the rest. They slowed, and then paused and turned to each other, an almost peaceful look stretching between them as if they had been waiting for this encounter. Their expressions soured as they turned gaping to Cutter, and they quickly righted their clothes and split from each other.

He didn't understand and didn't want to as he crossed the emptied field. The bow slid from his hands as he reached the ruin of Thorn Rock, where he began to dig. A slip of yellow cloth snaked from between two stones. He tore it free in a ragged bundle and held it high like Jackson with his dead rabbits.

"For our bounty," Cutter said. He did not search for Jackson's lucky arrow, only grabbed his sword and hatchet before heading back to the embers of the campfire. Jackson gathered his bow and followed. Fenner dogged behind them.

No one spoke another word.

Cutter offered the cloak to Baron Cogan and promised both the ghost of the ban and her mound of power were gone. The baron had no need to see Thorn Rock's ruin himself; he'd heard the howl cut short in the night. In gratitude, he offered payment in money or land, whatever the hunters liked.

Cutter refused the land, didn't wait to see what Jackson chose, and took the coin to a nearby inn. Spending money made him popular with the women, and that was all he wanted right now. The man who'd desired land, peace, and sons seemed a naïve, empty-headed ghost of himself he'd forgotten in the wilderness. Better to drink and journey and find women, and when one fiery lady couldn't keep herself from clawing onto him, he carried her to a back room and hiked up her dress.

And did nothing else.

"What's the matter, friend?" she asked, licking crooked teeth.

He didn't know. She was fleshy and wild, the kind of woman he could grab onto and plunge his tide into, but his blood lay idle, his member a dead worm.

He let her dress sink down her thighs. "Don't like you so much," he said, slipping out of the room.

And not the next woman, either. Or the next. The ladies in the castle's shadow failed to stir his blood. The painful stiffness from that night at Thorn Rock would not return.

The trouble haunted him at another village down the road, and another. Even in neighboring baronies, his lust shriveled. As the days slid by, he wondered if the women were truly the problem, or if a curse might have dogged him from Thorn Rock. At night, he dreamed of wailing in the wind, and Jackson's lucky arrow stood hard between his legs, but when Cutter woke, nothing had changed. If he ever found that damn arrow, he would burn it to ashes.

He had no plans to seek it out, or even return to Cappamore. When he crossed the murky wilderness borders by chance and found himself in that stretch of Ireland, every word by village or trader hinted Cutter's curse had infected the land too.

Since the spring of the wailing, Baron Cogan's cows had given stillborn calves, and half the hens' eggs were sour green pockets of rot. Rams would not mate with ewes, and the disinterested livestock only found their virility when traded to pastures outside of Cappamore. The incoming flocks of sheep would not breed.

Baron Cogan's wife died giving birth. Half the rumors said the child was not human and had torn the baroness apart, while others said the baron had killed her himself when the abominable creature slithered from her womb. No one knew what became of it.

Cutter aimed to put leagues between himself and Cappamore after that. A cursed man would not do for a cursed land, and mercenary companies always needed strong men. Word on the wind said the Christian nations would again raise arms to take Jerusalem, and this time they would win. In far off deserts, Cutter could forget Cappamore, Jackson, Thorn Rock, and he would never think on what kind of creature he'd really shot down that night.

Knowing would do him no good anyway. She was dead.

As he rode atop a reward-purchased horse for the southern port to leave Ireland for good, he spotted a man who might have been Fenner between two rowan trees at wilderness's edge. A small wild-haired child stood at his knees, her tiny hand clutching his fingers. No telling where she'd come from, or why she wandered the countryside with him, and they faded into the trees before Cutter could call out to ask.

She might have been the only new child in Cappamore since that night. At the port, sailors said no matter which women Baron Cogan invited to his castle after he put his wife in the ground, none grew pregnant. No children came to him that Cutter ever heard.

None to himself, either.

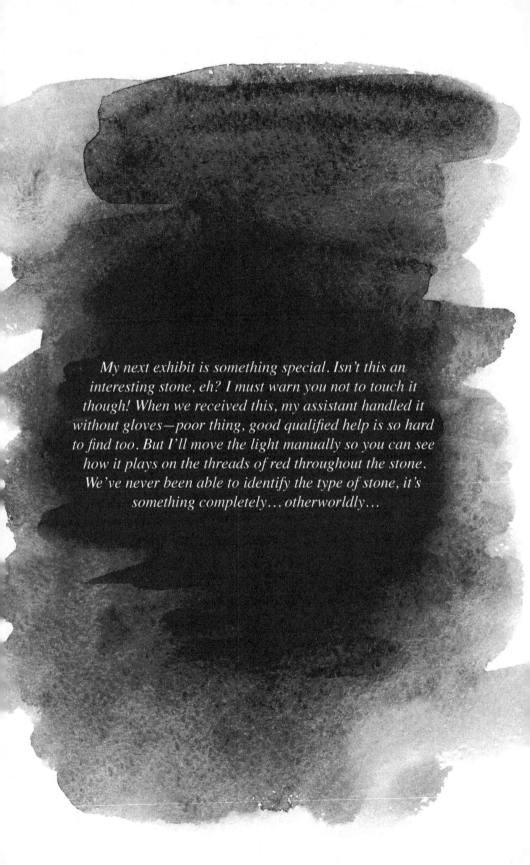

My next exhibit is something special. Isn't this an interesting stone, eh? I must warn you not to touch it though! When we received this, my assistant handled it without gloves—poor thing, good qualified help is so hard to find too. But I'll move the light manually so you can see how it plays on the threads of red throughout the stone. We've never been able to identify the type of stone, it's something completely... otherworldly...

IN EVERY DROP

Lindsey Ragsdale

he night covered our village.

It seeped into the leaves and roots of our trees. It crept, undisturbed, into corners. It smothered the insects, the birds, and the chittering monkeys, commanding silence. Nothing moved out there. The dark was safe. The quiet was soothing.

We didn't have long before the sun would rise again.

Izel clutched my fingers in her sweaty little fist. The only sounds in our hut were her panting in the heat and our mattress of rushes softly rustling any time one of us would turn over. "Mama," she whispered. Her breath was like hot sand against my face. "Is there water?"

"Not yet, *tum*," I whispered. *My love*. I stroked her hair with one hand and tucked a moist curl behind her ear. It was stifling inside, despite the darkness that surrounded us.

I didn't want to think about how warm the next day would be, as the sun-god K'inich Ajaw climbed higher and higher into the sky. We just had to wait. Wait like we had the past several days, rats in a trap. Wait for the hunter to set them free.

"Just a little longer. Why don't you play with your toys?" I didn't even suggest trying to slumber. The heat hung inside our hut like thick animal hides pressing down from all sides. Sleep was impossible. Izel pouted, but rolled over and picked up her menagerie of little clay animals.

"Mama, when is Papa back?"

"He is still gone, looking for help," I lied.

"When is he coming home?"

"Any day now, *tum*."

He was already home. I'd buried him, or the bones and ragged scraps of carcass that were left of his body, in the garden while Izel was asleep, days earlier. The sun dried my tears to salt tracks as I scrabbled in the dirt with my bare hands, grieving with gritted teeth to keep my hysterical screams from spilling out. I could never tell Izel what happened to her father.

She was all I had left, my little girl who chased butterflies and played in the mud. My fearless daughter who begged her father, Aapo, to take her to work every day, and wept when he kissed her goodbye. The jungle was no place for a child, with men cutting down trees and using sharp machetes to slice through vines, making way for our crops and livestock. Izel wanted to play with the boys and watch games of *pokta pok* instead of gardening and cooking with her mother. She loved the wilderness of the jungle that surrounded us, brought to life by Aapo's bedtime stories. Her favorite tales were about butterflies. Izel could always find the most beautiful monarchs, and they'd gather around her in a cloud, lighting on her face and fingers in the few moments she held still.

That's why it was so difficult to stay quiet these endless hours. When the heat came before the rainy season, the women of our village would awaken at night, when it was cooler. We'd light the village with torches and complete what tasks we could by moonlight, like fetching water and cooking. Women gathered by the riverbanks with laundry, taking turns scrubbing clothes with flat stones and hanging them for the sun to dry the following day. We would drag our heavy stone *metates* outdoors and grind corn, chatting as we dragged the *metlapil* stone up and down the rough surface, turning corn into soft flour for tortillas and masa. Our husbands slept, as herding and farming required sun and daylight, but many of our children would awaken and play outside, or help their mothers weave reed baskets. It was easier to work without sweat dripping down your face and the sun beating down on your head.

Izel was used to running around with her friends these cooler nights and sleeping during the day. The night used to be comforting, with soft firelight illuminating our conversations and work. Then, the darkness had been reassuring, like a dense blanket that protects from the cold. Now, that same blanket served to smother the few of us that were left. Though the village appeared deserted, some people still lingered, but it was too dangerous to gather in groups. Some hadn't fled yet. But most had disappeared.

I didn't dare fetch water from the nearby *dzonots* at night anymore. I didn't want to leave Izel awake and alone, and it was far too dangerous for her to come along. I went out during the hottest part of the day, when K'inich Ajaw was at his apex and Izel slept. We lived, if you could call this mad existence living, by the moon and the sun. When I did sleep, sometimes I hoped that the death-god Cizin would steal me away before I would wake.

A damp rock, edges worn smooth by little hands, was pressed into my palm. "Hold this for Papa," Izel whispered. A leather thong was wrapped around the stone. I closed my hand reluctantly around the cursed thing, wishing I could crush it into oblivion. It was no bigger than my thumb and was the last gift Izel's father would ever give her.

"I have a present for you, Izel," Aapo bellowed, pushing the

peccary skin aside at the doorway of our hut. He was covered in clay from a long day of clearing trees and brush, but his smile shone through the mess, a white slash across the deep brown dirt on his cheeks. Bits of leaves dotted his hair, which I'd comb out later as he bathed. My heart swelled with love as Izel ran into his arms and he scooped her up, throwing her in the air while she shrieked with delight.

My beautiful family.

"Let me see, let me see!" Izel pleaded when he landed her back on the ground. She tugged at his rawhide bag, and he knelt down, undoing the leather that sealed it shut.

"It better not be a new pet!" I huffed, teasing, as I hunched over my metate, grinding corn into a smooth flour.

He laughed. "No pets. Even you will like this, Akna." Aapo pulled out a small stone and held it up to the light shining through the doorway.

It was a limestone chip with unusual red veins running through it. The crimson flashed for a moment like sunlight skipping across water, and I gasped at the beauty of it. He gave it to Izel. "Look at this, Izel! I have never seen a stone like this before! I brought it home for you!"

I didn't like the look of it. I was reminded too much of blood, and of my grandmother's hands stained with cochinilla beetles as she used their scarlet carapaces to dye our clothing. It frightened me, seeing her hands covered in pigment. I thought she'd hurt herself the first time, and echoes of that first shock always resonated whenever I glimpsed redness where it wasn't supposed to be.

"Where did it come from?" I asked, standing up and stretching out the kinks in my back. Izel was gazing at the stone in wonder. Her attention was riveted, which was unusual for her, and she looked upon it with bright, almost feverish, eyes. The stone's veins seemed *to pulsate in the light, going from dark crimson to bright vermillion as she held the stone. My mouth grew dry and my hands trembled. A chill ran up my spine despite the balmy heat. I resumed grinding as Aapo continued, willing my hands to steady themselves.*

"We discovered an unmapped dzonot while clearing the jungle today. I climbed down to fill my jug with water, and found a small cave. Bits of limestone like these were scattered all over the ground. I took one piece and went back up to show the other men. Maybe they are worth something. But the workers didn't want to return with me when I showed them the rock. They asked me to throw it away. I knew Izel might like it, so I hid this one and brought it home." He ruffled Izel's hair, who was turning the stone over and over in her hands. "Thought it might bring good luck. I'll string it on a cord, so you can wear it always, tum." Vermillion glittered through her fingers.

The reluctant cry of a bird echoed through the trees outside. Dim, hazy light shone around the edges of our doorway, where an animal hide hung to block out the light. The sun was rising. It was time.

"Izel," I whispered. "Mama is going to get some water for us. I want you to stay here."

"No, I want to come," she said in a louder tone. "Let me come." Sudden fury kindled in her eyes, and she stood up. I flinched from her outburst, scuttling backwards across the bed before I could stop myself.

Izel's anger never ceased, despite how hot and exhausted we felt. The sooner I got water for the two of us, the better it would be for her. She would cool down and sleep, and I would continue foraging and searching the abandoned village huts in the light of day for anything useful. Closing my eyes, I took a deep breath before addressing Izel in a brighter tone.

"It is safe here, and I can walk more quickly than you."

"I want to see if Abund wants to play."

Abund was dead. I'd seen his body two days prior, limbs slashed and dangling from the tree by the village square. Flies crawled over his dried, cracked lips, and his eyes were gone, maggoty craters and black blood left where they'd been ripped from the sockets. I'd squeezed my own eyes shut and vomited on the ground at the sight of him. His ruined face still crawled through my nightmares.

"Abund is probably sleeping now. Would you like to sleep, too? Like a good girl?"

"No, I want to come," she began to whine, voice climbing in pitch. That was out of the question. I resorted to my last, desperate tactics.

"Eat some tortillas first, then we can go." I rose from the sodden reed-mat bed, wet from our perspiration, and rummaged in the woven basket by my *metate*. Two piles of tortillas lay there, wrapped separately. I'd cooked them myself. One pile was normal, the other had magnolia bark mixed into the dough. I took three tortillas from the drugged pile. After eating these, Izel would be sound asleep in minutes. "Here."

Izel slumped down onto the ground, face like a raincloud, but took the tortillas and began eating them slowly. I sat by her and combed my fingers through her hair. "Where is Mama's love for you?"

At first she was silent, only chewing, but looked up. "In every drop of rain," she mumbled, smiling a little.

"That's right," I said. "Every drop of rain."

It was my way of telling Izel I adored her endlessly. She was fascinated with the rain and one day had asked how many drops there were. *More drops than there are stars in the sky,* I'd said, holding her close. *And you know what?*

What, Mama?

My love for you is in every single drop, I'd replied, kissing the top of her head.

I waited impatiently, tidying our hut, sweeping the ground clean, airing out our mattress, and gathering laundry as the light through the doorway brightened. When I turned back to the bed, Izel lay curled up on her side, still clutching half of a remaining tortilla as she snored softly in sleep.

I hated sedating my daughter. It was dangerous, and it pained me, but I had no choice. This was the safest way. After arranging her comfortably on the reed mat while listening to her steady breathing, I picked up the basket of laundry and an empty jug I'd left by the bed, and walked out into the blazing sun.

I was alone, feeling naked in the clearing before our home. Five other huts ringed our family's part of the village, almost identical to ours, with high, sloped thatched roofs and walls made of hardened earth and rushes. Darkened doorways gaped wide like hungry mouths. My sister and her children had fled days before, along with several of my older cousins, taking their belongings with them. A few clay trinkets and scattered pieces of woven basket lay abandoned on the ground, covered in dust. There was no rain to wash them clean. We were the only ones left.

Droplets of sweat trickled down my neck. I'd tied up my dark, thick hair before stepping outside, and the light soaked every inch of skin it could reach. Each day seemed hotter than the last. K'inich Ajaw mocked us relentlessly with his shine, and yet again, I wondered how we'd angered the gods so much. How had it come to this? Families torn apart by fear and danger, water slipping through our fingers, while he blazed on from above, towering over everything, seeing all.

What did he see that made him curse us so?

I was exhausted. The sooner I got water, the sooner I could get back to Izel, and calm her through another day of heat and boredom. She was all I had now. Our family was dead or gone, and I had only her to live for. This was my burden and my privilege.

The creek lay many steps from our clearing, closer to the center of our village. Before, there'd been women and children laughing, talking, playing, scolding. The clinks of pottery as women cooked over the communal hearth, the animal cries of livestock. Smells of cooked corn and beans, sometimes beer and meat. No longer. The only sound now was the muffled padding of my feet over the hot, hard ground, and the calls of birds from the jungle's edge. I faintly heard the creek's bubbling as I drew closer.

Bits of pottery dotted the ground. I was careful not to cut my feet. A spilled basket of kernels, the birds pecking at them before taking flight as I passed. Broken tools scattered by the side of the path. Almost as if their wielders had been suddenly plucked off the ground by a giant claw. Their last thoughts fixed on whatever task they'd been working on, or minds wandering. Perhaps they'd been thinking of their own families.

I reached the creek and knelt to fill a jug, glancing at the sky. Izel would be asleep for a while longer. I could wash some clothes and blankets while here, and dry them back at the hut. I needed to work quickly, but it was safer in the daylight to be out in the open.

Footsteps. I heard them before I looked up. A woman holding an infant in a sling stood by the path. She must've been sheltering under the trees. Her face and clothes were dirty, and her baby's face was turned away, curly hair and one small ear poking out from the top of his bundle. My heart pounded with fear for them.

"Akna!" she called. "You are still here!"

I then recognized the filthy woman. Colel, who lived on the other side of the village. I'd seen her frequently in the weekly market, selling squash and beans. She'd had a baby recently, so I hadn't seen her before most of the village people left. My eyes darted to the foliage behind her, hoping to see anyone else, but she was alone. My heart broke for this poor woman. What happened to her husband, her family?

"Colel," I called out. "You have to leave this village."

"Do you know what has been happening?" she sobbed. I must've been the first person she'd seen in days. "It took my husband and my daughter. Why not me?" Colel's eyes were wide and bloodshot. She moved with stiff, halting steps towards me. Her entire body was quivering, like a deer that scents its hunter. She clasped her baby to her chest, shielding him with her arms. His little hands clutched at her breast, but he made no sound.

"I do not know," I lied. "It is not safe here. You need to go to Quirigua, to the north. Someone can help you there."

"Come with us," she said. "Please. We are both alone. We can go together."

"I am not alone," I said. I picked up my filled jug and took a step back. "Colel, go." My voice was loud in the sudden silence.

The birds stopped singing, the monkeys ceased their chittering. This pause chilled me, even in the heat. Something was about to change.

Something was wrong.

"Go," I rasped at Colel, who stared at me. "You need to go *now.*"

She reached towards me with dirt-stained hands, tears brimming in her eyes. "Help us, Akna. Please."

A rustling in the undergrowth, a few steps away, caught my attention. My head whipped around, catching a quick glimpse of a black tail slithering through the leaves. Cold lightning shot through my limbs.

We were too late. It was already here.

"Get out of here!" I screamed. The baby wailed, its piercing cry filling the silence. I'd heard that sound many times as a mother. Colel stumbled a few steps back. She wanted my help but I could do nothing. I knew what was about to come, and I knew it would happen, whether I tried to stop it or not. Their blood would spill on the dead, thirsty earth, but it wouldn't be enough.

An ominous thrumming rose from the trees. Low, menacing growling splintered the stillness around us. Only then did Colel turn away, holding her son to her chest, and begin staggering back towards the village. She scurried away, fear hastening her strides, her son whimpering in her arms. I braced myself.

From the trees, a dark form blurred past into the bright sunlight. It moved like smoke, slipping through space with practiced ease. A claw-tipped limb covered in black, silky fur lashed out and raked across Colel's retreating legs, leaving crimson rivers behind and sending a cloud of bloody mist into the air. She screamed in pain and surprise, and fell to her knees, back hunched over her child to protect him.

A black, hulking beast towered over her, claws outstretched and teeth bared. It towered almost as tall as the tree on the riverbank and stood on two hind legs, covering Akna with its massive shadow. Its tail flicked in a frenzy, as it prepared to pounce.

I darted to the riverbank, picked up a thick branch, and ran at the creature's back, screaming as the wood connected with its hairy bulk. It paid me no mind, entirely focused on its prey. The brittle wood shattered on impact, splinters tangling in the creature's fur while others pelted my face. I lurched forward and tripped, all the breath snatched from my chest as my body hit the ground. A sharp, sudden pain pierced my torso.

All I could do as I struggled for air was watch the furred limbs ripping and tearing into Colel, shreds of flesh and linen scattering upon the riverbank. Her screams were mixed with the creature's guttural sounds of pleasure and hunger. The baby's crying cut off abruptly but Colel's low moans of pain continued, as the beast hunched over her form, panting as it fed. Fleshy ribbons and entrails pulled and snapped free of the broken corpse on the ground, spattering meat on our surroundings. Groans of pleasure and a low purr thrummed from the beast's throat as a rotten, musty funk filled the air and my nostrils. At last I managed to draw a shaky breath and bellow, "Stop!"

The beast turned, back muscles rippling. Obsidian-sharp claws flexed from their sheaths, scattering tiny blood droplets to the ground. Short, jet black hair covered the hulking beast, darker stains indicating the spots in its coat. Gore dripped from its fangs, two carving knives set in the chasm of its mouth. A pink tongue darted out to lick clots from its muzzle. I shuddered as I looked into its flaming, glittering eyes narrowed in anger. The eyes widened, and the creature froze.

Bits of fur dropped to the ground, like leaves falling from a tree, creating a tapestry at our feet. The beast shrank and fell, convulsing and twitching as hooked claws retracted, limbs shortened, and its eyes became the brown, curious gaze I knew so well.

Izel lay in the pile of fur, sweaty and panting, her sweet face and soft hands riddled with bloody streaks. One hand was tightly clutching something, and her fingers relaxed to reveal the red-veined limestone hanging from its cord around her neck, currents pulsing with each deep breath she took. Her eyes closed again, and she twitched several times more before laying still.

I gathered my sleeping daughter to me, dust, blood, and all, and turned my back to what remained of Colel and her son. If the insects and jungle scavengers didn't get to their bodies first, I would bury them another time. The jug I took, but the basket I left to collect another day. As I carried Izel back to our hut, the sun beating down upon us, I said a quiet prayer under my breath, hating myself for envying the fate of Colel and her family. Cizin now reunited them.

Izel still clutched that unholy stone. Once, I'd taken it away, hiding it beneath the plants in our garden. Izel had grown pale and weak, coughing up blood until I'd frantically dug up the rock and placed it in her palm as she slept. She was better the next day, and I realized I couldn't change what my daughter had become. It had chosen her, for some reason unknown to me. I could only live with the truth, and pray each day was bearable, or that it wouldn't come at all. Hoping for death filled me with a bitter guilt; I was torn between a mother's love for my daughter and my horror at what she'd done.

Izel was heavier in my arms than I remembered. No wonder the drugged tortillas hadn't kept her asleep. The bit of magnolia was now too low for a child of her size. My little girl was growing up. Into a world that would never love her, but only fear her. Villages were abandoned, families were torn apart, and life would never be normal again. All because of Izel.

Was this worth it? Was my daughter worth all these innocent lives?

"Mama loves you so much, tum," I whispered into her ear. "In every drop of rain."

And every drop of blood.

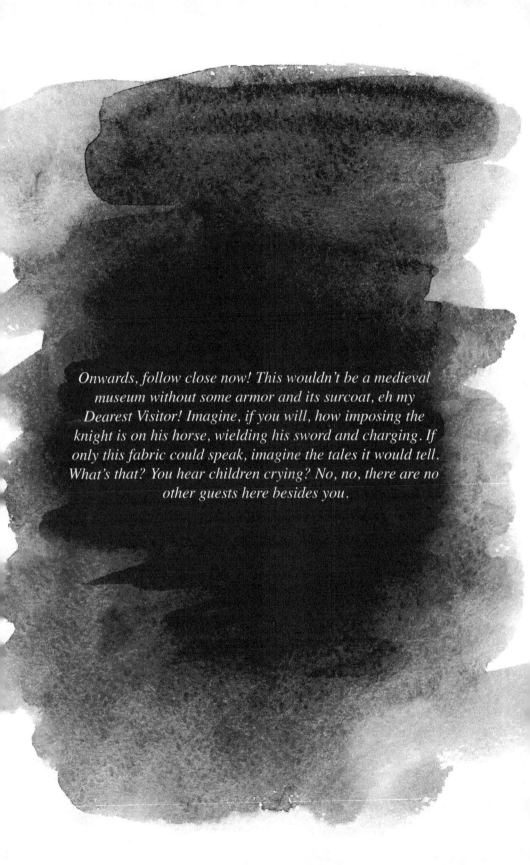

Onwards, follow close now! This wouldn't be a medieval museum without some armor and its surcoat, eh my Dearest Visitor! Imagine, if you will, how imposing the knight is on his horse, wielding his sword and charging. If only this fabric could speak, imagine the tales it would tell. What's that? You hear children crying? No, no, there are no other guests here besides you.

DEUS VULT

Ethan Yoder

he beast trudged through the wet earth, straining with each step to pull its hooves out of the fetid muck. From France to the Seljuk-occupied holy land and back again, the horse had dutifully carried its master. But now, so close to home, it could not bring itself to listen to a single command more. Sheets of freezing rain reflected the last remnants of sickly green twilight. The beast's rider attempted to will it onward, but his sharp kicks to its ribs were met only with the slapping sound of boot on hide. The rider dismounted and pulled at the reins, grinding the bridle into the chapped flesh of the horse's mouth. In return, the horse planted its hooves further into the dreck.

The surcoat that covered the knight's mail absorbed the rain like a sponge, each drop of water a tiny hammer blow driving him further into the liquid soil. At the start of his journey the coat had been a vibrant blue, marked by delicately sewn fleurs-de-lis of yellow. It was an elegant signifier of both dogma and privilege, but as months turned to years, the coat became tattered by the blowing desert sand and discolored by the blood of the dead. Now, as his journey neared its end, somewhere near the border of his home land, covered in mud and sopping wet, the coat didn't signify a damned thing.

The knight gritted his teeth and pulled the reins with both hands as hard as he could.

"Move, you bastard!"

His shoulders throbbed, the muscles clenching and bunching into agonizing sheets of granite below his neck. Then, like a bolt fired from a crossbow, a stabbing pain tore through his right hand and up his arm. The jolt of it forced him to release the leather strap and he fell backwards, splashing with a thud into the ice cold mud.

His mind fell further, careening through time and across continents before crashing into the cracked earth.

He was back there again, as real as the day it had happened. The high sun cooked the chapped flesh of his face and filled his lungs with invisible fire. He scrambled for his sword, but before he could reach it, the pommel of a Turkish kilij cracked into the soft tissue of his hand, rending bone from muscle, and muscle from sinew. The pain was consciousness destroying. It turned the knight's world to buzzing white. The buzzing turned to mist, and the mist to drops of rain, and he found himself back in the mud. The knight ripped off his gauntlets and dug his left thumb into the meat of his right palm. He massaged the muscle around the joints until the fire in his nerves began to dim.

A bolt of lightning cracked the sky with a deafening roar. The horse reared in terror, then slammed back to the ground and broke into a gallop. The knight rolled to the side as the beast passed him, a hoof trampling the earth inches from his face. He flopped to his belly and scrambled to his feet just in time to see the horse disappear into a dense thicket of trees. Had the knight more food in his belly, or a cup of ale, had he not felt the scalding cold so acutely in every part of his body, he might've mustered more concern. As it stood, all he could do was stand and stare as a single beleaguered sigh escaped his lips.

It was with that same indifference that he followed the horse's trail. Green undergrowth blanketed the forest floor like an emerald sea, making the monstrous trees, with their thick trunks and odd, angular branches, appear as the grasping hands of drowned giants. Rain leaked through the thick canopy in thin streams, like silver spider's silk. The knight's vision faded to flickering pointillism and the churning of shapes as the forest devoured the remaining light, but the knight was unmoved. All the things that plagued him had happened under the omnipotent watch of a burning sun in a cloudless sky.

From far in the distance, a whisper of a breeze washed over the knight, carrying with it a delicate, floral aroma that cut through the smell of decaying leaves and stopped him where he stood. So sweet, so intoxicating, so familiar—the memory of it so deeply buried in his mind that it took him a long moment to dig it out.

Wildflowers. It smelled similar—no, identical—to the wildflowers that grew in the fields that surrounded the country home where he was born. He could almost see the rolling hills dotted with beautiful purple blooms, almost feel the soft grass under his feet and the gentle kiss of the late morning sun, and almost hear his hound bark in the distance, a fierce protector and beloved childhood companion. As a boy, he had picked as many of the round, purple blooms as he could, binding them with twine into misshapen bouquets, dirt clods clinging to twisted roots. His mother lovingly accepted each one as if it were the most precious jewel.

The barest hint of a smile passed over the knight's face. That smell was the first thing in his entire accursed journey that reminded him of home. But there was another scent intermingling with it that he couldn't quite place. It was something long ago seen and forcefully forgotten, buried deep below — a thing that would have to be clawed out to be retrieved. The smile fell from his lips.

The knight followed the breeze north, feeling his way through the trees, stumbling on exposed roots and fallen branches, until the canopy began to thin, allowing white moonlight and rain to reach him. The forest's edge became visible in the distance, and beyond it several wisps of smoke snaked into the sky. The knight's pace quickened, first to a jog and then, as the trees cleared, a run. He breached the clearing, almost losing his foothold in the mud as he staggered to a stop. Each plume of smoke was tethered to the chimney of a small, decaying, straw-roofed house, two perpendicular rows of which lined the valley in front of him. At the end of the houses, a steep road twisted back up the hill, feeding into a fifteen-foot-tall mouth of twisted iron. The knight's breath hitched in his chest.

No. Not a mouth. A gate.

At first, the knight had trouble deciphering the structure ahead of him. Its walls were barricaded against the natural rock and it was difficult to tell where the stone ended and the castle began. Three spires stabbed upwards, piercing the sky. The middle spire was tallest, and the knight had to crane his neck to see its peak. There was no sign of life from inside. No lyre's song to fill the thick, night air. No whispered reconciliation or boisterous wailing of hymns. Not a single candle's light to illuminate the rows of ornate stained-glass windows that lined the façade like lifeless eyes, peering down to the village below and up to the crest of the hill where he stood.

The knight had never seen anything remotely like it. The structure was both church and castle, with the disparate parts of each butting up against one another, the lack of balance giving charge to the space around it.

Rain had eroded the hillside and made the already steep descent even more treacherous for the knight. Each footfall sunk deep into the mud and threatened to collapse the narrow path and send him careening to the rocks below. Yet despite this, he found it increasingly difficult to pull his gaze from the cyclopean castle in the distance. From the valley basin, the massive structure appeared even more monolithic.

The knight walked down the main path between the two rows of huts. He stopped when he noticed a stern-looking woman outside her meager dwelling, thin arms shaking as she lifted a large chamber pot and tipped the contents into the mud. Their eyes met, but the woman paused for only a moment to assess him, a loathful scowl crawling across her face. Before the knight could speak, she had already turned her back and started to hobble away.

"Wait!" the knight called.

She did so without turning back to face him, a visible tension creeping into her shoulders.

"I am looking for my horse. I am also in need of food and lodging for the night."

The woman relaxed and began to walk back into her house, the knight's willingness to ask for her help—to debase himself by doing so—not worthy of her attention. The insolence of it gutted him. She couldn't even be bothered to look at him—couldn't afford him that small dignity. Four steps cleared the distance between them. The knight grabbed her arm and pulled.

He squeezed with a force that turned his knuckles white.

"Woman, I am speaking to you."

She turned on her heel, spraying muddy water in the knight's direction, and pushed him with likely all the force her sinewed frame could muster.

The push barely moved the knight, but it set off bells in his head that cloaked all other sound. His vision turned to red smoke. As he ground his teeth together, tiny flecks of enamel broke free and crunched to wet mortar in his mouth. There was nothing else in that moment but rage. Rage and the fear that lurks beneath it.

Then he was back in the desert.

Steel splintered bone and turned bodies to meat.

Men begged for their lives in a foreign tongue.

Two pairs of eyes stared at him from the dark.

The knight and his fellow crusaders chanted the words they had been given by the pope and by God.

"Deus Vult."

And then he was back in the dark and the rain. Instinctively he loosened his hold on the woman's arm, and she pulled herself free.

"I said get your hands off me! If you weren't a knight, I might just—"

But the pounding of his heart blocked all external sound. His lungs greedily grasped for air. The world around him rocked side-to-side like a boat threatening to capsize, and a buzzing emptiness crept up his legs. He braced himself against the closest shack. The wood was soft from rot.

Small creaks, like the death cries of diseased birds, echoed from across the valley as villagers wrenched open their swollen and moldering shutters to peer at the source of the commotion.

"What's wrong with you?" the woman asked. "You had too much ale? You one of those that came back from the Crusades with a taste for the drink?"

"Haven't been drinking. Just hungry," the knight said.

"If you want to go begging for food, we've got none to give you," she said. "You'd need to go up and see the bishop."

"B—bishop?" the knight said, still dazed.

The woman said nothing, but regarded him with a disgust usually reserved for the burying of dead livestock on a hot summer's day.

"Yes, a bishop. What kind of knight never heard of a bishop before?"

One villager let out a single, pitiful laugh at the woman's comment, before falling into a fit of deep, phlegmy coughs.

The knight shook his head and the rest of the desert sand drained from his mind. The feeling returned to his legs. He straightened.

"I know what a bishop is. I'm asking what kind of bishop lives in a giant castle like that," the knight said.

"He's a bishop and a count," she said, "but we think of him as a bishop first, him being so holy. He does a fine job looking out for us, but we don't keep any extra for charity cases or undesirables."

A single brown drop clung to the edge of the woman's chamber pot.

"Well then, I won't bother you any longer," the knight said, and turned away.

"Wait. It won't do you any good to go up there."

The knight turned again. His body creaked with the effort, and his brow furrowed.

"I thought you said I needed to speak with the bishop?"

"I said you'd need to. I didn't say the bishop would speak with you."

"And why is that?"

"The bishop only speaks with those that have a special connection with God."

"A special connection with God?"

"Yeah, those of us who are pure and holy. They get to live with the bishop."

"What do you mean they live up there? As his servants?"

The woman narrowed her eyes, creating a landscape of thin cracks across her weathered face.

"As his congregation," she said.

"When do you see them?"

"We see them."

"So, any of you peasants that show a spiritual aptitude just leaves their life to live with a bishop?"

"Only those who haven't been corrupted by earthly goings on."

"And who among us hasn't been corrupted?"

"Why the children, of course."

For a brief moment the rain ceased, and only cold air filled the space between them.

"The children are taken from their parents?" the knight asked.

"Just the good ones. The ones that behave and learn their prayers and treat the bishop with respect no matter what he asks."

The woman cast a sharpened gaze backwards past the threshold of her ramshackle hut to the oppressive dark inside. It took a moment for the knight's vision to find purchase in the black, but slowly the outline of two small figures emerged. It was hard for the knight to see what they were, because in their meager countenance they seemed only a collection of the things they were not—tattered rags where there should've been warm clothes, sunken cheeks that should've been fat and rosy. When they met their mother's gaze, they both looked down and raised their hands in supplication.

The woman twisted her face in disgust.

"Don't act so humble. If you would've acted that way when it mattered, you'd be up there with your sister," she said, pointing a grubby, nailless finger at the castle on the hill. Now get out here. It's almost time."

The two children scuttled out of the dark shack and hid behind their mother. They peered at the knight with eyes both suspicious and pleading. All around them, the people of the village emerged from their gutted shacks and turned to look at the castle.

"What's happening?" the knight asked.

"You'll see," the woman said.

No one said a word. No one moved. The sound of ragged breath from infirm lungs and dripping water through moldy thatch were the only accompaniment to the bizarre spectacle. The smell of smoke, animal waste, and the rusted iron of his mail filled the knight's nose. Through the fog, he heard one of the villagers cry:

"Look, there she is! Well, don't just stand there. Wave to her."

A low, buzzing chatter rose amongst them. The knight's focus darted from villager to villager as subterranean joys surfaced on their faces. And then, one by one, candlelight flickered to life in each of the castle's windows. The light—soft, barely an ember at first—bloomed, pouring a kaleidoscope of colored light through the stained glass.

In each illuminated window, a small silhouette was pressed to the pane.

Each figure was indiscernible from the next, but every villager seemed to know which one was their son or daughter. They wept joyful tears and called to them. They wished them well and gave their love. Their prayers of jubilation filled the valley like wine in Christ's holy cup.

The silhouettes did not move.

The knight stared in confusion and disbelief. What were they seeing that he wasn't? He barely noticed the first tug on his surcoat. The second and third were a distant annoyance. The fourth was more forceful—pleading. He looked down and saw the two haggard children, red tendrils branching across whites of their eyes, staring into him. Tears flowed down their thin, dirtied faces.

The knight recoiled at the sight of them. The child who held firm to the coat was pulled forward into the mud. Something rattled deep within the knight's heart. Pity? Remorse? He could see the knowing fear, the dread of existence in their faces, and it reminded him of something of which he wouldn't allow himself to be reminded. Despite the child's low birth, the knight crouched to help pull them out of the muck. Their skin was cold down to the bone and what wasted muscle lay on top of it was wrapped in sallow gooseflesh.

The other child crawled to the side of their fallen sibling, and held them in their arms—an attempt to comfort in a world that would give none.

Quiet observance was the only reply the knight could muster, and he sat in that moment with the children for a long while—the distant light from the castle washing them in pale shades of red and blue.

The flame extinguished and plunged the silhouettes back into darkness. Both children ran back to their mother before she could notice they were gone, but in the spot where they had just stood, a small object lay, mashed and half submerged. It would've been unrecognizable to most, but the knight knew it instantly: a single purple wildflower.

A howling wind rose from the direction of the castle, its high-pitched roar sailing over the knight. It became clear to him in that moment where the smell of flowers had emanated from.

When the knight started up the steep path towards the castle gate, the townsfolk urged him to reconsider. When he did not, they called him a blasphemer and a devil. When he still kept going, they cried for the bishop to strike him down. When he reached the castle gate, their curses were a distant patter, indistinguishable from so many drops of rain.

As he crossed the threshold of the iron gate, he couldn't help but notice once again how it resembled the gaping maw of some unfathomable behemoth. The gate opened into a courtyard, stone walls rising into the sky around him, swollen vines crawling up them like blighted veins. Seven green wooden doors presented themselves to the knight, but he found with frustration that only the fourth was not bolted shut.

The knight entered into a dark corridor, the only illumination coming from underneath the dozens of doors on either side of the hall. The air was thick and warm, its odor sour and carrion. Thick straw lined the stone floor in front of him, but it felt unnaturally slick under his boot. He grabbed a handful. There was just enough light to see. The knight's knees threaten to buckle. Amidst the hay were thousands of strands of silken hair.

Human hair.

Child's hair.

The knight turned and ran to the door. Whatever this place, whoever this bishop, the knight did not belong there. When he rattled the lock, it would not open. He threw his shoulder into it, but it was sturdy of construction. In desperation, he unsheathed his sword and swung violently, first as a knight, and when it would not give, as a caged beast.

When he ceased, sword warped and chipped, panting, rivulets of sweat streaming down his neck, the rhythmic sound of beating on the door continued.

Knock.

Knock.

Knock.

It was coming from one of the doors down the hall. Someone on the other side of the threshold was trying to answer him.

The knight remembered the small silhouettes in the windows.

He ran, the cold stone of the castle echoing every hurried step and gasping breath and twisting them into a nightmare symphony of wretched fear. He turned the corner at the end of the hall but found that the interior was a network of endless arteries of gray brick. Every door the knight passed was locked. From behind some doors came muffled breathing. From behind other doors, there was only silence. From underneath all doors, the shadowed pacing of feet.

Then, like an old friend, it returned to him—the smell of wildflowers. Beautiful like before, but more vivid, like the memories lay on the edge of a knife. He followed the scent.

It led him down passageways and corridors, down holes in the earth, through doors that existed in the place between doors, and finally up a twisting staircase into the highest point of the tallest spire. It was so strong, the scent, that the knight could feel the flowers brushing against his ankles. It seeped between the cracks of the wooden door in front of him, cloyed his senses, made him forget everything except the vague notion of what he was sure it had at one time represented. But still in the back of his mind, he sensed something deeper to it, and the sweetness became saccharine, as if the flowery aroma was only there to cover something else.

The knight pushed the heavy oaken door, and it yielded with ease. The room was long, longer than he thought it should be, based on his cursory glances from before. That didn't matter though, because all that registered to the knight were the flowers. Thousands of wildflowers covered every inch of the room. They grew from between the stone tile, and sprouted from the mildewed tapestries on the wall.

And he allowed himself to remember what memories lived under the smell of wildflowers.

After Jerusalem had been sacked, after all the Turkish soldiers were dead or screaming for death through blood-filled mouths, the knight and the other men still felt God calling them to action. His presence buzzed at the napes of their necks. It passed through their darting eyes and shaking hands. He had given them their holy city—their shining beacon on the hill. Such a prize would require a greater offering. It was not for them to question predestination.

They found them hiding in their homes, huddled together in corners, clutching makeshift tools in defense. They clung to the small patches of darkness where the burning sun could not reach them.

The old.

The sick.

The women.

The children.

The Church's army formed lines and went house by house, breaking down every door, searching every room. It was methodical—clean. When the knight brought down his sword, his heart swelled with the gift of divine wisdom.

It wasn't until he reached the last room of the last house on the last street, that he smelled it. Wildflowers. *His* wildflowers. Powerful and vibrant. Just like the ones from his home. God was giving him a sign. Just as Jesus had shown his pierced palms to Thomas after the resurrection, or given Noah a rainbow after the great flood, the knight was receiving validation for his sacrifice.

The knight's mind swam with possibilities. Would it lead him to gold? Or perhaps to a secret Turkish cache of holy artifacts? He followed the smell around the room like a starving wolf, finding it strongest in the far corner of the room in the small area above a tattered, hand-woven rug. The knight flung the rug to the side and revealed, just as he knew it would, a trap door. A joyous, child-like smile covered his face as he ripped the door open to reveal his reward.

And was met with the terrified eyes of a little girl and her mother.

Their brown faces were covered in dust, except for the places where their tears had fallen. The little girl's soft fingers were wrapped around a small bouquet of purple flowers.

The knight didn't say anything and didn't comprehend for a long moment. He just looked at them, ghostly white. Smiling.

Then he started to scream.

As the knight brought down his sword, the mother pulled the child to her breast and held her there, as if through the act of holding, she could keep the girl's soul tethered for just a bit longer.

When the other men emerged from the homes of dead families, ankle deep in slick, warm blood, they felt closer to their god than they ever thought possible. The Lord had given them what was by their estimation the greatest gift they could be given: the moral and ethical imperative to kill all that could be killed. With that in their hearts, they began to chant those two hideous words.

"Deus Vult."

The knight dropped to his knees on the castle floor and vomited bile onto the black stone and winding flowers. His vision wavered for a moment, blurring and darkening before snapping back into focus at the sensation of someone else in the room. He felt the presence before he saw it, sitting in the corner watching him. A torch light burst into flame, the knight staggered to his feet, and pivoted as a small figure darted past him. When he turned back, he could see the bishop's eyes looking into him. Ropes of thick, green mucus oozed from under his eyelids. The bishop was naked, revealing his body to be long and impossibly thin, the sickly yellow pallor of his skin, interrupted at two dozen places by jagged gashes. Some of the wounds were crusted shut and others sagged open like slack mouths, the gray juice of spoiled meat running from their corners and revealing the pink sinew underneath.

The bishop didn't move but just followed the knight with his eyes. Another torch erupted in flame, and cast its shadows on the wall in bizarre and frenetic shapes. No, not just shadows. One of the things darted past him before disappearing into the darkness.

Then another.

And another.

Their little bodies, long since freed from their souls, were decomposing watercolor palettes of grays, greens, and purples. The longer their imprisonment, the greater the putrefaction of their small frames. Three of the woeful things attempted to follow their siblings, but were unable to bring forth suitable locomotion, and laid on the floor, gently tapping their shaved heads into the moistened brick. It was hard for the knight to tell that some of them had ever been children.

The dead things surrounded the bishop and then swarmed him. They covered him completely, a cocoon of swirling, rotten flesh. One by one, they faced the bishop, and for a moment it looked to the knight as if they were embracing the skeletal figure. Then, with horror, he realized what they were doing.

Small hands found their place in the gashes of his arms and legs, fumbling dully with bloated fingers. They pulled on the tendons and muscles, causing them to first spasm, then raise, then lower. Up and down. Left to right. Crude and mechanical at first, then smooth, then graceful. The bishop stretched his fingers and reached for a long garment on the floor. He began to stand—the puppet, but also the master.

The knight tried to think, tried to consider what options laid before him, but when he saw the bishop, he lost all parts of himself that knew any recourse but to stand and wait. Distantly he wondered how he could be so quick with his sword when it had been innocents at the end of his blade, but now, when confronted with real evil, he was struck impotent.

The bishop buttoned his vestments and took a giant, lurching step forward. He towered over the knight, a full seven feet tall, hunched and pulsating, pious and penitent. The bishop opened his mouth to speak, but only guttural bursts of phlegm came out. The mouth snapped shut just as quickly, teeth cracking into each other like a thunderclap. Two thin hands slid up into the wounds on either side of his neck, and the flesh under the bishop's throat began to pulse and jerk. This time when he opened his mouth to speak, his voice boomed with sound and fury. The knight barely heard the words. He didn't need to.

"Deus Vult."

God wills it.

When the bishop fell upon him, it was not with anger or malice. The bishop did not hate the knight or wish him harm. He felt only love for him, his brother in Christ, a holy warrior of the highest order. The bishop had no plans to kill him. He needed him. What is a shepherd without a dog to guard his flock? With a delicate hand he took the knight apart, bleeding thread by bleeding thread. He removed the knight's surcoat and cradled it to his chest. He ran his fingers across the surface and felt the almost imperceptible grains of sand and dirt that existed in the space between threads. The bishop delicately hung the coat from a hook on the wall. The knight wore a coat of crimson now. He would need no other sigil.

When the bishop brought him back together, it was in a new and frightening shape. The bishop took his communion from the leftover scraps of the knight's flesh, and when he shared with the knight, the knight took freely of it, feeling the power in the blood and smelling the sweet stench of wildflowers.

As the rain clouds cleared and the first rays of pastel light showered the village below, the inhabitants stood outside their rotting shacks and gazed up to the gray castle. This time, more than any other, they were sure they could feel it gazing back.

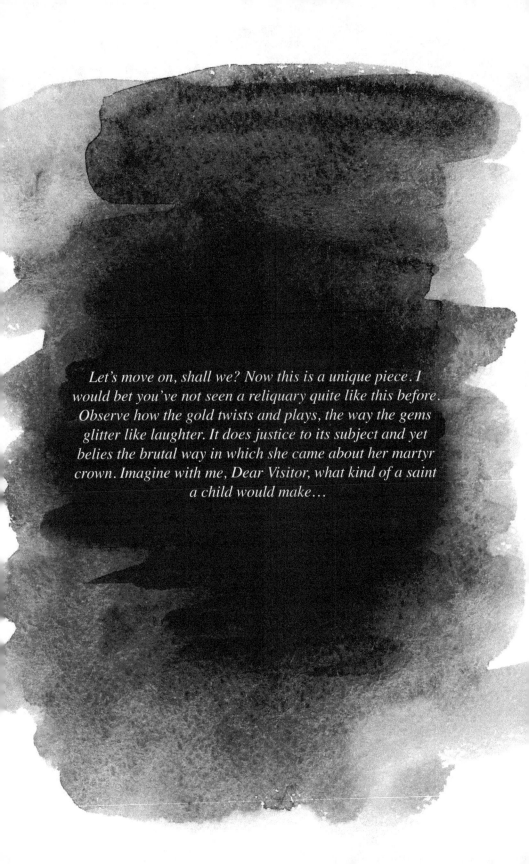

Let's move on, shall we? Now this is a unique piece. I would bet you've not seen a reliquary quite like this before. Observe how the gold twists and plays, the way the gems glitter like laughter. It does justice to its subject and yet belies the brutal way in which she came about her martyr crown. Imagine with me, Dear Visitor, what kind of a saint a child would make…

THE FINAL BOOK OF SAINTE FOY'S MIRACLES

M.E. Bronstein

I. About a Liberated Prisoner Whom Sainte Foy Strangled in His Sleep

uring my childhood I collected words my father did not know; when they spilled out, he beat me. I spied on trials, listened to oath-takers who stuffed their langue d'Oc with bits of Latin. I repeated after them, said juro tibi and videlicet and sine omni malo ingenio.

My vagabond father shepherded me from place to place. He stole silver spoons and horseshoes, loaves from bakehouses, and clothes from drying lines, and wound up imprisoned by a vexed chatelain who meant to hang him. My father prayed to Sainte Foy, and she loosened his fetters, and then his jailer (marvelous to say!) indulged in too much wine and left his door unlocked. I did not appreciate this miracle.

We made a pilgrimage to Conques—to give thanks to Sainte Foy. My father's favorite saint, a great patroness of the wretched and desperate, of beggars and thieves.

Conques is a silvery place cradled by green mountains and mist. Back then, it was peopled and busy and the streets smelled of stale sweat and burning chestnuts. The Abbey was pale yellow and gray, as though it wished to obscure itself in the intermittent fog and sun. Its famous doors and grillwork were riddled with the melted chains of former prisoners freed by Sainte Foy. And then a brilliant treasure glowed at the heart of so much cold limestone and iron: Sainte Foy's golden and bejeweled reliquary, containing a fragment of her skull. We were barred from her by a grating. (No wonder she sympathized with prisoners.)

Prior to this pilgrimage, I had only encountered martyrs' remains in boxes and sculptures of hands and feet. But a statue of a whole, unmarred (though very small) body now sat before us, enthroned and robed and crowned all in gold. And yet she also looked like driftwood; the chaos of gemstones scattered across her silhouette made her at once opulent and bedraggled, barnacled with brilliance. Her large enamel eyes stared past me. Four little globes of crystal shimmered atop the corners of her throne.

My father lit a candle for her. Many other candles flickered nearby, and reflected fire pulsed across her—gold on gold. My father prayed and fondled his silver crucifix peppered with seed pearls (another recent theft).

While he prayed, I followed the ambulatory around Sainte Foy. Her brilliance and candles freckled the flagstones and columns with light—which I chased. Pilgrims filled the choir, reflected candle-light ablaze in their pupils, and they ignored me. I pounced and caught a scrap of light—or almost did. It glowed on the back of my hand—then burned, like a true flame, no mere reflection, and I yelped, retreated, scampered back to my father. I told him Sainte Foy had burnt me and asked if we could go. He seized my hair, dragged my head toward his. He said, "Be still, be patient, or I will tell her to burn you again, I will tell her to blind you. She does that, you know—she blinds the wicked."

The thought was fleeting—I swear—but for the briefest instant, I wished he would die.

We stayed in Conques that evening, and in the morning, I woke to find my father dead.

But no, that could not be. He had defied death so often, how could my little wish kill him? But he remained leaden, weighty, no matter how I shook him, his neck and face bloated and purpled. His left hand curled like a dead spider on his chest, grasping his crucifix, his nails bloody and torn—

He had died struggling to wrest its chain from his swelling flesh.

My father's blood-pinked eyes protruded from their sockets like overripe pimples—and something moved, deep in their lifeless depths. I should have fled then, leaned closer instead, and a reminiscence of gold glittered behind his faded pupils. Just like the pilgrims in the choir. Gilded by their love for her. And I clutched my hand, where the memory of her light still itched, and I ran.

I left him there.

I had heard none of his struggle during the night. I had only dreamed of a child's distant laughter, buoyant and light as ribbons on a breeze.

II. How a Maiden Was Martyred and Later Encased in Gold

I have begun out of order. I ought to have initiated this account by discussing my unworthiness to record it.

Alan of Lille states that godly language does not shine like a gaudy medal. Nor should we exsanguinate our speech. Rather, medium tenuere beati — the blessed take the middle path — between splendid, wine-stained discourse and plain and bloodless expression.

Forgive my forays from the middle path into purplish and glittering avenues. Recall that my lapses are inspired by a radiant source: the Majesty of Sainte Foy.

I will provide a brief account of her martyrdom, for any readers who remain lamentably unfamiliar with her history.

Sainte Foy was martyred in the time of Diocletian. Her *Passio* states that she was no more than twelve years old. The prefect Dacian came to slaughter Christians; he summoned a patrician's daughter, who made the sign of the cross before him. The prefect advised that she pledge herself to the cult of Diana, and Foy refused. The prefect had Foy bound naked to a bronze grill and stoked hot coals beneath her. But then heaven thundered and a sudden rain doused the fire. Dacian had her beheaded. An unearthly aureola glowed about her severed head, and those who witnessed the maid's death understood that she had God's favor and they converted. And so Sainte Foy was crowned with the glory of martyrdom.

Dacian had her corpse cast into a swamp, and there it remained until the good bishop Dulcidius constructed a new basilica and a marble tomb to contain her remains. (Today blood still blooms out of her first burial ground in the swamp.) Her body and head have moved again and again. I believe it was in the time of Charles III that her skull found a worthy home in its present reliquary. Thereafter Sainte Foy earned fame for her miracles — recorded well before my time by the estimable Bernard of Angers, and others, who remain unnamed and unknown.

I was a foolish child when she earned my fear; now you will learn how I came to love her. And you will follow my example and give her your love, too — or risk her disappointment.

III. How a Verbose Young Man Vowed Himself to Sainte Foy's Service

After my father's death, I slept in the street and beheld a vision of Sainte Foy's Majesty. Her aureate shell flickered and shifted as though molten, aflame. She bloomed and glowed, no longer little—I had become the little one, and I quaked before her. She whispered, her voice so close, it almost perched on my shoulder, and she promised to intercede with the Lord on my father's behalf if I gave her what was rightly hers—what I owed her for the favor she had bestowed on me (freedom).

She showed my mind a picture: my father's silver crucifix.

I went on trembling as I awoke. No, no, I could not go back to him, to her. Her request had to be a trick—she wanted me to return, so that her glow might adhere itself to me, and I would not have that.

I left Conques. I traveled north and arrived at Chartres. I threw myself at the mercy of the Notre-Dame almonry.

The Abbot of Saint-Père collected orphans like me—I was sound and whole, preferable to the feeble and leprous children parents often abandon to monasteries. I lived and prayed and studied. I learned prayers full of lovely new words, which became a kind of nourishment to me.

But: her reach. It grew feebler, so far from home. But she never left me—not really.

Sometimes—gold and white, just out of view. Misplaced brilliance in the dark of my cell, the abbey's corridors. I would turn and it would vanish. But then: a faint echo, laughter, caught in the vaults. A tug at my habit, like a child's hand, but no one there.

I read all I could about Sainte Foy. Perhaps if I learned more, I could banish her, shake her off—something, anything. I read her *Passio*, the *Translatio*. I journeyed to the Vermandois to consult the library of Saint-Quentin, where Bernard of Angers once offered a copy of his Liber miraculorum to the canons Wantelme and Leowulf.

I savored the language of Bernard and others—their delicate circumlocutions around strange and wondrous events.

I pictured the red pool of rich vermillion as it flooded from the inkhorn of the girlchild's broken neck. The cooled embers of her eyes as she died. Her radiance veiled by swamp filth.

My father had pressed his thumbs into my throat, often threatened to break my neck, too.

Could I have been wrong? Perhaps her attentiveness to my wishes had been a kindness—or intended as one.

I attempted to discuss the matter with Father Barthélemy, but he distrusted my tales of southern saints and reliquaries; he spoke of idol-worship and I said nothing, corrected him in my heart, never out loud.

My mind approached the road to Conques, but always turned back.

I had a friend in the cloister garden—a magpie who frequented the quince tree. I considered him a sort of kinsman, because my brothers often called me Pica, deeming me garrulous as a magpie. And so, whenever I entered the garden to gather wort for a physic, we would regard each other, and I would say, "Hello, Pica, it is Pica."

That is, until one day, when sunset stained the heavens amber, and I found the quince tree empty of my friend. I circled the tree and found the magpie in a bloody pile, his wings broken. Sunlight gilded his eyes. I cradled my namesake between unsteady hands, which made his feathers shiver, as though he still lived—would he not awaken and fly away again? No, no—just like my father, he would not.

That evening, I dreamed of a child in a gown of white samite veined with gold threads. She knelt upon the earth, played knucklebones.

I kept my distance. Hoped she would not see me. That I could slip out of the dream again unnoticed. Dream-blood thundered through my ears. Her fingertips were pink with someone's death. Where had she found those knucklebones?

Sainte Foy looked up and said, "Won't you join my game?"

I froze. Did not answer.

She shook her head and said, "No, no, of course not. You are right. You've grown too old." She sounded disappointed—though unsurprised—by this error on my part. "When you think of me," she asked, "is it out of gratitude—or fear?"

I said nothing. She knew the answer already.

"The people of Conques do not think of me anymore, Pica," said Sainte Foy, "and I have fewer attendants and visitors today than I once did."

Could a saint grow lonely?

It seemed strange, that she would chafe against solitude. But she was a playful little martyr, who required company—to participate in her games, to make them real.

Sainte Foy collected her knucklebones, dropped them again.

"What shall I do?" I asked. "How should I serve you?"

"You failed me, refused me, so many years ago. Did you think I would forget? You owe me your dearest treasure. A sign of your true devotion. You will return to me and provide me with such a sign by Saint Augustine's Day."

She did not ask out of any special reverence for Saint Augustine; rather, his feast day happened to coincide with the anniversary my father's death.

And if I did not return? I dared not ask the question out loud, but she heard it anyway.

"And if you do not obey me, I shall treat you as I have treated your friend in the garden." Her fingers, so pink, so bright, like a normal child's hands, stained after plucking berries.

When I woke, I probed my neck, my wrists, my eyelids. No swelling, no pain. Everything in place, unmarred.

IV. On My Return to Conques and the Beggar Children There

When my father and I first journeyed to Conques, we crossed a narrow wooden footbridge over a hissing gorge. In the intervening years, it had been replaced by a stabler passage of stone, though the oxen that dragged carts across it twitched their ears and lowed as their passage resounded around them. My mule stamped and snorted. The misted air chilled us, as though we had entered a cave.

I found Conques as I remembered it—a cluster of gray buildings stacked somewhat precariously against a rich green hillside—but quieter. Only a few souls populated the streets, many of them recognizably pilgrims like myself, either come to pay their respects to Sainte Foy, or on their way to more famous altars on the Via Podiensis.

I had few possessions but treasured my little breviary, a girdle book that always dangled by my side. Elegant red-and-blue pen flourishes twined around its initials. Little monsters cavorted through its margins. I had decided that this would be my offering to Sainte Foy—and perhaps then she would be satisfied, at last, and leave me be.

Something like snow veiled my gaze as I approached the Abbey. Could it be her already? Blinding me, punishing me? But no—only one of my body's habitual complaints, when I neglected its needs. I sat at the road's edge. My vision cleared. I continued.

I found a clutch of beggar children outside—leeches that had laid themselves against the Abbey's ribs to suckle at its lifeblood. A haggard and dirty little maid approached me, palm outstretched. I gave her a denier and asked why it was so quiet here.

"It is always like this," she said.

"I have seen this place otherwise, full of activity."

"When was that, sir?"

"Before you were born, I suppose. But why do you linger here, if not to benefit from the thick assemblies that conglomerate about Sainte Foy?"

She stared; she had not understood me. I rephrased and simplified the question. Where had all of Sainte Foy's worshippers gone?

"Oh, people come," said the girl, "but then they go away again. Quickly."

Yes, yes, that felt true. Because, her miracles—they bite.

Bernard of Angers recounts that during a procession she once gave the gift of hearing to a deaf-mute, who then struggled to tear his bleeding ears from his head—for he had never heard any noise before, much less the racket of trumpets and cymbals that accompanied Sainte Foy's Majesty through the streets.

"She does not frighten you?" I asked the girl.

The child inspected the coin I had given her, like a diminutive merchant assessing a counterfeit. She said, "I bring her presents, and she protects me."

I did not ask where or how the girl acquired the "presents" in question. I held a breath in my chest, then entered the Abbey Church.

It had turned dark indoors, the pale limestone walls and vaults waxy and grayish with years of taper and torch smoke. Milky light spilled out of the tall windows and striped the long darkness of the nave. Sainte Foy glowed, a faded star in the distance.

Up close, she looked more corroded than I remembered, patches of dullness blooming across her surface, bruise-like. Ash, shed by her candles, encircled her gemstones.

I reached for my girdle book and found only a hunk of severed cloth. My breviary had been cut away. My purse was gone, too.

I went down on hands and knees, prayed that my possessions would reappear. They did not.

I scampered raggedly out, hoping to catch the beggar children, but they had left. I retreated indoors and followed a slow and unsteady path back to Sainte Foy. I explained that the treasure I meant to give her had been stolen. I hoped she would forgive me. I had no coin or jewels to speak of anymore. I begged her not to strangle me in my sleep.

V. A Brief Account of Miracles Recent and Old

There is a strange repetitiveness to many of Sainte Foy's miracles. They spiral into themselves. Bernard of Angers recounts the miracle of Guibert the Illuminated, whose godfather tore his eyes out. A dove appeared (or a magpie, some say) and plucked Guibert's bloodied eyes from the ground and flew to Conques with them. Guibert remained blind for many years—until he lit a candle for Sainte Foy, and then two pale berries fell from heaven and fitted themselves into his skull. His sight was restored. But then his restored sight led him to desire and lie with women, and Sainte Foy blinded him again. After he repented, she gave him back his sight. And so it went, Guibert's sight winking in and out in accordance with his fluctuating sin and virtue.

Once, Sainte Foy healed a hunchbacked girl, but the ungrateful maiden would not attend Sainte Foy's holy procession; she lingered before her loom instead, and Sainte Foy curved her back anew and locked her gnarled fingers around her shuttle. The girl repented and kept vigil for many nights (shuttle still in hand) until Sainte Foy unspooled her curled bones once more.

Gimon, prior of the Abbey, grew old and attended nightly to the candles on Sainte Foy's altar. She tormented him awake again and again, called him slothful and complained that her light was wavering out; yet every time he rose to do her bidding, he found her candles miraculously relit of their own accord, and he heard a child's laughter.

One almost imagines that Sainte Foy enjoys our phases of moral errantry. We are fish in the river of virtue, and when an unkind tide ejects us so that we lie flapping on the riverbank, she likes to wait before tossing us back into the water. Sometimes she extracts us from the water herself for the simple amusement of watching us twitch and writhe in the air of sin.

I wasted a day hunting for the beggar girl, whom I would have thrashed with a hazel switch, but I found no trace of her. I ought to have pitied the poor, hungry child—she could not have realized, could not have understood—but I would die because of her greed, or be blinded at the very least, Sainte Foy would take her revenge if I did not give her what I owed her, if I did not find her a treasure, and now I had none.

I begged for feed for my mule and myself. Fortunately, the people of Conques were accustomed to mendicants. And I acquired new tales of Sainte Foy as well as sustenance.

Many of the people I spoke to did not call her Sainte Foy, but referred to "Foy," as though they spoke of a mischievous young neighbor.

They had scarred fingers where their flesh had swollen and contracted as she needled at them for rings she coveted. Many were bald and said she had burnt their hair off. They told me of roofs consumed in fire, how they went blind overnight, then saw again. They spoke of imprisoned thieves who shed their chains and murdered their neighbors. And again and again: coffers depleted, treasures lost, deniers drawn like a trail of ants to the honeyed light in the Abbey. And now, she had taken almost everything and they had nothing left to give her. And yet, these kind folk—who offered me almonds, plums, and wine spiced with thyme—appeared unperturbed by these events; they laughed, and flecks of gold glittered deep in their eyes where her spirit had adhered itself.

Only one old man, his pupils dark and empty, muttered the word "demon," then touched the wooden cross at his breast (he said he once possessed a far finer one, but Sainte Foy had requested it from him in a vision years ago; he refused her, and shortly thereafter it vanished).

And what did I think? Was she a saint or a demon? Why commune through magpies rather than doves? What saint requires so much earthly payment?

I visited her nightly and prayed. Though a contained sickness writhed in my gut as I waited, waited for her to punish me, I stayed, and there was something good in the practice, in my prayer, it was good to slip back into Latin, into words I love, after simplifying my speech for the benefit of the townsfolk. I elaborated, embroidered around familiar prayers. Somehow I believed—I hoped—that would appease her a little.

And yet, she never answered me. And Saint Augustine's Day was fast approaching.

VI. How Sainte Foy Slew a Thief and Brought a Wretch Back to Life

I hadn't any coin to pay for a bed beneath a roof, so I slept in a meadow and tied my mule to an oak.

But late at night—the sound of a child's faint and birdlike tittering interrupted my sleep. I faded hazily back to wakefulness, drawn by the sound. And there—at the edge of the meadow—a hunched little shadow, the beggar girl, the child who had taken my breviary.

A miracle! On the eve of my defeat, she reappeared, and I would reacquire my treasure from her, I would bestow it upon its rightful owner: Sainte Foy. I lurched after the girl, who darted away, still giggling. She ran off among the trees.

I gave chase. Just ahead, leaves and pine needles broke beneath her footfalls as her laughter simmered through the shadows and dense summer air. But I was growing old and unaccustomed to children's games and their ridiculous chases. My breath grew labored, louder than her laughter, and soon I lost the sound of her; she was concealed by my own body's complaints, my joints crying out, my loquacious heartbeat. I came to a halt, bent and breathed. I listened, heard nothing but the usual sounds of the night: crickets, owls, wind. Perhaps she had been one of those apparitions that sometimes manifest between sleep and waking.

I returned to the meadow, defeated anew.

And there I found new company. Company I had most definitely not dreamed into being. A large man in a cloak was untying my mule, who stamped and snorted, alarmed by the unfamiliar presence.

I limped toward him, one knee reluctant to bear my weight. I cried out, hoped he might take pity.

"Please," I said.

A slice of silver spilled out of his cloak and directed itself at me.

I ought to have turned and run then. I continued toward him instead. I tripped and collapsed at his feet, where I clutched at his cloak and begged.

"Please," I said again, "leave me this sole means of conveyance—I have no coin, no means of returning to my home otherwise—"

"You talk too much," said the man. The cold edge of his dagger pressed against the tender span of flesh above my collarbone—which felt taught as a drum's skin, ready to break. And to make noise.

I cried out for help, again and again, and the knife slipped. The cloaked man gripped it more tightly and plunged it into my throat.

I must write this down or I will not believe my own recollection. I tore open like a gutted fish and a wet shadow puddled down my front. I collapsed upon the grass and could not move. I heard a fountain, sweetly bubbling—though I was nowhere near the Plô's sweet waters. Then I understood: the gentle gurgle in question emerged from my own person. I had become a spring of gore.

Just like her.

I prayed fiercely to her then. And for the first time, my prayer poured from a place of truth and love and understanding.

I do not care what you are, I thought, dead girl or martyr or demon. My savior or my tormentor.

But I am your loyal servant and I pray that you will help me.

But—treasure—what was my dearest treasure? I had no treasure to offer her, and she loved gold and jewels more than anything else.

I asked that she accept my words instead. I promised to engem her history with them.

A warm glow suffused the night, just as my murderer swung astride my mule. How to describe the indescribable? I was a bee in a hive, but my roof of honeycomb had melted, turned to a glowing mist, a fiery and honeyed fog of light. I saw the world through stained glass the color of amber, illumined by something far brighter than the sun we know. I felt like the eagle, the only creature allowed to contemplate sunlight without turning away.

And at the heart of that glow, I beheld a girl child in a white gown, her neck and wrists overladen with brilliant chains and jewels, her eyes bright and shining as the blade that had slain me.

Sainte Foy stood in my mule's path; the beast reared and the thief slipped from its back and lay in the dirt and dark at Sainte Foy's glowing feet. She kicked his gut several times, and he emitted a strange sound, rather as though Sainte Foy trampled upon punctured bagpipes. She knelt beside him and something squelched and tore, and when she stood upright again, she cradled a pair of bloodied eyes in the palm of her hand, and the heap of thief at her feet howled, and Foy kicked him again and he quieted.

"These baubles are of no use to you," she told him. "They make you covet what is not yours. I regret freeing you."

And then she came to me and addressed me.

I attempted to greet her; my blood gurgled instead.

Sainte Foy crouched and touched my neck. A warmth like liquor tingled behind my skin. A rosy scar still lingers at the base of my throat, to remind me of Sainte Foy's beneficence.

"Now, how will you serve me?" she said. "What treasure do you offer me?"

I babbled, I bubbled promises.

"Myself, and more importantly, my words," I said. "I pledge that I will write of your miracles, extend your fame, and so bring you company richer than my own."

I swore. Juro tibi. Sine omni malo ingenio.

Saint Augustine's Day has passed, and *her* feast day is soon to come, and I have much work to do.

Why should I not speak in gaudy medals?

How else should I turn the shade of a murdered child into a virgin martyr? Is there any other way to represent the miraculous nature of her actions? Otherwise she might appear a capricious child with a strange sense of humor. Only the alchemy of fine speech can transmute her games into gold.

And so I will read through this narrative again and rewrite it. I will proceed like the magpie and hop from one sentence to the next and collect the most glittering words and phrases. I will rewrite this tale and burnish it until it shines with a more heavenly light.

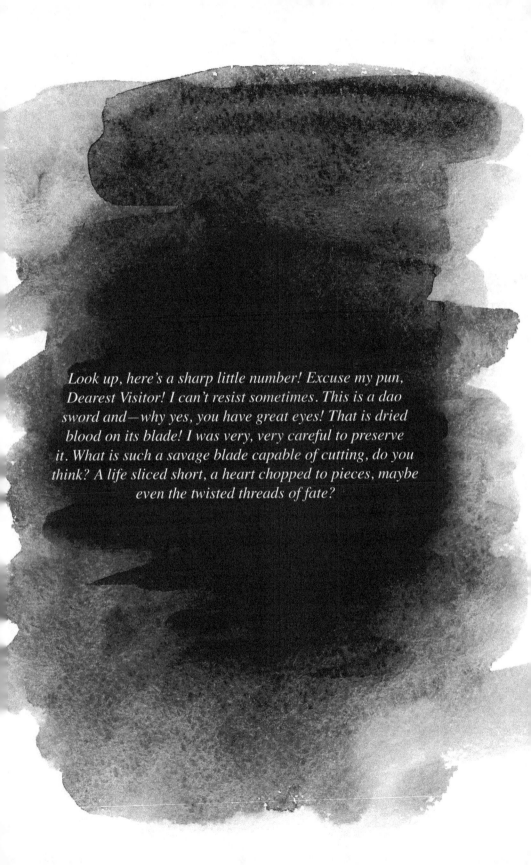

Look up, here's a sharp little number! Excuse my pun, Dearest Visitor! I can't resist sometimes. This is a dao sword and—why yes, you have great eyes! That is dried blood on its blade! I was very, very careful to preserve it. What is such a savage blade capable of cutting, do you think? A life sliced short, a heart chopped to pieces, maybe even the twisted threads of fate?

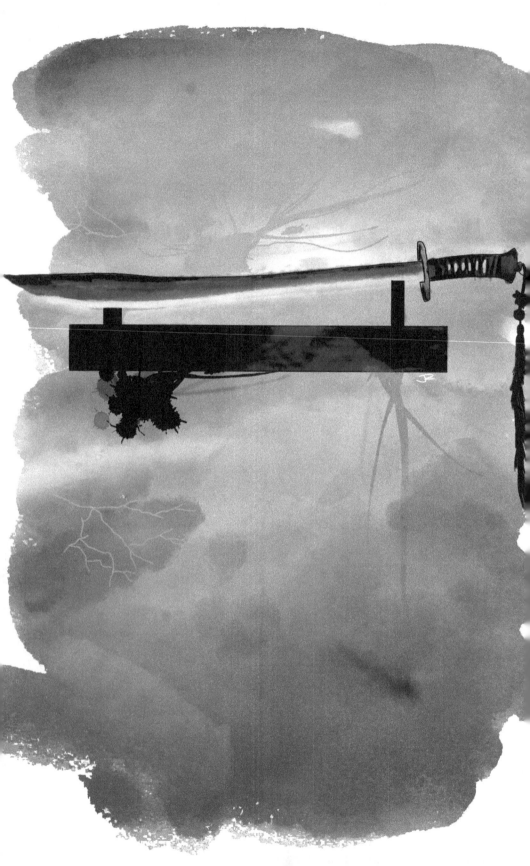

A DOWRY FOR YOUR HAND
Michelle Tang

he small lanterns encircled the weeping willow tree like a noose. Their flickering points of light resisted the creeping night, and drew the guests' eyes to the garden whenever polite conversation failed.

Lu Xian tore his own gaze away from the window and smiled at Ming Li's parents, perched on either side of their daughter. They'd traveled for some hours to reach Lu Xian's family in Yingtian, and their fine silk clothes were wrinkled with a patina of dust dulling their shine. The local matchmaker had claimed a sudden illness and, without her to ease the meeting between his parents and Ming Li's, the atmosphere was strained.

Ming Li's mother set down her tea. She pursed her lips in disapproval as she stared at the tree with its ring of tremulous illumination. "That tree doesn't need light to see, and doesn't appreciate such waste."

Lu Xian cleared his throat. "The stones in the courtyard are uneven, and the lanterns allow the servants to see where they step. It is practical, rather than decoration." The lie passed through his lips with the ease of practice. Once, he'd kept the garden unlit, for beautiful Wan Yue to pass through unseen.

"The way they are positioned, as if to keep the shadows at bay…" Ming Li's mother murmured. "I hope the garden is more beautiful in the sunlight." She shivered.

Lu Xian grabbed the opportunity and sprang to his feet. "I see the cold night air is affecting you. My apologies for not closing the windows sooner." He swung the wooden screens inward. Hesitated. A shadow, as large as a person, lurked beneath the willow tree.

He glanced at the position of the moon and shut the window louder than he'd intended. Ma Ma glanced at him from the corner of her eye as she refilled each guests' teacup, and the earthy scent of the looseleaf filled the room. She'd had the paper screens installed a few months ago, when Lu Xian had begged for something to separate him from the view of the garden at night.

His potential bride continued to look outward, though the stretched paper hid all details from view and diluted the tree's lanterns into watery yellow stains. Silence filled the room again as Lu Xian retook his seat. His left hand ached for a moment, perhaps injured in his haste to close the screens. *Speak of the dowry. It's getting late.*

"Have you heard much of the marriage ceremonies in the West? A merchant told us of something they call 'Hand-fast,' where a bride and a groom have their hands tied together. A symbol of their union." Lu Xian's father—Ba—asked the guests, as he shook his head.

"Do they use their hair as the rope?" Ming Li's father touched his own hair, bound atop his head.

Wan Yue had asked Lu Xian the same thing. *Think of something else.* To distract himself from thoughts of her, Lu Xian slid a finger beneath his thick jade bracelet to scratch at the skin beneath—the discussion made him feel like strands of hair tickled his own wrist.

"Not at all. In fact, as I understand it, they do not combine the couple's hair at all."

"Are there people outside?" Ming Li interrupted. Her mother gave a disapproving *tut,* but Lu Xian's interest in his potential bride increased when he heard her voice, deeper and more melodic than he'd expected.

"The wind through the garden rustles the leaves," Ma Ma said. "Sometimes, it sounds like voices."

Lu Xian kept his expression blank and wondered if the others could hear the whispers of his name floating on the breeze. He darted his tongue across his dry lips. Ming Li was a good match—she was pretty and demure, and her family had money. When they married, he could leave this cursed house with its garden full of memories and find peace in a new home, with his new bride's family.

"I find it hard to believe—" Ming Li's mother's eyebrows rose innocently as she spoke, "—that a handsome young man such as your son would not be promised to someone already."

"This boy? He is too plain to marry anyone except the most generous-hearted of women. Anyway, it was decided he would finish his schooling first." Ma Ma was adept at this: showing false humility, praising Ming Li, and reminding the prospective in-laws that Lu Xian had passed the civil service exams and would soon be employed in the government. She did not mention his foolish courtship of Wan Yue, of course. A family secret best kept buried. He suppressed another glance towards the garden.

Ming Li's father's eyes roved around the parlor, settling on the Dao sword displayed on the wall. "Which of you joined the army?"

"I did, for a short time. I could not return after my injury," Ba gestured to his leg and cursed the Mongols and their descendants, a mutter Lu Xian had heard so often it had become ritual-like.

The other man harrumphed as he smoothed his mustache. "The Dao was meant to be returned, though. With the cost to forge each blade, they even retrieve them from the bowels of the dead. I am surprised you would display it so proudly, this symbol of a vow not honored."

The wind whispered louder in the silence that fell over the room. From the garden, the tree creaked. Lu Xian tried to think of something to say, but the itching around his wrist had worsened. No longer a tickle on the surface, it seemed to lie deep beneath the skin, and Lu Xian scratched harder to reach it.

"That is a beautiful bracelet." Ming Li's mother gestured to his left arm, and Lu Xian pulled his fingers from beneath the jade.

"Thank you. It was a gift from my father." *Part of a bribe to discard a bride.* Beneath the deep-green band, ever cool to the touch, his skin stung. There was blood beneath his fingernails. He slipped his hand beneath a fold of his tunic. "And thank you for the lovely presents you brought for us. You are most thoughtful."

"Now that we are on the topic, perhaps we should talk dowry?" Ming Li's father put down his teacup and looked at Lu Xian's parents. With luck, they would come to an agreement quickly, and soon be on their way home.

The parents haggled as if over livestock, while Lu Xian and Ming Li squirmed.

Wan Yue had possessed no dowry. Her parents worked as servants to another family, as she had been to theirs. "This shall be your bride's gift to me," Lu Xian had whispered, caressing her cheek as they kissed. "And this." He'd inhaled her fragrance, the scent of sweet plums, as his hands had trailed lower. "And this." They'd coupled in the dead of night under the blanket of darkness, on the bench beneath the willow tree, the trailing fronds a shifting curtain that hid them from sight.

The memory evoked guilt, diluted by time and resentment. He hadn't slept well in months. Lu Xian felt stifled in this small room filled with strangers: stifled by past mistakes, by the glee of parents bartering their children's futures. Ming Li's eyes had found the beige paper screen once more. Lu Xian stood and moved towards the window. He could open it a crack, just enough to let a breeze stir the over-warm air inside.

"Lu Xian..."

He froze, one hand reaching outward. Had any of the guests heard? Ming Li shifted her gaze to the floor beside him. He thought she was being submissive, as was proper, but there was too keen a focus in her dark eyes. She stared at the base of the door. Unable to stop himself, he angled his head to look as well.

The room's light spilled out from the gap between door and floor, unbroken by the shadow of feet. And yet, the slide of coarse cloth shoes against the stone outside came to his ears. Once, he'd smiled at the sound, knowing Wan Yue would soon slip from the shadows into his arms. He'd loved to watch her walk towards him, graceful and occasionally unsteady on her tiny, bound feet, her steps small and careful, the rough *shush* of the material a contrast to the delicate poise of the woman.

"When we are married, all your slippers will be made of silk," he had promised her.

She had smiled up at him, her tapered fingers tracing the thin braid of onyx hair she'd tied around his wrist. "I do not need silk. It is enough to have you as my husband."

"I will never stray." He took a strand of his own long hair and bound their hands together.

A clatter on the floor by his feet startled Lu Xian out of his memory, and the negotiations around him broke off. His bracelet lay on the wooden floorboards, cracked in half.

"Better the jade than your body," Ma Ma said, but her face was troubled. "Today the jade took an injury meant for you."

He picked up the two halves. Perhaps he had banged it against something earlier. He was ever careless. But sweat bloomed down his back and prickled at his forehead.

"Come and sit down, Lu Xian. You look unwell." Ming Li's mother narrowed her eyes as she appraised him. She nudged her husband.

"Unwell? My son? Never. Why, until a few months ago, he slept with the windows wide open to the night air." Ba's voice filled the room, too loud and boisterous. Ma Ma gave him a warning look, and Ba closed his mouth.

The ache in Lu Xian's left hand worsened, until he bit his cheek to keep from crying out. Just when he could no longer bear it and moved to flee from the room, the pain left him. It was blissful for a moment, before worry set in. He could no longer feel the cuff of his shirt against the base of his wrist, nor his right hand cradling the other. Lu Xian tried to tap his fingertips against his thigh, then used his nails to pinch the thin webbing between left thumb and index finger. Nothing. It was as if the flesh no longer belonged to him. *Just endure a little longer. They'll leave soon enough.*

"Do we have an agreement, then?" Ba asked. He looked around the room.

Ming Li's eyes widened. "What is...your hand..."

Everyone turned to stare. Lu Xian stumbled to his feet, holding his numb hand in the air. "I don't know what's happening." The flesh had gone cool, the nail beds darkening to purple. As he watched, the skin turned gray. He moaned.

A sickly sweet smell rose from his hand. Ming Li gagged behind her silk sleeve, her father lunging to slam open the windows. The tree groaned. Leaves rustled like promises in the night.

"It's spreading." Ma Ma took hold of his diseased appendage, rubbing hard, as if the duskiness permeating his hand would come off like so much dirt. Skin sloughed instead, layers of dead skin sliding moistly away against the friction of her thumb. Black ichor seeped from the damaged tissue, and the smell of decay grew more pungent. In the furrow left by Ma Ma's thumb, dark mold peeked fuzzily between tendons shiny with slime.

"There, around my wrist—do you see it?" Lu Xian pointed at the raised line at the base of his hand, puckering the skin like a rope cinched too tightly around the waist. The others stared, eyes fearful.

"It is diseased," gasped Ming Li's mother. "I knew he looked sickly."

"I have seen this in the army, son." Ba's voice was too gentle for the horror in his expression. "The flesh has died, somehow. It will fester and kill you if it's not removed."

Lu Xian swallowed. He lurched across the room and took Ba's sword off the wall, its polished metal blade gleaming sharp and cold. "You must cut it off, quickly. Before it spreads."

Unconsciously, he had repeated his mother's words, spoken months ago. "You must end things quickly. Before word spreads." Strange how he mourned the loss of his own hand more than he had his future with Wan Yue. More than he had mourned Wan Yue herself. But then, he couldn't replace the hand.

"No!" Ma Ma cried. "Surely there is some medicine, some herb?"

"We do not have time. Look." He shoved his arm towards her. The hand had shriveled and dried, looking like meat left too long in the sun. "Please, before it takes the rest of me."

Ba looked at Ming Li's father, his moist eyes reflecting the lamplight as he reached out and slowly took the sword from Lu Xian's moist grip. "Please. Hold his hand fast."

The man tightened strong fingers around Lu Xian's left arm. Lu Xian's mind fled, chasing distant thoughts as if his body could follow. Hand amputation was done to punish thieves. What had he ever stolen?

Through the open window, the lantern lights around the tree flared, dancing wild and bright. Despite their glow, the weeping willow's shadow creeped past them, across the garden, stretching towards Lu Xian with creaks and whispers.

"Lu Xian…you promised."

Thwack. Skin and sinew split. One bone cracked. The pain scorched through Lu Xian's body, buckling his knees, ripping a cry from his throat. It was echoed by the women in the room, their wails and moans a chorus.

"One more. One more, son." Ba's voice was hoarse, and he wiped at his eyes with the back of his hand, smearing blood across his face like a woman's rouge.

It took two more strikes before his left hand thudded to the floor, as cold and lifeless as the jade band had been. Lu Xian's mind floated, black spots invading his sight, but even the peace of unconsciousness stretched beyond his reach, and he screamed until the scent of cooking flesh and smoldering blood filled his lungs and made him retch.

Ba dropped the extinguished lantern, the delicate paper drenched red. Around him, people shrieked and vomited.

From an inferno of great pain, Lu Xian stared at the severed appendage. Onyx threads peeked from the exposed meat of his wrist. He blinked to focus his eyes. On the floor, his hand was stuffed with hair, choked with it, strands weaving insidiously through muscle and into veins, like parasitic worms in the flesh of a fish.

Ma Ma, sleeve soaked with tears, bent towards it.

"Don't touch it." Lu Xian whispered. "Don't—"

"It is still a part of you. A part that grew inside me." She reached out. As her fingers grasped his severed hand, Ma Ma gasped. She clutched at her neck, eyes bulging, face reddening.

Outside, the willow creaked, loud and rhythmic, as if a great weight swung from its bough. Coarse cloth shoes *shushed* beside him, and the odor of rotting plums filled the parlor.

Lu Xian grabbed his shriveled hand from his mother's grip and threw it across the room. He held it only a moment, but the moment of contact was long enough: he was ripped out of the present, even the pain of his amputation dulling amidst the heartbreak and betrayal that ravaged him. Rough rope snapped tight against his throat, and his bound feet stepped off the bench to meet only air. As he hung, graceful legs jerking, the long leaves of the willow tree swayed around him like mourners at a funeral. He fell to the wood floor, his body his own again as he gulped for air, left arm hugged tight to his chest.

Ming Li's father supported both his daughter and wife as they fled, unsteady in their tiny, silk boots. Lu Xian's chance to escape the garden—to escape Wan Yue—left with them.

Ma Ma was gasping for air, one shaking breath chasing another, faster and faster. She fainted. Ba caught her, lowered her onto the floor, never looking away from the corner where the accursed hand lay.

Pain seared through Lu Xian's body. The significance of his loss, of his future prospects, dawned on him with rising horror. He stared out the window as he wept, cradling the stump of his wrist.

In the dark garden, the weeping willow tree fell silent. The lanterns extinguished one by one, their smoky tendrils floating upwards towards the heavens.

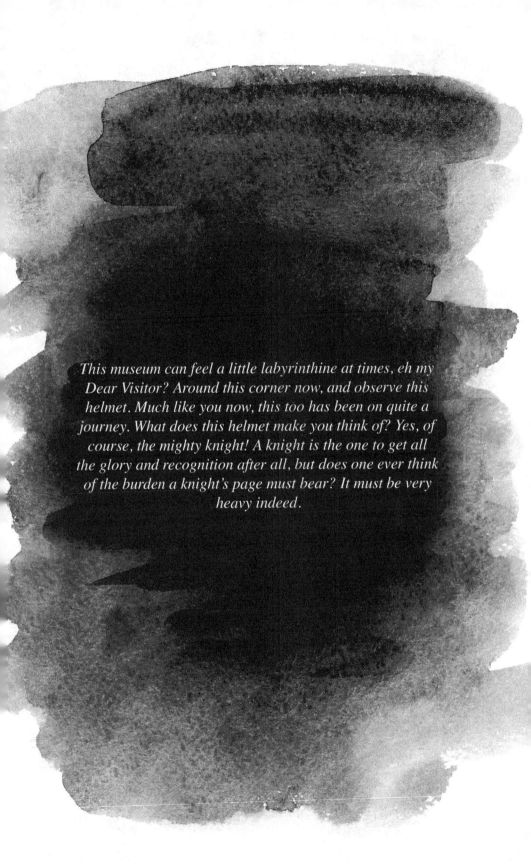

This museum can feel a little labyrinthine at times, eh my Dear Visitor? Around this corner now, and observe this helmet. Much like you now, this too has been on quite a journey. What does this helmet make you think of? Yes, of course, the mighty knight! A knight is the one to get all the glory and recognition after all, but does one ever think of the burden a knight's page must bear? It must be very heavy indeed.

THE MOUTH OF HELL

Cody Goodfellow

he sun did not set, so much as the twisted claws of mountains seemed to snatch it from the sky. Amid the gathering gloom in the ruins of their encampment, Olivier knelt before Brother Guion and bowed his head. "Bless me, father, for I have sinned most grievously. Will you hear my confession?"

Olivier bared his unclean thoughts and unworthy deeds in a fitful fury before baring the thorn in his soul, his failure to save his master. Though it clung to him like a fever, he could not speak of the evil dream that compelled him.

Brother Guion heard his confession and blessed him and the master's sword. Last, he pulled a small silver cross on a braided leather thong from beneath his tunic and hung it around the squire's neck.

"My son," said his confessor, "there is no cause for you to do this. You cannot bring him back..."

Olivier gave no reply as he donned a chainmail coif and hauberk and the bloodstained tabard that he'd washed in the stream. He buckled the sword high on his waist so it wouldn't drag in the dirt, then took up the bundle of his master's plate armor and climbed the trail winding up into the valley.

The sheer cliffs drew nearer, the way steeper, until he came round a rock outcropping to stand before the waterfall. More mist than falling water by the time it reached the pool in the hollow at the canyon's end, the falls seemed to sap the warmth from the air; but when a shift in the breeze parted the white cloud, the chill turned to an icy hand twisting in his vitals. Behind the misty veil, the weathered limestone wall was chiseled into the goggling visage of a devil. Jagged teeth lined the yawning maw of a low cave entrance that burrowed into the mountain.

Shifting the weight of the armor to his other shoulder, Olivier advanced on the cave. The pounding of his heart resounded in his ears, drowning out even the roaring waterfall, so did he not notice that Brother Guion no longer walked beside him until he turned to look over his shoulder.

The cleric stood watching from the far side of the winding stream. Olivier called his name, but couldn't hear his own voice. Lifting a hand in benediction, the confessor turned away.

Let him go. He needed no one who had no heart for this quest. He wondered if Guion would include this failure in his own next confession, if he would even see it as a sin.

The Lord's prayer on his lips, Olivier took a step inside the cave beneath the waterfall. A deep chill stole into his bones and the fetid stench of mold and damp earth closed over his face like wet wool.

"I shall fear no evil—"

His chattering teeth nearly bit through his tongue. He took another step. The armor seemed to grow heavier, dragging him towards the earth. He forced himself not to look back or stop. He moved not slowly, but with a battle barely won in every step.

None born of woman would have faced that portal with less terror in their hearts, had they any inkling that the crooked tunnels riddling this wilderness led directly to the inferno, and the domain of the deceiver.

His master, Sir Geoffroi d'Averoigne, had taken their small party through this godforsaken corner of the South precisely because the roads were said to be rife with bandits, though they encountered none. Travelers went missing, so an innkeeper at Aix had told them, as if the earth itself swallowed them up.

Seeking a Dominican monastery in this valley, they found only scattered broken stones where it once stood. The brothers of that lonely order were legended to guard the entrance to Hell, but they had been swept away by some forgotten disaster in decades past.

They found the countryside and the tiny neighboring village of Dents shut to them, save for a maid who gave them water and eggs, but urged them to move out of the valley before sunset.

Sir Geoffroi was sanguine about their peril; a godly man, he said over his wine, has no fear of Hell. Were they not on Avignon's business, executing the will of the true Pope? He had gone on crusade to Outremer and Constantinople, had served Christ. Sir Geoffroi had nothing to fear from the Devil, and they were under his protection.

In the hours before dawn, Olivier's master was bound and dragged off into the night along with the others, taken or slain by demons whose fiery breath burned down the camp. Olivier was struck a blow that knocked him senseless, while he suspected the only other survivors, Gilles and Brother Guion, his master's confessor, had run and hidden.

Gilles, the cowardly master of horse, fled with the few that hadn't bolted during the raid, leaving only Sir Geoffroi's squire and priest. Brother Guion wanted to fly to the nearest fortified village, but Olivier was steadfast. He would not abandon his master, even if the legends were true and he had been taken to Hell itself.

A commanding shout echoed out of the depths. Flattening against the wall, he pressed his steel burden to himself to still its clattering.

The voices were loud but indistinct; some chanted while another condemned someone who wept uncontrollably.

He laid down the bundle of armor. His fingers fumbled at the wet leather cords binding the bulky pieces, but he could not untangle them. If he put on the armor, was he not bearing false witness? If the guardians of the gate were not of this world, he needed only the cross.

Securing the bundle of armor so it hung from his shoulder, he reluctantly drew his master's sword from its scabbard and held it before him as he advanced down the throat of the cavern.

The walls were pitted with niches, cracks, hollows, and branching tunnels. The ceiling was daubed with obscene images in a white pigment that seemed to glow—crude humanoid forms with horns, dwarfed by their own pudenda. The orgiastic fresco circled around a massive, voluptuous female form with no head but great curving horns who seemed to gyrate and cavort in the fitful glow of a fire at the center of the grotto. Beside it, a circular pit exhaled a fetid breath of decay and incense.

Three bent forms in hooded patchwork rags stood over a fourth who huddled and wept with her head in her hands. Two chanted a prayer of sorts in cracked, ashen voices, their crooked hands licking out in cursing gestures. The third cracked a whip over the crying woman's head and roared, "Confess it, or go into fire unshriven!"

"I did nothing but take pity on those men, sisters! I cry you mercy..."

With a chill shiver, Olivier recognized her for the girl who'd given them provisions yesterday. Drawing himself upright, he stepped into the grotto with the sword upraised.

"Stop this! You are not clergy, you're not even men! By what right do you scourge this girl?" His voice quavered, but he found an anchor when he imagined his master saying those words.

The hooded hags bowed to Olivier. "Cry your pardon, young master," her voice dripping venom, "but we know our ways. This whore has consorted with travelers, and conspired to flee the valley with them, in exchange for the favors of her virtue."

"Aalis?" he called as he approached her, holding the sword out to the hags like a holy icon. "Come away, they'll not harm you."

Aalis stood and came closer, then slapped him across his face so he spun and nearly fell to his knees. "Shut your mouth, boy! What know you of harm? It's for your sake, I've been condemned!" Turning to the hags, she proclaimed, "I am still a maid! I never let him touch me."

The witch with the whip pointed two fingers at her and chuckled wetly. "If you tell true, you've no cause to fear. You'll be examined... below."

"Stand back, you witches and servants of Satan!" Olivier brandished his shining blade. "I do not recognize your authority."

"But we are the judges in this place," growled one of the hags. "The church has forsaken us, but not the mercy of the inferno. We winnow sinners from the select among the living, and Hell judges the dead... And you, little cockerel, are the dead!"

Olivier reached for Aalis's hand, but she fled behind the hags as if he, and not they, was her tormentor. The witch cracked the whip in his face, sending him scuttling backwards, his sword an empty threat. The armor overbalanced him, and he toppled into the pit.

He tumbled and rolled across a floor of crooked flagstones, the armor incurring as much harm as it deflected. He came to his senses looking up at the girl he'd tried to save.

"I rescued you," he said. "Why did *you* come here?"

"Why did you come here? Did I not warn you?"

Olivier cleaned his master's sword on his tabard. "I've come to rescue my master."

"Forget him." The girl turned away. "He is with the dead and has been judged."

Standing up, he sheathed the sword and took up the armor. "He doesn't belong here. This is a pit of sin, but—"

"Everyone who is here belongs here." She vanished into the dark, leaving him to follow her voice. "You have already damned us both."

They followed the tunnel to an octagonal chapel hewn out of the limestone. Worn wooden pews in concentric circles faced a barren altar, and a gilded confessional skulked in a niche beside the tunnel by which he'd entered.

Walls, ceiling, and columns were scabbed with mosaics of glittering tiles. In a parody of the Stations of the Cross, the mosaics showed the beautiful Lucifer scourged and driven through the streets of Heaven by an archangel torturer, flayed and degraded into a red beast, and finally crucified by his fellow angels, who wept with guilt and averted their eyes while God, depicted as Pontius Pilate, watched from on high and washed his hands.

"What is this place?" Olivier demanded.

Aalis cast a sour look at him. "Do you not know a chapel when you stand in one? We must make a clean breast of our sins and await judgment."

"I have confessed my sins and I fear no judgment," said the squire. "For my cause is just." Knocking upon the confessional, he drew back the curtain to find the penitent's bench empty, but he saw the profile of a bearded face behind the partition screen.

Olivier took the seat, resting the sword between his knees. "Father, bless me, I come upon an urgent mission to redeem one who was taken by mistake."

No answer came.

"My master, Sir Geoffroi d'Averoigne, is a righteous champion of the Church..."

A rustling, and a faint clink of metal.

"He was taken by devils...or men in the guise of devils and

dragged to this pit. If this be a place of judgment and torment for sinners, he must be released."

Keenly he sensed the presence behind the screen, yet it made no reply.

"In the Holy Church, I command you to release him, lest I seek him myself. I will not be moved. I beseech you to answer my plea."

Olivier reached for the screen and swept it aside.

Coins spilled over the lintel and clattered across the floor. He peered into the shadows and saw a dully gleaming rictus.

A mummified corpse sat in the confessional in rotted clerical robes. Buried up to its stooped shoulders in silver, coins, and cruder tithes, it leered at him without offering any counsel. A bloated rat incuriously looked up from gnawing on the yellowed parchment of the corpse's face.

What mockery of holiness was this? In a rage, Olivier struck out at the skull, knocking it off its pedestal of bone and sending it bouncing across the chapel floor.

As he leaned forward, he felt the bench beneath him fall away, and clutched at the frame of the partition. The seat had dropped to let him fall into yet another pit, out of which wafted the stench of an open sewer.

He stalked out of the confessional to find Aalis watching him. "Is there no priest here? Has God been forgotten in this place?"

"My village revolted against the tyranny of the Dominicans, burned their abbey, and paved our streets with its stones. The church forsook us long before I was born, but Hell remembers."

"For our sins, we are judged..."

"It was no fault of yours. I don't belong here. Nor do you."

"So now *you* are a judge of who belongs in Hell? What do you know of me? My father and my brothers took my virtue before I knew what it was, and I was beaten for speaking of it, and I knew it was no sin because no Devil ever came for them. But when my

love and I were to be married, he hoped to take me away from here...
He was taken down there, and God has not said a word. None who
sinned against me has paid, but for speaking to you, my family is
ruined, and I must face the confessional."

This was madness, but he saw in her eyes there were no words
that could restore her faith. "I am sorry, I didn't know—"

"And what *do* you know, sir squire? You cannot swing a sword or
recognize a church, yet you are so certain you are Christ's champion.
Your little god has forgotten us, sire, and I fear he has forgotten you, too."

Olivier caught his breath at such blasphemy from a rosy-cheeked
maid. "You shouldn't say that. You could—"

"I might go to Hell?" A bitter grin slashed her face and the light
in her eyes made them into coins. "And would you still rescue me,
brave sir knight? Or would you leave me to lie in the filth of my sin,
leave me to burn?"

He bit his lip, chagrined. She touched his face and leaned in so
close, he lost his next breath. "Away with me, sir knight. If you
would save someone, save me. Hell will claim us soon enough, and
anything we do now...is free."

Hot blood flushed his face where her lips brushed his cheek. "I
cannot abandon my master."

"I'm sorry. If you will not be turned aside, then you have judged
yourself." She pointed to the altar and a blind wall behind it, which
had slid back to reveal a passageway. "Go, and may your faith
deliver you from your sins."

He looked back at her once and the pain of a fleeting dream
almost stole his resolve. Aalis turned away and knelt before the
confessional, hiding her eyes until he'd lifted his burden of armor,
lit a torch from a lamp, and entered the black passage.

By guttering torchlight, he descended a flight of steep, narrow
stairs in a lopsided spiral flight that terminated at a narrow stone

bridge, barely the width of his feet, arching over an abyss. A looming giant, backlit by guttering flames, rose to stand and beckon him across.

Only glimpses and facets of his adversary leapt into the light. How fiercely its knurled, twisting horns stood out. How its face was a wilderness of jaws and jagged teeth.

Olivier considered. He struggled with warring impulses. He could not hope to cross the bridge bearing the armor, let alone to face the hulking devil on the other side in fair combat. But if he cut an imposing figure, perhaps he wouldn't have to.

Olivier retreated up the stairs and drew the sword. Cutting the thongs that bound it together, Olivier freed and then donned his master's armor.

The act was far more laborious and clumsy than when he'd assisted Sir Geoffroi with it, and when he'd cinched the final strap, the weight of it seemed to drag him down more than when he bore it on his back. He could scarcely see out the visor when he rose and approached the demon with sword upraised.

"Yield in the name of Christ, I command thee! I seek my master's rescue from this place and I shall not be moved!"

The demon waited for him to shuffle to the midpoint on the bridge. Then he reared up on cloven hooves, puffed out his cheeks and blew a gout of flames.

Olivier twisted away on the bridge so the splash of fire washed over his steel shoulder. Pressing blindly forward, he felt the flames engulf him. Burning oil cascading down his flanks, he thrust out blindly at the demon. A choking miasma of burning hair and flesh flooded the helmet over him. The metal squeaked and buckled as he roasted. Blisters welled up all over his limbs. Swinging in a blind fury, he lunged at the demon but stepped out onto only smoke and darkness, and plunged into the abyss.

Olivier fell into a river that was only half water. He found himself sinking, a flood of filth pouring into the armor and dragging him down into a putrid soup. He wallowed and struggled to reach the steep, rocky shore, where he collapsed.

His pain and exhaustion threatened to bear him away. He thought of his master and wondered what he would do.

Sir Geoffroi loved Christ above all others, though he frequently railed at the Church for its failure to adhere to or spread His lessons.

Well he remembered the day they came upon peasants walking in the road near Montségur in a silent line, one hand on the shoulder before him—eyeless, their faces chopped away to masks of bloody bone. They were sent to bear word that the Church had purged their village of all Manichee heretics, and to warn that their neighbors could expect the same on the morrow.

Sir Geoffroi offered them what comfort he could and then rode hard to the Manichee village, where they found a wayward crusade of cashiered mercenaries raiding and torching farmhouses on charges of heresy. He located the mob's commander and took him aside for a debate upon scripture. The man soon returned and summoned his men to decamp and return home. He no longer had a nose.

If such a man belonged in Hell, then Heaven must be empty. Olivier was steadfast that whether this be the Hell of the Bible or just some mad cave of torture, he would recover his master, dead or alive.

He did not realize he had nodded off until he caught himself looking up into the dark helm of Sir Geoffroi gazing down on him.

"Master?" he started, quite sure he still dreamt.

"So I am, boy. Give me the rest of this fine plate."

Olivier searched himself and found that half the armor had already been stripped from his befouled body. His assailant wore the helmet and the greaves, and held the master's heavy straight sword to Olivier's throat.

"Off with it! I must fly!" Aside from the hastily donned armor, the thief was naked, clothed only in mud. His manhood was gone, in its place a rude mouth of a wound.

A shadow passed over them and a growled curse from above. Torchlight caught his wild rolling eyes. The half-naked man whined in terror and struck the squire across the crown of his skull with the flat of the blade.

Olivier fell and nearly tumbled back into the river of sewage. He crawled on all fours after the thief, who nimbly scaled the sheer earthen wall and disappeared over the top with a madcap, ragged laugh.

Olivier haltingly pulled himself up the wall, finding rocky handholds under the mud and ascending to find himself atop a wall of a *bolgia* in a cavern so vast that its borders were obscured in gloom. Three more such walls ringed the cavern, separated by trenches bridged by narrow stone arches, in which something moved and made horrible sounds. At each bridge stood a devil who advanced on Olivier with a pike or barbed billhook.

Olivier cast about him as the devils drew closer. He had fared poorly in combat with one of them when he had a sword, but now —

A glint of torchlight flashed off his master's gleaming helm, in the trench below. Olivier tried to climb down after the fleeing thief. His footing betrayed him and he toppled into the trench. Bracing himself for yet another rough landing, he was instead buffeted and tossed on a squirming, thrashing sea of bodies.

Hands clasped his limbs, pawed at his armor, and probed his screaming face. Kicking away from them, he clung to a wall and found his footing, but the wave of bodies closed over him again, the wordless, gurgling moans of the dead filling his ears.

Pushing, striking them, he tried to pursue the thief. The damned souls gave bleating moans and fumbled for his face as if to put out his eyes with their grimy, taloned thumbs.

They fell away only when he found the breath to command them, "Unhand me, I am the son of Viscount Guidard d'Argonne!" Their moment of habitual confusion at the strident voice of a nobleman gave Olivier space to breathe, if not to move.

A wall of naked wraiths filled the trench, pale as mushrooms underneath the coating of their own filth. Their eyes put out and ears sheared off and Roman numerals inscribed in their backs with a branding iron, each was also scarred or maimed in some unique fashion that spoke of the myriad varieties of agony dealt out in this place.

Perhaps he was too late and he would find his master among these crippled shades. A jolt of panic at the thought set him parting the wall of damned souls with his mailed fists and staggering after the thief.

Bodies skulked away from Olivier's fists. He caught a flash of the master's sword as it plunged through the bloated belly of a living skeleton scarcely ten paces away. Olivier grappled with a faceless horror that shrieked as it pummeled him with the fingerless stumps of its hands.

Olivier screamed back at the apparition and shoved it aside, climbing over bodies and leaping headlong to throw his arms round the thief's neck and wrestle him to the floor of the trench.

"Mercy, my lord!" cried the thief. He bowed his head as Olivier snatched the helmet from it.

It was Gilles, the cowardly master of horse. "We were taken by these mad bastards and tortured for sins we never committed. Upon my name, I am a good Christian, young sire! I do not belong here!"

Olivier freed the sword from the blind man's belly and lifted it to cleave Gilles' skull, when the words struck him. He thought again of his master and all the many lessons in his every word and deed, and he sheathed the sword.

"Our master, who was likewise taken without cause. These madmen have made a hell on Earth."

"All men make their own hell on Earth," Gilles spat, "you fucking idiot. Because we know there's none down there...and we deserve one..."

"Perhaps you do, but our master does not. If you guide me to him, we will deliver you from this godforsaken place."

"*We?*" Gilles let loose a wickering, sickly laugh, then grabbed a fistful of Olivier's hair and pulled him close to whisper, "Saint Olivier, come to harrow Hell. We are the damned, sire! Down, they will see us!"

Olivier knelt and let whimpering blind men crawl over him. A roar and a flash of flame and the damned souls shrieked. Olivier struggled to get up, but the thief stepped on his neck and pressed him facedown in the muck.

"Masters!" Gilles cried in a cracked and pitiful voice, "I have him who has come amongst us blaspheming! I have him who would release the damned from our righteous judgment! I have him!"

Olivier trapped the foot and twisted it until the thief fell against the opposite wall of the trench. He picked up the sword and the helmet and tried to run, but a noose of braided hair dropped over his head and drew taut round his neck.

He kicked and danced on the air. Breath cut off, he flailed at black phantoms. A chuckling thing clothed in knives, with carrion breath and antlers sprouting from its eye-sockets and a lipless mouth with teeth filed to needles held him aloft by the twisting hair-rope, making him dance until he blacked out.

"My boy...I had such hope that you would not follow me."

Olivier had been so gulled at every turn by this place that he closed his eyes at the blasphemous vision that spoke so haltingly, bloody shreds on filed fangs. Even after all he'd seen, this was too much to bear.

"Master...no..."

How the naked strands of muscle twitched and strummed with each sibilant whisper. How danced the shadows of the bloody antlers of a stag, somehow screwed into its trepanned skull so that pus and blood drained into the fitfully blinking eyes. How it swayed on the hooks transfixing its back so that it hung suspended by leathern thongs from the low ceiling of this crypt. How the pair of hooded illuminators working by candlelight with globular glass lenses hung before their eyes inscribed with ink and quills what Olivier imagined must be some accounting of this monster's sins. They had already covered his body from ankles to armpits, and their relentless needles were about to converge at his breastbone.

All this he could see of this thing that could no longer count itself a man, and still look for his master, for surely this debased thing, this emperor of all sinners, could be any creature in Christendom but his master, Sir Geoffroi d'Averoigne.

He searched the crypt—for that it was, lined with reliquaries and moldering sculptures and mounds of bones and a flayed corpse in the last chair, at his own right hand.

Olivier was bound hand and foot with thick greasy ropes of braided hair, and he'd been stripped of his master's armor, which an eyeless wraith sat polishing.

"So you thought to rescue me, did you?" His master coughed an indulgent chuckle that set his ravaged body swaying.

"I might have, if I was not betrayed by a craven thief...Gilles, your master of horse."

"He was ever quick to seek advantage. He gave you up because he knows he is dead and amongst the damned. He is free to lie and steal and kill. By betraying you, he hoped to be elected to become an initiate. It is not a perfect system, but it could yield perfect sinners."

An illuminator pricked his master until he gasped, then dipped the needle in his blood to color the confession on his chest.

"Master, you do not belong here. This is unjust..."

"It is exactly just, by the law of man and God. I am the greatest sinner in this place. By my pride and my blind worship of self, I betrayed Christ. I am another Judas. I thought men could learn to think for themselves, even as I have seen them be less than beasts and never better."

"But all that you did was the work of Christ. You were his sword..."

"Then he is mad, and he should be here in my place. I went to war and spitted babes on a spear for my banner. I saved not a single soul. Here, at last, I might hope to atone.

"I withstood torture and yet challenged the master of this place to trial by combat. I won his skin and it was revealed to me..." Bloody tears streamed from his slitted eyes. "I sorely wish you hadn't come, but now you're here, they will make short work of your initiation. Your sins are not many, though so very large..."

"What can you mean, sir? My...initiation? What sin of mine could be so large as to merit this?"

"What was your sin? You placed your faith in me, for one. You thought yourself a hero, if not a martyr, for braving Hell itself to deliver your unjustly imprisoned master. But I was not dragged here by chance. For my sins, I was sent for. I was meant to be this place's master."

Olivier strained against his bonds, but they only gouged welts in his flesh. "No! It cannot be! We must flee, master, we must deliver word of this place to Avignon..."

"They know, you fool! These monks were forgotten and abandoned by the Roman curia that dispatched them into this wilderness. While others of their ilk idled and grew fat on the toil of their peasant subjects, these ones agonized to enforce the holy laws on the wayward pagans above us.

"Legend had it the caves underfoot led straight to Hell, yet sin, wickedness, and even devil worship ran unchecked in the village. The threat of Hell itself did not turn them from their depravity...so when the unruly peasants rebelled and burned them out, they made themselves into devils."

"But it's madness!"

"Of a sort, perhaps," Sir Geoffroi smiled without lips. "The visions that first inspired them came upon them when they took communion with black, moldy wafers. The mold brought the visions, but surely the Lord sent the mold—

"Whatever the cause, they heard the call, the new divine command to do God's work. They abandoned their scriptoriums and their cloisters to take a hand in taming the sin in this world. Their abbot made them see that if they did nothing to stem the flood of sin and blasphemy in the valley below, surely they would all burn in the inferno for all eternity.

"They are each of them saints and true martyrs, boy. They who came to doubt that Hell exists decided they must build it. They made devils of themselves that they might serve the Lord, as he whom the Lord loved best serves not in glory and jewels and light, but in shadow and shame.

"Think of it, Olivier. Not the fear of eternal damnation in stained glass or a priest's hollow promises, but in blood, fire, and iron. This region was once a warren of vice and heresy, but the mouth of Hell has spoken and the land is silent."

"Master, this is not what you taught me..."

"What *did* I teach you, then?"

"That it was the love of Christ that turned men away from sin."

Now his laughter set Geoffroi swaying so that the quills gouged deeply his flesh, spilling ink and blood. "I taught you all that you know, but you were not ready for all that *I* know. You'd have to see for yourself. I would not have had it this way.

"I wept that you would someday witness and cast your own heart and soul into the mad sport of war and know the answer to every priest's sermon ends in a pool of blood and a banquet for vultures. If the master of this world must be Satan, then let him rule, for we tremble on the edge of knowing there be no God at all."

Olivier choked on his disbelief. Everything he believed and lived for collapsing around him, turning in on himself in contempt for having been such a fool.

In his rage, he buried his nails in his palms until blood trickled from his fists.

"But I see that you hunger and thirst..." Sir Geoffroi growled in Latin and a strange procession filed into the crypt: blind living skeletons, starving to death and draped in the loose skin of precip-itous weight loss, brought out platters with chickens, joints of beef, mounds of ham and rabbit and brook trout, each more obscenely sumptuous than the last. Only when they had set all before him and he began to suspect this was a subtle form of torture in itself, did a servant cut his bonds.

He tore into a chicken with his bare hands, stuffing the meat into his mouth even as his belly rebelled at the sound of the sniffing nostrils, the smacking, toothless lips, the strands of saliva drooling from the slack mouths of the ravenous damned.

He could stop only when he felt his gorge rising and risked losing what he'd eaten. "I would have thought you would hate this place. I'd have thought you would burn it all down..." Olivier looked sidewise at a voluptuous naked woman wearing a blindfold and nun's wimple, come to fill his wine cup. While he feigned a longing leer at her, he slid a knife up his sleeve.

"It only wants a firmer hand, boy. That's why I was sent here. These punishments must be united to Heaven's great purpose. Much must be changed, before this place can become the model for the rest of Christendom.

"But with you here, we can reform this barbaric pit and its practices. If one were to add a sort of Purgatory, where the sins of living men were corporeally visited upon him, then released so their scars spoke of what awaited them, then you might see the healthy fear of sin's wages even in the benighted cities."

"What cities, sir?"

"Why, every city! A secret order of fanatical knights with extrajudicial powers to condemn sinners to Hell or Purgatory in every city in Christendom. We will show them the fire and burn away the dross until the Kingdom of God shines so bright as to shame the Sun."

Olivier thought of his father, whose face he could not remember and of whom he'd heard no word since he was bonded over to Sir Geoffroi. He thought of his master's lessons.

"I was sent to bring these madmen under the yoke of the Church, but out of their madness will come a New Jerusalem. A world without sin in thought or deed. How quick men would be to fly from sin, if they knew for a certainty that the fires of Hell burned just beneath their feet, if they knew that any sin they committed under cover of night would be found out, and punishment visited upon them before dawn? From the lowest peasant to the mightiest lord, even unto the clergy itself. If the fear of Hell were only real, what a paradise this would be."

"All of the world would be Hell, master. All free will gone…"

"What free will? What is a peasant free to do, but work or starve? What is a knight free to do, but fight and die? What freedom has any man, but the freedom to sacrifice and survive or perish?

"Do you not see? God invented the Devil so that Man would love God. And so, the Church invented Hell so that Man would love the Church. We cannot do the Lord's work if they do not live in mortal terror of us."

"We?"

"Oh yes, boy. You will be initiated, as I was."

Olivier pushed away the platter of chicken. The servant feinted as if to take it away, but then slapped Olivier so hard, he fell to the flagstones.

Sir Geoffroi's hand stretched out to offer a benediction. "Eat, for this is my body..."

Feet pinned Olivier down and hands trapped his head and forced a black communion wafer between his jaws, then sluiced it down his throat with a skin of alkaline wine. His eyes watered, his vision of Sir Geoffroi already doubling and deforming as hallucinations overwhelmed him.

"The world cares not and never did, for what you believe. It was easier for me than it should have been. I took pleasure in hurting them. That's why you would be perfect, because you take no pleasure in it...but you have shown...you would literally walk through Hell to save the Devil."

The damned souls lifted Olivier back into his chair. He feigned helpless convulsions until they withdrew their claws. "I would save you..." Olivier sprang from the floor and stabbed his master with the carving knife.

The monks tried to save him, but Sir Geoffroi laughed and pulled Olivier closer, even as he drove the knife deeper into his master's back. "A very...palpable hit. You...always learned quickly... Your faith...will serve this place well..."

"I will not," Olivier screamed in his master's face. "The Church cannot condone this… God would not allow it…"

"Don't you see, boy? There is no good or evil. There is no God but power. You can serve it, and become God's hand upon the earth, or you can defy it, and be truly damned."

"I thought you were the only good man in France…"

"I thought you were a good and proper son. Your disappointment is no deeper than mine…that I am right…"

"I'm sorry, master." Olivier took hold of the horns sprouting from Sir Geoffroi's brow and ripped them free. Twisting them in his hands so the arrays of points turned outward like two fistfuls of knives, he plunged them into his master's eyes to put out the fire of madness blooming therein.

Olivier backed away from his master's suspended corpse. The illuminators and the damned souls stood with heads bowed. Staggering away, staring into the labyrinths of his hands, he kicked over a brazier, sending a flood of blazing oil across the floor.

He followed a narrow passageway out of the crypt, taking the ascending path when it forked, until he emerged through a trapdoor in the dusty altar of the abandoned chapel of Dents.

The villagers were stirred to hysteria by his coming, for he raved that he had slain the Devil and that all the damned would be released from Hell, for the New Jerusalem was at hand.

Waited they had for this day, clinging to scraps of half-remembered scripture in preparation for the arrival of the messiah.

Weeping with grace, Aalis cleaned and tended his wounds. Howling with wordless fervor, they lifted him up on their shoulders and bore him through the streets to the hill overlooking the mouth of Hell. There they nailed him to a cross and raised it so that his word could be heard throughout the village, and for the days thereafter, until he fell silent, they knew that, for all their sins, God had not forgotten them.

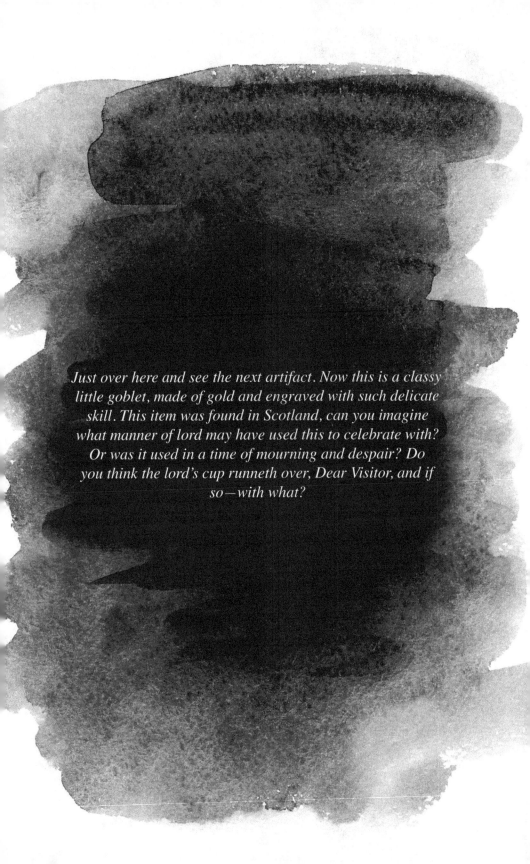

Just over here and see the next artifact. Now this is a classy little goblet, made of gold and engraved with such delicate skill. This item was found in Scotland, can you imagine what manner of lord may have used this to celebrate with? Or was it used in a time of mourning and despair? Do you think the lord's cup runneth over, Dear Visitor, and if so—with what?

THE LADY OF LEER CASTLE
Christopher O'Halloran

he devil can have the Scots, the English, and every other bastard with a boat," roared a large woman. The MacMahon mercenary pounded the haft of her axe on the oak table stretching along the hall. "Ireland belongs to the Irish, and I don't give a damn if our ancestors shagged the same women!"

The soldiers at Domnall's table gave a rousing cheer, bumped chests, and clapped shoulders fondly. Their tunics—uniform in their brown stains—made one undulating, joyous mass. Some of the brown was mead, but more was dried blood. Of their friends, yes, but of their foes in greater quantities.

The mercenaries from Clan MacMahon were brutal and effective. Hired by Clan Canain to defend the territories to the north of Leer Castle from Edward Bruce and his 'liberating' Scottish army, they fought for the promise of moderate wealth and a feast cooked with such rare spices as pepper, saffron, and ginger. Meats roasted in honey, tenderized with vinegar.

The scent of sweat and blood filled the hall. A modest fire crackled in the hearth, but the heat of the packed bodies did more than enough to turn the air stifling.

Domnall turned away smiling. His brother sat at the head table, glowering as usual. The man had cleared his home of invaders. What would it take to finally put a smile on his face?

When Domnall turned back to engage with his men, he caught Breccan watching him.

"How long is your brother going to keep us waiting?" Breccan asked. "My guts are in upheaval, and I'd like to see if these dilled veal balls are as satisfying as you claim."

As brother of the chief, Domnall Ó Canain wasn't required to fight alongside the soldiers, but he had made quick friends with the freckled mercenary Breccan and was loathe to see him off. Growing up in Leer Castle, Domnall knew how to fight—had been taught at his father's heavy hand. Staying behind would provide him safety, but what else?

Nothing beautiful came from safety.

"Hunger is the greatest spice, my friend," answered Domnall. He couldn't help but beam at Breccan. Domnall's affinity for the MacMahon mercenaries had grown strong over their trials, but Breccan shone like a midnight torch—and kindled in him the fires of a hundred. Something about his green eyes, his fair, freckled skin. His light brown hair falling to his shoulders.

There was a leaf caught in his locks. Domnall nearly mentioned it but held his tongue. It introduced a delicacy to the man who had sliced his way from one end of a glen to the other.

"*Friend?*" asked Breccan, smiling. His eyebrow lifted. "Is that what I am?"

Domnall rolled his shoulders and peered at his detached brother at the head of the dais. Fergus melted into his throne, his lady in red at his right hand. Her silk dress looked much too thin for the weather of the countryside, but not once had he seen her shiver.

If Domnall was honest, he didn't much like to look at the woman. No one spoke of her. She always seemed to be almost out of sight. Her presence was something of a blur. An aberration in one's vision. Until she desired visibility. In those cases, she drew every eye to her thin, crimson lips. The wet eyes beneath her sheer veil.

Behind her, an animal laid with its big head between the legs of her chair. Domnall couldn't quite get a clear image of it. If it was a dog, it was the shaggiest he had ever seen.

"We are friends until you make your decision." Domnall shuffled closer along the bench, leaning in to keep their conversation private. His heart beat fast at the intake of Breccan's scent: musky, wet, and natural like freshly turned soil. "Take me away."

"What would Fín think?" Breccan eased the longsword from his scabbard, showing a hint of the blade. Bright steel gleamed in the dark hall. Candlelight reflected off its sharp edge, orange where the lifeblood had previously stained it like wine. "Fín has been my only companion for so long."

Domnall reached a trembling hand forward and pushed the blade back into its scabbard.

"I can make friends with Fín," he said. "I *do* know my way around a sword."

"Don't I know it."

Domnall flushed. Breccan stared unabashedly at him, and it took everything in his power not to look away. Not to feel the shame beaten into him since he could remember.

"Why do you wish to leave so strongly?" Breccan asked. "You have it grand here. An honored position in the clan, safety in the coffers of your brother, and feasts fit for a king."

"Shows what you know." Domnall lifted a hand and began counting his arguments on his fingers. "One: my position is powerless—"

"Comfortable."

"Fuck your comfort."

Breccan grinned; Domnall melted but continued, bolstered by the reaction.

"Two: the coffers are not as sustained as Fergus would have everyone believe. Don't worry," he said when Breccan's eyebrows shot up, "you'll be paid. He's a man of his word."

Serving women circulated along the periphery of the hall, distributing tankards of wine to the mercenaries.

"And three," continued Domnall, feeling his own stomach growling. "Feasts are nothing without the right person with which to eat." Below the table, out of sight, he put his hand on Breccan's knee.

He wouldn't tell Breccan about how things at Leer Castle were slowly growing more and more corrupt. How an air of malevolence hung over their days, culminating in mischief at best and murder at worst.

Bags of kittens wantonly drowned in a stream and left upon the banks to be discovered by washerwomen.

Human waste smeared across the fabric in the shop of a tailor.

The murder of the widower Edrich Ó Hanlon and the defilement of all four of his children.

The loss of innocence. The death of beauty.

The perpetrators: no one and everyone. A neighbor, the barber, children. As if a poisoned well was turning the minds and souls around him dirty.

Domnall tried to avoid the filth. The violence was different from what he encountered on the battlefield and it was becoming overbearing. It wasn't soldiers attacking one another; it was the weak becoming prey. The vulnerable being excised like a perished fetus from a corpse.

Was it always there, and he was only now starting to notice it?

Even in this very hall—a room for revelry and sharing bread—a locked and sealed trap door had been recently laid into the floor in front of the dais. Beneath it, an oubliette. A room for the dissidents of the clan to be dropped into and forgotten. A room of bones over which the Ó Canains celebrated.

Fergus alone controlled the lever that opened that trapdoor, all with his lady in red at his side. Her animal at her seat.

What was that thing? Its vague form hurt his head...

Breccan looked from one of Domnall's eyes to the other. The minor movement made Breccan's green eyes twinkle. Diamonds within the emerald. He took a tankard from a serving tray.

"We can read beneath the stars," said Domnall. "More than the Bible."

"I can't read," said Breccan.

"I'll read to you."

"Life with me will be dangerous."

Domnall reached for a tankard of his own.

"I welcome it." He'd take danger over evil.

The serving woman jerked away from Domnall.

"My lord," she said. "The chief insists you drink from the private reserve."

She offered an ornate, pewter goblet. On it were engraved three, plump, overfed swallows above a horse, saddled, bridled, and in a state of noble arrogance. The regal banner of a clan that occupied Leer Castle in days past. Once mighty and rich, now a nameless family lost to the annals of time. Chewed up by this place, leaving behind only trinkets and silverware.

"I wish to drink with my men," said Domnall. "If I am to fight alongside them, I will drink alongside them."

She would not let him have the same wine the others drank.

"My apologies," she said, "but my lord *insists*. Forgive me, but he says he doesn't mind you playing soldier, but a member of your standing must hold his head higher."

Domnall opened his mouth to argue, but Breccan covered his hand with his own.

"Thank you," he said, taking Domnall's goblet for him. "Battle fatigue has made our prince forget himself."

The serving lady curtsied before gliding away.

"Drink," said Breccan, putting Domnall's cup before him. "Let it be your last taste of royalty." He tapped his tankard against Domnall's goblet. "Tomorrow, you taste the road. May you live to regret it."

With a wink, he took a hearty drink of his wine.

Domnall sipped his own so as not to leave Breccan in the lurch. As he lifted the goblet to his mouth, the tail of the saddled horse engraved in the pewter twitched. And did the wing of the middle swallow ruffle?

A trick of the light. The torch-flame behind him twinkled in the metal.

"Lord, that's sweet." Breccan grimaced.

The hall fell silent. Domnall looked to the dais.

His brother stood. His braided beard fell to his chest. Narrow streaks of gray shot through the dark hair. The brutality of his reign wore him thin.

"Men," he said, his voice booming in the hall. "Women. You have fought valiantly for your country. Doing what is necessary to push back the Scottish invaders."

"Demons," shouted one soldier with a monstrous burp. The other mercenaries roared.

Fergus smiled, the expression not reaching his eyes. God, he looked tired. Did the turmoil of war keep him awake nights, or was that his red lady?

"Demons," Fergus repeated. "Aye. Devils and monsters. Always lurking. Always looking to take. Always looking to destroy kin and country." He looked to the lady in red. Beneath the dusky veil, her long hair cascaded in waves, only slightly darker than her maroon dress. She met his eyes, stoic. Her thin lips pursed slightly.

"A toast," he said, lifting his goblet. "To Ireland. To Leer Castle, may it stand with the support of Clan MacMahon."

With a resounding chorus of "hear, hear!" the mercenaries drank the proffered wine. It wasn't the best Clan Canain had to offer, but it was surely better than the mead and other swill they drank on the battlefield.

The rumble died under Fergus's steely gaze.

"War," he said, "is expensive. Feeding an army drains the coffers. The services of Clan MacMahon do not come cheap."

"Aye," called a man wearing MacMahon colors, "but we're worth every penny."

"Now he'll explain he must cancel the feast," Breccan whispered to Domnall.

Domnall turned to his friend, opened his mouth, and—instead of speaking—yawned.

"Don't let us keep you awake, my—"

Breccan's words caught in his throat. He blinked rapidly. His eyes turned bloodshot before Domnall. Red spilled into the whites of those orbs.

While Breccan stared at him, eyes wide and mouth gasping like a land fallen trout, Domnall's own eyelids took on weight. They closed slowly as Breccan's stretched to their widest.

Domnall panicked. His limbs felt as if clad in layers of mail. Moving them took enormous effort.

Breccan was choking. On what? Air? Wine?

Stay awake, Domnall told himself. He needed to get help for

his friend.

Breccan grabbed at his tunic, face slick with sweat. His freckles were specks of dirt in the slime coating his body. An unseen fire consumed them, baking the hall.

They collapsed together, Domnall growing drowsy as his man began to die.

As they all began to die.

Every MacMahon mercenary fell, clutching their throats. Some held weapons, their only feeble defense against attack. A large MacMahon woman couldn't hold her broad axe for long. She let it fall. It landed blade down, separating her toes from her right foot.

The soldier worth every penny brandished his dagger, fearful and foeless.

"My heart," he muttered. "It gallops..."

He staggered, hand against the table for stability. Perhaps in an effort to pin his heart down, he spun the dagger in his hand, shrieked into the cacophony of the dying soldiers like a banshee, and planted it into his chest. He fell onto his back, the dagger jutting skyward like a single foxglove flower sapped of all color.

"No..."

Domnall tried to drag Breccan towards him, but his spirit was flagging. Slipping from him like the last wisps of smoke from an extinguished flame. He crawled towards Breccan instead and collapsed on his chest.

How could this be it? How could the danger of their life together catch up to them before it even began? Breccan was dying.

Domnall laid on his man. He couldn't follow him into the grave; they had sampled different vintages. But he would not die alone. Domnall could walk him to Saint Peter. Hand him off with a kind word.

"I'm here, my friend. I have you."

Breccan's jaw clenched, unspoken words battering at the gates of his teeth. Domnall placed his hand on his cheek, wiping the tears away, clearing the drool from the corners of his mouth.

"Shhh," he said, throat tight. "I have you."

He looked into Breccan's eyes. Those marvelous greens were almost completely dark. Only a sliver of color—the rest devoured by hungry pupils chewing up the surrounding irises.

Domnall looked towards the dais. Only one man could have done this. A man who would go to any lengths to keep his clan a head above the rest.

Fergus looked out over the hall, surveying his work. The servers stood behind him, doing their best not to witness the death sentence they had each dispensed.

"Brother," Domnall grunted. It took all he had to even lift his head, but he did so. Raised it so Fergus could receive the condemnation in his gaze.

Their eyes met. For all the rage Domnall exuded in his flagging state, he received not a drop of emotion from Fergus.

The lady in red stood at his side. Her bright-red, thin lips spread across her face. Malice twinkled in her eyes, shining through her thin veil. She whispered something to the beast at her feet. It was the first time Domnall witnessed her speak, but her words were lost. Cotton packed his ears; one foot was firmly in slumber.

Snorting rumbled out of the silence. The frantic snuffling of some farm animal. A pig rooting for truffles.

It was no pig.

It was nothing of this world.

He yelled at his legs to move, to push him away from the advancing monster, but his body was no longer his. His voice was gone. A scream was too much effort.

The sheep-sized creature clopped among the bodies. It dug its face into the neck of a dying man, biting with teeth not meant to tear flesh. It tugged, stretching the skin while the man batted feebly at its hideous face. He moaned, red foam spilling from his mouth. His eyes rolled.

The flesh of his neck tore. Blood sprayed in a thick rope. It stained the creature's fur while it chewed with a mouth designed for grazing.

It trod over the mercenary's body, caring not where it placed its hooves. Domnall's last sight before slipping into sleep was of the creature lifting up onto its hind legs, then bringing its hooves down on the stomach of the dying man. Stomping his entrails up and out of his mouth. A meal served after all.

The creature ate.

Domnall willingly let go of consciousness. Anything not to see that face.

Domnall woke in a pile of the dead. Men and women who survived the slaughter of war only to be cut down in spite of a guest rite that should have protected them. The hall smelled of shit and the final exhalations of his friends. Without their liveliness—their revelry—it was colder than a bog's winter clutch. He closed his eyes, not able to rectify his existence.

Something grabbed his ankle.

The creature. That sheep with the face of—

He opened his eyes and lifted his head. It wasn't the deformed creature nibbling at his leg. It was only a serving maid pulling what she thought was a dead body towards the oubliette.

She gasped, not expecting such vitality from a corpse.

Domnall tugged his legs out of her grasp and scrambled to his feet.

"What," he stammered. "Stop!"

Some of the women looked at him, but most went about their business. Two of them dragged the now-toeless woman's large form to the gaping hole before the great table. Each held one trunk-like leg. They rested her shoulders against one lip of the hole, then dropped her in.

Domnall expected a heavy thud—the crunch of bones, the wet splat of impact after such a fall—but of course hers wasn't the only body in the oubliette.

Judging by the lack of corpses in the hall, the hole was near to full with them.

Heart racing, Domnall spun around.

"Breccan," he said, mouth dry. "Breccan!"

His friend remained where he fell, eyes fixed on the spot where Domnall had lain before being tugged awake.

Domnall fell to his knees at his side.

"Wake up, my friend." Tears stung his eyes, but he brushed them away. His chin quivered. That emotion Fergus taunted him over when they were young. That their father tried to beat out of him.

Friend? Is that what I am?

"Wake up...my love."

No words roused him. Shaking didn't work. He was no sleeping maid, to be awoken by love's true kiss. He was just one more casualty of a desperate chief who'd do whatever it took to hold onto power. The most recent atrocity of a castle built on blood.

He leaned towards Breccan and kissed him. There was nobody here to take that away. To hell with the maids. To hell with the mercenaries piled like driftwood in that lightless hole.

This was the only moment they had. Domnall cradled Breccan's face in his hands and kissed him one last time.

Beneath the table, Breccan's ordinary, wooden mug lay next to Domnall's pewter goblet. The three swallows over the regal horse were as still as the bodies in the oubliette. No flap of the wings. No shiver before taking off. They were trapped in Leer Castle.

They were all trapped in Leer Castle.

"I'm sorry," he whispered. Fresh tears fell onto that freckled face. He closed Breccan's eyes, then stood, brandishing Fín. The edge of the sword sang as he pulled it from the scabbard.

"Back," he roared. "Release them!"

The serving maids gawped at him. They held the limbs of the soldiers, struck by indecision.

Domnall swung Fín into a bench. It splintered, caving down the middle. With a grunt, he wrenched the heavy longsword free and swung again, cleaving the bench fully in twain.

The maids muttered, dropped the bodies they carried, and took hurried steps back.

"Out," he spat. "To your quarters, and pray I don't feel the same rage when I see your faces next."

His chance at peace was dashed like a ship upon rocky shores. Violence followed him wherever he went.

Fín's leather grip throbbed in his fingers. The cross-guard butted against his hand as if Breccan reaching out from beyond the veil. His chest heaved with his breath. All the strength the wine stole returned once more—with interest.

What choice did he have but to give in? To become one more instrument of Leer Castle?

Fergus stood before his huddled masses. The denizens of Leer Castle and its territories had gathered in the church. Their odor filled the cavernous chapel. They murmured like rats, crawling over each other.

"The mercenaries of Clan MacMahon fought bravely," he announced. "They won us the battle against Bruce's Brutes and the dreaded Scots. But the casualties were grave."

Peasants gasped.

"Many lost their lives on the battlefield. Those that survived are returning to Monaghan to have their wounds treated. Look on them as angels. They knew the sacrifice they were making. They did it for Ireland."

"They did it for the money," shouted a gnarled woman, swaddled babe in her arms.

"Aye," conceded Fergus. "Their services were not free. But let us not discount their honor. Let it be known that Clan Canain and Clan MacMahon will forever be allies."

Domnall moved as if in a dream, slipping past the guards who knew him so well. As if he had never woken from the tainted wine Fergus served him. Almost casually—like driving a serving wedge into soft cake—he pushed Fín's point into his brother's back, cutting his sermon short.

The sword tore a hole in the thick tunic, parted skin and muscle, and entered his brother's body. He watched Fín sink further and further, the action irredeemable.

His heart, aflame only moments prior, froze. What was he doing?

Murder—in a chapel. Fratricide. Regicide! Before the eyes of God and those he lived amongst. Kith and kin.

He pushed forward, unable to stop himself. Driven by a bloodlust unlike any experienced in battle. A strange, silent demand for destruction. A force his father—and later, Fergus—had tried to goad out of his sensitive disposition.

Fín shuddered against Fergus's spine. Bone scraped the blade, but Domnall pushed, horrified at the punishment he enacted against his will.

With a sudden slip, the sword punched through his brother's sternum.

Fergus grunted. His head tilted like that of a hound. He examined the sword erupting from his chest. His braided beard rested on the flat of the blade like hanging vines.

Domnall put a hand on his brother's neck. He could save things. He could stop them from going any further. Men survived being impaled. It wasn't unheard of. If he had missed the delicate organs—

Breccan...

His freckles. His green eyes. The life lost. The future they could have had. Away from Leer Castle. Away from the fog of hostility infusing every stone and every rivet.

A gasp rippled through the peasants. They recoiled, immobilized by the sheer number of bodies packed in the church.

Fergus's lady in red looked on, examining the scene with the impartial gaze of an undertaker.

Friend?

"Brother," Fergus whispered.

Is that what I am?

Domnall twisted the blade. It chewed up his brother's insides. Blood poured out in fresh droves. The front of Fergus's tunic. Down between his shoulder blades. It poured over Domnall's hand wrapped firmly around Fín's hilt, steaming and pleasant. A sticky puddle formed at their feet, inching around their boots.

Fergus coughed, and it gushed from his mouth. It sprayed over the gathered citizens, coating the gnarled woman and her baby in scarlet.

Her shriek started the chaos. Every man, woman, and child rushed toward the vestibule. The slow were crushed underfoot by the mass of humanity. Screams came from every corner.

A candle toppled. Flames spread along carpets and banners. Smoke billowed up stained glass. Bodies clogged every exit. The trapped and injured burned alike, begging God for mercy. Hell's fire answered their prayers.

Domnall lowered his brother to the ground. Blood flowed from the chief's mouth, dark as wine.

"Why?" Domnall asked, his throat tight. It didn't matter. Not really.

"Couldn't afford to pay," Fergus said, as simple as suggesting they till the wheat fields early this season. "Did it for the clan."

"You didn't have to—" Domnall coughed on the smoke. It thickened around them. He didn't care anymore. There was no coming back from this. Their clan was as doomed as that of the horse and sparrows.

"Always so naïve," Fergus said.

"And you were always a bastard."

"She whispered to me," Fergus said. "Guided me. Her brutality— her clutch on the land...I couldn't tell her no. Her creature..."

He sighed. His eyes rolled left and right.

Something freed him. All tension eased from his face. Though he was dying, he looked more alive than he had since the red lady had appeared by his side. It was as if Fín unleashed something in the chief. As if driving the blade through his body broke the shackles keeping him under her thumb.

"Gave you a chance," Fergus said. "A chance to escape. Slip out of her clutches." He groaned. "You should have left."

"She's gone now," said Domnall. "It's just us."

Fergus smiled.

"We murdered her child. Grandfather or *his* father... Doesn't matter. Captured her, put a baby in her, then put a knife in the whelp as soon as it fell out of her." Fergus winced. Blood seeped from the corners of his mouth. "We pay for their transgression. They slaughtered it, and we...we will continue to pay." He shook his head. His words were coming slower. "She's never gone, brother. Her and that damned creature. Where they go, blood follows." He closed his eyes. "She's your problem now."

His chest sank a final time. One last breath tumbled from his lips to join the billowing smoke.

Flames burned without remorse. The screams died off. A sweet smell of roast boar drifted through the air on an undercurrent of burning hair. Domnall's stomach turned. The poison had come *before* the feast. The food prepared for the soldiers—if it existed in the first place—went uneaten.

Boar sounded divine.

Domnall sat against the pulpit. His eyes watered from the smoke. There was a hollow space in him, a wake left behind in the departure of the quiet rage.

I ruined us, he thought.

Something pulled at his leg. He looked and regretted it immediately.

It had the body of a sheep, large and thick. Its wool was dark gray, dirty and mottled like turned flesh. A streak of red ran along its body from where it had feasted on the mercenary's neck.

With blunt teeth, it clenched Domnall's ankle.

The face of a baby looked up at him. Dark eyes, holes for nostrils set in a pale, dead countenance. Wrinkled, old in one moment, young the next. The stench of decay rose from deep inside its throat.

It displayed its broad, flat teeth and groaned at Domnall.

He screamed.

"Hush, child," said a voice from above. The red lady leaned over him, resting her delicate hands on his shoulders. Her veil brushed against his forehead like the web of a spider. "We'll make sure you're safe. Right, pet?"

The creature moaned and pulled Domnall.

He scrambled, trying to find purchase on the stone floor.

"Let me die," Domnall cried. "I want to die!"

"No, no," said the lady in red. He heard her voice in his head; her thin, crimson lips never moved. She only smiled behind the wisp of a veil, her eyebrows angled in mischief. "I need ears. What is a whisper with no one to hear it?"

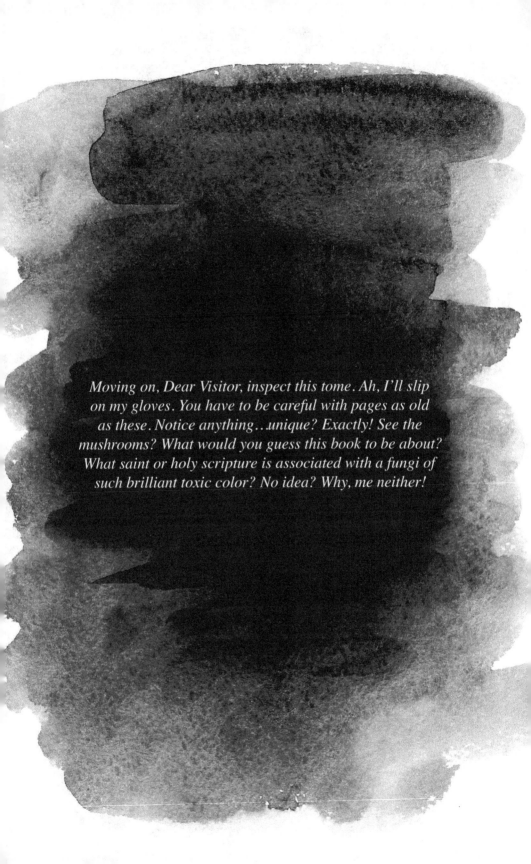

Moving on, Dear Visitor, inspect this tome. Ah, I'll slip on my gloves. You have to be careful with pages as old as these. Notice anything...unique? Exactly! See the mushrooms? What would you guess this book to be about? What saint or holy scripture is associated with a fungi of such brilliant toxic color? No idea? Why, me neither!

SCHIZZARE

Bridget D. Brave

he page turned, and where there should have been an expanse of unmarred creamy white, Pietro instead found a blemish on the sheet, near the corner. Mold, he thought, or maybe a stain from food or drink. It was the strangest, most brilliant color, a sort of hypnotic blue with spots the shade of fresh elderberries.

It looked rather like a mushroom.

He ran his thumb over the smudge, surprised to find it still wet to the touch, the blue and purple pattern transferring onto his skin. Pietro searched the wide wooden lectern for the culprit. He sought each corner and then finally the ceiling when he found nothing that could satisfy. His eyes again found the mark on the paper, and Pietro realized it didn't look like a mushroom. It *was* a mushroom, rendered in inks that could not have possibly come from his supply. He glanced suspiciously at the other two men in the room, both bent closely over their own work, the scratching of their pens the only sound in the space. Was this meant to be amusing? Something they did to rile him, or perhaps to bring him a smile in the unease of settling into his new home, his new life?

He had heard that some of the brothers once left gifts for initiates to lift their spirits while they were learning the ways of their new calling. That sort of comfort-act seemed unlikely of Novice-master Francesco. The elder monk was terminally serious at all times. He realized he was staring when Francesco's face settled into an unpleasant frown. No. Not Francesco.

Perhaps Antoni, then. The flush overtook his ears, and Pietro was glad for the dim of the library. He looked up and noted Francesco's pointed stare. Their mentor did not care for him and his young friend; that much was certain. He had felt the weight of the disapproving looks when they dared to laugh during a quiet moment, or sat too closely on a bench. Antoni was shy and more reserved than Pietro, but he was the only semblance of a companion Pietro had in this stone fortress, tucked away from the rest of society. Would Antoni leave a drawing like this, for him to find? A secret joke to be shared between the two of them? Or perhaps a message, some deeper meaning behind a mushroom of impossible color that he would explain once the two of them found themselves alone?

Later, in the dark of the hall, their breath intermingling in the close space, he thought to ask him.

"Mushroom?" Antoni whispered, with the barest trace of laughter. "Why would I paint a mushroom in your book?"

It wasn't a question Pietro felt capable of answering. All of his theories seemed ridiculous, now that the man he'd suspected of leaving him secret messages stood an arm's length from him. Despite how close they had grown in these past months, Pietro could not possibly admit why he had hoped Antoni was leaving him secret messages. "Someone put it there."

"Or perhaps some*thing*." Antoni's teeth glinted in the dark as he grinned. He was endlessly fascinated with macabre stories of secret witches stealing into the dark of bedrooms to tempt young men with all manner of things. Something he carried from his time before these halls, when a sister was still alive to share such sinister secrets in the long winters of Antoni's sickly childhood.

"Are you to start another of your demon tales, meant to give me a sleepless night?"

"Demons are *real*, brother," Antoni's voice was barely a whisper, but the jovial tone crept through as he raised his eyebrow. "Do the Discourses of Mark, Matthew, Luke not mention them by name?"

Pietro, raised in the city, did not harbor the superstitions of Antoni's village in the hills, nor did he take the subject of ghouls and demons as lightheartedly. He thought himself smugly superior in this regard, although he was loath to admit it. "Many things are. Are you saying a demon stole into the library to sketch fungi in my work?"

Antoni laughed, an honest laugh. "You will devil it out."

"And pray not to find the actual devil."

They both laughed then, clapping their hands over their mouths before someone could disapprove.

The next evening, after he had finished his meager meal and more than his fill of beer, Pietro sat again at his desk and opened the book in question.

There was a fresh mushroom on the corner of the next page. This one appeared taller than the last, with a cap that was becoming bulbous and full the way mushrooms do when they are near ready for a harvest. He turned back to the prior evening's work. There was no doubt it was drawn by the same hand—the careful curve of the stalk where it would meet the ground, had the artist thought to include soil, and the thatchy marks of the underside of the cap. While small, it was incredibly realistic, bearing the hallmarks of a master craftsman.

As the monks wrapped their tomes in linen for the night, he managed to catch Antoni's eye, indicating with a slight incline of the head that he wished to speak. At the table just behind Antoni, Francesco grimaced, his face growing ever more creased in the flickering light. Pietro swallowed the lump in his throat and hastily gathered up his book in his arms, making his way to the subjugate's wing. In the hall outside their quarters, he lifted a candle to the page.

"It is a mushroom," Antoni said wryly.

"And you have not painted this?"

"Why," the man asked again, patiently, "would I paint a mushroom in your book?" The question hung between them in the candles' flicker, breathless and anticipatory.

The fungi haunted Pietro for a full week, growing ever larger and more vivid, threatening to overtake the entirety of each page. An itch developed at the base of his neck. This itch grew into a harsh whisper that scratched against his skin, disturbed his sleep, drove his appetite from him. As the sleepless nights continued, the whisper crescendoed into an irritating buzz he could no longer ignore. *Find me. Know me.*

How would he explain this particular illustration, when interrogated by Francesco? Flora and fauna were commonplace in certain works, but this was a retelling of the story of Saint Peter. Saint Peter hadn't a mushroom anywhere in his story, as far as Pietro knew, and certainly not one prominent enough to warrant this many renderings. He was certain he would be accused of wastefulness. A high sin indeed with the growing scarcity of vellum. The winter had been harsh, and their own stock had dwindled when the mountain pass turned more ice than road. To give oneself over to frivolousness would come with consequences.

The mushroom cared not for the scarcity of vellum. It continued to appear as he sat down to each new page, each night, and it continued to grow. On the seventh evening, the sheer size of the mushroom was given new gravity, when Pietro found two figures sketched standing beneath it. Two figures in familiar garb—deep brown, roughspun robes with woven belts lined in green thread. The figures were facing away from one another with their hands extended behind them. The hands were clasped together. His heart thundering, he closed the book and again examined the room around him. The others had their heads bent forward, paying no mind to the panicked brother in their midst. He opened the book again, examining the two figures. The one on the left clenched a fist at his chest, his face upturned. The monk to the right, slightly taller, held a quill.

Pietro could not help but feel these figures were familiar. The clenched fist, the tilted head—were these not mannerisms he had often caught himself admiring from across a room? It was a gesture the tow-headed Antoni frequently made, when something was surprising, or delicious, or particularly overwhelming. It was a distinguishing movement, a mannerism that always caught his eye. Pietro found it hopelessly endearing.

The itch returned to the back of his neck, whispering promises he could not dare to dream. *Find me. Take me.*

In the hall, the flickering torch causing shadows to play across the page, Antoni made a low laugh. "Is that meant to be me?"

"I am not sure," Pietro stammered. "It certainly looks like you."

"Because he has straw-colored hair?"

"Because of many things I find familiar."

There was a long beat of silence.

"You have drawn me into the tale of Saint Peter." Antoni's voice was quiet, almost coy.

"I have drawn nothing!" Pietro exclaimed. "I thought you left these."

"I promise you, I have not touched that book. This is the first time I have been near it since you showed me last."

Pietro frowned in the semi-dark. Someone was drawing on his pages. Someone who knew his secret thoughts. How often had he imagined what it would feel like, the press of Antoni's palm against his own? Pietro's grip on the tome went damp, his hands shaky at the very thought.

Antoni's brow wrinkled. "Have you left it anywhere that might allow someone to draw in it?"

Pietro looked down at his work. "I was too afraid I would misplace it. I keep it in my room if I am not inscribing."

"Whoever is doing this is going to great lengths to send you a message. One you are clearly ignoring. That is why they are drawing it larger, don't you see?" Antoni sighed, his hand absentmindedly scratching at his chest. "It depicts the two of us, standing beneath it. It must be the size of a tree." He paused his scratching. "I think we should go to the cellars."

"Why?"

"If we are to understand the meaning behind the mushroom, we must go to where the mushrooms *are*. Where do mushrooms grow? In the dank, dark places. It is much too cold and snowy for any to be popping up outside. Maybe your mushroom is there, in the cellars below."

"There are rats in the cellar," Pietro said with derision.

"There are rats in the scullery, and you still eat the bread. If we find rats in the cellar, that means there are certainly things growing. Rats don't much care for places without any food, you know. More reason to see."

Despite his reservations, Pietro followed Antoni into the cellar, carefully feeling his way down the slime-slicked stone as the surrounding air grew cold and damp. Antoni's mullein torch provided their only light, giving off the scent of pine and cinnamon. He claimed it helped keep the vermin away, as they did not care for the smell. Pietro had his doubts. It smelled a great deal like a cheery hearth with a fresh loaf of bread baking. Why the rats would flee from the prospect was beyond his comprehension.

The main cellar was a dirt floor affair, with stone walls that curved into a domed ceiling. He had heard that they once made the beer here, years before he was born, before they realized that the damp caused the brew to turn to sour more often than it produced ambrosia. The brewing facilities moved to the drier cheese caves in the rocky expanse behind the chapel, and this cellar fell into disuse and dust. The space now was dark, with barrels, bottles and jars in various states of decay piled haphazardly in each corner. Some of these heaps so decrepit that they nearly appeared alive—knitted together with lichen and cobweb until they formed bizarre, hulking shapes that threatened to lurch toward the pair the moment their back was turned. Pietro shivered at the thought. He glanced over at the man beside him, feeling the flush threaten again when he realized Antoni was staring directly at him.

"Are you frightened?" Antoni asked, not unkindly.

"Just...ill at ease."

Antoni smiled again, his hand over his heart. "I swear to protect you. Look near the crevices in the walls," he said, lifting his torch to follow the stone. "If there is anything sprouting, that will be the likely location." Antoni raised the torch higher, sending the shadows jumping against the walls. A large pile of detritus appeared to stir in the changing light. Pietro stepped backward involuntarily. In a moment so fluid it seemed preordained, the warmth of Antoni's hand slipped into his own, their fingers lacing tightly together. Each man stood stock still, eyes facing walls opposite one another, focused only on the two hands clasped behind their backs. Pietro heard Antoni's breath hitch, as if the man were about to speak.

That was when he noticed the faint purplish blue glow emanating from the corner. Behind the pile of discarded wood and old rags he had mistaken for a lurking monster, something was giving off light. He knew what it was before he saw it fully.

A small, but brilliantly colored mushroom.

In his excitement, he let go of Antoni's hand. That was when the moment came, a moment not unlike how he had long imagined divine intervention must feel. A rush of heat, the howling sensation of wind in his ears, and the words forming in his mind more than in the realm of his hearing.

SWALLOW IT WHOLE.

Pietro bent sharply at the waist and took the mushroom firmly in his grip. It released from the wall with a satisfying *pop.*

There was the momentary sensation of choking as the muscles of his throat threatened to force the spongy flesh back up. Pietro fought the urge and felt his slippery prize slide down his gullet.

In the cold gray light of the pre-dawn, they sat on adjacent benches in the prayer garden.

"Are you angry with me?" Pietro asked.

"Of course not."

"I still do not know why I did that."

"Of course not."

Pietro was embarrassed in a way he found himself unable to articulate. He was not sure how to explain that he just knew what he had to do, and that he could not help but do it. Antoni's complaints and worries had mostly been over the possible danger. He knew that was ridiculous. There was no pang in his gut. No sour taste on the back of his tongue. Nothing to indicate the fungus was working its way into his bloodstream, poisoning him.

Antoni appeared less reassured. Instead he seemed genuinely disturbed by what had transpired in the cellars. Whether it was the consumption of the mushroom, or the moment that they had shared that unnerved him was immaterial. Pietro could not separate the two in his mind. Somehow swallowing the mushroom had confirmed everything he had hoped. The sketch was meant for him as a sort of instruction. To show him what he must do to attain Antoni's touch.

The vellum that evening did not contain a mushroom. The page was blank.

Pietro flipped back to the page prior, looking at the way the blue-speckled cap seemed to shine with a light of its own, almost as it had in that dank room. Beneath it stood the couple, hands clasped, rather...rather similar to the way he and Antoni had stood in the moment before he first spotted it. No, not similar. Identical.

Pietro waited until Francesco had left the room before he approached Antoni's lectern. "Do you believe in prophecy, brother?"

Antoni looked uneasy. "I suppose I do. Why?"

"The drawing in the book. We were standing exactly like that, when I found the mushroom. With our hands..."

Antoni frowned. "Is your book telling you to swallow another mushroom?"

"There is nothing in the book tonight. As if that was the end of it. I thought it odd, that is all."

"I will agree that it was odd. But perhaps it is for the best. What if it was a demon, after all?"

Pietro considered this. It was possible that it was some sort of temptation from the beyond. If so, it had granted him one of his deepest desires. Whenever his mind wandered, Antoni's fingers, slender and cool, entwined in his own. The feeling was still so fresh as to arouse physical discomfort.

For a week, his life continued on undisturbed. The same routine of wake, work, pray, eat, write, sleep continued until the seventh day when he opened his manuscript and found, in the same glowing colors, a small mushroom. Pietro felt his heart lurch in his chest violently. He could hardly wait to tell Antoni.

"So our mushroom demon was not vanquished by consumption?"

Pietro smiled in spite of himself. "I suppose not."

The next evening, the mushroom appeared again. Slightly larger. It gave him the most unexpected feeling of contentment to see it there, still in existence when he thought it lost forever. This continued until another week had passed, when he witnessed the mushroom once again nearly overtaking the page. There, beneath its spreading cap, were two figures kneeling facing one another. He flipped back to the prior sketch and then returned to this new image. There was no doubt they were the same two.

For the first time since his arrival, Pietro skipped the evening meal.

"I believe," he said to Antoni later, once they were alone, "that perhaps I was meant to find it."

"Are you feeling well? You looked quite pale today, and you missed your supper. Where were you?" He raised his eyebrows. "You mean to look again?" Antoni's voice rang of disbelief.

They crept down into the cellar single file, Pietro rushing ahead the moment the unearthly glow became visible. It grew in the same place as before, blue and almost pulsing in the dim when he dropped to his knees before it. He heard Antoni nervously shift behind him. "Another grew in the same area."

"Not the same area, brother," Pietro whispered. "In the exact same spot. Almost as if...almost as if it is the same one. Sprung again to life."

"Do mushrooms return from the dead?"

"This one has," his voice was reverent.

Antoni shivered. "I think you should leave it where it grows, then. It does not appear ready to leave."

Pietro sat silently, staring at the pulsing glow. "I wonder what it wants."

"Wants?" An edge of hysteria crept into Antoni's voice. "It wants nothing, except maybe to go on being a mushroom. Undisturbed."

"Why? Do you still think it poisonous?"

"Pietro." His blood sang at hearing Antoni speak his name. "You are not thinking of swallowing it again, are you?"

Pietro did not answer, remaining on the ground. He heard Antoni dropping to his knees beside him, felt Antoni's hand rest upon his own. *This is the second time we touched,* Pietro thought. "Promise me you will not swallow another mushroom. Please."

Silence.

"Will you pray with me?" Antoni asked.

Though he thought the idea ridiculous, Pietro nodded. They bent their heads toward one another, the air from their fevered prayer warming their joined hands.

Afterward, he allowed Antoni to lead him back up the stairs, the mushroom momentarily forgotten in the revelation of their touch.

Twice he had watched the mushroom grow on a page. Twice it had shown him and Antoni together, closer than they ever dared to stand on the floors above, under their masters' watchful eyes. *Twice* now. But this time the mushroom image stayed the same. Day after day, it was the same picture of the mushroom appearing on the page, with the two brother monks kneeling in sacred prayer beneath its spreading dome. Why wasn't it disappearing as it had before? What had been the catalyst?

He found himself lying awake most nights, sleep remaining elusive as he turned the idea over and over in his mind. He absent-mindedly rubbed at his arms, his shoulders, the skin on his lower back, noting how dry the mountain air made his flesh feel. As he sat, staring sightlessly across the table above his uneaten breakfast, he began to understand. The idea at first was almost amusing, then became something more, something that took root and wove itself into the deeper recesses of his mind. *Of course.* He had to destroy it. Obliterate the mushroom completely to allow it to grow and cast a new spell.

After the lights of the hall had extinguished and all had settled into the peaceful quiet of sleep, Pietro slipped into the cellars. On hands and knees, he stared at the mushroom, waiting. There was no pronouncement. He lifted it to the level of his eye and waited. The mushroom stayed intact. Pietro frowned and crushed it in his fist. When he opened his fingers, it sprung back to its original shape. Feeling the rise of frustration, Pietro dropped the mushroom to the floor and ground it under his heel. The mushroom, dirtier than when he dropped it, nevertheless bloomed back to life. A cold wave of panic rushed up his spine. If he could not destroy the fungus, how could he coax the wall to grow another?

EAT IT.

He plucked the mushroom back up, and before he could think better of it, popped it into his mouth, chewed, and swallowed.

Seven days later, a tiny mushroom appeared on his page. The thrill of excitement came once again. Each morning he rose and stretched his aching body, scratching at the flakes of skin that must have appeared while he slept. Each night he picked at his bread, ever watchful for the bell signaling the end of the evening meal, pointedly ignoring the curious stares of Antoni at the other end of the table.

Finally, on the seventh night, the mushroom had reached its full height, nearly overtaking all of the vellum page. Beneath it, again, were the two figures. One now clasped the other from behind, his arms snaked around the first man's abdomen.

"Would you take a walk with me?" Pietro asked as they left vespers.

Antoni nodded, his face concerned. "I think the fresh air might do you a world of good, brother. You look worse than before. You have barely been eating, I have noticed."

This was true. Pietro's distraction had not diminished as he delved into the mushroom mystery. Most moments between his official responsibilities, he could be found sitting passively, staring at nothing, a forgotten cup or book or a nibbled-at hunk of bread discarded in his lap.

"I am worried about you. I think that whoever is leaving you these messages means to do you harm. Why else would they continue while you grow thin and hunched over? Why would they not put an end to this flight of fancy when it interferes with your apprenticeship? It can only be because they mean to make you fail, to drive you mad. I know you mocked my idea of demonic intent, but evil dwells in the hearts and minds of men as surely as it lives in the kingdom of hell. I am curious how you write considering the state of your hands."

Pietro glanced down at the cracked, flaking skin. "They have been dry, as of late."

"They look like they are withering and dying. If you..." He

paused when Pietro turned not toward the doors of the main hall but to the left. "Do you mean to take me back to the cellar?" Antoni asked warily.

"I have something I must show you."

They descended the steps in silence, ducking to pass through the door into the domed room beyond. There, in the dark corner, the unearthly blue glow beckoned. "You wanted to show me this?" Antoni blinked. "I have seen this before."

"No. Yes. You have seen it. But not in this incarnation."

"Incarnation? Are you telling me you destroyed the last one?"

"I tried. It would not seem to mash out as easily as I had hoped."

"You ate it," Antoni said matter-of-factly. "I should have known. Your skin. The pallor in your complexion. The way you pick at meals. You look like you haven't slept in a week, behaving like a skittish kitten when anyone draws too near. You have been poisoned. We should tell Francesco."

"I am not poisoned." The words came out as a harsh spit he didn't intend. Antoni recoiled instinctively. "If I were poisoned I would have expired long before this night."

"Is this why you have brought me here, then? To show me how *well* you are?"

"I brought you here because this is the only place we ever touch."

Antoni was quiet for a moment. "I wish you would not say these things."

"Because you are ashamed of love."

Antoni flinched as if Pietro had slapped him. "I wish you would not say that as well." His hand clenched into a fist at his chest, worrying the fabric of his robe beneath his fingers. "You ask things of me that are not possible."

"All I ask is for your time."

"You ask far more than that. You ask for promises I cannot make."

Pietro made a dismissive sound. "I never asked you to *promise* me anything."

"But you would like to."

Pietro did not respond.

"Pietro, I *do* love you. As my brother."

"You know that is not what I mean."

"You *are* my brother. In God," Antoni said, his eyes failing to convey the resoluteness his voice had attempted. "There is no greater intimacy. Do not ask me for more." He reached out his hand. "Come, let us see Brother Francesco. I'm sure there is something he can give you to help with your stomach, to help you sleep."

"I do not need to see the Novice-master."

Antoni shook his head. "Leave the mushroom alone for now. At least until you have had some rest. You might have had enough to sicken you. One more might be your undoing."

Pietro leaned forward, as if to give in and follow his fellow monk up the stairs. Then he lunged. Antoni realized what he was doing too late. He caught him awkwardly at the waist as Pietro groped for the mushroom in the dark. Antoni tried to pull Pietro back upright but Pietro was already shoving the fungus into his mouth and chewing aggressively. Antoni held on for a moment, his face pressed against Pietro's back.

"If you are so determined to kill yourself, I will not stand around and watch it," he said, his voice muffled by the rough fabric of Pietro's tunic. He took several deep breaths against Pietro's spine before letting his arms fall. Then he turned his back and made his way up the stairs without another word.

Antoni did not seek him out the next morning. He did not allow a space beside him for Pietro in the chapel, nor did he meet his questioning gaze in the dining hall. Pietro was not sure how to soothe this, but the whispers he heard at night assured him that the mushroom would show what would happen next. He just had to bide his time.

He knew it would be a week until he saw the sketch again, and then a week longer until he knew what would come to pass.

With this knowledge, and without the company of Antoni, he found the passing of days particularly tiresome. There was no reason to rise from his bed early to attend to his duties in the garden, nor to attend the reading of scripture in the chapel. Those events marked the passage of time in each day, and passage of time was something he would much rather let slip by. Instead, he stayed in his room, begging sick when the other brethren finally sought him out. He was left largely alone after that, save two meals delivered daily to his door. Pietro sat on his bed between feedings, staring at the blank pages of his tome, waiting.

A week passed, his arms appeared ever more spindly as the flesh beneath his fingernails retracted, the skin around his eyes grew taut, giving him a hollow, translucent appearance. He heard again the strange whispers, now coming from the darkened corners of his room at night. While he was unable to discern the exact words, he believed fervently that he knew what they foretold.

Then the mushroom appeared.

On the seventh night following, the mushroom again spread its cap across the page. In the shadow beneath he saw himself, gaunt and grayed, seated with his back against the stalk. In his arms lay Antoni, gazing up at him with a wide-eyed expression. He traced the image with fingers wrapped in bandages long past their cleanliness, leaving faint streaks of watery blood behind.

Pietro slammed the book closed and took in a shuddery breath. *At last.*

He descended the stairs, nearly losing his footing in his mad dash to find the glowing cap. But no such glimmer greeted him in the dark. In the corner he found Antoni, curled beside the wall, his robes caked with damp earth and dust. Pietro dropped onto his hands and knees and crawled close, exhaling sharply with relief when the other man stirred. Antoni shifted with a jerky movement, as if his arms were restrained, slumping into Pietro and nearly knocking them both over. Pietro clumsily turned him in order to hold Antoni upright. Holding the body gave rise to a violent revulsion Pietro tried to swallow back down. Antoni's bluish lips pulled back into an unnatural grimace, his breathing shallow, his arms retracted against his chest as if they had been withered by years in the grave. As he held Antoni, Pietro heard rasps within the dirty robes, the sound of husks crumbling beneath his hands.

"I thought…I thought that if one had only sickened you, perhaps I could eat it first. Prevent…stop you from taking in another." Antoni tried to smile, the result a sickening combination of cracking skin and bared teeth, the roots exposed in bleeding gums. "My constitution is not as strong."

Pietro opened his mouth to speak, then stopped as Antoni's body spasmed then went rigid. Antoni stared up at Pietro, his eyes wide with fear. "I am sorry. I was *wrong*. It *was* a prophecy," he whispered. "Just not the one you wished for."

Antoni shivered, and was gone.

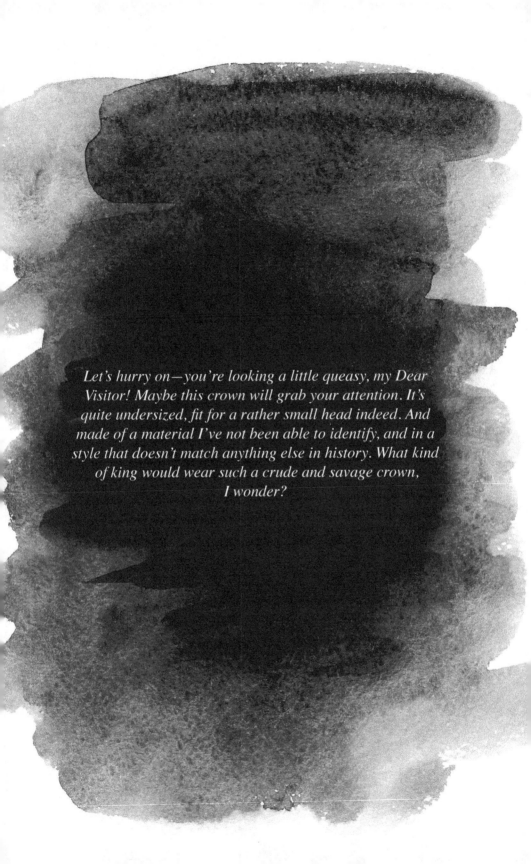

Let's hurry on—you're looking a little queasy, my Dear Visitor! Maybe this crown will grab your attention. It's quite undersized, fit for a rather small head indeed. And made of a material I've not been able to identify, and in a style that doesn't match anything else in history. What kind of king would wear such a crude and savage crown, I wonder?

THE KING OF YOUTH VS. THE KNIGHT OF DEATH

Patrick Barb

 hen they placed the flimsy crown, woven from black sheep's wool, on the head of the boy who became the King of Youth, it hardened to ebony-tinged iron. At his command, the children of Courbefy in Limousin took up arms and expelled their elders from the royal fortress meant to protect the tiny hamlet.

One month and a fortnight passed with no end in sight to their frenzied revelries. Stores of salted meats and grain, intended to sustain the nobility in lean winter months or in times of siege, dwindled to scraps and crumbs.

The more cautious children, viewing the festivities from obscure corners or whispering against the walls, let the celebrations proceed unquestioned. No one raised objections regarding the King. Or if they did, they never spoke of them near the boy monarch and his loyalists.

As another day broke, the onyx-hued crown sat snug on the King's brow. Blood trickled down the boy's pale and sunken cheeks, hardening into a black crust like a centipede's shell. Storm-cloud eyes stared at the sleeping children around him.

On the fortress walls, cocks crowed, signaling the arrival of a cold, unforgiving morning.

"Attention. Attention."

The King spoke his command from the banquet hall dais. The first to be roused by the regent's words was Amadon, a nobleman's son wearing a pig's severed head over his own because the King told him to, sitting in the place of the royal advisor.

With a muffled voice straining to resonate past layers of pig flesh, he cried, "Long live the King of Youth!"

The King nodded to the pig-headed lad. "Thank you, Amadon."

A sharp-angled leering grin sliced the corners of the King's lips, making him look like some hunched-over gargoyle. For a moment, those still waking experienced a shared uncertainty about time, location, and the cause to which they'd committed themselves. If pressed, those affected might confess to a momentary belief in the potential for the King's terrible smile to swallow his thin face whole.

Some went further, sharing an indulgent hallucinatory vision of the King of Youth devouring the hall, starting with himself and then consuming everything surrounding in an impossible sequence of annihilation.

"My subjects," he said, "they're sending someone to kill your King. And he'll kill every one of you who'd stand and protect me. They call this monster 'The Knight of Death.' I've seen the white helm covering his face, like my vision of our initial triumph when you plucked me from the crowd and set this black crown upon my head."

The children's voices rose in protest.

No!

They'd never!

They couldn't!

We're children!

"We all die for something," the King of Youth said, "Tell me, how many of you will die for me?"

The water frothed black, bubbling from the first of two holy wells on the border between the forest and the farmlands. While his advisors shook and trembled, Duke Bernart, the vassal lord of Courbefy, mouthed a silent thanks. It appeared they'd performed the corruption ritual as instructed.

He hoped the results proved positive at the second holy well also. After all, the Witch living in exile by the leper colony at this other site had promised them a solution to the problem of this new King of Youth, the mysterious boy who took the silly Carnival "title" far too seriously and who wielded power over the hamlet's young, compelling them to fight in his name. Should the summoning fail and the hamlet lose two of its holy sites, the Duke feared his time in power would come to a swift and definitive end.

Whispers tickled the insides of his ears. It was as though unseen hobgoblins or faeries hidden away in the hood of the Duke's cloak spoke foul curses to him alone.

In the already shattering pieces of his soul, the Duke understood the maddening voices as a tiny percentage of the price he and all the elders seemed destined to pay.

"What have we done, my lord?" one of the pious asked, keeping their distance from the corrupted well.

Branches snapped under foot. The wind howled, like the keening wail of a succubus in heat.

"We've done what was necessary, " the Duke answered. "We've

done what God wouldn't."

Among the whispers in his ears, the Duke picked out the rasping voice of the old Witch outlining the summoning ceremony from the shadows of her briar-covered cottage, the lone dwelling situated close to the village's forsaken leper colony. No touch of the divine came from her blistered lips, of that the Duke was certain.

A trembling hand broke through the tree line. The youthful messenger, a man but barely, with smooth cheeks and lineless palms, appeared closer to wearing swaddling clothes than resting in a coffin. As a result, many of the elders' hands dropped to the pommels of their weapons when he came into view.

The messenger's hands gripped his knees, and sweat fell from his shivering form to dampen the dying remnants of wild grass. "Your lordship, the other well...the water runs black. The Duchess awaits your return."

With the messenger's interruption, a degree of courage returned to some. Izarn, Courbefy's master-of-arms, positioned himself behind the arch of the well, facing the Duke. "My lord, extract us from this devil's bargain. Give our precious children a chance to shake off whatever spell this rabble-rousing 'King' has cast upon them and—"

But before Izarn finished his breathless delivery of a speech clearly long in the planning, the Duke raised an open hand and closed it, signaling for silence. "We've given them weeks. You've seen the wounds our womenfolk tend. Inflicted by children on our trained men and those untrained peasants you *encouraged* to enlist in our cause alike. No one is spared. And now, those burns and open sores from boiling lard? The poor souls affected won't last the next few days!"

Despite the rising passion in the Duke's voice, Izarn, hard-headed as the helmets in his armory, pressed on. "But not all the children are so far-gone to commit such heinous acts, Bernart! Someone like my Amadon—"

The Duke reached across the black water, seizing the master-of-arms below his cloak, and ripping the man's days-old, sweat-soaked shirt from his chest. Fading yellow bruises and blackened scabs mapped islands of pain across the man's chest.

"The same Amadon who left these marks when he and the others brought their howling parade past our sleeping sentries and rampaged through our quarters, expelling us from the fortress?"

Before Izarn could reply, a mace smashed through the curved stone arch of the corrupted well. Ancient masonry crumbled to dust, further muddying the already clouded water. Both the Duke and the weapons master leaped back from the sudden attack. The sound of swords drawn echoed through the clearing.

Shattered limestone particles swirled, and, in blasphemous harmony matched the black-and-gray clouds, tattered like old crones' shawls, that darkened the afternoon sky. Peering through the sudden darkness, the Duke went to meet the eyes of whomever dared further deface the holy site.

He abandoned any notion of facing the intruder when he realized who stood before them. Instead, he motioned for Izarn to stand down.

The Intruder. The Interloper.

A beast in the approximate form of a man, standing at the height of a large, upright bear—with a thickness of body to match his ursine counterpart. Armor-clad from feet to head, wearing something closer to full-bodied jousting armor than the typical mercenary's helm and light leather ensemble. Stranger still, the color of this armor. No shining silver or burnished bronze turned green and red from rust and wear. The armor appeared white—like bleached bones under an unforgiving summer sun.

When the Duke's eyes made it to the man's snow-white helmet, the vent-holes through which ragged breaths escaped appeared as the blackened gaps between a skull's teeth, picked clean of skin and meat. The enormous stranger's eyes were hidden from view in his helm, but armor rattled slightly with the slow twitch of his head to the side, as though a giant had risen from the earth to consider the Duke and his retinue like ants.

The black water of the fountain sluiced off the stranger's armor plating. As the water returned to the ruin well of the fountain, so too did the Duke find his voice again.

"The Knight of Death."

Speaking the name, he fought the twin urges to flee and to defecate in his tights where he stood. "We, the elders of Courbefy, require your services."

Fina Geralda found certainty in one thing: something wicked plagued the children of Courbefy.

Like the others, she'd allowed excitement to overtake her on the first night of Carnival with the initial coronation of the King of Youth—the boy who everyone knew, but no one remembered. The seizure of the fortress came off like a Passion play where child and adult played prescribed roles, going through the motions. Carnival served as a time for merriment and madcap anarchy, a time for release before the coming of Lent. She'd seen no harm at the beginning, even if she chose to take a restrained role in the proceedings.

Her opinion changed when she caught the eye of the King of Youth at the start of the second week. He'd called her into his council chambers and said, "You look like a girl who asks questions. A question is as dangerous as a sword or ax or arrow when wielded properly. So, Girl Who Asks Questions, ask your question of the King of Youth."

Without hesitation, she rose to meet the challenge. "What happens when Lent comes? What happens when Carnival ends and your reign is over?"

The King of Youth pursed his lips and hissed. "Two questions! Three questions!" he shouted. Amadon, before he wore the pig's head, and some other boys and girls eager to curry favor rushed into the King's chamber. Before they'd laid a hand on her, Fina Geralda made her exit. Moving as though the other children posed no threat to her.

The King of Youth was a different matter.

Following her menacing encounter with the King, Fina strived to keep her distance, stopping short of attempting an escape from the fortress. She doubted her chances of survival, and she wouldn't risk her sister's safety besides. Since their mother died at Fina's birth, she'd carried a self-perceived sense of sacred obligation, and acted on it via the care and mothering of her rebellious older sister, Saissa.

In the fortress, Fina wanted nothing more than to keep her head down and survive. So, when Saissa and her peasant lover skipped a royal summons, resulting in Fina being tasked with tracking them down and bringing them before the King, the young girl's stomach flipped and flopped. Like a fish pulled gasping from a creek.

Wandering the empty upper corridors, a sense of dread like she'd experienced in her not-so-private audience with the King of Youth took hold of Fina Geralda. She called her sister's name. "Saissa?"

From the corner of her eye, Fina caught a glimpse of white. Like smoke moving toward her. Closer, closer.

But when she turned around, she found no one waiting.

In the banquet hall, the King's latest coronation ended. Fina pictured Pig-Headed Amadon pretending to place the ebony crown on the boy king's head. *But never taking the crown off. The black coronet remains forever on the King's head.*

The sound of pipe and drum accompanied by the tinkling,

meandering notes of some apprentice bard on a hand-me-down harp penetrated the stone flooring on which Fina Geralda treaded.

"Saissa?" she asked again.

She'd known of her sister's secret liaisons with a peasant boy. And she also knew of the sickness greeting Saissa for the past few days. The older girl blamed the revelries of previous evenings, but Fina had her doubts. Given more time, she believed her sister's belly would soon swell with new life.

If true, Fina wished nothing but happiness for Saissa. She never envisioned such a future for herself, but she'd never begrudged her loved one that next milestone in life.

Fina stopped at a sound like thunderclouds rolling heavy through a melee thick with armored knights held on tournament grounds. She turned to where she believed the noise originated, though achieving certainty in the echo chamber of the empty hallway proved difficult.

She'd made the wrong choice.

Again, no one greeted her.

When Fina turned around, her feet tangled in the fringe of the garderobe's curtain. Blood smears marred the masonry. The peasant boy with which her sister had her dalliances lay against the far wall of the garderobe, stained tights around his ankle and chest cavity carved open with brutal inefficiency. But the sight of her sister crammed into the garderobe's hole from which the castle waste was expelled brought a low, trembling sob to Fina's lips. The ruin of Saissa's beautiful face extended from the upper jaw to the top of her head.

Fina imagined whoever had committed those twin atrocities climbing up through the waste and surprising the lovers, wrenching up with their weapon inside her sister's mouth. The stone floor of the garderobe provided further evidence of what had occurred. Teeth and brains and waste. And a silver pendant—the one their late mother left to Saissa—sitting amid the gore.

At once, every fear or doubt cast aside while the King of Youth held court came rushing forward, manifested in the aftermath of physical violence revealed to Fina. This time, when she heard the rattle and clank of armor, it came from in front of her. Close enough so she knew the wearer could reach out and grab her.

Just like that.

As though he sensed the girl's realization dawning, a giant clad in gore-drenched tournament armor lunged from his makeshift abattoir. Fina slipped on the messy remnants of her sister and her sister's lover. Palms stinging and stars in her eyes, she screamed. A primal release. She whipped her head to the side, watching the slow, deliberate progress of the armored killer. He wore blood and entrails as heraldic symbols, his white armor stained brown and crimson. He moved like a nightmare, skipping between moments. Armored joints staying statue-still, yet he came closer and closer. Even baptized in blood, the man-beast's identity was no secret from Fina as she recalled the warning issued by the King of Youth.

Fina pulled herself up and fled across the castle.

The Knight of Death followed.

The Duke instructed those left behind at the first shattered well to clean the site and to prepare to retake the fortress once the damned Knight of Death, with armor white and heart coal-black, removed the King of Youth and smashed the children's defenses.

Still, he suspected Izarn might rouse a sizable faction to forgo the assigned cleanup at the well and ride hard to the fortress. Many gathered at the site were parents like the master-of-arms and shared in his belief that their presence could save their offspring from the

Knight of Death's rampage. And who would those parents listen to? After all, Duke Bernart and Duchess Talesa had no children of their own.

So, how could we possibly understand?

But the Duke set suspected treasons aside for the moment. More urgent matters required his attention. Approaching the second well, he called for his bride. "Talesa! Talesa!"

No answer came, but a sense of ill foreboding threatened to overtake the Duke. So, he rode on.

By the wooden walled encampment where Courbefy once exiled individuals dying from leprosy, the Duke found his Duchess.

She lay sprawled across the path. Black dirt and blacker blood caked her body as though her own shadow held her to the ground. Even in such a pitiable, inhuman state, the Duchess's form was unmistakable to her paramour. A twisting trail of dried blood led away from her neck and a ragged wound marked the place where her head once sat.

The Duke discovered his Talesa's severed head, eyes swollen shut and crusted over with more blood, lips slack and wormy, resting in the Witch's lap. The crone lifted the Duchess's head, cradling it to her wrinkled bosom. She kissed the bloodied forehead. Then, the Witch grinned at the Duke. One by one her yellowed teeth dropped from rotten gums to litter the blood-stained earth.

"The Knight of Death finished this before he came to you," she said, her words clear despite her toothless maw. "Did your messenger not have a chance to tell you?"

Broken by the sight of his beloved, the Duke fell to his knees before the Witch. "This King of Youth, this Knight of Death, who are they, Witch? *What* are they?"

The hag shook her head, then pointed to herself and said, "No, no, no. You're asking the wrong question, Duke. Instead, ask, 'Who am *I?*'"

She took a hand, nails missing from the beds of her fingers and dripping sticky with the Duchess's blood, then rubbed crimson serum across the stretched-out skin of her bare stomach. The sigils painted in his bride's blood glowed on the Witch's parchment-texture skin with white-hot intensity, blinding the Duke temporarily.

But as his vision returned, the truth appeared…

The remains of Amadon the Pig-Headed Boy sat in disarray on a massive serving platter on the dais in front of the King of Youth. With a lipless grin, the regent sucked on his teeth and used two hand axes pulled from the armory to slice off golden brown hunks of roasted thigh meat, plunking a serving down on the plate of his newest advisor, some merchant's daughter.

"Oh, Amadon, imagine your father's disappointment to learn you shared the key to his armory with me…tsk and tsk and tsk again. But you have not used up your usefulness yet. You'll make a fine meal for your fellows. Won't he?"

The new advisor looked up and nodded her agreement, a subtle declaration of fealty compared to Amadon's previous fawning.

The girl lifted a hunk of Amadon-meat to lips already glistening with juices and fat drippings from her earlier servings. Teeth tore into gamey flesh. Around the banquet hall, the Courbefy children feasted on their former compatriot.

When Fina Geralda entered the hall, her modest dress hung in tatters from her shoulders, scouring wounds crisscrossing exposed flesh. Deep pools wept red courtesy of the Knight of Death's mace. Fina grabbed the two closest young men, a pair idling by the open doorway. Rigaut and Guiral, she remembered their names. They'd prepared to take their holy orders but got caught in the madness of this singular Carnival season, like all other children.

With strength surprising to the two would-be holy men, Fina pulled them to her and gestured at the wooden beam used to bar the double-doored entryway. "Come! Help! The door!" She shouted in explosive syllables. Dry-mouthed, the tastes of copper and death tainted her tongue.

On the other side of the room, watching from the catbird's seat, the King of Youth took note of this interruption.

With less than lady-like language, Fina roused her impromptu recruits to action. As she and Rigaut pulled the doors closed by their worn brass-ringed handles, Guiral slid the wooden board into place locking all the children inside the hall. Turning their backs to the door, the young men regarded Fina with fog-shrouded concern. "Fina Geralda, what troubles you?" Rigaut asked.

"Can't you see we're safe here?" Guiral followed.

Fina found all eyes in the banquet hall on her. Even the dead eyes of Amadon the Pig-Headed Boy appeared to gaze in lifeless contemplation of Fina Geralda.

"I..."

But before she finished, the doors splintered as though struck by a boulder. A thick chunk of oak sheared away at impact, slamming forward and splitting poor Guiral's head.

The Knight of Death slashed through the remnants of the door, gaining entry to the hall. His free gauntleted hand wrapped around Rigaut's throat, lifting the lad off the floor. A squeeze crushed his esophagus. Then, the Knight tossed the ragdoll-limp boy into the air.

When he came down, Rigaut's face met the viscera-packed spikes on the Knight of Death's mace.

Fina Geralda screamed again. She took in the vast bloody nightmare scene into which she'd arrived. After the brutal horror unleashed by the Knight of Death in the upper hall, she picked out young men, women, boys, girls, some of them mere babes fresh from suckling at their mother's teat, foul with human flesh on their ragged, overexcited breaths. Blood stained tunics abounded, as though she'd found herself before an audience of tiny butchers.

Her scream died at the back of her throat, so what followed sounded more like the last laugh of a dying court jester. Temporary madness dug its claws in and Fina needed all of her focus to drive it from its perch.

Blocking out the other side of the horror show for the moment, Fina focused on finding the next place to run, the next place to hide. She needed somewhere she'd gain the upper hand, a place to get her bearings before making her subsequent move.

One place appeared suitable for the task...

The dais and the makeshift dining throne of the King of Youth.

The time for hesitation and second-guessing expired when the Knight of Death extracted his mace from Rigaut's ruined skull. Even as blood ran down and across the stone floor, filling the cracks in red, Fina ran. All around her, the other children rose from their seats. But as the Knight of Death swung his mace with wild abandon, catching random youths with the sharp-tipped edges of the club, the children lacked a corresponding urgency.

The Knight of Death hammered those youths left in a daze along his path to the King. His victims whimpered or screamed at the impact of his mace against their emaciated bodies draped in blood-drenched cloth. They crumpled to the floor, bleeding, crying, or dying, depending on the severity of the blow struck. But no one ran away. No one huddled together in protective circles. No one tried to hide. No one fought back. Like addle-brained cows or sheep raised for slaughter, they let death happen as though they had no concept of an alternative.

Nearing the dais, Fina pushed some of the sleepwalking children, trying to get past them but also hoping to goad them to action. "Move! Move! He'll kill everyone!"

But her words had no impact.

In the staccato silences of the Knight of Death's one-man rampage, a cry sounded from outside the fortress's walls. A thunderous show of force loud enough for those in the hall to hear. Swords beating against shields. Strained gasping cries of grown men pulling siege towers into place. The elders of Courbefy, following the Knight of Death, prepared to take back what they believed theirs.

At the sound of this reinvigorated siege, others, like Fina, on the cusp of leaving childhood behind, broke free from the King's enchanting spell. They ran through the shattered remnants of the banquet hall doors. For a moment, unnoticed or forgotten by the Knight of Death, Fina considered whether she'd better double back and seek relief from the Courbefy elders as well.

The King of Youth remained seated, even as his subjects died around him. Torn skin and face meat weighed down the Knight of Death's mace. When wayward young crossed his path, the brute scooped them up in his arm and threw them forward with enough force to break limbs and shatter spines. Soon, he rode on a tide of beaten, broken, bleeding young bodies, ready to crash at the feet of the King.

Not until the Knight wrenched off the arm of some stout boy of thirteen and flung it at the dais, knocking the King's latest advisor back with such force the back of her head exploded against the stone floor, did the regent rise from his throne and issue a command.

"Defend your King."

The Knight of Death continued his relentless quest. But Fina Geralda, who'd taken the long way around and tread on tiptoes through the blood and brains of the dead merchant's daughter behind the dais, paused long enough to assess the field of carnage.

She wondered who'd defend the King when so many of the older children had either already fallen victim to the Knight's rampage or fled from the castle, trying to make peace with their betrayed elders.

Even then, the shrieks and pleas rising from below the fortress suggested the escaping children weren't received with the forgiveness they might've expected.

So who would defend the King of Youth against the Knight of Death?

Like the squeaking battle cries of mice, tiny voices rose in a chorus of blind rage. Fina sought their source; but it wasn't until she looked down that she found them. Children—not like her or her sister—but the sort who should have been playing under their mothers' skirts. Many were not even old enough to work in the fields. These small ones grasped butcher's knives and the smiths' smallest hammers.

They swarmed the Knight of Death. Stabbing, striking, and, where they lacked weapons, biting and pinching. Countless numbers of frothing mad children covered the Knight of Death so it looked as though he wore a coat of goblins.

The King clapped his hands in wicked delight.

Still thinking herself out of sight, hiding behind the corpse of poor Amadon the Pig-Headed Boy, Fina Geralda watched the King of Youth delight in the sacrifices made in his name. Equal to her terror toward the Knight of Death, anger raged inside Fina directed at the evil King. Her lips moved, starting a curse under her breath.

Then, she bristled as the boy king's dark-circled eyes stared her down like he'd eavesdropped on the very contemplations in her head. He waved a long, crooked finger back and forth in front of his face. Admonishing the young woman. "Ah, ah, it's not time fo—"

The King's words were cut short when the Knight's hands wrapped around his neck and pulled him into the fray. But before he fell, the King grabbed the twin axes from his table.

As the Knight brought his mace down, the King of Youth slashed both axes around in sweeping arcs. The blades, slick with congealed juices, struck the Knight's armor and sent up dazzling sparks. Undeterred, the Knight of Death struck again.

The King crossed his axes and blocked the follow-up blow. Wooden splinters from the thick ax handles flew into both combatants' faces. The King let tears of crimson trickle down his corpse-pale face. They mingled with the black-crusted blood from the wound inflicted by the crown.

Isolated with more corpses on the dais, watching the breathless combat unfold between the unstoppable Knight of Death and the uncanny King of Youth, Fina found herself mesmerized by the dark crown on the King's bobbing head. The absence of light, like a starless sky, pulled her focus toward the object.

The Knight shoved the King hard against the edge of the raised platform. His head struck wood with the black crown saving his life. Wood and iron clashed, ringing out like church bells. The jagged hoops rising over the boy's stringy hair lay close enough so Fina need only stretch out her hand and pull loose the crown.

But the King brought his head up fast and spat a pink mixture of his blood and saliva. The phlegmy wad flew through the narrow eye holes of the Knight's helmet. Caught off-guard, the ogre of a man stumbled backward, on his heels for the first time. Smelling weakness and growling as *his* bestial nature came through, the King threw his thin-limbed body at the Knight.

With his two axes, the King swung away at the Knight's neck and shoulders. Like some performing bear on its last legs under attack from overeager corpse flies, the Knight fought with gauntleted hands too slow to deflect the lithe monarch's maneuvers. Soon, Fina trembled, wishing to throw her hands over her ears to block the thunderous sounds of the King's assault.

At last, he wedged one ax blade under the Knight's helmet and then the other. He pushed up, straining until his pale face turned purple. Then, the Knight's helmet came free. So great was the unleashed pressure, the helmet flew across the banquet hall impaling its bevor through the chest of Izarn the weapons master. Leader of an aborted charge into the hall, Izarn fell forward with such force the Knight's helm bulged through the skin of his back.

Those elders who'd joined Izarn turned tail at his sudden demise and fled from the fortress.

On the other side of the hall, the King laughed. His head tilted back, eyes dancing mad, he reveled in the appearance of the Knight of Death's true face.

Because, despite the bulk of his armor and the monstrous proportions they portrayed, the Knight of Death's face—boyish, malnourished, haunting—showed a perfect match for the King of Youth's.

Fina gasped to see the twin visages.

With preternatural awareness, the King turned at the sound of Fina Geralda's gasp.

But not fast enough.

Eyes burning with fiery hatred, the King understood too late, the bad luck into which he'd fallen. Loosened in his brawl with the Knight of Death, the black crown no longer rested on his head. Fina held the black circle, squeezing the iron band so tight her blood ran like stigmata onto the dais.

"Give me my crown!"

The King's shouted command came from two mouths at once. From the boy-ruler Fina feared and from the unmasked Knight of Death. Like echoes in a graveyard, confused spirits unsure of where their souls reside. The King in front and the Knight behind, lined up in a near-perfect row.

Certainly perfect for what came next. Fina thrust the crown forward with its jagged, spiked hoops leading the way. She aimed for the head of the King, shouting, "You may have it. And you may wear it back in Hell!"

She leaped from the dais to the floor, momentum adding inhuman force to her blow. The black crown sliced through the skull of the King, then drove through the exposed face of the Knight of Death.

Blood flowed thick and black from the wounds of Knight and King. And the maiden who'd dealt the killing blow collapsed exhausted over them both.

With the cursed land of Courbefy having taken everything from him, Duke Bernart gave into the siren's song of violence. He'd held it back for so long, trying to lead his people, to outmaneuver his enemies. Finally, he understood how out of his depth he was.

His blade sliced through skin, muscle, and bone, severing the Witch's head from her foul body. With this act of vengeance, the Duke remained numb. Like a cold hand massaged his heart. Even the horror from the Witch smiling when the blade hacked through her spinal column came through as a dull ebbing pain.

Her head fell beside the Duchess's. Where the latter head remained still, eyes forever shut, the crone's eyes flicked open and she ran her serpent's tongue along blistered lips.

"You live?" the Duke asked, without fear or panic but with a restless acceptance of the mad sights before him.

"I've lived. I've died," the Witch answered between throaty, bullfrog cackles. Her headless body stood and scooped up her head, then the Duchess's. Cradling them both where before she'd held the head of the Duke's Talesa alone.

"Long before they gifted you this post in Courbefy, leprosy took hold and tore this village apart."

As if to punctuate her statement, the Witch's body broke apart, limbs sloughing off like dead skin. Until the Duke stood in silence before a pile of parts, squirming, grasping blind across the blood-soaked earth.

Still, the Witch continued, unrelenting. "I caught the sickness. But not the babe growing inside my belly. My sweet baby boy-to-be. I told them. I told them again and again. A mother knows!

"They wouldn't even bring me here to the colony, instead they held me in the tall grasses, away from the village. They cut me open and severed the cord connecting me to the life I'd carried.

"They held him and he wailed for me. Strong, healthy. A mother knows.

"But they blamed me for the black fate that befell the village. Instead of letting me hold my son, they let his blood run down on me. Then, they burned him and left me to fall apart inside and out.

"My last words spoken were a curse. Damning the bastards of Courbefy for denying a mother the chance to see her child grow, to see what he'd become."

The Duke found his voice. "All this death for one child?"

"All this for the death of his infinite possibility. Who knows what my baby boy could've become? Mayhaps a brave knight fighting with fearless abandon. Or...a king."

Trying to catch the eye of the Duke as realization sank upon him, the Witch's eyes rolled back white, and a hoarse cackle escaped her ruined lips. "They'll fight, *my* King of Youth and *my* Knight of Death, because that's what you people enjoy. The young, the dead, and the fighting. But it means nothing which one wins and which one loses. It's all an illusion. No, what matters to me is how many of your subjects are swept up by my illusion—how many lose all they hold precious for a chance to stop or to embrace my 'sons.' And yet, you managed both, o mighty Du—"

The Duke brought his boot through the top of the Witch's head even as the voices rose to a banshee's scream. Unceasing ululations shook his head until he wanted nothing more than to rip it off and toss it away. Instead, he shed his armor, let his weapons fall, then stripped his garments as well. Bare as a newborn, he walked through the open gate of the leper colony, surrendering Courbefy to whatever forces sought to lay claim to the land.

Fina Geralda stumbled through the ruins of the fortress, holding tight to the black crown of the King of Youth. Outside the fortification, children and adults wandered—dreamers pulled with violent finality into the land of the waking. Finding her father alive, Fina took an unsteady step forward to greet him.

Then another and another. Her heart pounding in her chest, she called out "Papa! Papa!"

He offered a small, probing smile to his youngest daughter. His expression one of cautious hope. Then, a chorus of other voices crying out, "Papa, Papa! Mama, Mama!" rose to join Fina's call. The urgent voices blended into a cacophonous barrage. She walked with arms extended, ready for her father's embrace.

Something burst from the blood-soaked earth, pulling itself through soil and rubble, birthing itself again. A two-headed creature in white armor, sunken eyes of a lifeless youth, vernix coating dripping down twin smiling faces.

The black crown fell from Fina's hand, returning to the King.

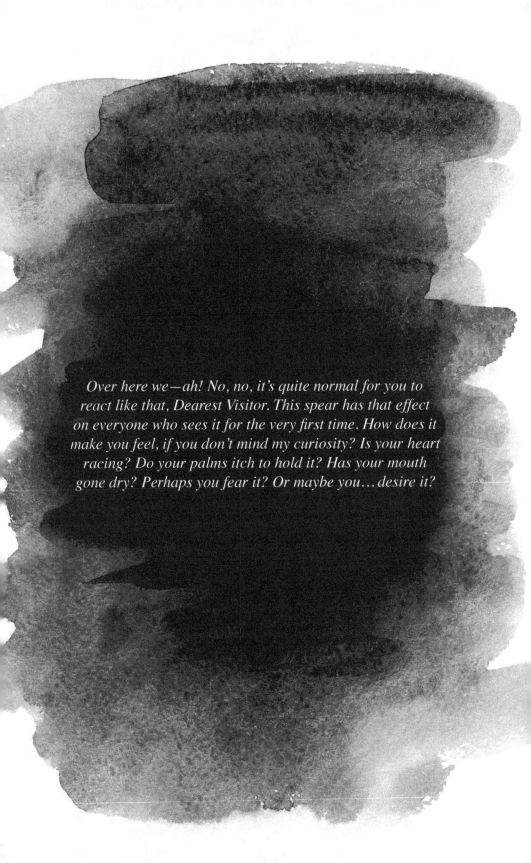

Over here we—ah! No, no, it's quite normal for you to react like that, Dearest Visitor. This spear has that effect on everyone who sees it for the very first time. How does it make you feel, if you don't mind my curiosity? Is your heart racing? Do your palms itch to hold it? Has your mouth gone dry? Perhaps you fear it? Or maybe you…desire it?

THE FORGOTTEN VALLEY

C.B. Jones

saleah likes to wake first, before all the others. In the pre-dawn morning, the darkened silhouettes of the towers serve as landmarks and borders, keeping her from walking too close to the canyon's edge. Everything is silent, too early for the din of conversation that will echo off the canyon walls. At this hour, the desert air is crisp and Tsaleah is invigorated by it all: the solitude and dark and cold.

At her destination, Tsaleah walks the rows of seedlings, down slopes and across terraces, clutching a clay canteen, its surface smooth against her calloused hands. Covered in the ornate interlocking black-and-white patterns designed by her grandmother, the canteen has carried water for years. It nourishes the staples known as The Three Sisters—corn, beans, squash—one drop of water at a time.

Tsaleah will spend hours here, pacing the rows before the sun's early light casts its unforgiving rays over this harsh land. She will drip water onto the same plants multiple times throughout her rounds, never wasting a drop. This is a land where water is sacred, a land where excess of anything is a luxury.

As far back as she can remember, Tsaleah and her family have tended these fields. Tsaleah counts the spring and summer days by the crops' progress, the leaves brushing first against her ankles, then her knees, her waist and beyond. She has done this since the corn towered over her by the middle of the growing season. Now, in her twentieth year, this only happens near harvest time.

The men of the village help in these duties, but they also go on hunts and scouting patrols. Sometimes, Tsaleah wishes to join them, to see what they see. Sometimes she gets the sense that the younger ones go out on such patrols to mess about. How often they return with too little bounty and too little to say.

Tsaleah watches one of the younger men, Taawa, at the return of many such hunts. He is tall and handsome. Oftentimes, he notices her watching him, gives her a sly smile.

He is coming up in ranks, the envy of those in his age group, and has graduated to hunting with the older men. Even now, he appears to stand in equal stature among them, if not taller.

On the most recent return he walks with an antelope slung over his broad shoulders. There is a crowd around them, buzzed chatter. The men regale the townsfolk with the story of how Taawa killed the beast, how he ran on feet swift as lightning.

Under a black sky crowded with stars, their mouths and bodies meet. With an intimate knowledge of the land, the hardest boulder can be the softest pallet for two young lovers. There is a right way to lay so that the smooth surface cradles the contours of the body.

His breath quickens in her ear, and she anticipates what follows, wonders what would happen if she were to lock her ankles around him, if she kept him from withdrawing like he's done every previous time. From the knowledge she's picked up from the older women in town, she knows that this is her most fertile time. She knows it would work.

How easy it would be to fall into this life, though. The life expected, the life predestined. She would carry his child and she would become his wife and from this they would settle into their preordained roles. It would be a good life. A life ordained by the Creator.

But no, she refuses to trick him into this.

This is where her thoughts lie as she stares up at the sky, miles from here and now. It startles her when he jerks back suddenly with a cry and spills his seed onto the sand.

Taawa breathes heavily for a while, saying nothing. He returns his coverings and gives her hand a squeeze, disappears into the night.

Tsaleah waits by herself, lying on the smooth sandstone, still warm against her bare back from the heat of the day. She stares up at the sky, her ancestors staring back. A long line of people who did what they were supposed to, did what they had to. Even though it's never been a strong desire for her, Tsaleah wonders if it is time for her to do the same. If not Taawa, then somebody else. There are other men in town and plenty of other opportunities for courtship.

Her thoughts are interrupted by the snapping of brush. Footsteps. Across the canyon she sees a shadowy figure, tall and gaunt. But only for an instant. Forcing her eyes to focus, it's gone. A trick of the mind, she tells herself. A mule deer, perhaps.

Later that week, Tsaleah finds herself deep in the canyon with her mother, near the city's center. Her mother is offering pottery for trade, something insubstantial, looking for something that will strike her fancy. This is a trip for fun and pleasure. They pass turkeys in pens, and her mother swipes a loose feather. She has been collecting them for a rainy day.

Tsaleah sees them from afar. There is Nova, the niece of one of the holy leaders. Her family lives in one of the towers. Her dad has status within the town, one of the heads of the council. Nova has a beauty that is intimidating, a smile to be envious of. She is talking with Taawa. They are laughing, standing too close. Something burns deep within Tsaleah. She tries to tamp out these embers in her gut, but they only flare up when she sees Taawa touch Nova's arm.

Tsaleah notices a single piece of turquoise hanging on a cord off Nova's neck, a piece of jewelry she envies. She already has so much more than Tsaleah. How could she possibly take more?

That night, Tsaleah waits at their usual spot, a rocky shelf over-looking an empty section of canyon. Taawa never arrives. From far across the canyon, Tsaleah sees another tall figure. Long arms moving in the moonlight, a beckoning. Tsaleah hurries back to her family's quarters. She will not return to this spot again.

The next morning, while walking the rows, the thoughts burrow in her brain. Neglecting her tasks, she takes time to draw pictures in the sand: her and Taawa together. She takes care to draw a tower far off in the distance, no Nova to be seen.

I could have had him by now, she thinks. *If I had shown any inkling of wanting a family with him, he would have acquiesced. We could have our own home, our own area of land. We would wait for Taawa on the canyon edge for him to return from the hunt and when he did he would run up to us with joy, hoisting our child on his shoulders.*

Tsaleah shakes her head and spits on the sand tracing she has created. She thinks on how the heart places more value on something once it cannot have it.

How can she compete? Nova has a powerful beauty, her straight black hair and smooth skin, the charismatic smile, and the way her eyes dance. Close in age, Tsaleah has always admired Nova, remembers how she would sometimes work alongside her and the others in the fields. Maybe this was out of boredom or maybe this was a political ploy, but she did the work with genuine joy and interest.

In her head she sees them together. His hands on Nova's wide hips as they make love on the top of the tower, closer to the stars than she and Taawa had ever been. How the turquoise piece would dangle between her breasts, Taawa's eyes mesmerized by the way it would glance off the skin with the movement of their bodies. Tsaleah could only wish and wish for such a feeling, the tower and the status and all she would never have.

She finds a secluded corner of the field and sinks to her knees, tears stinging her eyes. Finding a fist sized stone, she picks it up and tries not to imagine their faces in the dirt as she pounds it over and over into the ground until her fingers bleed. And for the moment, she feels fine once again.

Tsaleah spends nights in the shadows, out of sight. She watches them and their secret meetings. It is a courtship similar to her and Taawa's earlier days. There are light touches and shared conversations, laughter, but no union of the flesh. Not yet. But Tsaleah knows that it is coming and her stomach fills with the hot ash of jealousy.

On another night of watching, it happens. She sees the two lovers enter the tower during the darkest hour of night. It doesn't happen at the top of the tower like she's always envisioned, but rather on the second floor, one of the rooms of worship. Tsaleah is close enough to the building that she can hear Nova's soft cries and moans of pleasure emanate from the window.

When it's over and enough time has passed, Nova leaves the tower first, through the main entrance. She scans the surroundings and motions for Taawa that it is safe to leave. He exits and they part their separate ways.

Over the next week, the routine stays the same. Always, Nova leaves the tower first, Taawa following after.

Tsaleah's days are filled with waiting and rumination. There is so much yearning within her that she feels as if it will swallow her whole. On many occasions, she goes to the fields forgetting to fill the canteen, trampling seedlings, distracted by the repeating thoughts in her head.

Every day, she waits for night, hoping that this will be the night that it stops, so that *she* can stop.

Waiting at the usual spot for the suitor that will never come, a memory returns to her, a story she had heard as a child.

Her father had sat around a campfire with several of the men from camp. Somehow, she managed to convince him to let her stay up on this particular night. He tousled her hair periodically as she sat by his side. The talk of the secret world of adults floated over her head, confounding and indecipherable. That is until one of the more mischievous men from town took notice of her and shushed the others.

"Has young Tsaleah heard of the forgotten valley?" he asked.

The other men smiled in anticipation, looked toward her father.

"No, she is too young for such tales," her father said, waving a dismissive hand.

"I want to hear, Papa," she said.

"Yes, papa, she wants to *hear*," the mischievous man said.

Her father said nothing.

The mischievous man began to speak in a low voice, "A two-day's journey away there is talk of a place where our kind once lived. They lived in harmony and there was food aplenty. Corn grew in stalks as high as three men. Water flowed in knee deep streams year-round. Deer roamed the canyons unafraid and would walk right up to the slaughter. Nobody wanted for anything."

Tsaleah looked at her father for some sort of permission to keep listening. He only stared into the fire.

The mischievous man continued, "Yet nothing so good can last forever. An enemy appeared, something in the night. Not unlike the night we find ourselves sitting in this very instant."

Tsaleah looked over her shoulder, out into the dark. The tongues of flame from the campfire cast dancing shadows.

"People began to disappear. Children snatched from their beds. There were sightings of beings, tall beings. *Giants*. These giants were cannibals. The townspeople were afraid. More people disappeared. The giants were becoming emboldened. They could be seen during the day, on the edge of the village.

"The bravest men mounted several attacks, but the giants were too strong. The villagers could not leave this land of plenty. They refused to be driven out. A solution was formed. They would build their dwellings high up in the cliffs. Ladders could be withdrawn in the evening as the people took refuge. They would be safe at night in these perches way up high.

"And they were for a time. The village's council and holy men looked for a long-term solution. The high priest knew of an item that would finally defeat the giants. It was a spear of the straightest juniper, adorned with shards of turquoise. Blood drawn from the palms of holy men painted its shaft. The spear's tip was blessed by the highest of moons.

"The spear, it worked. It pierced the bodies of the giants like they were nothing, like their skin was corn husk. At the end, every one of the giants was slayed, their blood soaking into the canyon floor.

"It was not without cost. Perhaps their blood was poison. Perhaps it was a bargain from the spear itself. For the water of the canyon dried up. The crops would not grow. A famine set in the village. Many left, but some did not. There are tales that those that did not leave turned to cannibalism, acquiring a taste for the human flesh just like the giants themselves.

"The spear, it still remains there to this day. It is under the watchful eye of a shaman, the last one from this time. A powerful weapon that can grant any wish at a cost. That is what I hear."

Nobody spoke. They watched Tsaleah, awaiting her reaction.

"Is it true?" she asked, looking to her father.

"Of course it is true," the mischievous man said. "The giants still exist to this day as well. They look for children who waste food and do not mind their fathers, and then they snatch them from their beds. They do not like *good* children. Good children do not taste as sweet."

"Enough," her father finally spoke. "Tsaleah, go to bed."

"Can you walk me?" she asked. "I need protection from the giants."

There was a roar of laughter around the fire at this and her father walked with her into the night.

Recalling this story, Tsaleah knows what she needs: *a powerful weapon that can grant any wish.*

On sandals made of yucca fibers, Tsaleah treks toward the horizon. The hour is early, well before dawn. A quarter of a moon provides all the illumination she needs. She must leave well before the sun to avoid the field's early risers, to put in as much distance before the unforgiving heat of the desert day.

The day before her departure, she sips water at all hours and fills her canteen. Around her waist she wears a belt and pouch full of pine nuts and strips of dried venison. She makes good time. As the sky begins to lighten, the towers of the town are imperceptible blots on the landscape.

During the hottest part of the day, she takes shelter under a rocky outcropping, sinking into a cool crevice of damp earth. An excitement fills her. This is so much better than farming and tending the crops. Even if the journey does not yield anything, this will not have been a waste.

Another dawn rises on her. She is descending, cliff walls springing up around her. She must hurry to beat the punishing heat. The last spot of water was miles ago, a murky spring where she quenched her thirst, taking care to wrench the water through a fibrous cloth to filter it into her canteen.

It's hours before she sees the first evidence. On a sandstone cliff in a bend in the canyon, there are etchings into the wall itself. There are spirals and waves, silhouettes of antelope and humanoid figures with triangular bodies. On the margins of the etchings are more figures, much taller than the rest.

It is here when she realizes the silence of the place. No birds sing. Even the wind seems to have stopped blowing. Despite a recent respite at a spring, her mouth is suddenly parched. Despite the shade of the canyon, beads of sweat form on her brow.

They were calling me here, she thinks.

It is not too late to turn back. Nothing will be lost. But nothing will be gained, either. She will return to the town, her family's dwelling, and those fields. She will learn to be satisfied with what she has.

No.

Further she walks. She looks to the canyon walls, searching for more signs of life. Deeper into the canyon, where there are patches of ground that the sunlight never reaches, she sees the ancient village. High above on a ledge and under a sandstone overhang is a constructed wall, bricks similar to those of her own village. Black windows. How could anyone possibly get up there?

The longer she stares at the rocky face, the more the details reveal themselves. High above the cottonwood trees, there is a vast stretch of adobe structures. More walls, more buildings, more windows blinking into blackness. And above the village, the canyon walls yawn further into the sky, curving forward and back.

But here, there is a slant that she could easily climb to get to the first level, a rocky shelf that lies below the village on the cliff. She scampers up. There are piles of broken rock, crumblings from the cliff up above that have fallen and shattered onto the landing she now stands on.

A sheer sandstone wall four times her height is all that separates her from the abandoned village above. She thinks of calling out, but she is deterred by the unnerving silence and the thoughts of those giants lurking in some dark fissure in the canyon walls.

Investigating the smooth wall, Tsaleah finds a foothold. And another. If she could just put one foot here and another there, then surely she could hoist herself up the rest of the way. This must be the way it was done all those years ago, when they didn't have the ladders available.

Her toes grip the first foothold, and she reaches above. She's done such maneuvers many times back home; the granary of her village is in an out-of-the-way place.

Ghosts.

That's what she thinks of when she reaches the level of the village. This area is nestled into an alcove, more buildings stretching further back to the canyon walls. Their yawning entryways welcome her with silence. She sweeps the perimeter, giving the windows and doors a wide berth, lest any lurking cannibal emerges from within. A garbage pit lies at the outskirts of the village, full of ancient, dried corn cobs and pottery shards. Several long bones can be seen jutting from the dirt.

Enough light is present to see inside the first building she examines, enough light to see the former inhabitants and their hollow eye sockets, the ladders of their exposed ribs. They are stacked in neat rows, nothing but bones, varying heights. Adults and children. A family perhaps. An entire lineage. A chill erupts from the base of Tsaleah's neck, oozes down her spine.

Some of the other buildings display similar scenes, while others are empty. She spies a beautiful turquoise necklace amongst the bones of another home and is tempted to take it, but the thought is fleeting. A human skull, half-buried in the dirt, smiles with shattered jaw and yellowed teeth.

Nestled between two adobe walls, she sees the borders of rocks forming a circle. A kiva, and at its center, a ladder juts from a rectangular opening of impenetrable shadow. The scent of fresh burning sage wafts from the opening. A haze of smoke blends with the afternoon light. Tsaleah's heart races. This is it. She takes a deep breath, kneels down and grips the ladder's handles, sinks her foot to the first rung, descends into darkness.

Her feet hit the dusty floor, motes dancing with the sage smoke up the solid shaft of light that angles through the opening. Tsaleah jumps when her eyes adjust to the round dark room, and she sees him. He sits cross legged, just beyond that light, an ember of sage smoldering before him. His long white hair is translucent and cascades upon his spindly shoulders. It glows almost as brightly as his eyes, white as bone, smooth stones nestled into the ancient crags of his face.

"Why do you come?" he asks, his voice sounding like a thousand dry sorrows.

Tsaleah pauses. "I come for the spear."

He laughs, a sound like the crunching of bird wings echoing through the curved walls of the kiva. "Child, you do not know what you seek."

"This is true," Tsaleah says.

The ancient man chuckles.

"I am not sure what I want, but I do know that I want more than I have," says Tsaleah.

"So shall they all. Is something missing?"

"Something is missing. I thought something was missing before, but now it's worse than ever," says Tsaleah.

"The heart values least what it already has and values most what it does not have. This is second only to the value of something that it had once and lost," the man says.

"Yes," Tsaleah says.

"Well, if you come for the spear, then it is simple: I will give you the spear." The ancient man reaches behind him. The long weapon materializes from the shadows. He holds it before him, the shaft thinner than Tsaleah has imagined. It is almost as thin as his skeletal arms.

Tsaleah reaches for it, but he abruptly pulls it close to his chest.

"Not yet," he says. "You must know some things first." His voice grows lower.

"This spear can puncture the sky.

It can steal the wind.

It can stab the air from lovers' lungs, taking away all vows and affirmations.

Not only in death, but beyond.

"This spear is a needle.

It can sew the fabric of reality, stitch a new blanket from the shreds that it creates.

This spear does not concern itself with timelines or cause and effect.

You may pay the price well before you see any reward.

"This spear can pierce the stoniest of walls and the hardest of hearts.

It will draw blood from a canyon and sand from a river.

It can steal hours from the days and give years to lives unlived.

It can name the world and take the title from that which is.

"This spear can have a price.

Do not draw it, unless you are ready.

Do not wield it, unless you are sure.

Do not touch it, unless your intentions are pure."

Before Tsaleah can react, his arm crosses an impossible distance, and he grabs her wrist with a strength that belies his skeletal frame. Long bony fingers coil like vines around her wrist. He yanks her forward, and she flies toward him like a rag doll. It's this close when she realizes how sharp his teeth are, a mouth full of jagged shards of broken pottery.

She wonders, were he to stand, how tall would he be? How much had those crossed legs folded in on themselves? This close to him, she realizes how long his torso is. She wonders if he will be the last thing she sees and thinks: *maybe this wasn't worth it after all.*

He turns her right hand over, palm up. From there he runs the sharp edge of the spear tip in the flesh of her hand. Blood wells up and runs down her wrist. He shoves the shaft of the spear firmly into her grasp, a sizzling sound emanating from her wound as it closes shut.

"Go," he says.

And she does.

On a ledge far above the canyon floor, Tsaleah keeps the spear tucked away and hidden. She checks it daily. It sings to her, hums in her veins, fills her mind with a song that she cannot control.

And one early morning, when she catches a tall, looming shadow out of the corner of her eye, she knows what she must do.

On the day of the last night, she goes to her hiding place. She uncovers the spear. It's automatic at this point. She cannot stop herself from reaching for it, the shaft in her hands like it was meant to be there all along.

Night falls, and from the shadows she waits, the spear steady in her hands.

When the couple exits the tower with their relaxed and easy gait, the spear flies through the air.

It happens before any of them can know it. Tsaleah's movements are guided by forces unknown to her, her muscles firing while her brain screams, no. The spear never had a choice to not be thrown once she took up her post and pointed it at the door.

The tip pierces Taawa just to the left of his breastbone. It slides perfectly between two ribs, puncturing his lung and stabbing his heart. He never knows what hits him.

Tsaleah stands in shock, looking at what she has done. The blood drains from her head and sends her to her knees.

It isn't supposed to be this way. This cannot be it. This spear is no mere weapon. It was to hold a power greater than imagined, a shift into a reality where Tsaleah has all that she wants, a reality where Tsaleah knows what she wants and wants what she has.

Do not draw it unless you are ready.

For some reason—whether from complacency or no longer caring—Taawa was the first to cross the tower's threshold and into the open night air. Nova was right behind him.

Do not wield it unless you are sure.

Tsaleah scampers towards Taawa, crying his name. A high-pitched rasping breath escapes his quivering lips, the last he'll ever take. Tsaleah feels his broad chest, absent of heartbeat. She stares into his eyes, absent of life. The world falls out from under Tsaleah. Eagles scream from her lungs, a despairing cry to the heavens.

But there is no time for grieving alone.

"Tsaleah!" Nova cries in a sorrowful rage.

Tsaleah looks up to see her rushing toward her, face contorted.

You may pay the price well before you see any reward.

Nova is now at Taawa's side. She feels his still chest, touches his face.

Anger overtakes Nova and her hands are on Tsaleah's throat, knees on her chest. Tsaleah struggles against her, scraps for air, slaps at her face.

Releasing a hand from Tsaleah's throat, Nova grasps in the dark for a blunt object, her fingers brushing up against a stone. Clutching it, she raises it high and underneath her, Tsaleah chokes out pleas for mercy, pleas that fall on deaf and vengeful ears. With the first blow, Tsaleah feels her jaw give way, teeth breaking loose in her mouth, her face a muzzle of pain.

Nova raises the rock again, her eyes aflame with a holy rage.

Yet a divine distraction breaks through Nova's bloodlust. To the left of her, something is happening. Anchored into Taawa's chest like a flagpole, the shaft of the spear vibrates. It pulses with light and sends out harmonious tones. There is a flash of lightning, a bolt of pure energy from the sky. It strikes the spear's shaft.

And in the brilliant light their vision is lost, and they are blinded.

Blinded to all before the moment and shortly thereafter.

When sight returns and the scene returns to focus, there is only them.

Nova and Tsaleah, standing apart in the dark. Tsaleah's wounds now healed, her lips no longer bloodied.

The spear, once buried in Taawa's chest, is gone.

And Taawa…was there ever even a Taawa?

Will the village remember the fastest young buck in a generation, the young man who would surely grow up to be one of the greats?

Because at this moment, Nova and Tsaleah do not. At this moment, he is already bonedust beneath their feet. At this moment, their eyes are glued to each other, pupils locked in pupils. They step toward one another, fingers intertwining.

It's different when it's just the two of them. There is no community relying on the sum of their individual contributions. If they want to take off, they take off. They are determined to see as much as they can. Long forays into wilderness and land untamed, yet always circling back to a secluded area they call their own. Home is a corner tucked high away up the walls of the canyon behind walls of cotton-woods, in an abandoned dwelling, down a valley long forgotten.

Despite their wanderlust, they feel tied to this land. They couldn't leave. Its rough edges are imprinted on their palms and fingertips in the form of callus. Its dry air inflates their lungs, and its grit is in their blood.

They grow The Three Sisters, just like they always have. They value water, just like they always have. They watch the stars, just like they always have. But they do it all together.

In the summer months, they spend their nights out on the rocky canyon rim above the place they call home. There they lie together in each other's arms, underneath an incomprehensible array of stars, sharing their bodies' warmth in opposition to the cool desert night.

It's on one of these peaceful nights when Tsaleah lingers back by their quarters. Nova has gotten a head start, is waiting for her at their usual spot.

Canteen in hand, Tsaleah makes her way up the snaking path that leads to the canyon rim. The crescent of moon provides ample illumination.

Above her, several rocks skitter down the canyon wall and something crashes through the brush. A shadow moves just over the rim, the faintest of movements.

"Nova?" Tsaleah calls out to the darkness.

There is only silence.

Tsaleah's pulse quickens, hammers in her chest. She thinks of what happened the last time the spear was used, all those years ago. Picking up the pace, she ascends to the rim. Once there, she sees Nova's shadowy silhouette, hunched over the spot where she normally lies. But the silhouette unfolds, standing at its full height, taller than Nova or anyone Tsaleah's ever seen.

Now, Tsaleah sees the crumpled mass at its feet. The tall figure turns. With eyes that catch all the slivered moon's light, it fixates on Tsaleah. White shining orbs glowing from a face on high.

And in the dark, fear turns to fury, trepidation to determination. Tsaleah bends her knees, readies her stance, and sprints. She sprints toward her lover, toward that which would take it away, toward the legend she will become.

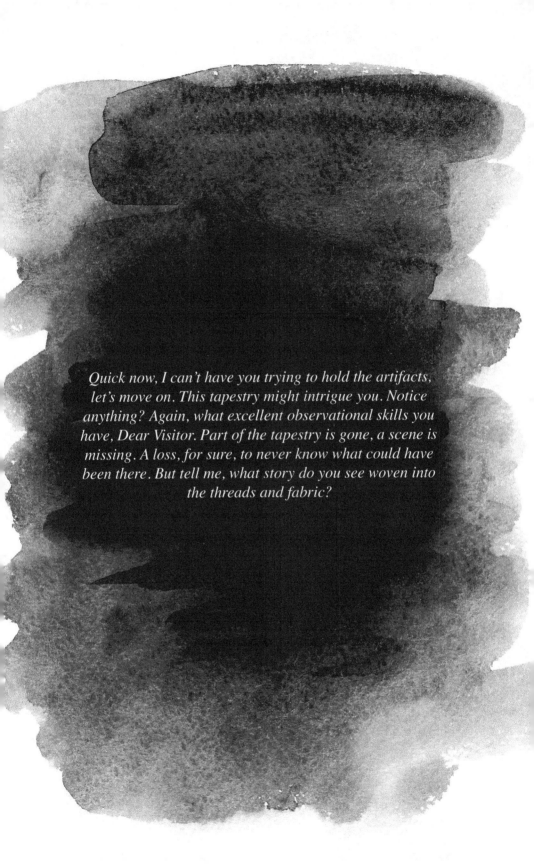

Quick now, I can't have you trying to hold the artifacts, let's move on. This tapestry might intrigue you. Notice anything? Again, what excellent observational skills you have, Dear Visitor. Part of the tapestry is gone, a scene is missing. A loss, for sure, to never know what could have been there. But tell me, what story do you see woven into the threads and fabric?

THE FOURTH SCENE

Brian Evenson

y Lord, I followed your father's instructions to the letter, though where there was nothing in his words to guide me I was of necessity forced to take my own counsel. I say this in no wise as justification for what I have done. Rather, let it be seen as indication that, if I have done wrong, it is due solely to my own foibles. Your father, may he rest in peace, is not deserving of blame.

If I beseech you to grant me a last request, I do so with full knowledge of my own unworthiness. I shall make my request nonetheless, but for you to understand why you should grant it, I must first report on the task your father assigned me. Did I complete it? Yes. In a manner of speaking, at least.

I fear my words have already become muddled, that I have allowed my thoughts to outpace them as I dictate to the revered brother stationed just outside the cell door. Yet how can I properly gather my thoughts here, in the condition I am now in? I can only endeavor to do the best I can, and beg your indulgence for those moments when I fail.

I shall begin at the beginning. Would you believe I knew nothing of the tapestry, my Lord, until I was called into your father's presence and commanded to tell him what I saw? I was puzzled by this request, and confused above all at being addressed by your father. I suppose had I not been the guard on duty that night any guard would have served just as well. I shifted the shaft of my halberd from one hand to the other, peered in the direction your father gestured at the curtain-like stretch of fabric that ran along the wall behind him.

"A tapestry, my Lord," I said to him.

"Of course it's a tapestry," your father said, disgusted. He turned to his advisor, stationed just beside the throne. The simplicity of the advisor's robes were belied by the ornate gold rings encrusting his fingers. "Can you believe this fellow?" your father said.

"He is but a guard, my Lord," his advisor said. "What can one expect from him?"

Your father turned back to me. "What I was asking was: What images do you see rendered within?"

I frowned and asked your father's leave to move closer. With a wave of a hand your father gave me leave. I stepped forward, looked more carefully at the tapestry.

At first I felt there was nothing to see, that the tapestry was a mere gray, featureless expanse. But then, as I stared, I began to see something more, a pattern beginning to arise. I noticed a lone strand of silk dyed red and I followed it with my eyes, saw how it wound subtly through the weave, all but invisible, like a rivulet of blood glimpsed from a great distance. Then I began to make out many shadings to the gray that I had originally construed to be strictly one color. Suddenly, I perceived the tapestry to be separated into three distinct scenes.

I stepped closer to the first scene and squinted. And then, abruptly, details began to emerge. It was an odd sensation, as if the tapestry were only organizing itself into an image under my gaze. I sharply drew in my breath.

"There!" your father said, eagerly. "What is it? What do you see?"

"I see the castle," I said. "Drawbridge raised, battlements deserted..."

"Yes," your father said. "Go on."

"There are letters in the sky above, but I am not schooled in reading."

"Don't concern yourself with those. Go on," said the king again, impatiently.

"A knight comes from a distance, through a waste, approaching those gates."

"You shall be that knight," your father said. The advisor beside him frowned.

"My Lord?" I said, and then I took a closer look at the knight and saw his face did indeed resemble mine. I tried not to reveal my surprise.

"Continue," he said.

The longer I looked, the clearer it became that this knight *was* me. "There's nothing more here," I said.

"Well then," your father said. "Proceed to the next scene."

I stepped to the next scene and examined it. It showed the inside of an underground chamber, manmade, the knight hesitating on the edge of it. I saw, awaiting the knight, a figure I had never seen before: an unnatural creature, a monster. It had no head, yet still stood erect, as if alive. An eye adorned each shoulder, sunk into the muscle but gazing balefully out of the tapestry. The middle of its chest was split by a mouth running from nipple to nipple.

I told your father what I saw. "You see?" he said to his advisor. "A blemmyae. The fellow sees it too. He *is* the knight." He said to me: "What else?"

"That is all, my Lord," I claimed.

It was not all. But what I saw I did not feel it wise to share with him, my Lord. Instead, for what I felt to be my own safety, I lied. Or, rather, told only a portion of the truth.

What I did not dare mention was that this monster, this blemmyae, held by the hair the severed crowned head of a king. A head which, quite remarkably, resembled your father's.

I remember your father stared at me for a long time. *Perhaps you too have glimpsed this image of your own decapitated head,* I thought at the time.

But he said nothing of this, instead shooing me along to the last scene. "What do you see?"

Here was the throne room of the castle. Piled in the room's center was a heap of treasure. The knight stood with his back to the viewer, framed in the doorway, hesitant to enter.

"Treasure, yes," said the king. "Wealth beyond measure."

"Yes, my Lord."

"Tell me," your father said, tapping a finger against his lips. "Does the image in the tapestry suggest what will happen once the knight enters this treasure room?"

"It does not, my Lord."

"It leaves the story unfinished," he said. "Go to the end of the tapestry," he said. "Examine the edge. Tell me what you see."

I walked to the end of the tapestry and felt along the edge. It was frayed, irregular.

"It has been cut, my Lord."

He nodded. "There is more to this story," he said. "There is an ending scene. We do not know what it depicts. But you, my knight-to-be, shall live it and find out."

And so it began. Your father stood and bade his advisor hand him an ornamental sword, and with this he knighted me. He commanded me to go forth, to search far and wide until I had found the castle depicted in the tapestry. This was, I confess, a command that I felt held a secret trap or trick. I was so sure that he had not said what he had said that I respectfully begged him to repeat it.

"Are you sure he's the man, my Lord?" asked the advisor. "He seems a bit dimwitted."

But the king, with a shake of the head, simply repeated what he had said. "Find the castle," he said, "kill the guardian, and bring the treasure back to me." He gestured to the tapestry. "Finish the story."

"No matter the consequences?" I asked.

"No matter the consequences."

I bowed deeply, my head spinning, and prepared to withdraw. Before I could, your father asked, "Do you know how to kill him?"

For a brief moment, I was unsure what he meant.

"Pardon, my Lord?"

Your father laughed. "How can you expect a pardon before I know what crime you have committed?"

"My Lord, I…"

But he waved me into silence. "A little joke," he said. "And not a particularly good one. I meant the fellow holding the lantern. The—" he turned to his advisor, who whispered to him the word he had forgotten "—blemmyae. Do you know how to kill him?"

I was so shocked that he believed the severed head of a king to be a lantern that I could not trust my own voice. I shook my head.

"Stab its eyes out first," your father advised me. "This will make it harder for it to find you. Above all, don't let it take hold of you. A creature like that is surely strong enough to tear a man's head from his body."

If you are the sort of royal child who grew up hearing tales of brave knights and perilous quests and glorious treasures—and what other sort of royal child is there, truly?—I suppose that you have expectations for how things went for me. Perhaps I wandered far and wide through the kingdom without success, then far and wide through neighboring kingdoms, spiraling further and further away from here until, at last, in the depths of despair and at the end of my strength, I found the enchanted castle at last. Or perhaps I aided a traveler on the road who proved in fact to be no ordinary traveler but a magical being in disguise. You know the stories, no doubt, far better than I. They seem to me, unlettered though I am, to always involve nearly insurmountable difficulties which are nonetheless surmounted in a way that makes the completion of the quest, when finally achieved, all the sweeter.

But it was not like that for me. I found the castle almost immediately, because it was this very castle. I had only to ride out through the gate and turn and look back to confirm that, yes, your father's castle was exactly the castle I had seen in the tapestry. Indeed, when your father had asked what I saw, I had told him *I see the castle,* by which I meant *your castle, the castle we are standing in.* But he did not perceive the castle in the tapestry to be his own. How was it, I wondered, that he could not connect the one with the other?

I have asked myself that same question many times since, while sitting here in darkness. Perhaps your father was enchanted. Or perhaps it was as simple as inattention on his part. A king has the luxury not to notice things, particularly if, like your father, he only traveled outside when safely enclosed in the royal box. Or perhaps it was even simpler: he did not want to see. That, too, is a luxury reserved for the powerful by those who surround them.

In any case, I confirmed that it was indeed the same castle. And then I wondered what I should do next. Should I leave and pretend to look for the castle I had already found, perhaps never to return? Should I return to the throne room immediately and explain to the king what he had not noticed about the castle in the tapestry and risk losing my life?

I did neither of those things. Instead, I dismounted and walked back toward the gates, just as the knight on the tapestry had done. I supposed I half-expected a blemmyae to appear, but nothing happened, nothing at all. I walked toward the castle, and then I entered, and then I stood in the courtyard, unsure of where to go or what to do.

In the end, instead of going to see the king I followed the advice of the second scene and descended into the vaults below the castle. I was not sure what I would find there, but I felt an impulse drawing me toward the door leading down and I gave into it. I took a torch from the box near the door and lit it off of the torch in the wall sconce, and then went down the dark, musty stairs.

I descended without seeing a soul, hearing only my own echoing footsteps and the sound of the torch. The first floor of the vaults was filled with hogsheads of beer, casks of wine, dry stores. The floors were thick with dust, with cleaner paths tracked through where servants had come and gone. The air smelled sour. I heard the scurrying of mice as they hid, the hissing of the torch, nothing more. In the back of the storerooms I found an iron-banded door. It was locked, but the key had been left in the lock on this side. It was nothing to turn it and go through.

The staircase hidden behind the door was narrower, descending in a dizzying spiral. As I descended, the air grew cold and the rock of the walls became slick with moisture and moss. I went down and down, starting to feel slightly confused.

When at last the stairs ended, I found myself at the beginning of a hallway. I stepped into it and saw that it was lined with cells, a dozen or so on either side. I walked forward, and saw that the cells were unlocked and, for all intents and purposes unoccupied. Some were bare, others had only a collection of mildewed straw and scattered bones. This proved to be the case with every cell except the last.

In that cell was a body. It lay on the floor, upon a heap of sodden straw. It was missing its head. It was, I saw, recently dead: it had not yet begun to rot.

Holding the torch high above my head, I stepped closer to get a better look.

At that moment, the body began to move. The skin of its shoulder suddenly seemed to tear apart and I saw a gleam there, on first one shoulder then on both, that it took me a moment to realize were eyes. The body sat up. "Ah," the mouth in the chest said, in a strange, thick voice. "You've finally come."

Even though I had seen the tapestry and had from it a sense of what the blemmyae looked like, to see it in person was almost too much to bear. My mouth grew dry, and I could not catch my breath. My eyes did not know where to settle, and kept moving again and again from eye to eye to missing head and back around. It made me dizzy to even look at him. The creature looked at once wrong, deformed, but also somehow simultaneously right, as if it occupied this body in exactly the way the body was meant to be occupied, and it could not be otherwise.

"How can you exist?" I couldn't help but ask.

He came a little closer to the bars. "I haven't always been like this," he said. "Once I was like you."

"What happened?" I asked.

He chose not to answer this question.

"How long have you been here?" I tried.

"A very long time," he claimed. "Many, many years."

"What do you eat? How have you survived?"

He shook his head. "You seem to believe this is an ordinary place, but it is anything but ordinary. You have seen the tapestry?"

I nodded. In looking at him, my gaze fled from the eye on one shoulder to the eye on the other and back again.

"But not the fourth scene."

"Not the fourth scene," I confirmed.

The mouth in his chest smiled. "I didn't see it either. Can you imagine what that fourth scene might depict?"

I hesitated. I did not know for certain, but I had some idea because of the royal head the blemmyae had been carrying in the tapestry. I gave a short, reluctant nod. I could, at very least, imagine it.

"Good," he said. "I will tell you now, there is no fighting against fate. I tried, and perhaps you will try too. But even if you do you will not escape your fate."

"You want me to release you so that you can kill the king," I said.

"In a manner of speaking."

"I will not release you."

"In the end you won't be able to help it. It is your fate. Just as it was my own."

I shook my head. I was turning to go, when he sprang with unnatural speed to the bars of his cell, thrusting his arm through and grabbing my wrist. His grip was tight as iron and though I tried, I could not break it. I dropped the torch on the floor and tried desperately to draw my sword, but before I could manage it something began to change.

I do not know how to describe it exactly, except to say that I felt myself leaking out of my own body and into the fingers of his hand. At the same time, I felt something surging up in my mind, growing stronger and stronger and taking form, taking shape, crowding me out, and suddenly I realized it was him. For a moment I could not move, and then it was as if I was looking through two sets of eyes at once: I was looking through my own eyes at the creature grabbing my wrist, and looking too at myself through the creature's eyes. My body felt wrong, unfamiliar and familiar at once, as if I suddenly the accord body and mind had had no longer exists. I saw my own arm try to break free and felt it, but felt too that I was not the one moving it. When I did make an effort to move it, I was terrified to see that the arm of the creature moved instead. It was disconcerting and confusing, and it left me effectively paralyzed.

And then I blinked and the doubled vision was gone. I was once again seeing with only one set of eyes, the pair belonging to the blemmyae in the cell.

I watched my body as it stood outside the cell and pried the fingers of the stunned blemmyae, my fingers now, off its wrist. And then it stepped back out of reach.

"I'm sorry about this," he was saying through my body's mouth. "If I could change our fate, I would. I will, however, do more for you than was done for me. I will leave the iron-banded door above open. Perhaps someone will find and release you."

And then my body's mouth smiled and my body left, taking the torch with it, leaving me in darkness while it went to decapitate the king.

That is, largely, my part of the story. I gather from the questions the reverend brother posed to me that he did just as promised, that he went upstairs and decapitated not just the king but his advisor and guards too, then opened the key to the treasure vaults and removed what he wanted, and then left. You will not see him again. He did keep his promise and left the door open which is why, eventually, I was found. And, because of the images on the tapestry, blamed for your father's death.

What did that missing fourth scene depict? I cannot say for certain, but permit me to speculate. It could be one of two things. If I had to guess, I would say it depicts the very cell I now occupy. A knight stands outside of it, his face contorted with pain, while a strange, headless creature within the cell grabs his wrist. The ghost of the knight overlaps the figure of the blemmyae and the ghost of the blemmyae overlaps that of the knight.

But there is another possibility, a distant one. I did not think to examine the leftmost edge of the tapestry, not being encouraged by your father to do so, but I wonder if I were to examine it now, if I would find that it was frayed as the rightmost edge. Perhaps there is no missing scene, and the tapestry was meant to be hung somehow in a circle, its edges touching, with the third panel leading again into the first, making one eternal round.

The reverend brother who records this has told me of the whispered story, long disbelieved, of how your great-grandfather was killed by a blemmyae, and of how this creature was locked in the vaults below the castle until, abruptly, he vanished. Perhaps that was why your father became so excited when the tapestry came into his possession. Might I ask: Where did he procure that tapestry? I imagine that that too will be difficult to trace, that in the end it will seem as if it happened almost by magic. Soon, if it hasn't happened already, the tapestry will vanish as mysteriously as it first appeared and only reappear later, when it is again needed.

My Lord, a blemmyae killed your father, but he was dressed in the skin of a man, dressed in the skin I used to wear. This skin I now wear is not who I really am. If you execute me, you will be killing an innocent man.

But even if you execute me, I am certain after the axe descends I will find myself back here, in this cell, somehow alive. I will remain imprisoned here for decades, surviving somehow without eating or drinking, until you are dead, until your son and heir is grown and has had a son of his own, until what happened to your father has largely become legend. And then one day the tapestry will reappear and soon after a knight will be chosen and will make his way down here and the cycle will begin all over again.

Break the curse, my Lord, release me. Open this cell and let me go free. I will be of no bother to you. I will go far, far away. I will leave the confines of civilization and live as a creature free and wild. If God is merciful—and of this I fear I have my doubts—the magic that is in the tapestry will not be enough to reach me and bring me back. I beseech you: help me replace that imagined fourth scene with another.

Or if this message falls upon deaf ears, as it almost certainly is sure to do, do one thing for me: read this record to your son every year upon his birthday. Let him know his fate early so he and whoever the next knight will be might somehow avoid it. He does not have me to fear: he has only the tapestry to fear.

But I doubt if, comfortably ensconced in your own notion of what the world is, you will concede even that. In which case, when the time comes, I shall look forward to meeting your son. As I take what fate has allotted me, I promise you, my Lord, that I shall do my best to make his demise painless.

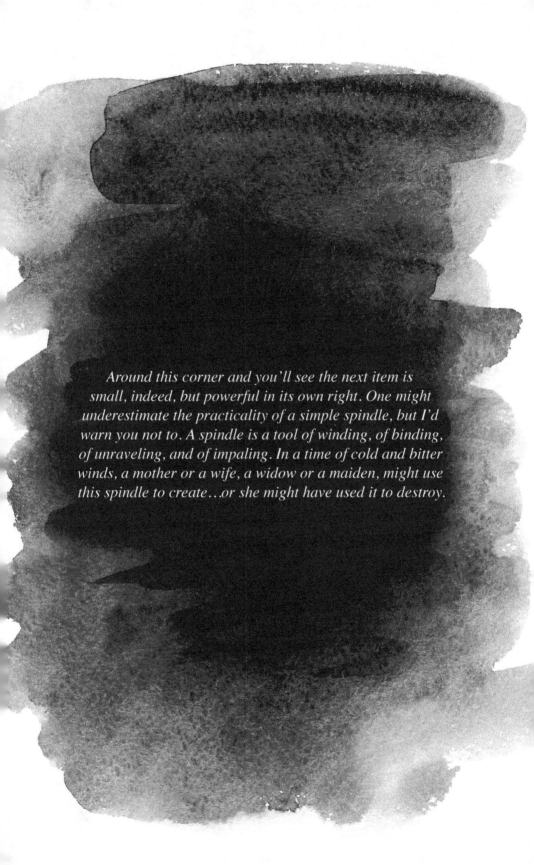

Around this corner and you'll see the next item is small, indeed, but powerful in its own right. One might underestimate the practicality of a simple spindle, but I'd warn you not to. A spindle is a tool of winding, of binding, of unraveling, and of impaling. In a time of cold and bitter winds, a mother or a wife, a widow or a maiden, might use this spindle to create…or she might have used it to destroy.

WHITE OWL

Stevie Edwards

Our story begins in a small town outside Regensberg, known to those around it as the most obedient place this side of the Stone Bridge. The husbands woke before sunrise and worked hard throughout the day, traveling up and down the Danube to provide the surrounding towns with fresh meat, crisp fruit wines, and new shoes on their feet. The wives worked hard tending to their homes, ensuring all was cleaned and the dinner made for when their husbands returned. The children played and filled the town with joyous sounds, but also knew when to be quiet and to do their chores. They were God-fearing people, which meant that they were free.

No one spoke out of turn. No one missed daily service. The men did what God asked of them and the wives did what the men asked. Especially during the town's most celebrated time of the year: Epiphany. A time to celebrate the joining of God and Jesus, and the destiny that awaits all who believe.

Oda was a good wife, a devoted mother, and a revered baker. Every year, her family was given the honor of providing the town's tortell. She'd spent the week hunched over the hearth, mixing the fresh flour and creating the cake, delicately hiding the small Christ figurine her son had crafted deep within its center. It was evening now, and she had stolen away to the moor behind the town to be alone. The wind whipped into her face, and she pulled her cloak tighter, smiling out at the glistening snow atop the rusty green and brown peat and taking a long breath of cool air, gooseflesh erupting across her skin. On this evening, the women and girls were expected to line the streets of their small town and watch over the parade that marked the countdown to Epiphany. And Oda had done her duty, had huddled with her friends along the dirt path. But as the parade started and the hustle-and-bustle enraptured the crowd, she took her moment to duck away, as she often did, to have a moment for herself, in the crisp, clean air of the moor that lay only a few yards behind her home.

A warm, yellow light shone out of the back window of her home across the grass where her husband and his friends shared glasses of wassail. The sounds of laughter and the raucous parade drifted around her but did not shake her from the drunkenness of her own surroundings. The snow had begun falling faster and enveloped her in a white blanket. She was enraptured by winter's beauty, so much so that it was not until she heard a twig snap behind her that she realized she was not alone.

Oda turned around quickly, and her gooseflesh returned.

A masked figure hovered behind her, menacing and unmoving. The falling snow changed from peaceful to violent, catching in her eyelashes and making it hard for her to see. Her frantic wipes of her eyes were futile and with every swipe, whatever was in front of her loomed closer.

Oda knew she had been caught. And now He had sent for her. Her whole body shook uncontrollably; the fear wrapped around her and choked her like a vice. She begged and pleaded, promising that she was just taking a walk and not practicing again. But it was all for nothing, for she always knew that this face would be the last she would ever see.

The monstrous figure lunged towards Oda with a childish roar and began to tickle her. The monster removed its mask and became nothing but a boy. Oda's boy.

The Parade of Perchta's Boys, they called it.

She had worked for weeks on end crafting the intricate mask for her son to wear. He had loved it so much that he had been wearing it to bed every night. How could she not have recognized him?

Her son broke out into laughter as he pulled his mask back on. She laughed nervously with him, and as she watched him run back toward the road, disappearing in the snowy landscape and rejoining his friends in the parade, she hoped that he did not tell his father where he had seen her tonight.

She took this as a sign to return, sticking her tongue out and catching a few final flakes of snow on her walk back. Her body was bathed in cold sweat, and she shivered in the cool wind, trying to slow her breathing and compose herself before joining the crowd. The warm glow coming from her home where her husband had been minutes ago had gone dark, which put some urgency into her step. She knew if he caught her out here, he would not be as easily assuaged as her son. He would assume the worst, and she would bear the full weight of those assumptions.

When she reached the edge of her home, she felt a similar presence behind her again. Her arms went up in feigned terror, in an attempt to play a more active role in her son's game. She turned around dramatically, pressing her back against the timber frame and raising her hands in mock fear. The same mask looked back at her again but, for a moment, she thought the figure seemed a bit taller than before. Adrenaline coursed through her body, and she looked around for an escape, cursing herself for backing into a corner. But the figure seemed to loom all around her, suffocating her with its presence.

The moor was quiet. Empty. And the noises of the parade would drown out any screams.

Something glinted in the moonlight out of the corner of her eye, and the figure began to speak.

"I have been sent for you,
 for you have not been true.
And for the God you forsake,
Your life I soon shall take."

The monster reached for the glinting object as Oda's fear became real. Before she had a chance to move, the long blade pressed her harder into the wall. Her eyes met the deep sockets of the figure, and recognition flashed on her face as the blade slashed across her stomach. She dropped to her knees, clutching the gash in her skin and trying to keep herself from spilling out onto the ground like a basket piled too high with bread, the steaming heat of the entrails enveloping her like a wet, warm hug.

As the figure walked away, Oda did not dare to scream for help. Instead, she prayed one last time, to a God who was no longer listening, in hopes that she would be long dead before her disgrace was discovered. The last thing she heard was the flapping of wings and a shrill, pained shriek.

Bertina squirmed, feeling waves of heat wash over her even though it was January. After Sunday service, the men and women separated outside the church and spoke about what a great sermon it had been, how sad it was that Oda was gone, and that there was nothing they could have done to save her from her proclivities towards paganism. Bertina smiled and nodded, amazed at how quickly Oda's former friends turned on her.

"My husband never trusted her," said one of the townswomen.

"Mine refused to let me seek her help and I am certainly glad I listened to him," said another.

No matter what they said, Bertina knew that Oda had helped them all at one point or another. Women in the town were quick to ask her to cure their sick baby or to bless their crops. Even Bertina had gone to her for help, and she remembered the time fondly. She sought her and shared her most shameful secret: her inability to conceive a child. Oda welcomed her with open arms and, after a couple months of mugwort and late-night trips to the moor, told her that her problem was not in her body but in her mind. Bertina knew that she was right. After only a short time together, Oda had exposed a truth long hidden, buried deep within the recesses of her soul since the eve of her thirteenth birthday. She had barely begun to bleed before her father arranged for her to be married, spending all that he had saved to give her a good life. Bertina loved her father too much to say no and, later, feared her husband too much to say the same. After that revelation, Oda and Bertina became treasured friends bonded through their secrets, and spent many nights together crying, laughing, and, for a few small moments, safe in each other's arms.

"How quickly you all forget what Oda has done for you," Bertina started, looking each woman in the eye as she continued. "She was selflessly devoted to taking care of her husband and children."

A silence washed over the group.

"And do you not remember how she baked bread and handed it out to those less fortunate than her, even though she barely had anything herself?"

The silence grew deeper, the women looked downcast. None of them, including Bertina, noticed that the men had also grown quiet as well.

"Out of all of us, it does not make sense that a monster who punishes the lazy would murder one of the most hardworking women in the town!"

Her husband's large hand suddenly clamped around her wrist.

"Time for us to go home."

Later that night, Bertina wrapped her cloak around her battered body and walked the length of the moor, stopping as she spotted a beautiful white owl perched on a fence post. The owl seemed to be looking right into her eyes, beckoning her to come closer. The gaze felt familiar, so she approached tentatively, and when the owl did not fly away, she reached out and touched it.

It was now the eve of Epiphany, and Bertina's house was bustling. Much of the town was gathered in her home and her husband sat in a chair in front of the hearth, surrounded by a circle of enraptured children. He was telling them the story of the Witch.

He told them that she was at least eight feet tall, disgustingly ugly, and had one absurdly large foot, a foot so large that it would distract you while she pulled out the knife that was hidden under her skirt. If you were a bad person who did not obey orders and live a good Christian life, she would slit open your belly, eating your entrails and stuffing you full of straw. But if you were good, she would only visit you while you slept, leaving a silver coin in your shoe as a reward and a reminder that she was always watching.

There was a pang in Bertina's chest as she watched her husband interact with the group who looked upon him like he was their king. She knew that the night would not only remind him how badly he wanted to be a father but how she was to blame for this shortcoming.

Near the end of the story, he stood up and growled, playfully tackling one of the kids to the ground.

"I have been sent for you,
for you have not been true.
And for the God you forsake,
your life I soon shall take."

Hearing the rhyme, the kids all screamed and laughed, running away as her husband chased them around the room, repeating the phrase over and over. She balked at the show being put on in front of her and remembered a story her mother had told her on the eve of her marriage. That the Witch was once a positive presence, a guardian. But in the hopes of stripping her of her power, the Catholics had taken her name and turned it into something evil and ugly, banishing her to the shadows. Bertina's mother begged her that night not to suffer the same fate. And so far in her marriage, she had let her mother down. So, in that moment, with fear and the anticipation of her husband's wrath coursing through her body, Bertina spoke her mind.

"The Witch does not speak!" she blurted out. "Her voice was stolen from her. You have it all wrong."

The room just continued in its multiple conversations, but her husband's eyes told her that she had been heard while the eyes of the others looked away.

After all their guests had left, her husband led her to their bed.

"Tell me: what else do you know about this witch that I apparently do not?" he asked, but it was not a question meant to be answered. "I bet it was your mother who put that nonsense in your head."

He dug his nails into the skin of her forearm and pushed her downwards.

"I just wish I could have met her. Your mother. So that I could have killed her before she had the chance to give birth to such a disgraceful daughter."

He spat at her, the glob of wet bubbles landing next to her thigh.

"The Witch serves God. Serves *me*. She disposes of those who do not do as they are told, rids the town of their failures." His coarse fingers laced themselves around the neck of her nightgown and yanked hard, popping the buttons at the back. "And need I remind you again that a woman of your age who cannot even manage to give her husband a child deserves to be sliced open and have those worthless organs ripped out of her."

A finger menacingly trailed across her naked stomach.

"If your silent witch does not kill you soon, I will happily do it myself."

Bertina closed her eyes as he lowered himself on top of her and imagined herself as the white owl, flying freely over the snow.

Bertina walked alone outside again, wrapped in her cloak. She wandered mindlessly in the biting night air and eventually found herself standing where Oda's body had been discovered. But she was not alone after all. A figure stood before her, about eight feet tall with a foot slightly larger than the other. They were wearing matted white furs from their neck to their knees, and while their face was not beautiful, it was not scary either. It was an amalgamation of too many features, everything too prominent but blended at the same time. Bertina felt like each time she looked at them, the face changed. But those eyes. Their eyes felt like coming home.

The figure gazed at Bertina softly and sympathetically. They placed their hands on her shoulders, pushing her against the same timber frame that Oda had been butchered against only days before. Their hands moved to her face, lightly tucking her hair behind her ears before moving down to her stomach. Their touch was gentle, apologetic. Bertina should have been scared, but she felt at peace.

The figure placed a hand into their cloak and produced a golden spindle that sparkled like nothing Bertina had ever seen before in her life. It was pristine and incredibly sharp, gleaming like it had never been used. Gripping the circular base, the figure brought the spindle to her stomach and opened her cloak with their other hand. Their eyes locked with Bertina's and almost seemed to be asking for permission for what had to be done. She nodded, accepting her fate, the spindle pushing into her soft skin.

As her stomach began to open, Bertina did not feel any pain. She felt release, like all the things she had been carrying around for so long had now been emptied out. Once the crescent cut was complete, the figure pulled the incision wide, and stuck their hands inside. She looked up to the sky, listening as the figure worked away, pulling out her insides and placing them gently on the ground. Looking down, Bertina watched the figure coil her intestines into a pile, the heat of the organs causing steam to rise from the snow. She kept watching as pieces of herself were removed until there was nothing left but a bloody pink pile at her feet.

Suddenly, the figure began filling her back up. They stuffed stones, sticks, peat, and grass into her gaping hole of a stomach. Every few handfuls, the figure would pick up a section of entrails, sliding their hands along to collect all the blood and viscous fluid to help stick together the natural materials. Their hands smeared one last layer of sticky organic wetness across her stomach, stuffing the materials in tightly. Then, the spindle reappeared, and the figure used it to sew the wound back up, as if nothing had been done at all.

Bertina awoke in her bed, her hands immediately reaching for her stomach. There was nothing there. No trace of the encounter that had felt so vivid in her mind.

Her hands roamed over her bare stomach, her skin soft and firm as before. But if she put pressure in just the right place, she swore she could feel the blades of straw scratching at her from the inside. She had glimpsed freedom in the moment, and now that it turned out not to be true, her life felt heavier than ever.

She went through the motions of the day and accompanied her husband to the feast of Epiphany, but everything felt wrong. She did not want to eat or drink. The women gathered around the table whinnied over her and suggested that she may be a mother yet. She worried that maybe Oda had been mistaken, that her body had betrayed her and opened itself up to her husband's wish.

The laughing around the table felt like daggers in her ears, piercing into her brain and making her squirm. Her eyes kept lingering on the knife beside her plate, and she resisted the urge to grab it and slash herself open, to prove that she was empty. Instead, she cradled her head in her hands, moaning and mumbling to herself. Her husband's threatening hand squeezed her knee, but she brushed it off and stood, pushing her chair back and running out into the night air as the women in the room looked on in sympathy and recognition.

She walked and walked and walked, tears streaming down her face. She found herself at Oda's home and gently pushed open the door, stepped inside and headed to the small cupboard in which Oda hid her supplies. She knew that with all the goading, her husband would be more eager than ever, and she would need something strong to help her survive the night. Opening the cupboard door, she saw Oda's son's mask hung up on the wall and, beside it, another mask, similar in style but a bit larger in size, and much unlike the other, it was caked in dried blood.

She ran to the moor, hoping that what she had just seen was not true. The snow was falling heavily from the sky and adding to her disorientation.

The Witch did not exist, but evil did.

She dropped to her knees, crying out into the openness for the figure from her dream to return.

"Please!" Bertina wailed, her voice getting whipped around her in a snowy frenzy. "I need your help! I need you to be real!"

At that same moment, she felt a presence behind her. She slowly moved to stand up, her arms bracing on each side. But she did not feel the same sense of calm from her dream. Instead, the air was ominously tense, and her labored breathing was deafening in her ears. Suddenly, there was a violent tug on the back of her cloak, wrenching her back up onto her feet. She spun around and found her husband staring at her, anger swirling furiously in his eyes.

"You," he growled, sending her stumbling backwards. "You are an embarrassment. A humiliation. And to act that way in front of the congregation? Unacceptable."

He reached behind his head and pulled down the same mask she had seen only minutes ago, the dried blood seeming to be reinvigorated against the white snow. A long blade gleamed in his other hand and Bertina's chest heaved with sobs and with grief as she stared down the same fate as her friend.

Her husband slashed violently at her stomach, cutting deep inside her. But the sound was wrong, and both paused when they heard it.

Instead of the wet sound of organs and blood, there was just the *thunk* of stones and the quiet rustling of sticks and leaves as the cold wind pulled at what was inside her. She felt small objects cascading over her feet and looked down to see nothing but stone, sticks, peat, and grass spilling out of her wound. Her husband saw it, too, and his face went pale and clammy.

Bertina looked up at him and smiled as the screech of a white owl sounded overhead. The owl appeared, digging its claws into Bertina's husband's shoulders and he cried out in pain. He tried to shake the animal off, but it just dug its talons in deeper. The owl released him and flew into his face, wrapping its talons around his right eye. There was a loud pop, followed by her husband's screams as the owl ripped his eye clean out of the socket, squishing it and dropping it onto his shoulder. As the owl positioned itself to continue its assault, Bertina yelled for it to stop.

The owl paused and flew onto the ground, looking up at Bertina for confirmation. As her husband clutched at the cavernous hole where his eye used to be, the owl transformed, becoming the figure that Bertina knew had been real. The figure produced the golden spindle, and Bertina placed her hands around it, asking silently for permission to use the object that had saved her nights ago. The figure nodded and released the spindle into her hands.

She felt a power she had never felt before, gripping the circular base and walking over to her husband. He tried to run, but she raked the spindle down his back, slicing through skin, muscle, and bone. Her husband fell and tried to sit up, attempting to scurry away from her. Bertina pushed him down and straddled him, making sure he saw her one last time before she plunged the sharp needle into the center of his remaining eye. She pushed and pushed with all her might, burying the object as deep as she could. She then spread her fingers over the eye socket and slowly pulled the spindle back out as creamy liquid covered her hand. She stood, leaving him screaming on the ground, and turned back to join the figure a few yards away.

Bertina handed the spindle back to the figure and thanked them. The figure held Bertina's hand and led her deep into the moor. Once far enough inside, the figure put Bertina back together. They carefully removed the stuffing that had saved her life. Then, they took a jug of water and gently washed the debris from her insides, the two of them never losing eye contact. The water felt cool on her body and she was overwhelmed with the moment, as if the figure was washing away her past and creating her anew. Once they had finished, they took the cloth bag they had been carrying on their back and placed it on the ground, opening it to reveal Bertina's missing parts. The figure replaced them meticulously, putting them back exactly as they had been. Once the job was finished, they sewed her back up, and Bertina finally felt, for the first time in a long time, whole.

The figure sat back, exhausted from the task. They bowed their head and reached out their hand, pointing the way home. Bertina looked at the figure's outstretched hand and grabbed it in her own, pulling it towards her and holding it gently in her lap. The figure smiled and held up their other hand, slowly opening their palm and revealing the spindle, gold and gleaming.

It was an offering.

A chance.

A welcome home.

Bertina returned the figure's smile. Her choice had been made.

A group of children gathered around their grandmother's feet on the Eve of Epiphany, begging her to tell their favorite story. The one about the strong-minded princess, trapped in the castle with the terrifying monster that was everywhere but nowhere at the same time. About the Witch who, on some nights, can still be seen walking in twilight, a golden spindle in her hand and a white owl leading the way.

The grandmother sighed and obliged, settling in her chair and clasping her hands in her lap.

This story begins in a small town outside Regensberg.

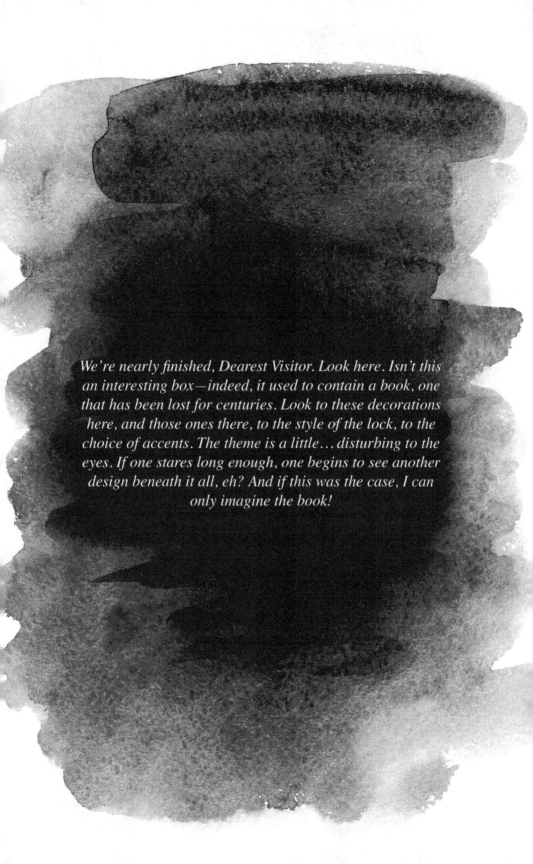

We're nearly finished, Dearest Visitor. Look here. Isn't this an interesting box—indeed, it used to contain a book, one that has been lost for centuries. Look to these decorations here, and those ones there, to the style of the lock, to the choice of accents. The theme is a little…disturbing to the eyes. If one stares long enough, one begins to see another design beneath it all, eh? And if this was the case, I can only imagine the book!

A DARK QUADRIVIUM
David Worn

"In the district of Toulouse a damnable heresy has lately arisen, which, after the nature of a canker, gradually diffusing itself over the neighboring places, hath already infected vast numbers throughout Gascony and other provinces... Wherefore, we command the bishops, and all God's priests resident in those parts, to be vigilant, and to inhibit, under pain of anathema, all persons from sheltering in their territories or presuming to protect the known followers of such heresy."
—Condemnation of the Albigensians at The Council of Tours of 1163.

As soon as William saw the heretics' ancient codex, he knew he had to be the one to decipher it. The book itself was in a poor state; its leather cover had deteriorated, and the cords of its binding had long ago come undone. Were it not for the metal clasps that bound it shut, it would have surely come apart. Sitting at the rear of the room with the abbey's monks, William found his gaze returning again and again to the book and to the strange reliquary in which it had been sealed for unknown centuries.

The interrogation of the Albigensian heretics took place in the relative warmth of the abbey's calefactory. Inside, between two fires, a large table had been arranged for the council members. On the table itself lay the Albigensians' reliquary, its lock broken, and its front panel slid aside to reveal the codex.

The Bishop of Durham, a small, serious man whose talents lay more in diocesan politics than in devotion to the Gospel, served as the mouthpiece of the council. For the first hour of the interrogation, the bishop had questioned the Albigensian captives on their flight from the Languedoc and of the circumstances surrounding their arrival in England. The captives, bound to each other by thick ropes and weak from hunger, gave only the most perfunctory of responses. Seeing that this was getting them nowhere, the bishop turned to the question of the reliquary the Albigensians had traveled with, and specifically, to the nature of the tome that had been locked inside.

"This codex you carry, what is it?" said the bishop, holding the object high in the air for the members of the council to see.

"It's just a book. It has no worth," said the heretics' leader, a man by the name of Gerard de Carcassonne.

"He lies," interjected a heavily accented voice from somewhere behind the council.

William leaned forward to get a better look at the gruff Cistercian abbot who dared interrupt the bishop. He had heard it said that it was this man, the Abbot Henry de Marcy, who had pursued the heretics and their relic from Francia all the way to England. This Francian abbot did not look like any clergyman William had ever met. Far younger than most men of his rank, his robes were dirty and his beard unkempt from weeks of travel. More than that, he exuded a physicality that William found vaguely threatening in a clergyman.

At the head of the council table, the Archbishop of York fixed the abbot with a stern look. "Abbot de Marcy, you are here as a guest to these proceedings. You will refrain from interrupting the council or be removed."

"My apologies, Your Grace. However, he lies. This book is their version of a Bible."

Turning to face the heretics, the bishop asked, "Is this true?"

Gerard said nothing.

"Did you know that your captors at Oxford tried to read it?" asked the bishop. At this, Gerard tensed. "Unfortunately, the Augustinians are better scholars of ale than of ancient texts."

A flicker of laughter passed around the room until the archbishop raised a hand to quiet the assembly.

"However," the bishop continued, "we have among us an ecclesiastical scholar skilled in the sacred languages."

The bishop gestured at William, who approached to retrieve the codex. Handing it to him, the bishop leaned in and said in a low voice, "Find me proof of their heresy so we can get this rotten show over with."

Returning to his seat, William thought that it was true, he was well versed in the ancient languages. However, his true passion was that quadrivium of mathematical arts of the type practiced in the schools at Oxford and Paris. As William studied the codex, the bishop continued to press the heretics' leader on its contents. Lost in the pages, William failed to notice the Abbot de Marcy silently inserting himself into the seat next to him.

"What do you see in there?" the abbot whispered.

"Father Abbot, I do not think it appropriate—"

"Listen, I have tracked these heretics for months only to lose them to your people. You will tell me what it says, or we shall find ourselves in a...*désaccord.*"

"I...I don't yet know," stammered William. "These passages contain scripture, but here, the drawings and panels. They should not be a part of a manuscript this old. And these here," William gestured to another of the pages, "these are astronomical diagrams. Is it not incredible?"

"Father Abbot, the council," whispered the monk who sat beside them. William and the Abbot looked up from the codex to find the bishop glaring at them.

"Let me repeat the question," said the bishop. "Does the book contain heresy?"

"My Lord, I will need more time. However, I can tell you this. The codex is...very old. Five hundred years at the least. Curiously, it's written in several languages. Latin, Greek, Aramaic, some Hebrew. Some passages appear to be extracts from the Greek New Testament. Also, there's something else that's quite interesting."

"Yes?" The bishop leaned forward.

"It's illuminated."

From the council table, the Bishop of Worcester, a man whose girth suggested that he enjoyed peasant tithes perhaps more than others, slammed his large, hairy fist against the table. "This is a waste of time! So what if it's illuminated? All of my damned books have little pictures in them."

"My Lord," began William, "manuscripts of this age are never illuminated. That invention came later."

"Bah. Enough of all this talk. Torture them already!" replied the Bishop of Worcester.

At the front of the assembly, the Bishop of Durham sighed and turned to the archbishop, who nodded his assent. From the fire by the council table, the bishop retrieved a glowing hot iron and approached an elderly Albigensian man, frail and thin from weeks in captivity. Gerard betrayed no emotion as the bishop raised the implement toward the captive's forehead. Unable to escape, the old man whimpered.

A frightened young man stepped forward. "Stop! I'll tell you what you want."

"No!" cried Gerard.

The bishop lowered the iron. "Speak boy. What is this book?"

"It's called the *Codex Primis*. Gerard says it is forbidden to read it. We had to get it out of Carcassonne."

"Why?" asked the bishop.

"The Cistercians have been trying to get the Franks to invade our cities. We had to get the codex away. Its existence is proof of…"

"Proof of what?"

The boy looked to Gerard for help, no longer certain that this was the right course. However, Gerard's gaze was fixed on William and the codex. A bead of sweat slowly dripped down his brow.

The bishop, growing impatient, approached the elderly man again, bringing the hot iron within inches of his face. The man appeared too despondent to resist and merely closed his eyes. The young Albigensian spoke again, more frantically this time.

"It proves that your church is wrong, and your god is a false one!"

"Blasphemy!" exclaimed the Bishop of Worcester.

Paying him no heed, the bishop bade the boy continue.

"I swear I know nothing more. We never even had the key to the reliquary lock!"

In the silence that followed, William looked up from the book and spoke.

"Your Grace, My Lords, if I may. I've been examining more of the pages. It is a most peculiar manuscript. There are diagrams and symbols alongside the scripture. Some of it appears to be a kind of arithmetic. I would be able to give you a better account if I could bring the codex to the abbey library and compare it with the books there."

The bishop dismissed him with a wave, no longer needing him now that the boy had provided evidence of the group's heretical beliefs.

As William rose to leave, Gerard surged forward, straining against his bonds.

"Do not translate that book!" He turned from William to face the archbishop. "Your Grace, I beg of you. The codex is dangerous. Reading it opens your thoughts to—"

Gerard saw the scorn and disbelief painted on the faces of the council.

"You fools! You don't understand. Your gospels and catechisms are all backwards. The God of Good did not create this world. He cares not for us. It is the Children of the God of the Dark that are our true creators. They are here now, listening. Always beside us, hiding between moments—in the smallest parts of it! They await only for one of us foolish enough to light the path."

The Bishop of Worcester stared at Gerard, his mouth agape, but this time it was the archbishop himself who cried out, "Enough! I have heard enough of this blasphemy. Members of the council, it is time to decide the fate of these Albigensians."

Around him the council members gathered. After several minutes of agitated discussion, the bishop turned towards Gerard and proclaimed:

"It is the decree of this council, convocated by order of the Archbishop of Canterbury on this day of January the 22nd in this year of Our Lord 1166 that you, the people known as the Albigenses, have testified as to your faith and are pronounced and adjudged to be heretics. This conviction we make upon the authority of the Gospel and the New Testament, for is it not said in Galatians 'If any man preach any other Gospel unto you than that ye have received, let him be accursed'?"

The bishop smiled at the captives. "Therefore, as punishment, you are to receive the brand of heretic upon your forehead, whereupon you will be banished from these lands by which means as to be decided by our will and pleasure."

Finally alone with the strange Albigensian codex, William was momentarily unsure where to begin. Carefully placing the broken reliquary on a desk, he took his lamp and examined the shelves and display cases of the abbey's library. He was impressed; he had not expected the Cistercian's abbey to have acquired a collection of such breadth. Among their books he found Nichomachus's *Introduction to Arithmetic* in the original Greek, a copy of Euclid's *Elements,* and three of the five volumes of Adelard of Bath's translation of the great Algorithmi's *Totum Quadrivium.* For the codex's biblical passages, he was surprised to find a copy of the famed *Codex Alexandrinus* containing the oldest recording of the Greek Old and New Testaments. This book, as befitting its rarity, was chained to a display case. Rather than walk back and forth, William pushed his desk next to the case, the screeching sound of wood on stone echoing off the library walls. He paused momentarily, listening to see if anyone had been stirred by the noise. Satisfied that the abbey still slept, he sat at the desk, slid back the front panel and removed the heretics' codex from the reliquary. With the binding long since undone, he had no way of knowing if the loose pages were in any sort of order. Spreading them out across the desk, he began to study them.

Like many of his fellow scholars at the priory, William had joined the clergy for the opportunities it provided to engage in higher forms of learning. Unlike Oxford, Yorkshire did not have schools that operated outside of the Church, and so his knowledge of the languages of the ancient world stemmed primarily from his ecclesiastical studies. Nevertheless, over the years he had grown into something of a local authority on the quadrivium of mathematical arts, particularly those of arithmetic and geometry. And so, he had been confident that little in the heretics' ancient codex would be beyond his ken.

Reading through the loose pages of vellum, he found himself unsettled by their contents. Some pages contained scripture lifted straight from the Greek New Testament. However, comparing these to their twin in the *Codex Alexandrinus,* William found subtle differences in word use. Together, these variations compounded so that entire verses could be seen as casting doubt on the divinity of Christ and of the virgin birth.

On other pages, he found passages with no equal in the sacred texts he was familiar with and therefore must have originated from the Albigensians themselves or some precursor sect. Several of these were disturbing to read for they contested the most basic doctrines of the Church such as the omnipotence of God or the necessity of baptism. Despite his attempt at scholarly detachment, he found himself racing through these passages. Next, he came upon a set of pages devoted to the quadrivium. He smiled to himself as he read these. This mixture of scripture and natural philosophy was unlike anything he'd ever read. He thought of the nascent schools in Oxford and wondered if the insights gleaned from this manuscript could be a means of joining their ranks. Of finally leaving the priory.

As he continued to study the codex, he began to notice formulae and strange diagrams hidden in some of the illustrations and decorative panels. At other times, the calligraphic ornamentation itself appeared to hide sequences of numbers and arithmetic symbols. As he transcribed these, he occasionally paused to consult another book, troubled by the implications of what he was finding. Not because of the language, for he understood the Greek numerical system that was represented here and was able to decipher the occasional Aramaic numbers. Instead, it was the sheer complexity of the operations alluded to in the diagrams and script.

For example, on one such page he found an illustration of a red robed figure holding a staff that terminated in an exquisite drawing of an armillary sphere. The sphere itself was of astounding complexity, its rings—meticulously rendered in gold leaf—glinted in the flickering lamplight. The figure's expressionless eyes looked upon a particular ring of the sphere and, angling the book to get a better view, William noticed something different about the ring. In it, he observed concealed writing that was only revealed when held at just the right angle to the light. William gasped in amazement at the discovery. For in this ring, he found equations and formulae describing astronomical calculations that simply could not have existed when the codex was written.

He found similar formulae hidden in other illustrations, and on each page, a red robed figure, the direction of its gaze a clue for where to look. It was almost as if the figures were lighting a path intended just for him. So many of these new insights went beyond the geometry of Euclid, the arithmetic of the Algorists, or even the new algebra of the Arabs. William's pulse quickened as he examined his notes, the pieces sliding into place. And in the unconscious darkness at the back of his mind, a new quadrivium was beginning to take form.

As the night wore on, William continued to toil at deciphering the manuscript. Having already absorbed every one of its pages, he returned to the beginning of the codex and read again. It was during this second reading that he noticed something strange: a string of new passages. At first, he assumed that he must have missed these during his first reading. However, as the number of unfamiliar passages grew, he slowly realized that it was the pages themselves that had changed.

Examining these altered pages, he found entirely new sections and drawings. Among these, were a series of detailed illustrations of bodily organs and tissues, something he knew of only in words from having once read Galen's *On the Usefulness of the Parts of the Body*. These disturbed him. Illustrations of the interior of the body were forbidden by the Church and witnessing them in this manner, labeled and meticulously drawn, made him keenly aware of the corporeal fragility of his own body. He felt himself not as a body inhabited by a divine soul, but as a wet, gurgling mass of blood and viscera. He hastened to turn the page.

On the next set of pages, he found passages dealing with the Albigensians' creation myths and their system of heretical dualism, believing in both a Good God and an Evil one. More exciting than these, however, were a series of new images, at once more beautiful and more unsettling than the blood-red figures that came before.

The new illustrations were unlike anything he'd ever seen. The evident skill and technique was far beyond even the greatest illuminations of the Markyate Psalter or of the Lichfield Gospels. In contrast to the restless style of art that was common in the manuscripts produced at Canterbury and Winchester, the figures in these drawings stood motionless. However, they were far from lifeless. The shadows along their faces produced an impression of depth and curvature that was so strong, that William felt he could reach out and caress them. In each image, the shadows combined to create a perception of inky depth that he'd never hithertofore thought possible. The buildings and landscapes were unprecedented, their scale shrinking towards the distance, racing to reach some unseen terminus. The intuitive understanding of geometry that must be necessary to produce these masterpieces left William humbled and awestruck. He could fall into these landscapes; such was the illusion created by the darkening shadows and steady contraction of objects towards the horizon. Not that he ever would, for with a mounting sense of dread, he began to piece together the meaning of the drawings whose technique had distracted him.

William was no stranger to the darker side of religious scripture. The Book of Revelation, the Gospel of Nicodemus, the various apocrypha. Descriptions of hell and of those below, none of these were new to him. Nevertheless, the scene depicted in the illumination sent a shiver down his spine. Muted landscapes dotted by tenebrous caverns and the ruins of acropoleis. Dark brown clouds, as those born of a great fire, billowing above stark windowless citadels that reached towards the horizon. All of it bathed in geometric planes of shadows. And in the towers and parapets stood the same red-robed figures as before, only now no longer locked to a single plane, but alive with depth. However, it was not these figures that had filled William with dread, but the children. Spilling from the shadows, in every part of the illumination, were small children. Or so they appeared at first glance, but William perceived that the proportions were all wrong; they were more like those of fully grown men than of children. In some parts of the image, the children gathered in a semicircle around a number of more adult forms. Forcing himself to look more closely, he winced in disgust as he ascertained the nature of the transgressive acts that were being committed. They were ripping women and men apart. In one section, a group of them could be seen placing dismembered heads into large fleshy sacs as others gathered limbs and torsos in enormous carts. His mind recoiled at the savagery. He was about to turn the page when something about the ruined bodies stayed his hand. The heads...their eyes closed as if asleep, the expression upon their faces, not tortured, but blank. William thought back to what the Albigensian leader had said at the interrogation. That man was created not by God, but by the Children. He understood now. The children in the scene weren't dismembering the bodies but... assembling them. Joining the parts together. A genesis without God.

For the first time that night, William realized that the codex might be dangerous. He looked at his notes and considered stopping. What he had learned was enough. He was gathering up the pages when, underneath the illuminations, on a half-covered page, a strange series of lines caught his eye. No, not strange at all. A musical stave with neumes as for a chant! He lifted the page and beneath it he found more musical notations, then a series of new arithmetic diagrams. A table of multiplication, not for Roman numerals as would be expected, but for Arabic ones. Descriptions of unknown astronomical calculations. A set of geometric axioms so advanced he only half understood them. These segments of the quadrivium lured him back to the codex, the unsettling illumination of moments ago, forgotten in the thrill of discovery.

As William continued to work back and forth through the manuscript, the transformations no longer hid from him. New layers of text came into focus beneath the old. Different languages superimposed upon one another. He drew himself closer to the book, his fear forgotten, marveling at what he saw. Greek upon Latin upon Hebrew and Arabic all appearing on the page.

And underneath it all, another language like nothing he'd ever seen. Symbols and ideograms fused together in shapes that spiraled before him. At first, indecipherable, then, slowly...his mind opened. A language of transformation! So beautiful. Each symbol describing a semiotic flow through which a single meaning could be transformed into dozens—no hundreds of new thoughts! Compared to this, the languages of men were so limited. And so too must be their minds. But this...this *primis scriptum*.

This was truth.

And it was his alone. Sitting up, William felt a strength flowing from this knowledge. His hands no longer trembled. If his stomach quivered, it was in excitement and not apprehension.

Through the language he learned to think in new ways. He began to see the world as space. Everything in it existing at some definite position. The movement of things merely an illusion necessary for the broken minds of men, incapable as they were of perceiving that time was also a dimension of things.

But William saw. He saw too that there could be more dimensions. So many more. And through the strange flow logic of the symbols, he learned that, like meaning, so too could a thing be transformed. And that these transformations could move a thing from a being of smaller dimensions to one of larger dimensions. As souls to heaven. However, he also saw, with a growing unease, that the inverse was not possible. Not without something becoming distorted or lost. And where, he thought, would these lost pieces go?

Looking up, William realized he no longer needed the codex to see. The new language was revealed to him on every surface. The walls, the table, the pages of other books. Opening one of these at his desk, he found new meanings emerged as the words shifted and the layers upon layers of arcane script unveiled themselves to him. Inside an illuminated Bible, he found the pictures and panels contracting and dilating upon themselves, the symbols transforming according to hidden rules that he alone grasped. Latin was meaningless to him now. So limited. Instead, he saw the flow of meaning through the text, like water flowing through a landscape. And in the darkest part of the illustrations, he saw something else. Faces, not quite that of men, but not quite that of children. For their eyes were ancient.

He recognized them as the Children from the illumination. Revealed by the new language and interwoven into the sacred books. Has it always been so? Had they been there from the very start? Encoded in the movement of man's primitive symbology? Surviving translation after translation. Waiting for him.

His body gave a half-hearted shudder, an echo of how he felt when he first saw the illumination. His mind, however, was no longer repulsed by them. He understood that the new language he now thought in belonged to them. And he wanted more of it.

At his desk, he opened another book, Euclid's *Elements*. Its original intent no longer mattered, for in it he saw the new language take shape over the old, bringing forth the true geometries that were only implicit in Euclid's propositions. He felt this knowledge enter his thoughts, pushing everything else aside.

He should stop.

William's sureness waned for he suddenly understood that now, this was the moment. His mind sat upon a precipice. He thought of his companions at the priory back in Yorkshire, of his beloved sister. He would lose them all if he didn't turn back.

But he had to know more.

And so he allowed the flow logic of the symbols to carry him down into the abyss. William clutched at his head. The vertigo of aeons opening before him. Shapes and colors that were once familiar now evoked new meanings. The oak of the desk, the flickering light of his lamp, the way the folds in his robes created valleys of shadows. Each of these impressions came to him as a concept. A memory of his past, or a sensation he had once experienced. Every object in the room conjured up entire fields of ideas and memories and sensations all joined in a manifold of meaning.

The lamp on his desk was the squabbling of the diocese and the scorn of the peasants as they brought the monks their tithe. The cold stone of the library walls was the smell of his sweat and the decay of rotting leaves from when he was bedridden last autumn. The musty odor of the books was God's love and the Sacrament and his mother's touch when he was still a child. The Codex Primis was...

He paused.

The codex brought no new sensations, stood for no memories. From it, he felt instead only a cold darkness. And in that darkness, a terrible vision. A world remade. The Children would return to their creation and use the crude bodies of men as clay. They would strum the hidden geometries and stretch the minds of men into new dimensions of thought as their language had done to him. The finite range of William's own experience prior to this day lay splayed out before him, small and pitiful. He hated it for its limitations. But these limits would shackle him no more.

William's heart raced and his pupils dilated into darkness as his mind finally broke on the shores of a new quadrivium.

In the shadows, beyond the lamplight, there was movement. They were here now. Perhaps they had always been here. The wrinkles around the eyes of their young faces hinted at the passage of aeons.

"Are you real?"

No answer. Of course, they wouldn't answer. Beings such as these did not converse with mortal men.

"I need to see more."

Yes, there was so much more to see. He could feel them whispering the mysteries of the cosmos, calling to him from the darkness. He just needed the right parts.

Carefully examining his fingers and hands, lifting his robes to examine his feet, his calves, his groin, he wondered at the strange logic of it all. He felt more than thought of his body as simply a collection of assembled pieces. All of God's creation, merely an amalgam of parts hastily arranged and smothered in sweat and innervated by blood and all of it housed in a skeletal puppet draped in flesh. And yet, as abhorrent as he now found himself, he knew that some of those same parts would be needed if ever he was to truly see.

While the abbey slept, William made his way to the kitchens. At the back, he found the cupboard with the tools the monks used for the slaughtering of game. William was not a butcher, he had only a rudimentary idea of what he would need, but he followed the flow of meaning through the symbols on the walls, the tables, and they guided him. A long sharp knife for cutting. One for skinning. A mallet for crushing bone. And a pair of meat hooks to hold everything in place.

Creeping back through the empty kitchen, William passed through the cloister in the direction of the abbey's church. He knew that there would be a monk there overnight preparing the liturgical items for morning mass. Inside the church, he found the monk sleeping on a pew, his head tilted back and snoring. Without breaking his stride, William approached along the adjoining row and, in a single motion, plunged a knife into the exposed neck of the sleeping monk. The monk's eyes opened in a flash, and his hands scrambled to his throat. He gurgled a cry, but William paid him little notice.

He had work to do.

With a meat hook in each hand, he plunged them into the monk's shoulders and pulled his body off the pew and across the floor towards the sacristy. With its supply of water and its sacred cups and chalices, this would be an ideal place for him to work uninterrupted. Dragging the body into the chamber, he hoisted it onto the priest's desk. Looking around by the dim light of a single burning candle, he found two lamps and a tinderbox. All around him, symbols formed like fog over the blank surfaces of the room. He ached to stop and learn from them, but he knew that there was so much more he would be permitted to see if he could just be patient and retrieve the right parts.

Removing the monk's robes and tunic, he punctured the soft flesh of his belly, cutting across his sternum. Using the smaller knife, he roughly removed the layers of skin and fat, exposing the ribcage. What he needed was in there. Cutting away the muscle, he formed a passage just below the ribs, big enough for his hand to pass. Reaching in, he rooted around pulling out what wasn't securely attached, and cutting at anything that was. Finally, he found what he needed. Removing the spleen, he placed it in a chalice and examined it. The still warm organ appeared to breathe as shapes and symbols formed in layers over its surface. William knew what he had to do. Using the small knife, he delicately split the organ into two halves, careful to follow its folds and sulci. Once complete, he searched the vestibule for the cincture to the priest's robes for mass. Finding it, he leaned back, placing the two halves of the monk's spleen over his own eyes and fixed them to his head using the cincture.

Looking around the room, at first all he saw was darkness. But then, slowly, the contours of the walls, the desk and ceiling came into focus. Unmarred by darkness or light, he could see their true shapes. And they were terrible. Everything made of a crude pulsing matter. What his whole life he thought of as solid objects, he now saw them for the lies they were.

The world was held together by the thinnest of threads. Aristotle had been wrong to reject the existence of a void. William saw emptiness manifest. Its awesome volume pockmarked by tiny islands of atomic substances bound to one another by a fragile webbing.

The desk. A thing he could touch and pound his fist against, was nothing but a field of decay as weak bonds struggled to hold the pieces together. And yet, in that void, in the spaces between things, between the webs and the glowing imperfect spheres of crude matter, he saw them. They were there, in between and all around. They beckoned to him. He could join them. Or is it that they could join him?

He needed only to provide more parts.

It was before sunrise the following morning when the Abbot de Marcy and his men returned from the woods where they'd left the heretics to die in the cold. Tired and hungry from riding through the night, the abbot made his way to the kitchens for food and drink. In the entrance, he knelt to examine a dark stain on the stone floor.

"Blood," he stated to his men.

They soon found other dark trails coming from different parts of the abbey and followed them into the church.

"Father Abbot, over there."

The abbot looked in the direction the monk was pointing and saw shadows moving on the face of the altar. As they crept forwards, one of the monks struck something on the floor, and it slid into the altar with a metallic clang. The abbot knelt to pick up the object—a knife, its edge still wet with blood.

"Holy Mother of God!" exclaimed one of the monks, startling the abbot.

Following his gaze, he saw a man in a blood splattered tunic emerge from the sacristy. As he drew nearer, the abbot saw that there was something horribly wrong with the man's face. Covering the figure's eyes was a dark piece of glistening flesh, held in place by some form of cincture. The figure turned to face the abbot, seeming to stare directly at him as though he could see through the blindfold of meat upon his face.

"Father Abbot, come inside and see."

The abbot recognized the man's voice as that of the scholar William. A deep feeling of religious dread rose in him as he recalled the Albigensian leader Gerard's warning.

As William moved away from the entrance, they saw into the

interior of the chamber. On a large table, the corpulent body of the Bishop of Worcester lay splayed open. Blood drained and flesh hung from an enormous cavity carved into his chest. The scraps of his anatomy glistened like pools of deep water, the flickering lamplight unable to penetrate their murky red depths. From the stomach, something brown and soft leaked out. Wet strands mingling with the blood and filth of the bishop's stomach. Bread. The bishop's stomach had been filled with bread, and now it oozed and plopped onto the floor with the rest of him. Earlier, William had surprised the Bishop of Worcester in the kitchens as the latter crept about for a middle of the night meal. The abbot's eyes were drawn to something else that was off about the body. The arms. The bishop's arms were strangely small and limp. Then the abbot realized with a jolt that their bones had been removed.

What dark liturgy had he interrupted? Turning from the horror in the room to its architect, the Abbot de Marcy pointed his knife at William.

"What have you done?"

William stopped his advance.

"You have to see it."

The abbot, confused, stole another glance at the room. There, beyond the corpse of the bishop, a dark structure loomed. What his mind had mercifully mistaken for shadows, he now saw more clearly, and his stomach churned upon witnessing what the mad scholar had wrought.

Then, Henry de Marcy, Abbot of Hautecomb, the man who would one day be offered the papal crown, cried out in rage. For what he saw in the sacristy was an affront to God. This archway of flesh and bone and vital organs. Of dead faces and stretched skin. Its yawning maw seemed to reach out for him through the sacristy doorway. Part of him yearned to be inside of it, to experience the ecstasy of vertigo as he fell into its depths. However, another part—the stronger one—the one driven by his devotion to Christ, this part resisted. This part told him that William's desecration could not be permitted to exist.

Something inside the structure shifted. Flesh tore open and the abbot's eyes widened in horror as blood began to rain down from the structure onto the floor of the sacristy. In front of him, William smiled, his arms raised in rapture.

"The path is lit."

With a roar, the abbot charged. His knife plunged into the scholar's stomach as they tumbled to the ground. Recovering from their terror, his monks scrambled to him. They tried to hold William down, but the scholar possessed an unholy strength. He threw off the abbot with one arm and strangled one of the monks with the other. Then, in one fell swoop, William plunged his fingers into the soft of the monk's throat and tore out what lay inside.

The remaining two monks retreated when the abbot's knife pierced through William's throat from behind. Without pausing to see the effect, the abbot lashed out again and again, stabbing the scholar in the chest, the face, and in the meat that covered his eyes.

When at last William was still, the abbot turned to gaze at the thing in the sacristy. The air seemed to vibrate as a low hum resonated throughout the church.

Inside the chamber, the air was humid and oppressive. Blood and organs littered the floor and the body of the bishop lay putrid and leaking. But it was William's creation that horrified them beyond all else. Connected to the walls on either side by wet strands of flesh and sinew was an insane structure of bone and skin and the insides of men. The pieces interlocked to form an archway tall enough for a man to enter. Closer to it now, the abbot found it hard to countenance; its skeletal configuration was all wrong. The angles of blackened bone and the gradual darkening of the strands of flesh hinted at an impossible depth. Not three feet behind the structure was a solid wall, and yet, the pieces appeared to converge towards some paradoxical distance…a trick! He had fallen prey to an artist's vulgar deception. As he moved off center from the structure, the illusion collapsed.

Studying the archway, the abbot looked for a way to destroy it. Above him, he saw, in a row at the top of the arch, six disembodied heads encaged in bone along with several large fleshy sacs, the contents of which his mind refused to consider. Underneath, blood and other bodily fluids spilled down in slow viscous sheets, creating a red veil of ichor. Staring through it, the abbot saw into a darkness. And there, in between shadows, small child-like faces stared back at him.

The closest of them raised an arm. Its hand pierced through the veil of liquid raining from above. Gray skinned fingers crept forward. The abbot watched, momentarily transfixed by this dark miracle, as the small hand steadily approached his abdomen. Stepping back, he looked around the room. There, by the desk, he saw what he needed—the bishop's blood splattered crosier.

"*Hoc est Christi dominio!*" shouted the abbot.

In rage, he swung the staff into the bones, hacked at the sinew and bashed the lifeless faces in the arch above. His monks joined him, beating at the structure with whatever implements they could find. So loud was the sound of their attacks, they failed to notice a torn and bleeding William standing behind them.

"No!" he cried.

The men turned, but it was too late. William plowed into the closest monk, and they fell towards the veil. The hand, sensing something close, grabbed at the monk, pulling both men inside. Their limbs tore at the border of the veil. A leg fell to the ground in front of the abbot, blood spurting onto his robes. The child's hand emerged again, faster this time. The arm growing longer as if recon-stituted by the fresh blood. Then, the face of a child that was not a child slowly broke the surface of the veil. Its eyes were closed as it birthed itself into their world.

The abbot continued his onslaught, when his crosier shattered, and he was left with nothing.

"Help me!" he cried to the remaining monk.

Together, they strained to lift a heavy tabernacle. With a heave, they threw it into the apex of the archway. A piece broke and bodies and organs spilled from the fleshsacs above. The veil broke into several rivulets. Where spaces appeared, the creature's gray skin cracked open, like splitting firewood. From its mouth came a howl of pain, the cry stretched and corrupted as the sound clawed its way out from behind the veil. The child, cracked and torn, retreated back into the darkness. The structure collapsed and, all at once, the humming ceased.

That evening, long after the remaining members of the council had visited the church and seen for themselves what had transpired, the Abbot de Marcy, the Archbishop of York, and the Bishop of Durham met in private.

"I hope now you see the extreme threat that these heretics pose and how close we came to ruin," said the abbot.

"If what you say happened is true. That there are things that await us in the dark," the bishop tightened his grip on the cross at his neck, "then, did the Albigensians speak true? Is the God of Abraham not the true creator?"

"Stop this blasphemy!" cried the archbishop. "This is the Church of the living God, and it is the pillar and ground of truth."

The archbishop paused, allowing his anger to wash over them.

"We will hide all traces of what happened here. Have the monks wall up the sacristy and tell no one of what lies inside."

"Your Grace, that is a wise decision. However, we must do more than that," said the abbot.

"Say what you mean."

The abbot had been preparing for this moment. Although, they hadn't seen what he'd seen, hadn't witnessed what had nearly come through the veil. The aftermath had been gruesome enough and his role in stopping it was clear to all. This was his chance to gain powerful allies.

"Bernard de Clairvaux, the founder of the Cistercian order, believed that a crusade against the Languedoc was the only way to eliminate this heresy. He was unable to convince the clergy and nobles of his day. However, times have changed. The last crusade was twenty years ago and the *Comtes* and *Seigneurs* grow tired of hearing of the conquests of their fathers."

The abbot leaned closer.

"The Francian nobility hunger for land and the spoils of conquest. They need only the Pope's approval. Were a certain archbishop of England, affronted by the presence of Albigensians on his shores, to call on the Pope for a crusade, well...that might be enough. Then, with God at our side, we will cleanse the whole of the Languedoc, burn their churches to the ground, and put them all to stake."

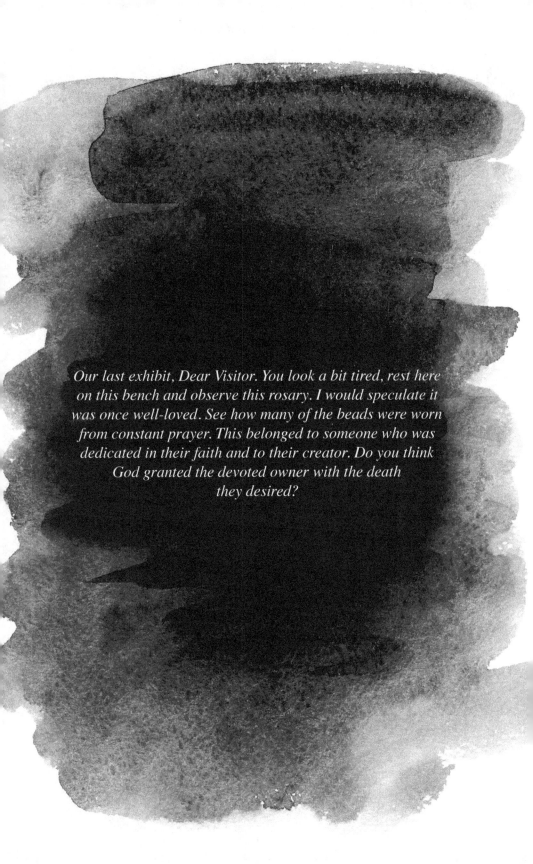

Our last exhibit, Dear Visitor. You look a bit tired, rest here
on this bench and observe this rosary. I would speculate it
was once well-loved. See how many of the beads were worn
from constant prayer. This belonged to someone who was
dedicated in their faith and to their creator. Do you think
God granted the devoted owner with the death
they desired?

THE LAI OF THE DANSE MACABRE

Jessica Peter

In fair Bretagne there was a town,
right where the sun in France sunk down.
With craggy cliffs o'er em'rald seas,
it crouched against the vicious breeze.

And in this town upon the bluffs,
surrounded by the forests rough,
there lived a woman named Camille,
so decent, faithful, kind, genteel.
For her, the only man was God,
a love which ofttimes saw her awed.
She chose a life that most would not:
entombed alone, but not forgot.
An anchoress, you see, does this;
most strange, mais oui, it gives them bliss.
She got herself bricked in a cell,
and kept the townsfolk out of Hell.
But as all know, life is fleeting;
when Death comes, there is no cheating.

And while Camille could evil bide,
the townsfolk danced until they died.

While I was writing down these lais,
I fixed upon this dancing craze.
Et moi, je suis Renée de France,
e'en I cannot ignore the danse.
I strive for candor, my quill true,
so thus I share this truth with you.
This tale will make your stomach churn,
yet p'raps that is for what you yearn.
A theme of Death will I reveal,
so let's get back to our Camille.

She seemed to be a normal youth,
but fateful visions showed her truth.
She dreamt of trumpets, fire, blood,
a horse so pale that stamped in mud.
From Revelations in her dreams,
she would awake with awful screams.
But as those thoughts grew ever dark,
her fam'ly's glee 'came truly stark:
their daughter must be holy born,
an honor not to be forsworn.
She aged through youth, remained intact;
engrossed in faith, she made a pact.
And when sixteen she formed a choice
in which her fam'ly did rejoice.
A choice profound, severe, and bold:
to live within an anchorhold.

So through the church, the Bishop came,
the townsfolk too, with hope and flame,

a somber group most funereal,
as final prayers giv'n to Camille.
An anchoress is living dead;
and dear Camille possessed no dread.
This was her young life's hope, you see;
to be confined, her soul set free.
Though also not yet Paradise,
to get there she'd pay any price.

She smiled stepping in the cell,
the place where she'd forever dwell.
The townsfolk helped her out once more
by bricking up the only door.
With windows, only three, alas—
the first into the church for Mass
then one for food and one for town—
her faith ensured she'd ne'er break down.
An altar was her one true friend.
Her soul, it soared; her body penned.

Camille was happy, humble, true,
that spartan cell now all she knew.
She spent her days in quiet prayer,
her dark dreams of the End now fair.
Her life was busy, filled with aid;
she helped all those who with her prayed.
She answered any questions asked,
about the future or the past.
She prayed Hail Marys with her beads
and helped the townsfolk with their needs.

Her cozy, pleasant, simple room
would one day serve for her a tomb.

So from the plot where she would lay,
she'd dig a scoop of dirt each day;
With comfort in her waiting grave,
in many ways Camille was brave.

But then Death came, and all was wrong.
For Death did come with dance and song.

One morn the town with mist was wreathed,
"Oh Corpus Christi," Camille breathed.
'Twas not His body that she saw:
it was a corpse, 'gainst nat'ral law.
It scrabbled up through churchyard dirt,
unfurled upright, as if alert.
The thing only a skeleton,
it cracked its neck and t'ward town spun.
Somehow, the grimy bones, they stood.
Camille still thought she'd fight with *good*.
It had been long dead, that is true,
but now it walked, it shook off dew.
Camille, she screamed, she struck the wall,
but there was no response at all.
The town, it slept, not knowing this,
naiveté is never bliss.

The baker woke, and walked 'cross town,
he didn't know the corpse was 'round.
Camille, she shouted, called his name,
but still it happened, all the same.
The corpse, that vile crusty thing,
it struck the baker with one swing.
The baker with his eyes all glazed,
began to hum like he was crazed.

This time Camille she screamed in vain.
At least the baker showed no pain.
Instead, he held the skeleton,
embracing, man and Hell as one.
They stumbled, then began to dance,
the baker in his humming trance.
Then humming turned to songs aloud,
the baker sang out harsh and proud.
Camille, she feared what had begun,
if started, 'twould persist 'til done.

As townsfolk all began to wake,
mais oui, Death's thirst could not be slaked.
Then graves split open, something stirred,
the bodies *by choice* disinterred.
As they emerged, they came, they came.
Camille once knew them all by name.
Cadavers shambling, dropping skin,
and skeletons with wild grins.
A dreadful shambles left behind,
as loose limbs in the brush 'came twined.

The corpses lumbered to the square.
The townsfolk too without a care.
You might expect they'd run away,
but no, they happ'ly joined the fray.
They greeted bodies as if friends,
despite their dripping, stinking ends.
While to each other they all walked,
the door of Death, it was unlocked.
The townsfolk came, no second glances,
and with the dead began their dances!

Camille knew not what she could do.
The town would have to see this through.
The danse macabre can't be stopped,
not even if the town all dropped.

Then at her window did appear,
her servant, holding food. "I feared,"
Camille she said, "You'd joined the throng."
Her servant, shivered, heard the song.
He said, "What is this going on?"
"I hope they'll only dance 'til dawn."
She didn't want to scare the lad,
but if he left, she would be glad.
"And what am I to do?" he said.
She sighed. "Just try to dodge the dead."
Then pulling out her beaded strand,
"Please take these, pray, avoid that band."
But then just as he left her space,
a vacant grin crept o'er his face.
He grabbed a partner, once a priest,
and spun around with the deceased.
His dancing, mad, had no restraint,
he even called out to the saints.

The dancing grew yet more deranged,
as living partners were exchanged.
The bony limbs flailed on the wind,
with human arms they paired and twinned.

A recent corpse with organs fresh,
it gripped the blacksmith, sloughing flesh.
The blacksmith had a lovely time,
he sang out, swathed in sticky slime.

One bony body fell apart,
its partner stacked it in a cart.
A juicy eyeball rolled away,
no gore would stop this pleasant day.
A baby sat out on the road,
the mother hadn't even slowed.
Instead she grasped a body too,
enamored with this old dead crew,
her partner haggard, rawboned, gaunt.
Camille was forced to watch the jaunt.
She clenched her jaw while dripping sweat,
and wiped her brow as she did fret.
The corpses for Camille cared naught,
as living dead, without the rot.
Now on her own, helpless too,
her power only at the pew,
she prayed for hours as she knelt,
to disentangle horror felt.

Her prayers did nothing to the thrall,
and someone even had the gall,
to keep a beat with some old drum,
that steady beat, it made her numb.
The townsfolk shouted and they wailed,
Camille then knew that she had failed.

The danse continued, day and night.
The townsfolk fell, gave up the fight.
As day to night and back again.
Camille she prayed, but just in vain.
As tears ran down Camille's fair cheek,
she wished her strength was not so meek:

What is the point of piety,
if you can't save society?
As they collapsed from Death most foul,
her stomach gave a horrid growl.

Camille kept up her silent prayers.
Until one morn she viewed the square:
the Dead they lumbered t'ward their graves,
with not a care for prior slaves.
She stood and cheered; she'd dreamt of this,
her heart expanded, nearing bliss.
But then she saw: no person stirred.
no life nor sound, not e'en a word.
She was too late, they all were dead,
despite her hopes, not one had fled.
She'd seen herself as one renowned,
but when need came, she was here bound.
She bent her head to pray some more,
though haunted by the blocked-off door.
The town was now so quiet, still,
her doubts now crept, a horrid chill.
Alone, enclosed in that small cell;
what once was Heaven now was Hell.

There was a town in fair Bretagne,
which took on *that* dance most profane.
While waves still lap against its shores,
the town's been mangled, ripped, and torn.

Now you may see this tale's appeal,
but curious, what of Camille?
Well, trav'lers found the town all dead;
it caused them such horrendous dread
to see these people, once alive,
unknowing of their final jive.
The bodies scattered through the square;
the stench of death hung in the air.
They buried each and ev'ry one,
with fear it'd take them 'fore 'twas done.

But first they stumbled on her room;
they hoped 'gainst hope 'twas not a tomb.
They cleared the bricks from her small cell,
and hoped for life—it could be well.
Camille she lay, devout and brave,
inside her loosely hand-dug grave.
She'd starved, bien sûr, now truly dead.
The trav'lers bowed, though wished they'd fled.
'Twas clear that she had dealt with doubt,
her scratches on the stones throughout.

What did we learn from this affair?
That life and death are never fair.
As ever, Death comes for us all;
just pray you're ready when he calls.
Get out and live, not just stand by.
You too might dance until you die.

Ah yes, wipe your tears. I have a tissue in my pocket, I think. We are at the exit now, tips happily accepted, if you are so generous! I hope you have enjoyed your tour of my humble little museum. Each exhibit was curated with care, as I am sure you noticed. You are, of course, welcome back anytime. History is always willing, always waiting. For history is a hungry leviathan, and it consumes all in the course of time, leaving nothing but dust and memories of those who lived before. And you and I can only hope to observe and to reflect on it, safely, far from its maw, until it is our turn to pass into the gullet of history, churned into the finest of dust. So yes, Esteemed Visitor. Be a dear and come back. Bring your friends. Bring your family. Until then, I'll be waiting.

CONTRIBUTOR BIOGRAPHIES

P.L. McMillan
Editor

A writer of all thing murderous, macabre, and monstrous,
P.L. McMillan has been published in over a dozen magazines
and anthologies. To her, every shadow is an entryway to
a deeper look into the black heart of the world and every
night she rides with the mocking and friendly ghouls on the
night-wind, bringing back dark stories to share with those
brave enough to read them. You can find her publications and
blog at https://plmcmillan.com/

Solomon Forse
Editor

The founder of HOWL Society, Solomon also plays guitar
in the Lovecraftian metal band Crafteon and teaches high
school English on the western slope of the Rocky Mountains.
Check out his latest fiction appearing in the *Howls From Hell*
anthology, *MYTHIC* Issue 18, and *Boneyard Soup Magazine*
Vol. 1, Issue 4. Follow him on Twitter @SolomonForse.

Christopher Buehlman
Foreword

A writer and performer based in St. Petersburg, Florida, he is the
winner of the 2007 Bridport Prize in Poetry and a finalist for the
2008 Forward Prize for best poem (UK). He spent his twenties and
thirties touring renaissance festivals with his very popular show
Christophe the Insultor, Verbal Mercenary. He holds a bachelor's
degree in French Language from Florida State University, where
he minored in history. He enjoys theater, independent films, chess,
archery, running, cooking with lots of garlic, and thick, inky,
bone-dry red wines with sediment at the bottom.

Caleb Stephens
The Crowing

Caleb Stephens is a dark fiction author writing from somewhere deep in the Colorado mountains. His short stories have appeared in multiple publications and podcasts, including *The Dread Machine*, *MetaStellar*, *Suspense Magazine*, *Scare You To Sleep*, and more. His short story "The Wallpaper Man" is forthcoming as a short film from Falconer Film & Media. You can learn more at www.calebstephensauthor.com and follow him on Twitter @cstephensauthor.

Philippa Evans
Angelus

Philippa Evans was born in South Africa, where she spent several years teaching and studying history, ancient Greek, and Latin. She moved to Scotland after completing her master's degree in Classics, and now lives and writes in Edinburgh. You can read more of her work in *Vastarien* (Grimscribe Press). She is also the co-creator of the ongoing history/comedy podcast Everything Is Awful Forever (https://awfulforever.com/).

J.L. Kiefer
Palette

J. L. Kiefer is a contributor to *Louisville Magazine*, where she has won several Society of Professional Journalism awards. She has also won several awards for her fiction, including the Editors' Award for Emerging Writers from Miracle Monocle. Her creative and journalistic work have appeared in *The White Squirrel*, *Whisky Advocate*, and *The Voice Tribune*. She is a supporting member of the Horror Writers Association. (https://www.jennykiefer.com)

Peter Ong Cook
Brother Cornelius

Peter Ong Cook is a proudly Filipino-American writer
residing in Los Angeles. He was raised on used paperbacks,
VHS rentals, and syndicated television. His dog, a husky
rescue, howls every time he steps away from home.

Hailey Piper
In Thrall to This Good Earth

Hailey Piper is the author of *The Worm and His Kings*, *Queen of
Teeth*, *Unfortunate Elements of My Anatomy*, and other books of
horror. She is an active member of the Horror Writers Association,
with over seventy short stories appearing in publications such
Year's Best Hardcore Horror, Pseudopod, Dark Matter Magazine,
Daily Science Fiction, Flash Fiction Online, and elsewhere. She
lives with her wife in Maryland, where they spend weekends
raising the dead. Find her at www.haileypiper.com or on Twitter
via @HaileyPiperSays.

Lindsey Ragsdale
In Every Drop

Lindsey lives in Chicago, IL. In 2021, her short story "A
Fistful of Murder" was published in *Howls from Hell: A
Horror Anthology*. She would like to thank AJ Meyer for
recommending valuable research sources, specifically *The
Maya* by Michael D. Coe and Stephen Houston, and his
historical feedback, which helped this story come to life.

Ethan Yoder
Deus Vult

"Deus Vult" is Ethan's first publication. He was the recipient of a coveted gold star from his third grade teacher for his short story "The Turkeynator," a Thanksgiving themed retelling of James Cameron's classic 1992 film *Terminator 2: Judgement Day*. Follow him on Twitter @edyoder.

M.E. Bronstein
The Final Book of Sainte Foy's Miracles

M.E. Bronstein is a PhD student in Comparative Literature who writes horror and dark fantasy when she should be working on her dissertation. Her writing has appeared or is forthcoming in *Beneath Ceaseless Skies; Miscreations: Gods, Monstrosities & Other Horrors; Other Terrors: An Inclusive Anthology;* and elsewhere. You can find her at mebronstein.com.

Michelle Tang
A Dowry for Your Hand

Michelle Tang writes speculative fiction from Ontario, Canada, where she lives with her husband and children. Her short stories have been published in several anthologies, including *Terrifying Ghosts, Night Terrors, vol. 2*, and *Negative Space: an Anthology of Survival Horror*. When she's not writing, Michelle can be found playing video games, drinking bubble tea, or watching horror movies from between her fingers.

Cody Goodfellow
The Mouth of Hell

Cody Goodfellow has written eight novels and five collections of short stories, and edits the hyperpulp zine Forbidden Futures. His writing has been favored with three Wonderland Book Awards for excellence in Bizarro fiction. His comics work has appeared in Mystery Meat, Dark Horse's Creepy and Slow Death Zero. As an actor, he has appeared in numerous TV shows, videos by Anthrax and Beck, and a Days Inn commercial. He also wrote, co-produced and scored the Lovecraftian hygiene films Baby Got Bass and Stay At Home Dad, which can be viewed on YouTube. He "lives" in San Diego, California.

Christopher O'Halloran
The Lady of Leer Castle

HWA member and HOWL Society admin, Chris is a milk-slinging, Canadian actor-turned-author with work published or forthcoming from *HellBound Books*, *Tales to Terrify*, *The Dread Machine*, and the anthologies *Howls from Hell* and *Bloodlines*. Despite transitioning to writing, Chris still puts his acting diploma to use; he acts like a fool for chuckles from his wife and son in British Columbia. Fans of stories about vein-removal and Phoenix-women against the patriarchy can visit COauthor.ca for stories, reviews, and updates on his upcoming novel, Pushing Daisy. Contact him there or on twitter @Burgleinfernal.

Bridget D. Brave
Schizzare

A HOWLS Devotee, Bridget's publishing career is largely restricted to the news variety, with one magazine editor declaring her given name "the worst pseudonym I've ever seen." She is new to the horror game, after learning that people who are constantly terrified should really consider writing about it. Hailing from the cornfields of Illinois, she has lived in various places around the country and is still searching for the place that feels like home. Currently residing in the Upper Left of the USA, Bridget is professionally trained as an attorney, but is getting better.

Patrick Barb
The King of Youth vs. The Knight of Death

Patrick Barb is an author of weird, dark, and horrifying tales, currently living (and trying not to freeze to death) in Saint Paul, Minnesota. His short fiction appears in *Diabolical Plots*, the *Humans are the Problem* anthology, and *Boneyard Soup Magazine*, among other publications. His debut novella *Gargantuana's Ghost* is coming from Grey Matter Press in August 2022. In addition, he is an Active member of the Horror Writers Association. For more of his work, visit patrickbarb.com or follow him at twitter.com/pbarb.

C.B. Jones
The Forgotten Valley

C.B. Jones is an author from somewhere in the middle of America. His work has appeared on *The NoSleep Podcast* and in *Cosmic Horror Monthly*. His debut novel, *The Rules of the Road* was released in 2021. He is a citizen of the Cherokee Nation. He can be found at www.therulesoftheroad.net

Brian Evenson
The Fourth Scene

Brian Evenson is the author of a dozen books of fiction, most recently the story collection The *Glassy Burning Floor of Hell* (2021). His previous collection, *Song for the Unraveling of the World* (2019), won the Shirley Jackson Award and the World Fantasy Award and was a finalist for the Los Angeles Times' Ray Bradbury Prize. He is the recipient of three O. Henry Prizes, an NEA fellowship, and a Guggenheim Award. His work has been translated into more than a dozen languages. He lives in Los Angeles and teaches in the Critical Studies Program at CalArts.

Stevie Edwards
White Owl

Stevie Edwards is a recovering academic who lives with her two wiener dogs in Ontario, Canada. She is a reader for *Uncharted Magazine* and a proud member of the HOWL Society. If you'd like to know more about her thoughts on writing, reality tv, and living life as a queer, fat protagonist, you can find her on Twitter @stephanieadele_.

David Worn
A Dark Quadrivium

David Worn is a scientist by day and sometimes horror writer by night. A longtime lover of all things horror, he may have been inspired to enter academe by the portrayal of grad students and scientists in movies like *Prince of Darkness* and *Altered States*. It is perhaps fitting that his first publication would be something of an homage to those two films. When not making up spooky stories with his kids, David enjoys graphic design, modular synthesis and showing up weeks late to book discussions in HOWLS. You can find him on Instagram @worncassettes.

Jessica Peter
The Lai of the Danse Macabre

Jessica Peter lives in the often gritty, ex-Steel City of Hamilton, Ontario, Canada with her partner and their two black cats. Her stories and poems all tend toward the dark, the uncanny, or the absurd. Beyond writing, she's a social worker and a health researcher and loves veggie gardening, craft beer, playing ukulele, and seeing the whole world. Find her on Twitter @jessicapeter1 or at www.jessicapeter.net.

Molly Halstead
Artist

Molly is a graphic designer and book fanatic who spends her day fighting with Adobe products and evenings reading horror. When creating in her free time, she focuses on book and magazine design, as well as traditional bookmaking and relief printmaking. She lives in North Carolina with her husband and two cats.

Hanne Byrd
Artist

Hoping to eventually manage her own gallery, Hanne is a self-taught artist who works primarily in pen and ink but also experiments with many different media forms. Her art expresses the movement of life and emotions, intending to captivate the viewer's imagination through careful manipulation of lines and contrast. You can find more of her work on DeviantArt at HanneKGallery.

Leah Gharbaharan
Artist

Leah is a graphic designer and illustrator working in Cape Town. Using both traditional and digital media, her illustrative work draws on the natural world and expresses her interest in disruption and patterns of change. Her work can be found on Instagram @schism.art

Joe Radkins
Artist

A father of two little Jedis and a husband to an amazing woman, Joe is an aspiring illustrator who works in all mediums. He currently lives in Pennsylvania fulfilling art commissions and is addicted to anything horror and Marvel. More of his art and commissions can be found on his Instagram @thecinemaddiction.

Maia Weir
Artist

Maia's goal in every medium is to tell a compelling story. Whether the players are human, architectural, or shades of gray, she invites you to explore meticulously created dimensions of narrative. Educated and experienced in applied arts, she is passionate about animation, illustration, installation art, writing, jewelry design, and more. She works to uplift herself and other artists through the matrix of artistic expression.

Iona Vorster
Artist

During the day, Iona works as a concept artist in the video game industry across mobile and console titles. At night she devours, dissects, and contemplates all things horror. She hopes to keep combining her nighttime and daytime interests in the future. You can find her professional work online at www.ionavorster.com

ACKNOWLEDGMENTS

A very special acknowledgement goes to the writers of HOWL Society. Forty-three members participated in workshopping their medieval pieces over three months, with four separate deadlines, and a resounding nine critiques on each piece. While by the numbers it might seem we would eventually hit a tooth-and-nail, winner-takes-all Hunger Games, instead we were brought together. We celebrated small successes, commiserated over finicky formatting, shared more medieval butt trumpet memes than you'd expect could possibly exist, and consequently built a community. While not every piece from the workshop made it into this anthology, we expect to see them out in the world in other markets soon. We would also like to give a particular thank you to Chris O'Halloran, who had the difficult job of wrangling writers, calming minor panics, and relaying the necessary details between the editors and the writing room (and he was definitely never forced to eat a pinecone).

—Jessica Peter

It's been an amazing evolution for the writing community of HOWL Society. When HOWLS started two years ago, it was a simple book club that was meant to keep members sane during lockdown. From there, the Writer's Corner channel was born, small at first but passionate, and it grew. Hell, it exploded. From a crawl, to a run, to producing HOWL Society's first anthology, Howls From Hell, in 2021—and now we're here. As the editors for Howls From the Dark Ages, we couldn't have done it without the support of every member of HOWL Society. It would be impossible to recognize every last person—both of the Discord server and the greater horror community—who have not only contributed to the creation of this anthology but to the success and spirit of HOWL Society itself, but you know who you are, and we thank you for everything.

There are a few people that have been pivotal in the maintenance of the Discord community and the nitty gritty of this anthology. To these heavy lifters, we would like to offer an extra salty thank you: the community mods, Mantis Shrimp, Queen Maeve, Chris O'Halloran; the artists, Hanne Byrd, Leah Gharbaharan, Joe Radkins, Maia Weir, and Iona Vorster; our design guru Molly Halstead; the sensitivity readers and spot-checkers, Cryptid, Schism, bunttriple, TKettle, EvF, and vagrant; Salisbury Hardman; J.L. Kiefer for her lewdly vampiric award-making skills, and Christopher Buehlman for our foreword.

It was an honor to act as co-editors for Howls From the Dark Ages, and we can't wait to see what the HOWL Society writing community does next!

—P.L. McMillan & Solomon Forse

ABOUT THE HORROR-OBSESSED WRITING AND LITERATURE SOCIETY

HOWL Society, located on Discord, is the most active horror book club on the web. With hundreds of members, the club offers readers the chance to join a supportive community where they can enjoy books alongside other horror-lovers while engaging in meaningful discussions and forming long-lasting friendships. Aside from serving as an organized platform for discussing books, HOWL Society is also home to a tight-knit group of horror writers. Additionally, members can participate in tangential conversations about horror films, horror games, and much more. Because the club aims to provide equal access to all readers and writers around the world, membership is 100% free.

The Book Club

- No membership fees

- All club activity for HOWL Society takes place on Discord

- Each month, club members vote on the horror titles that will be read in the following month

- The club reads one book per week, members obtaining copies of physical books, ebooks, or audiobooks according to their preferences

- Members are not expected to read every title

- Each book is separated into three sections and assigned to an individual channel

- Discussions for each section initiate on Mondays, Wednesdays, and Fridays at 12:00 p.m. EST

- During discussion, members use spoiler tags to ensure a safe discussion for those who choose to read at their own pace

- At the end of each discussion, members may participate in a survey to share a personal blurb which may later appear in the official HOWL Society review

Learn more at howlsociety.com.

A Note on the Type

This book was set in Times, named after *The Times* newspaper and designed by Stanley Morison in 1932. The heading font is set in Metamorphous and draws on Romanesque, Gothic, and Renaissance type inspirations and was designed by James Grieshaber. The drop caps at the beginning of each chapter are based on Victorian Gingerbread Initials from around 1890, and were digitized by Dieter Steffmann, Kreuztal. The space break illustration was designed by mariia_fr on Freepik.

Also published by HOWL Society Press:

Praise for Howls From Hell

"Quality horror by true believers—who can write. What more can you ask for?"
—Stephen Graham Jones, *New York Times* bestselling author
of *The Only Good Indians*

"No two stories are alike in this carefully curated anthology—a chorus of fresh voices unafraid to search the depths of hell for the darkest horror and gouge it onto the page."

—Laurel Hightower, author of *Crossroads*

"An anthology for horror devotees by horror devotees, Howls From Hell first pays homage to horror's venerable tropes, then blows them away."

—J.D. Horn, *Wall Street Journal* bestselling author of
The King of Bones and Ashes

Howls From Hell gifts us with sixteen imaginative nightmares from some of the freshest voices emerging in horror and dark fiction. The stories in this collection are fierce and delightfully wicked. I'm certain we're going to be reading a lot from these writers for years to come.

—Cynthia Pelayo, two-time Bram Stoker
Award-nominated poet and author

Printed in the USA
CPSIA information can be obtained
at www.ICGtesting.com
LVHW051152091123
763265LV00074B/2522